Return
To Edisto

Books by Lin Stepp

Novels:
The Foster Girls
Tell Me About Orchard Hollow
For Six Good Reasons
Delia's Place
Second Hand Rose
Down by the River
Makin' Miracles
Saving Laurel Springs
Welcome Back
Daddy's Girl
Lost Inheritance
The Interlude
Happy Valley

The Edisto Trilogy:
Claire at Edisto
Return to Edisto

Christmas Novella:
A Smoky Mountain Gift
In *When the Snow Falls*

Regional Guidebooks
Co-Authored with J.L. Stepp:
The Afternoon Hiker
Discovering Tennessee State Parks

Return To Edisto

BOOK 2 OF THE EDISTO TRILOGY

LIN STEPP

MOUNTAIN HILL PRESS

Cover design: Katherine E. Stepp
Interior design: J. L. Stepp, Mountain Hill Press
Editor: Elizabeth S. James
Cover photo and map design: Lin M. Stepp

Library of Congress Cataloging-in-Publication Data

Stepp, Lin
Return to Edisto: Second novel in the Edisto trilogy / Lin Stepp

ISBN: 978-1-7343883-2-9
First Mountain Hill Press Trade Paperback Printing: April 2020

eISBN: 978-1-7343883-3-6
First Mountain Hill Press Electronic Edition: April 2020

1. Women—Southern States—Fiction 2. South Carolina - Coastal - Fiction
3. Contemporary Romance—Inspirational—Fiction. I. Title

Library of Congress Control Number: 2020901099

This book is dedicated to....

Karen Carter, owner of the Edisto Island Bookstore on Edisto Island, South Carolina. This inviting island booksore—with its friendly staff and resident cat Emily Grace—has been our family's favorite "book stop" since the 1980s when it opened. Plan to stop by and visit on your next trip to the Lowcountry.

Thanks also to the Edisto Chamber of Commerce, who welcomed me to the island at my last visit with this wonderful sign announcing my signing at the Edisto Island Bookstore. The Chamber staff and its members work hard to promote and protect the quality of life of the island and its local businesses.

ACKNOWLEDGMENTS

"Thankfulness is the beginning of gratitude." – Henri F. Amiel

Thanks to everyone on Edisto Island who shared stories and memories with me on our vacations to the island since the 1980s, helping me to know the island better and making its people and history come alive.

Special gratitude to the Edisto Library and the Edisto Bookstore where I found, bought, or studied many books about Edisto's history....and to all those at the Edisto Museum, local shops, restaurants, marinas, bike shop, resort, and golf club who shared local stories with me and made me feel at home on Edisto.

Thanks to Mr. Bell, who owned Bell Buoy Seafood, for all the great stories and great seafood every summer until his shop closed.

Thanks to Cheryl and Mickey Van Metre, originally from Tennessee, who invited us into their Edisto Island home and shared stories with us about their years on the island.

Thanks to Babe and Gerri Hutto, who owned a home on the Point at Edisto near our favorite "beach camp" for over thirty years, and who always welcomed us with friendship to the island every summer.

Last but not least, special thanks to those who work so hard behind the scenes with expertise, dedication, and love to always make my books the best they can be:
___ Elizabeth S. James, copyeditor and editorial advisor
___ J.L. Stepp, production design and proofing
___ Jim Palmer, final proofreader
___ Katherine Stepp, cover design and graphics

And to all my fans Thank You for continuing to love my books!
Without you, where would I be?... Please keep reading!

To God be the glory, great things He hath done.

A BRIEF EDISTO HISTORY

2000 BC	Archaic cultures inhabited the island
1550s	Edistow Indians lived on the island
1663	SC Colony founded by King of England
	Lord Proprietors granted lands from Charles II
1700-1770s	Plantations grew, importing rice and indigo
1775-1783	Rev War; planters fled; property destroyed
1780s-1860s	Plantations thrived growing cotton
1800s	Edingsville Beach formed for wealthy planters
1861-1865	Civil War years; slaves freed; property destroyed
1870s	Many families returned; cotton still a big crop
1893	Hurricane destroyed Edingsville Beach
1920s	Boll weevil ended cotton production
	Drawbridge to island replaced Dawhoo Ferry
	Intercoastal Waterway dredged, linking rivers
	Truck farming and fishing grew on the island
1925	Resort development on Edisto expanded
	Early cottages built, no electricity or water
1935	Edisto Beach State Park built with CCC help
	Palmetto Boulevard paved for cars
1940	Hurricane destroyed most all homes on Edisto
1941-1945	WWII slowed growth; military patrolled island
	Coast Guard patrolled park; reports of spies
	Edisto S.C. Hwy 174 straightened and paved
1950s	Development on Edisto Beach resumed
1954	Big pier built near park entrance; later burned
1959	Hurricane Gracie did heavy damage
	Groins built to hold sand, stop erosion
1970s	Edisto tourism grew and expanded
1973	Oristo resort and golf course opened
1976	Beach changed fr Charleston to Colleton Co
	Remaining Island stayed in Charleston Co
	Many businesses and beach homes built
1976	Fairfield Resorts bought Oristo Ridge
1993	McKinley Washington replaced drawbridge
2006	Fairfield Resort bought by Wyndham
2008	Botany Bay wildlife preserve opened
	Growth continued with beauty remaining

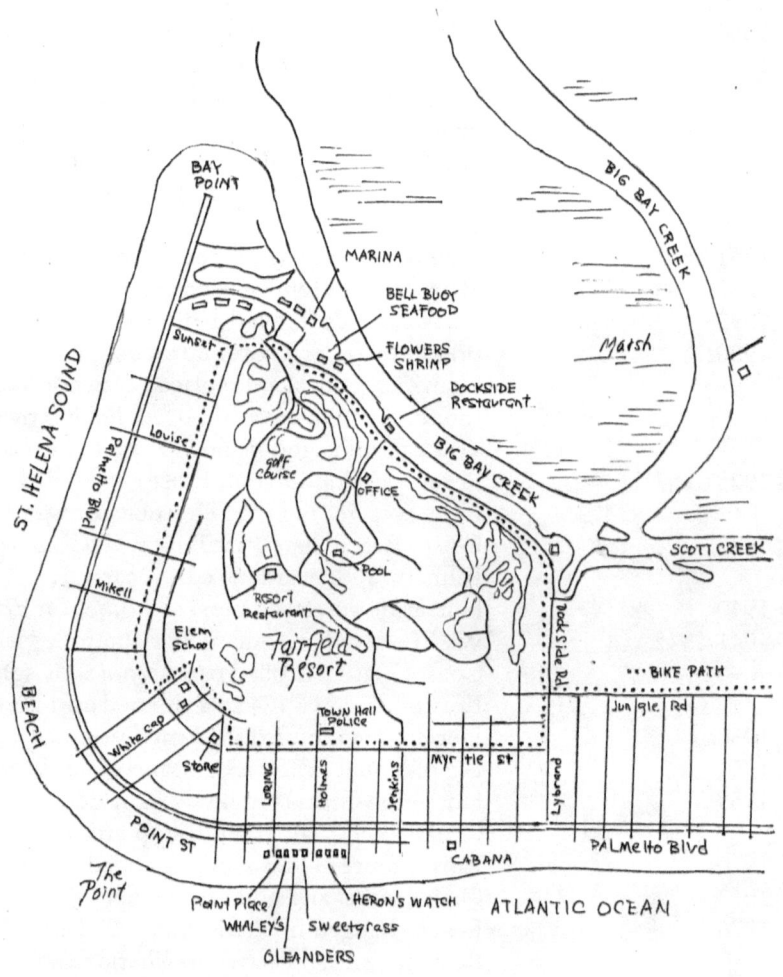

2002 Map of
Edisto Beach

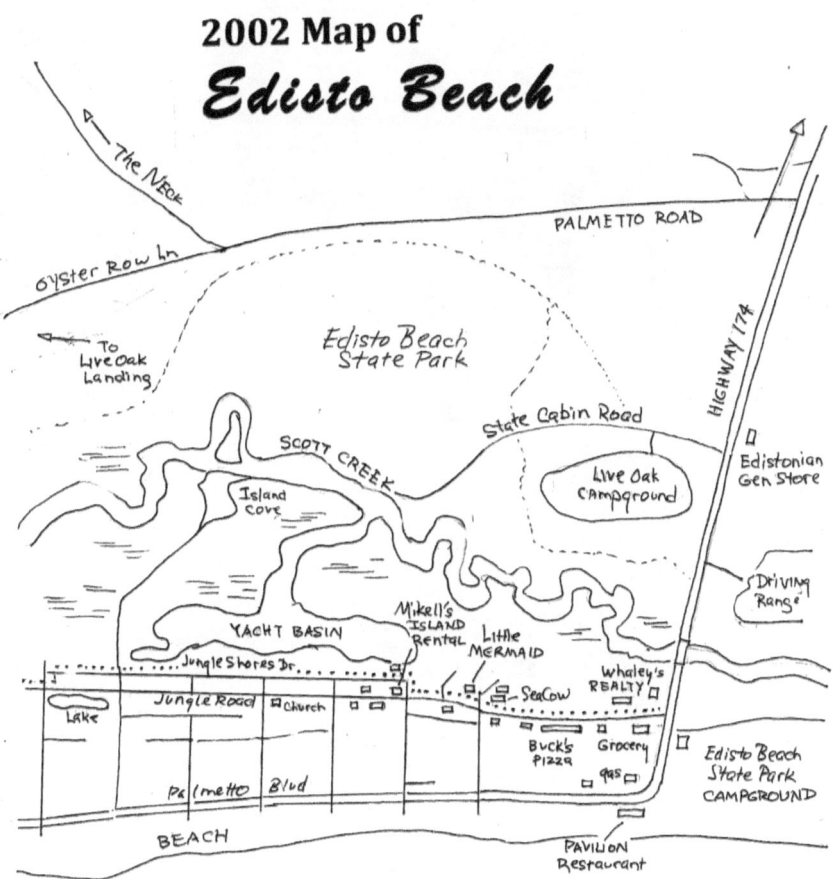

The Neck

PALMETTO ROAD

Oyster Row Ln

To
Live Oak
Landing

Edisto Beach
State Park

HIGHWAY 174

State Cabin Road

SCOTT CREEK

Live Oak
Campground

Edistonian
Gen Store

Island
Cove

Driving
Range

Mikell's
Island
Rental

YACHT BASIN

Little
MERMAID

Jungle Shores Dr.

Whaley's
REALTY

SeaCow

Lake

Jungle Road

Church

Buck's
Pizza

Grocery

Edisto Beach
State Park
CAMPGROUND

gas

Palmetto Blvd

BEACH

PAVILION
Restaurant

ATLANTIC OCEAN

CHAPTER 1

August 2002

Mary Helen smiled for the first time, in nearly two days and seven hundred sixty-five miles of driving, at the "Welcome to Hollywood" sign on the side of the highway. Not Hollywood, California, of course, but Hollywood, South Carolina, a small, rural backwoods town not far from Charleston. She could remember her father making jokes and singing jingles about the town's name when they'd driven through on their way to the beach. That's where Mary Helen headed now, to Edisto Beach, where her family had vacationed since her earliest memories, and where she, her mother, and sister lived after her father's death seventeen years ago. Grieved and heartbroken, they'd retreated to Edisto in 1985, when her father, Reverend Charles Avery, died unexpectedly sitting at his desk in the church. She'd been nine, her sister Suki five. The beach helped to sooth their hurt and sorrow then, and Mary Helen hoped it would do the same for her now.

The Hollywood sign also reminded Mary Helen she hadn't called her sister. She always tried to call Suki before one of her sister's performances. Pulling over at a gas station Mary Helen dug out her cell phone. She knew she wouldn't be able to get very reliable service at the beach but hoped she could still catch a signal this close to Charleston.

"Hi, Suki," she said when she heard her sister's voice. "I just drove into Hollywood and was thinking about you."

"You're here?" Suki almost squealed. "You're here in Hollywood?"

Mary Helen laughed. "No, I'm in Hollywood, South Carolina, not far from Edisto. But I'm envious of you being in Hollywood, California. I wanted to wish you success in your performance tonight with the Los Angeles Symphony Orchestra. You're on your way now playing with big orchestras in your first concert tour. What are you playing tonight?"

"The orchestra is performing at Walt Disney Concert Hall so they're doing Disney classics for this show. I get to do *Waltz of the Flowers* from the Disney movie *Fantasia*," she answered.

"That's the Tchaikovsky piece you wanted to play at your first performance in Beaufort when you were little."

"I remember." She changed the subject. "Now tell me what you're doing heading to Edisto? Is everything all right?"

"Why should something be wrong? Don't you think even a workaholic like me needs a vacation now and then? Aren't you always telling me that?" Mary Helen had no intention of dumping problems on Suki before a show.

"Well, yeah, but…"

"So I'm taking a break. It seemed like a good time."

There was a small silence. "I wish I could be there with you. Edisto is our happy place."

"Playing piano is your happy place, too. You know that." Mary Helen shifted the subject again. "What have you been doing since you flew into Hollywood? Anything fun?"

"Jonah took me around to see the tourist spots when we flew in yesterday. It was so much fun." Her voice softened.

"You like him," Mary Helen said, picking up on her voice change.

"Well, he's my manager and agent. Of course I like him."

"Stop being professional. This is your sister you're talking to, and I can hear in your voice you like him more than just as your agent and manager."

She hesitated. "Well, maybe a little. He's really handsome and charming and always so sweet to me."

Mary Helen shook her head listening to Suki babble on. "Take your time. Remember what we've learned about handsome, charming men."

"Oh, Mary Helen, not everyone who is handsome and charming is unfaithful and unreliable."

"Perhaps, but my experiences have certainly taught me to be wary." She paused. "You be careful with that tender heart of yours."

"I will. I promise."

Mary Helen heard a voice in the background before Suki could say more.

"I need to go," Suki said.

"Sure. Knock 'em dead, you hear? Remember our slogan: Be so good they can't forget you."

Suki's voice softened once more. "Thanks for calling, Mary Helen."

"I'll try to call when I can. Email me if your itinerary changes."

"I will. Give everyone at Edisto—and Mom and Parker—my love."

Mary Helen frowned. "Look, I haven't told Mom and Parker or anyone else I'm heading to the island yet. I wanted to surprise them. So don't say anything, okay?"

"Sure." Someone spoke in the background again. "Oops. Make-up is waiting for me."

"Go get ready to play. I'll talk to you soon."

"Love you, Mary Helen," Suki said, making kissing sounds before hanging up.

"She's such a little kid yet," Mary Helen said to herself before tucking her phone away and pulling back out on the highway. It was only thirty-six miles to Edisto now, about a half hour's drive.

A short time later Mary Helen crossed the Intracoastal Waterway on the McKinley Washington Bridge, a high, arched causeway connecting the mainland to Edisto Island. Even though the new bridge had been open since 1993, Mary Helen still missed the old Dawhoo swing bridge. The wide causeway over the marshes and river made access to the island easier, but it had also brought more tourists and more commerce to Edisto.

Not far from the bridge, Mary Helen pulled her Camry into a parking spot in front of Helton's Store. She needed a few groceries for the beach house and didn't want to stop at the larger Piggly Wiggly down at the beach where she might run into people she knew. Helton's, an island icon, was an old battered grocery with a tin awning over the front porch, a red trimmed screen door, and vintage 7Up and Dr Pepper signs in the window. As typical, two locals played checkers on the porch, their board balanced on a barrel top.

The men studied her with curiosity as she walked up on the porch. In designer clothes with a blue silk blouse, fitted white slacks, trendy sandals, and a Chanel bag, Mary Helen knew she looked like someone from "off" island.

Helton's was a neighborhood gathering spot, especially for the African American community, and Mary Helen could hear the hum of conversation around her as she pushed open the front door of the store. She picked up a basket inside and loaded it with breakfast items plus a few staples and perishables she knew she wouldn't find at the beach house. At the checkout counter a familiar dark face lit with a big smile as Mary Helen put her basket on the counter.

"Well, glory be, if it isn't my girl Mary Helen." The small black woman moved around the counter in a flash to give her a hug. "I didn't know you were at Edisto, child. I cleaned over at your folks' place at Oleanders this morning and didn't see any sign of anyone visiting."

"I just drove over the bridge and am heading to the house now," Mary Helen explained. She hadn't counted on Kizzy Helton being at the store but pulled up a smile for her.

"You still living up north in New Jersey?" Kizzy's husband Lewis asked, walking over from shelving canned goods to ring up her purchases.

"Yes. I thought I'd come to the island for a late summer getaway." Mary Helen pasted another smile on her face for Lewis.

Kizzy's eyes narrowed, studying her. "Your mama know you're

here? She didn't say nothing to me about you coming."

Mary Helen pulled a credit card from her purse to pay Lewis for her groceries. "I decided impulsively to come down," she answered, knowing it never a good idea to lie to Kizzy. "I thought I might surprise her."

"Hmmm." Kizzy put a hand to Mary Helen's face, lifting her chin until she could look in her eyes. "You've been hurt, girl." She stroked a hand gently over Mary Helen's cheek. "But don't you worry none. The island is a good place for healing and the good Lord lives strong here. He'll help you work things through."

Mary Helen bit her lip, trying not to let tears leak out at the kind words. Kizzy had always been intuitive about things.

"I'll stop by at the first of the week when I'm over to clean at Isabel's to check on you." Kizzy patted Mary Helen's arm. "I'll bring you one of my lemon pies you like so much."

"You don't need to go to all that trouble." Mary Helen picked up the groceries Lewis had finished bagging.

Kizzy waved off her protest. "You know it's my joy."

She followed Mary Helen to the door and out on the porch, walking with her to the car. After Mary Helen put her groceries inside and climbed in, Kizzy put a hand on the door before Mary Helen closed it, leaning over to study Mary Helen's face once more.

"You're a preacher's girl, but I'm seeing you've drifted off and away from your faith. Leaning only to your own understanding won't help you find the best answers at this time." She paused, shaking her head. "You know the One who's got the best answers for everything, girl. You may be mad at Him right now and think He hasn't been watching out for you like He should, but it's you that's distanced yourself from Him. You do a little seeking and you'll find Him drawing near again."

Mary Helen mumbled something in reply as Kizzy closed her car door. Pulling out onto the highway, she started crying and wept all the way to the beach house at Oleanders, hardly noticing the familiar scenery along the way. All the emotions she'd pushed down and held back this week seemed to suddenly overtake her.

"So much for the wisdom of stopping at Helton's," she muttered to herself as she hauled groceries and belongings into the beach house a little later.

It seemed odd arriving at Oleanders without her mother, her sister, Parker, and a welcoming committee of friends and neighbors. But Mary Helen needed some time alone before facing them all. Life had a way of blindsiding you when you least expected it, and no matter how wise and mature you thought you'd become, those hits always hurt for a time. This one had been a doozey.

The comfort of the beach house and the sound of the ocean behind it began to do its magic quickly on her heart and mind. With a little smile, she took load after load of her belongings upstairs to her old bedroom, with Suki's room just across the hall.

Oleanders, on Point Street, was a typical beach house on stilts, white with black shutters and doors, with an inviting shady porch on front and a seductive screened porch on back providing dazzling views of the ocean behind it. After her mother and her Uncle Parker married, they all moved to Parker's big home in Beaufort, near his antique business downtown, but they continued coming to the beach house most weekends and spent many holidays here.

In her teens, Mary Helen worked for Isabel Compton at The Little Mermaid every summer and stayed full time at Oleanders. She'd updated her bedroom at the beach house then, moving out some of the girlish furnishings, but never had the heart to change much. The furniture and twin beds were basically the same as always, except for new bedspreads and wallpaper. Favorite books, mementos, and photos filled the bookshelves against one wall, and Mary Helen's old Cabbage Patch doll Evie Dawn still sat on a rocker by the bed, along with a favorite worn teddy bear she'd fondly named Hector.

Mary Helen tucked away her clothes in the drawers and closet quickly, set up her Mac laptop on her desk, and put her toiletries in the bathroom. A few other boxes she left unpacked for now. Downstairs, she stashed her groceries away in the kitchen and checked the pantry to see what items her mother and Parker had left behind. Then she let herself out onto the screened porch to gaze down the quiet beach pathway leading to the Atlantic Ocean.

Exhausted from the trip, and the stressful adrenalin high she'd run on for the last week, Mary Helen dropped into a wicker chair on the porch. She leaned her head back, letting the panic and worry of the last days drain gradually out of her. Safe here, she could decide what to do next about her life. It wasn't as though she'd died or anything, it simply felt like it. A line from one of her mother's books slipped into her mind: Every time a dream dies, a part of you dies, too.

Scenes from the past week seeped into her mind and Mary Helen let the tears stream down her face again. She wasn't the crying type, like Suki, but the events of the week and the strain of it, coupled with Kizzy Helton's words seemed to open up a huge pocket of grief inside her. She let herself sob as emotions swamped her, knowing the release probably good for her, while hating herself for giving in to tears.

"I can't remember the last time I saw you cry," a voice from the doorway said.

Immediately recognizing the voice, Mary Helen hated to even open her eyes. She knew who it was. "Go away, J.T. I don't feel like company."

"Looks like you might need some though."

She heard the screen door shut and his steps walk across the porch. Opening one eye a little, she saw him drop into a chair beside hers.

"I really don't want to talk to you right now."

"Give it up, Mary Helen. I'm not leaving."

She made a valiant effort to rein in her emotions and wiped at her face.

J.T. handed her a handkerchief from his back pocket.

"No one carries handkerchiefs around anymore," she said, taking it and mopping at her face.

"I work with bikes at the shop at lot. Bikes have grease, oil, and dirt on them. Handkerchiefs work better than flimsy little tissues."

She glanced with alarm at the handkerchief she'd been swabbing over her face.

He laughed, an old familiar sound that took her back to childhood and a hundred memories. "Don't worry. It's clean."

Mary Helen leaned her head back against the chair again, trying to settle herself.

"What are you doing here?" he asked. "Your folks didn't tell me you were coming down. I drop by every day or two and check on the house for Parker. He didn't mention you were coming."

"Maybe he forgot to tell you."

"And maybe you forgot to tell him."

"I decided to come somewhat impulsively." She snapped the words. "What business is it of yours anyway, J.T. Mikell?"

He laughed again. "That sounds more like the old Mary Helen Avery I remember. Smart tongue. Quick comeback."

"I really would prefer some time alone tonight," she said again.

"Have you eaten?" he asked.

Her jaw clenched. "No, but I'll fix something in a little while when I get hungry. I stopped to pick up a few groceries."

"I have a better idea." He stood up. "There's a big pizza in my car I just picked up after closing the shop. We'll share it." He started toward the door. "I saw the lights on as I drove down Point Street toward my place and I pulled in the driveway to check the house. The pizza should still be hot."

Watching him head out the door, Mary Helen wished she could figure out a way to talk him out of coming back with the pizza but knew the idea useless. Obviously along with everything else, she'd have to put up with J.T. Mikell tonight as well. Funny how she'd forgotten to think out how coming back to the beach house for a time would put her in J.T.'s path again. Oh, well. As she'd recently learned, there were worse evils to contend with.

CHAPTER 2

Friday had proved a busy day at the bike store on Jungle Road but J.T. finally managed to close at 6:00. The summer tourist traffic was winding down in mid August, with many schools back in session now, but on the weekends the crowds picked up again. He couldn't complain when rentals of bikes, golf carts, kayaks, paddleboards, and more flew out the door with the tourist crowd every day. Business at Mikell's Island Rental and at their Dock Store on the Yacht Basin behind it grew every year.

Too tired to think about cooking, J.T. snagged a pizza at Buck's to carry home with him. He planned to sit out on the porch with his feet up to enjoy it. Even though it wasn't dark yet, J.T. noticed the lights at Oleanders as he drove past. He turned around in his own driveway, two houses away, to head back to see if Parker had come down from Beaufort, but saw an unfamiliar car when he pulled in the drive. Spotting the New Jersey license plates his heart tripped, like it always did whenever he thought of Mary Helen Avery. Dang woman. You'd think he'd be past thinking about her by now.

Hearing noise on the back porch, J.T. started up the steps quietly. Tourists often tried to take over an empty beach house for an afternoon or a free overnight. However, the sobbing he heard as he drew near the door caused him to pause. Mary Helen sat on the porch, crying like her heart was breaking. The last time he'd seen her cry like that was when she'd thrown his class ring back at him, and stormed out of his life.

He headed into the screened porch now, knowing he probably wouldn't be welcome. But sparring with Mary Helen Avery was nothing new to him. He'd put up with it to share a little time with her. It troubled him she was so upset, too.

As expected, he had to battle past her surly efforts to get rid of him, but he was purposed to stay. Posing the idea of sharing pizza with her, J.T. sprinted down to his car to retrieve it and then back to drop it on the table on the porch, overlooking her disinterested expression.

"Got any colas in the house?" he asked, noticing she'd wiped the last of her tears away now and put on a stubborn look instead.

She shrugged. "In the refrigerator."

Knowing the kitchen at Oleanders as well as his own, J.T. went inside, located a couple of colas and paper plates, filled two glasses with ice and then carried them back outside on a metal tray he found by the refrigerator.

He dropped into a chair at the table and opened the pizza box, letting the smell of it drift into the air. He put a few pieces on each plate, sure that Mary Helen would break down at the sight of a Buck's pizza again. Pepperoni with double cheese had always been her favorite—and his.

She shook her head in resignation. "You knew I wouldn't be able to resist this." She walked over to sit in the chair opposite his, picking up a piece of the pizza with a small smile.

"Why should you resist? I bought a large pizza with a coupon special—plenty to share."

She took a bite and closed her eyes in appreciation. "It's been a long time since I enjoyed a Buck's pizza."

"It's been a long time since you were at the island."

He studied her, without making a point of it. Tall, five foot ten at least, Mary Helen stood almost nose-to-nose with him. He'd always liked that. She was still slim and leggy, with the olive skin he remembered, the same pageboy dark hair with thick bangs, and those chocolate brown eyes flashing with intelligence and emotion.

"Are you through checking me out?" she asked between bites.

He grinned at her candor. "Yeah. You look good, if a little pale."

"I don't live on the beach anymore. I live in New Jersey in the city."

He shrugged. "I guess somebody has to live there. Glad it's not me."

She rolled her eyes.

"You ready to tell me what you're doing here—showing up unexpectedly and sitting out on the porch crying?"

"No." She frowned at him.

"Do Parker and your mom know you're here?"

"No. I wanted a little time to myself before I called them."

"To lick your wounds?"

"Wouldn't you?" she challenged.

"I suppose I might, if I knew what brought you here." He poured out more cola into his glass. "Parker and Claire will soon hear you've arrived. Elaine and Pete Whaley, next door, are out of town but they'll be back after the weekend. You know Elaine will call Claire as soon as she sees you're here if Isabel doesn't spot your car and call her first."

Mary Helen glanced toward the Whaley's house on the right of Oleanders and then to Isabel's on the left. "How is Isabel?"

"Good but getting a little older."

"She's not sick or anything is she?" Mary Helen asked in alarm. "Is she still working at the Mermaid?"

"She's fine," he assured her. "And she'll be glad to see you."

"I look forward to seeing her, too." She glanced toward Isabel's place again. "She so impacted my life. I can't say how much."

"She's one of a kind." J.T. flipped open the pizza box again to get out another slice.

"How is your family, J.T.?" Mary Helen asked, as if suddenly remembering the good manners her mother Claire instilled in her.

"Fine," he answered. "Since my Mikell grandparents are getting older, Mom and Dad built a new place on Peters Point Road near theirs."

"Near the old Mikell plantation?"

"Yeah. I'm living in the family beach house by myself now." He crossed an ankle over his leg, getting more comfortable. "We didn't want to sell Point Place and I wanted to stay there. Mom and Dad still come over to enjoy the beach and hang out. My brother Ryder, his wife Jennifer, and their kids Kaylee and Russell drive up from Savannah now and then, too."

She smiled. "It's funny to think of Ryder as a responsible adult and accountant, married with kids."

"Well, time passes. People grow up."

She glanced out toward the beach. "It seems like only the other day we were all out on the beach playing. All of us only kids."

It wasn't like Mary Helen to wax sentimental. Something really upsetting must have happened for her to show this soft side.

She glanced across the table at him. "You still look the same."

He grinned at her. "Still tall, dark, and handsome?"

"Maybe." She shrugged. "And definitely with the same arrogant attitude and devil-may-care grin." She let her eyes drift over him and then put out a hand to touch his cheek. "The same dimples, too." Her voice softened for a moment but then she straightened and turned away.

"I talked to Suki this afternoon," she said, changing the subject, not wanting to reveal any old feelings she might still harbor for him.

"How is she?" he asked in an equally casual voice, hoping she wouldn't see how much her touch affected him. He'd wanted to snatch her hand and kiss it but steeled himself not to.

"Suki was in Hollywood, California, when I called, and I was in Hollywood up the road." Her mouth tweaked in a smile. "Ironic, huh?"

J.T. laughed. "I remember we always used to sing that old show tune 'Hooray for Hollywood' every time we drove through the town." He sang a bit of it in remembrance, making her laugh.

"I thought of that old song, driving through," she admitted.

"What was Suki doing in California?"

"Playing with an orchestra, the Los Angeles Symphony, at the Disney Concert Hall. She graduated college in May and started her first concert tour in June. She's mostly playing with different orchestras around the U.S., traveling a lot, and then practicing in between. The agency she signed with in New York helped her find an apartment there. Mother and Parker went up to help her move in. She isn't far from my place in Short Hills, New Jersey, when she's home. I can take the New Jersey Transit Midtown Direct line into the city and be there in about an hour. We've been able to get together a little more when she's in town, but we both work a lot. She practices hours and hours every day when she's home and my schedule is hectic, too."

J.T. saw her face change when she mentioned her work, her eyes dropping away from his.

He glanced out toward the ocean. "The day is winding down. Let's take a walk on the beach before it gets dark." His eyes drifted over her. "You got anything less gorgeous to wear? Like shorts and an old knit shirt or something? You look too nice for the beach in that city girl outfit." He wiggled his eyebrows. "Not that you don't look good."

She stood up. "I brought shorts, and a walk would be good. I drove all day today and much of yesterday getting here." She started toward the door. "Put the pizza stuff up while I run upstairs to change."

"Sure." He watched her from the back as she headed inside, his eyes sliding over her again, before he gathered up their plates and glasses.

She came back in a few minutes in tan shorts, an old striped shirt, and flip-flops, looking more like the Mary Helen he remembered from the past.

J.T. resisted an impulse to take her hand as they walked down the sandy pathway behind Oleanders, past the old cabana and out onto the beach. It was easy to drift back in his mind to earlier times, but a lot of years had passed since he and Mary Helen Avery walked the beach as children and later as sweethearts in their teens. She'd turned twenty-six in January, hardly the girl of those past years, and he'd turned twenty-eight in May. How had so much time slipped away?

"What are you thinking about?" she asked.

"About how time has slipped away," he answered candidly.

She pulled off her flip-flops to carry them. "I always feel like a kid again at the beach though." She headed toward the water to wade, a grin spreading across her face.

They talked about childhood memories walking up the beach, avoiding any discussion of the latter years when they'd quarreled and when things went wrong between them. J.T. was glad to talk of happier times, glad to see her forget for a time whatever troubles brought her here.

On the way back down the beach though, he began to probe. He knew Mary Helen the type to hold things in, even when they needed to be aired out.

"So what happened in New Jersey to send you running to the beach?"

She frowned at him. "That's none of your business, J.T."

"Let me guess," he said, keeping pace with her long strides easily. "I bet you had a quarrel with a sweetheart."

"Not hardly." She snapped the words out. "I don't have a sweetheart right now." She made the word sweetheart sound silly when she said it, and J.T. grinned, glad to know she had no special boyfriend in her life.

"Then maybe you got fired. Stole a few too many paper clips on the job, embezzled a little money and are afraid they'll find out."

She glared at him. "I have never been fired from a job. Never."

"Then maybe you quit," he said, watching her grow testy now with the subject of her job. "Maybe the work was too hard for you or maybe someone hurt your little feelings." He smirked at the flush growing on her face. "Maybe you got a big crush on your boss but he didn't return your sweet affections, or maybe your boss put some moves on you that you didn't like."

"It wasn't like that," she all but shouted, turning on him with red spots in each cheek. "And Wendell Hembree was a married man. Married to the owner's daughter with two kids almost as old as me. The idea made me sick."

She stalked off down the beach now with tears dripping down her face.

J.T. caught up with her, grabbed her, and turned her into his arms. "I'm sorry. I know I provoked you into saying more than you wanted to."

She jerked away from him, hugging herself with her arms. "You are so mean."

"Maybe, but you need to talk about this." He dragged her over to sit beside him on one of the benches by a beach access point. "Tell me what happened. Okay?"

She leaned over and dropped her head into her hands. "It was awful. Wendell Hembree is the Corporate Merchandise Buyer with Adopt-Me-Dolls where I work in New Jersey. He met with me at the corporate office in Millburn to tell me what a great job he thought I'd done since coming to work for the company after college."

J.T. heard her breath catch as she looked back, remembering.

"I was hired as the Visual Merchandiser for Adopt-Me-Doll's Short Hills Mall store near Milburn and then got promoted to a Regional Merchandising Manager position." She sat up, continuing her story. "I started handling two other stores as a part of my regular responsibilities, traveling to the store at Menlo Park Mall in Edison and to another at Cherry Hill Mall. Each of these smaller stores had only a part-time visual merchandiser so I travelled to each about twice a month to help change out their store displays and to prepare for upcoming events."

She turned to J.T. "You probably didn't know all this, but I loved my job. It's what I studied for. I always wanted to work in retail." She paused, closing her eyes for a minute. "I got my degree to be a Visual Merchandiser and was thrilled when I got the job with

Adopt-Me-Dolls. I loved their concept of creating dolls that girls could adopt. The company owner, Donald McCrary, was raised abroad by missionary parents. He and his wife Marlene both had a heart for children in underprivileged areas of the world. They actually created their first dolls to link people with the needs of children in orphanages they held an interest in. They always gave a percentage of profits back to those orphanages from store sales and they still do that. Isn't that great?"

He nodded.

She sighed heavily, looking out toward the ocean. "I always felt so good being part of a company like that. I worked huge hours, lots of nights, and traveled extensively but I know I did a good job for the company. I wanted to stay with Adopt-Me-Dolls and move up with them. But I yearned to have more of a hand in the buying and in creating the displays. Often I had good ideas about potential store displays I thought would be fabulous but those above me held different notions. So I had to go along."

She hugged herself as if cold. "When Wendell Hembree approached me with the idea of working as a Liaison Merchandise Buyer with him, to travel to shows and help select displays and merchandise more directly, I was thrilled. He said Rita Sacco, my store manager at Short Hills, and the assistant manager, Lila Arquette, could cover for me when I needed to travel to a trade show or event. I knew Wendell's Assistant Merchandise Buyer left the company unexpectedly in early July and thought I might move into her position if I did well, get a higher salary and more responsibility. So I said yes, even knowing it would be hard to carry more workload."

"But Wendell Hembree had a little more in mind with your new job?" J.T. asked, remembering her earlier comments.

She wrapped her arms tighter around herself and rocked on the bench with her eyes closed. "I can still remember every minute of that day," she whispered the words. "He called me over to his office in Millburn on Monday. The main corporate offices were in a marvelous old building downtown. The first Adopt-Me-Dolls store started there, outgrew its location, and then moved to a bigger space in the Short Hills Mall outside of Millburn. If I'd moved up with the company I'd have worked in an office in Millburn. It's a pretty, charming town. The old Adopt-Me-Dolls Museum is on the ground floor of corporate, too, filled with dolls and the story of how the company started."

J.T. tried to stay patient and wait for Mary Helen to get to the point of her story. "So this Hembree called you in for another meeting on Monday?" he prompted.

"Yes. He told me about the itinerary of the first trade show we were traveling to together. Pointed at a sheet of travel arrangements on his desk, some airline tickets, hotel brochures. He flipped a hotel brochure open to show me pictures of the somewhat lavish rooms there."

She squeezed her eyes closed at the memory. "He was sitting across from me, not behind his desk. I remember our knees were almost touching. Then he said in a lower voice, 'We're going to make some nice memories at these shows, Mary Helen. The beds at this hotel have satin sheets.'"

Mary Helen looked at J.T. with panicked eyes. "At first I thought I hadn't heard him right, that I misunderstood, but then he ran his hand up my skirt. Right up my bare leg." Her breath hitched. "I jerked away; I was so shocked. I remember shaking my head back and forth saying no. He laughed a nasty little laugh and said, 'Surely you didn't think this new liaison position came without perks layered in? You're not that naïve. With only four years on the job, you didn't really believe a promotion like this would come without expectations?'" He squeezed my knee, and said, 'The term liaison implies a close working connection, Mary Helen.'"

She closed her eyes on the memory. "I sat there so stunned. I thought I'd simply die."

His heart went out to her. "What did you do?"

"I told him this type of relationship couldn't work for me, that I expected no inappropriate behavior if we traveled together. I also suggested the McCrarys would not approve of his actions.

He reminded me with a smirk that he was married to a McCrary, that they'd hardly believe me over him. He threatened me, saying he'd tell the McCrarys I was the one who approached him, trying to move my way up in the company by offering sexual favors."

"What a creep. Did you call his hand?"

"No. Maybe I should have but I was in such shock." She shook her head, biting her lip. "I realized, too, that no matter what happened, he'd still be in a top position with the company. He'd been married forever to the McCrary's daughter Donna and I liked her. I hated the idea of being the person who might hurt their marriage, cause trouble in their family. I didn't want to be painted with that awful brush."

"So you cut out?"

"Sort of. I stood up and told him I needed to get back to the office at Short Hills for a meeting. All I could think of was how much I wanted to get out of that room. He didn't seem to care he'd upset me, just grinned as I left, saying he'd see me Monday to head to the airport with him. I guess he assumed I intended to go along with his plan."

J.T. shook his head, grinning. "Well, obviously since you're here, you don't plan to play hanky-panky on Monday with Mr. Hembree."

"You can make your little jokes." She frowned at him. "But it was awful. I kept thinking I would figure out a way to handle the situation, but I never did. So by midweek, I decided to simply pick up my check early on Thursday, take a personal day on Friday, and leave town. I didn't see any other answer."

"You were in a spot. This guy sounds like a player, and he might have made things tough for you."

"I'm sure he would have. So I ran and quit. Isn't that cowardly?"

He shrugged. "Sometimes the wisest thing to do is to know when to turn tail and run, Mary Helen."

"Do you think I was wrong?"

"No. I think you acted smart. There are other jobs. You might have left without much notice, but I'm sure you know people at the company who will speak well for you, give you a good reference."

She nodded, tears dripping again. "I still feel so dirty."

"Well, stop that." He pulled her against him. "You were simply a young girl put in a tough spot by a rich, corporate creep. I'll bet the girl before you left for the same reason. You're probably not the first he's put in this position."

She drew back, eyes wide. "I never thought of that. Kimberly Harding did leave unexpectedly. I never heard any reason for why she left, only that it put the company in a difficult position."

"I want you to quit beating yourself up over this." J.T. reached out to stroke her hair. "You see movies all the time where things like this happen. You know a lot of men use their wealth and corporate positions to force favors. You simply chose not to play. Good for you."

She sniffed. "I was so scared all week. Scared he'd show up at my office, touch me again, or do something else creepy. I kept remembering him running his hand up my leg and how awful it was. He was old enough to be my father. He had two sons near my age, a nice wife, a great position in the company, and good in-laws that put him to work in their business. I respected him. The whole week was a nightmare until I could get away."

"I assume you left some nice resignation letters behind."

She straightened and wiped her face. "I did. I'm sure I'll get emails and calls wanting more explanation, but I thanked everyone for the opportunity to work at Adopt-Me-Dolls, said I was grateful for all I learned, wished them all the best." She waved a hand. "I handled it diplomatically."

"Still they'll wonder about it. If they know you at all, they know you wouldn't cut out for no reason."

"Maybe."

They sat quietly for a few moments, each thinking their own thoughts. J.T. sat envisioning his hands around Wendell Hembree's neck, furious the man played on the innocence of a nice girl like Mary Helen. Acted so nasty with her. Hurt her. Threatened her. Scared her. She deserved better.

"I'm sorry I dumped all this on you," Mary Helen said at last.

"I'm not. I pushed for it. You needed to talk about it."

She looked away.

"Look, I know I may not be the best person for you to confide all this to, but you know I care for you. And it won't go further."

"I do know that." She gave him a small smile. "I think I feel better for talking to someone about it, too. I couldn't talk to anyone at work and most of my friends worked with me. I didn't want to confide in anyone else about what Wendell Hembree did, either. The Hembrees are rich and influential in Milburn and Short Hills, as are the McCrarys. It would have tempted anyone I confided in to gossip. Plus I felt trashy for anyone to know what he did."

"Will you tell your mother?" he asked.

She winced. "I will probably need to."

"Tell your mother and Parker and don't feel ashamed to tell anyone else either. You didn't do anything to encourage Hembree to act like a slimeball the way he did. Be sure you know that."

"You've been sweet to me tonight, J.T."

He grinned at her. "Keep that in mind the next time you get mad at me."

She stood up. "We'd better head back to the house. You need to work tomorrow and I'm really tired. I think I'll go to bed early."

He stopped at the bottom of the steps to the back porch of Oleanders. "Saturday is busy at the shop. But I'll come by to see you after work."

"You don't need to. I'll be all right."

"Maybe I want to. I can pick up some fresh shrimp at Belle Buoy Seafood, maybe some crab cakes that we can stick in the oven."

"The ones Mrs. Belle makes?"

"The same."

"Well, then." She smiled. "I'll make salad, bread, and a dessert."

"Sounds like a plan," he said.

J.T. headed to his car, feeling happier than he had in a long time. Maybe if Mary Helen stayed around for a while, he could mend some fences with her. He certainly hoped so.

CHAPTER 3

Mary Helen slept surprisingly well after the trauma of her week and the long trip to Edisto. She grudgingly admitted J.T.'s visit helped. He was the last person she'd have chosen to talk with about anything personal, especially something humiliating and awful, but he'd goaded her into sharing and she felt better after she did. Funny how things worked out sometime.

Dressed in jeans shorts and a red sleeveless tank top, she stood in the kitchen at Oleanders now making breakfast. Her internal alarm clock, used to early morning work hours, seldom let her indulge in much extra sleep, even on a holiday.

Hearing steps and a knock at the back door, Mary Helen glanced toward the doorway to see Isabel Compton letting herself into the kitchen, dressed typically in one of her long floral skirt outfits.

"What a welcome sight," Isabel said, heading across the kitchen to wrap Mary Helen in a hug. "When did you get here?"

"Last night."

"And when were you planning to come see me?"

Mary Helen smiled at her old friend. "This morning, but you beat me to it."

"I couldn't wait once Ezra told me he saw a blue car with New Jersey tags over here." She glanced toward the stove. "You better watch your omelet."

Mary Helen turned to flip it in the skillet. "Want half of it?"

"Absolutely." Isabel grinned. "What can I do to help?"

"Pop a couple of slices of wheat bread in the toaster, get some butter and jam from the refrigerator, and pour coffee."

Mary Helen turned back to the stove to finish cooking the omelet and then split it onto two plates, bringing them to the kitchen table along with some silverware. Before sitting down across from Isabel she poured milk into a cute cream pitcher that looked like a happy cow.

Isabel laughed. "I always feel Claire's fanciful spirit in this house even when she isn't here." Her eyes studied Mary Helen. "I rather expected to find Claire here with you this morning."

"She doesn't know I'm here."

"Well, that explains why I didn't know you were coming." She poured a little cream in her coffee. "I expect there's a story."

"There is—a lengthy one."

"Well, let's eat first, and then you can tell me if you want."

Mary Helen loved that practical, matter-of-fact aspect about Isabel Compton. Little surprised her and she had a way of making everything seem commonplace, even life's uncertain, upsetting, and traumatic events.

She glanced at Isabel's familiar tanned face, full of life and intelligence, her gray eyes wise, never missing anything. She wore her dark hair, sprinkled with white now, pinned in the familiar bun at the base of her neck and she still dressed with a bit of casual flamboyance.

"How's Suki?" Isabel asked after eating most of her breakfast.

"Good. I talked to her last night before her performance with the Los Angeles Symphony in California. She'd flown in the day before and, around practicing, managed to get out to see some of the sights around Hollywood."

Isabel sipped at her coffee. "It's still hard for me to imagine that child grown up. But not you." She grinned at Mary Helen. "You were always grown up for your age, such a wise, confident little thing even at nine when you first came to Edisto. Talented too. And you always knew what you wanted."

"Well, you don't always get what you want in life."

Isabel finished her last bite of omelet before answering. "Life's a funny thing. Sometimes the things we think we want don't turn out to be the things we need."

"Maybe."

Isabel continued her thoughts. "I planned to marry Harlin Dean Boone but he ran off with my cousin Dorinne. Harlin later ran off with Dorinne's best friend and then with his secretary, so I count myself fortunate I met and married Ezra instead and didn't get what I thought I wanted."

She paused to spread a little blackberry jam on her toast. "When Ezra and I married, most women tended to stay home to raise children after marriage, and I expected to do that, too. However, children weren't in the cards for us and instead I inherited my family's little beach house on Jungle Road. I turned it into a lovely children's store, The Little Mermaid, which I've enjoyed immensely. In general, I was never particularly fond of children on a full-time basis, so I feel rather glad with how things turned out. I doubt the traditional homemaker role would have suited me well, even though I thought at one point it was what I really wanted. But I actually needed more from life." She glanced toward Mary Helen with a sunny smile. "I'm a good example of how things turn out as they should."

"I didn't know those things about you."

"Well, we don't always know everything about others, even when we think we do."

Mary Helen considered this, finishing her breakfast.

Isabel tapped a nail on the table after a time. "You seem overly quiet and rather wilted, Mary Helen. That's unlike you, so I'm assuming someone or something disrupted the life course you thought you had so well planned."

"Yes. Someone did, and rather shockingly," Mary Helen admitted, getting up to pour herself another cup of coffee. "I assume you want to hear about it?"

"Of course. A good story is exactly what I need to kick off what would otherwise be another simply ordinary day."

Mary Helen laughed despite herself. "Well, my story is hardly ordinary and that's a fact." She told Isabel then all she'd told J.T. the night before, glad she'd cried out most of her tears with him and could tell it without so much drama and emotion.

When she finished, Isabel reached out a hand to cover hers. "Well, that is a dreadful story for sure, and you were certainly in a spot with that disreputable man." She shook her head. "I am so sorry you had such an awful experience, and I'm certain there is a special place in hell for men like that who try to take advantage of young girls."

Mary Helen smirked. "That's a nice idea to consider right now."

"Hmmm, your younger self would have kicked Wendell Hembree in the shin and stormed up to the McCrarys' office to report him."

Mary Helen bit her lip. "Should I have done that?"

"Absolutely not. It would have been reactive."

Relieved, Mary Helen sighed. "I tried to remember what you taught me, to always give a bad situation three days before acting."

"Smart girl to remember that. Otherwise, you'd be sitting here fired, further humiliated, and without good references to help you find another job you might like."

"J.T. said the same thing," Mary Helen said before thinking.

Isabel lifted an eyebrow. "Since when have you been known to take counsel from J.T. Mikell or to even talk to him at length?"

Mary Helen looked away from Isabel. "He saw the lights at Oleanders last night and stopped to check on the house." She lifted her chin. "I couldn't get rid of him and while walking on the beach later he provoked me into telling him why I was here."

Isabel laughed. "You know I've always liked J.T."

"Actually, he was surprisingly kind when I needed it."

"You've always tended to overlook his worth." Isabel finished her own coffee and got up to pour another cup. "What are your plans now?"

She sighed. "I'll need to job hunt again, update my resume, see if my old college department and professors know of any opportunities. I can tap contacts I've made over the last four years, too. There are several similar, rival companies to Adopt-Me-Dolls I can explore, like American Girl, Mattel, and Madame Alexander." She hesitated. "Because Adopt-Me-Dolls also handles toys, clothing, and other children's items, that experience could open broader doors I might be interested in, too."

"I remember that big Adopt-Me-Dolls store you worked for in New Jersey. Ezra and I enjoyed visiting it when we came to see you on that trip to New York we took a couple of years ago. It was a massive store, with not only dolls, clothing, and toys but a Sweet Shop, Bistro, party room, doll repair shop, and more. I picked up a few ideas there to bring back to my little store here on the island."

"I really loved working there. If I hadn't liked it so much, this situation wouldn't be as sorrowful."

"That's a good point, but another opportunity will open."

"It might take me months to find the right thing though," Mary Helen added.

Isabel got up to freshen her coffee. "Do you plan to stay here at Oleanders or in Beaufort with Parker and your mother while you job search—or will you go back to your apartment in New Jersey?"

Mary Helen crossed her arms. "I am *not* going back to New Jersey. That's for certain. My lease is up next month and I told them I wouldn't renew. It was a furnished apartment, so I had no furniture there anyway. I packed up everything I owned and brought it with me. It's pitiful that I'd accumulated so little that I could pack it in my car or simply drop unneeded items at a thrift store without any remorse. I worked all the time, put in so many hours. Merchandisers have to go into the store evenings to change displays, rework the store windows, or set up promotions. I kept thinking I'd find more time for other things but never did."

"Work can become all consuming if you let it."

"Well, you don't need to give me that talk about working too much. I've already given it to myself. I gave everything I had to Adopt-Me-Dolls and what do I have to show for it now?" She knew her tone sounded bitter but didn't care.

"Actually you have four good years of work experience with a major company with increasing responsibility and raises to note on your resume. You also have new skills and a greater maturity. Surely you're not feeling so sorry for yourself you can't see that?"

Mary Helen leaned back and made a face. "I know. I'm just feeling down right now and wondering what I'm going to do with myself. Mother would paint or write to entertain herself and stay busy. Suki would play the piano. What will I do to fill the time? I'm used to being busy and working."

Isabel smiled. "How delightful that you should mention that. The girl I've had working at the Mermaid for the summer is going back to college this weekend. I was dreading working all the store hours by myself. You can come help me out. I'd love you to start on Monday if you would. Ezra and I might take another little cruise while you're here, as well. It's rare I have anyone to work for me that I can leave the store with to get away for a week or two."

Mary Helen got up to put their dishes in the sink. She heard Isabel tap her fingers on the table as if still thinking.

"Of course, if working at the Mermaid is too lowly for you now, I'd certainly understand," Isabel added. "You've grown used to bigger things and bigger responsibilities."

Mary Helen turned around to look at Isabel, feeling close to tear. "I'm touched you would want me. Please don't think otherwise. I can't tell you how much it means to me for you to offer me work at a time like this."

Isabel's voice softened. "And why wouldn't I? You're the best employee I've ever had. I'll title you store manager so you can put it on your resume as a nice interim position." She grinned. "Besides I do expect you to fully manage the store after all the experience you've gained. I'm not getting any younger. I'm in my seventies now, and the store could use some freshening and new ideas. I'm sure another business will snatch you up eventually, but I selfishly hope it doesn't happen too soon. It will be a joy to share your company again."

"Thank you, Isabel." Mary Helen moved across the kitchen to

hug her.

"Let's not get sappy." Isabel pushed her away. "Keep in mind I'm taking advantage of your situation. I hope Parker and Claire won't mind you staying here at the beach house rather than with them in Beaufort."

"I'm sure they'll come over to the island often."

Isabel glanced at the clock. "Speaking of work, I need to head to the store to open for the day. And you need to call your mother." She paused, tapping her chin thoughtfully. "It might also be a good idea to let your manager at Adopt-Me-Dolls, and possibly the company human resource director, know you've taken a store manager's job near your family. You can tell them you felt a little homesick for everyone here." She laughed. "Don't you let them think for a minute you're down here feeling sorry for yourself in some way. I imagine they're wondering why you left so abruptly."

"Do you think they'll figure out why I left?"

Isabel snorted. "I doubt it. I don't imagine Wendell Hembree will suddenly feel a sweep of deep remorse for his bad behavior and come forward to confess all, do you?"

Mary Helen bit back a laugh despite herself. "No, I don't imagine so."

Isabel stood and started toward the door. "Life will go on, sweet thing. You'll see. And this season will have its joys. Time with your family. Time with old friends like Jane. She'll be thrilled to see you. Time to enjoy the beach and get your peace back. It won't be all bad."

"I know, and I'm feeling better already. Thank you."

"Good, and remember to thank J.T., too. I wish I could have been a fly on the wall for that little get together last night."

Mary Helen flushed. "We only talked, Isabel."

"Well, sweet talk and sweet nothings are nice, just like the old Brenda Lee song. I always did like that song." Isabel let herself out the door and started down the stairs.

Mary Helen laughed and went to call her mother. It was still early, and she had plenty of time to drive to Beaufort and catch lunch with Claire and Parker before she needed to get back for dinner with J.T. Maybe she'd stop at the rental store and offer to take him out to dinner somewhere nice. Like Isabel said, she did owe him a thank you.

CHAPTER 4

J.T. kept glancing at the clock throughout the next day thinking about Mary Helen. Her story kept slipping through his mind. He knew after she got over the shock of what happened at her job that she'd start looking for another. Then she'd go away again and he'd hardly ever see her. She might even head back to New Jersey this week. She had an apartment there and might try to find work nearby. The suburban township where she lived sat close to several large cities, like Newark, Jersey City, and New York. Mary Helen always said, even in high school, she never wanted to spend her life in a small town like Edisto. Or even Beaufort. She'd wanted bigger. It was one of the things they often fought about.

To keep his restlessness at bay he loaded and delivered bikes around the island in the afternoon. Leon Johnson, his assistant manager, waved at him as he walked back in the shop.

"It was nice of you to run those bike deliveries out so Carlos could go home to check on his wife," Leon said from behind the register where he sat on a wooden stool.

"How is Maria?" J.T. asked.

"Doing good, I hear. Her gall bladder surgery went well, and Carlos already brought her home. With these new laparoscopic procedures, people get to go home the same day of their surgery now."

J. T. dropped paperwork relating to the bike deliveries on the desk by the register. "Well, tell him to take off whatever time he needs while she's getting better. We can shuffle jobs around to cover for him."

Leon glanced over the papers. "You missed a couple of your admirers while you were gone." He flashed J.T. a big grin. "You're a fine looking man and you sure do have a gift with the ladies."

J.T. frowned. "You're a good looking man yourself." He leaned against the counter across from Leon.

"Most of our tourist trade are white folks, and I'm a black man—and a married one, too." He held up his left hand to point to his ring.

"I'll bet it was that bunch of college girls staying at the Branson rental up the road that came by again." J.T. shook his head. "I'll be glad when they head back to school tomorrow. They've been stalking me most all week."

Leon laughed. "Yeah, they came by. So did that blond chick you've had a few dates with. She seemed to think you might be going out with her tonight. Pushy woman." He scratched his head. "She lives on the island but I keep forgetting her name."

"Gracie Byrd," J.T. offered, rolling his eyes.

"Doesn't sound like you're too taken with her."

"No, and it was probably a mistake to go out with her at all," he said, doubly sorry for doing that with Mary Helen back now.

"She is a looker, though," Leon said. "How long have you known her?"

"I've known Gracie since we were kids. Grew up with her. I didn't think much about going out with her a few times when she moved back here. She was going through a hard time, recently divorced, and seemed at loose ends. We just hung out a little."

Leon pushed his glasses down and looked at J.T. over the top of them. "Well, from how she acts, she seems to think there's more going on."

"Yeah, well, that's Gracie. She always likes to create her own realities."

"Hmmm. You might want to shy away from that one," Leon advised. "Women like that can cause trouble."

"Tell me about it," J.T. mumbled, a sweep of past memories

waltzing through his mind.

The shop door opened to let a group of customers in. As usual, they had questions—wanting to know things about the island, asking for restaurant recommendations or entertainment ideas. Most picked up gift items in the surf shop, too. Behind them a young couple came in the door wanting to rent bikes and an older man came in hoping to rent an umbrella. You'd think most folks would think to bring umbrellas to the beach but many didn't.

J.T. pitched in to help Leon handle business, with the store busy, and the rest of the afternoon moved along quickly. At about five, he glanced up to see Mary Helen walk in the door. And whoa! She wore a dress—a flirty buttercup yellow sundress with a low scoop neck. His breath caught at the sight.

"Hey," she said, breezing over to the counter.

"Hey yourself. Nice dress. You look good."

She sent him one of those rare knockout smiles of hers. "You like it?" She swirled around so he could admire the dress. "I bought it in Beaufort today shopping with Mother. She said I needed some beach clothes, that I looked like someone from "off" island rather than a local."

"Well, it's a different look from the New Jersey merchandiser."

Leon cleared his throat and J.T. looked up to catch his curious expression. Obviously, introductions were in order.

"Leon," J.T. said, "this is Mary Helen Avery. She's Claire Avery's daughter and is visiting here from New Jersey." He turned to Claire next. "Claire, this is Leon Johnson, my store manager and very good friend."

Leon reached out a hand to take Mary Helen's. "I'm pleased to meet you. My wife Vernita often talks about you."

Mary Helen's eyes brightened. "I'm pleased to meet you, too, and tickled to know Vernita lives here on Edisto again. We lost touch over the years but I'd love to see her. We played together as girls. Her mother Kizzy always brought her when she cleaned at Oleanders and sometimes I visited at Kizzy and Lewis's place. Vernita and I had the best times together."

"I've heard some of those stories." He laughed.

Mary Helen turned toward J.T. and put a hand on her hip. "You didn't tell me Vernita was back on the island."

"We haven't had much time to talk and catch up yet," he answered. "You only got here last night."

"You have a point." She blushed, obviously remembering what they *had* talked about last night. "Actually, that's why I stopped by. I thought instead of us eating at the house tonight that I'd take you out to dinner as a thank you for being so nice to me last night."

Seeing Leon's eyebrows raise a notch, she added, "J.T. and I haven't always gotten along, but I had a bad day yesterday—in fact a rather difficult week—and he was really sweet to me."

J.T. watched Leon smirk. Mary Helen was never one to tiptoe around a delicate issue.

"We're not very busy now in the shop," Leon put in. "Why don't you leave early, J.T.? I wouldn't want you to miss out on a date night opportunity with a pretty girl."

J.T.'s eyes skimmed over Mary Helen again. "Yeah, I think I'll do that."

Mary Helen glanced around the shop. "Why don't you show me around first before we leave?" she asked. "I haven't been in the rental shop in a long time. If your Dad and Mom are working at the Dock Store or in the office, I'd love to say hello to them, too."

J.T. nodded. "Dad's out at the Dock Store working today and I think Mom's in the store office. I know they'd love to see you."

He also knew he'd like to figure out over dinner what caused this huge transition in Mary Helen since last night. That weepy, panicked girl he'd comforted at Oleanders seemed to have totally disappeared.

Mary Helen began to wander around the store. "I remember when Mikell's Island Rentals was only in this one building before your family added the other shop behind it on the Yacht Basin." She paused to pick up a pair of sunglasses from one of the store shelves to examine them. "In fact, that area on the water was still being developed in the 1980s."

"That's right. The island has grown." He led Mary Helen through the store and out the back door. A pathway led across the street to the new office building and then wound its way along a weathered walkway to the marina on Yacht Basin, the water beyond it sparkling in the sunshine.

Mary Helen paused to shade her eyes, looking toward the marina.

J.T. stopped, too. "We already owned the property behind this store all the way to the water but we didn't develop it until about five years ago. Dad saw the potential then for expanding and added the marina and Dock Store. At the store people can rent boats, jet skis, or kayaks and then put them right in the water after renting them. You remember a tributary from the Yacht Basin winds through the marshes to Scott Creek, into Big Bay Creek and the St. Helena Sound, and straight into the ocean."

"I remember. Your dad used to take us through all those back water routes in his boat."

"The new office building you see across the street used to be an old beach house." He gestured to the colorful building. "As you can see, we painted it aqua blue to match the main bike shop on Jungle Road."

She smiled. "I remember your mom used to work in the little office room upstairs over the bike shop. Your dad did, too. It was a real crunch."

"It was," he agreed. "Mom and Dad have their own separate offices now in the new building. There's even a third office Ryder uses when he comes up from Savannah to do the accounts."

"It's wonderful how the business has grown."

J.T. bit his tongue not to mention how she'd once called their rental business poky and marveled at why he wanted to stay at Edisto to work when so many better opportunities waited out in the world. He also wondered again why she was so cheerful today after her dark mood yesterday.

"Where do you want to eat dinner?" he asked instead, keeping his thoughts to himself.

"I'm hoping you'll drive me over to the Charleston Crabhouse," she said, stooping to pick up a shell on the sandy path. "The one on James Island on the Wappoo Creek. I haven't been there in a long time. I want to be very touristy, sit by the window looking out on the creek, watch the boats, and order one of their seafood platters."

"I can go for that." He turned her to face him then, studying her eyes. "You seem a lot better today than last night."

"Yes, and you helped with that. Isabel did, too, this morning." She glanced toward the office building. A dark haired woman headed out of the door, waving at them. Mary Helen waved back, starting toward her. "I'll tell you more about that later."

"Mary Helen Avery, you're a sight for sore eyes." Lula Mikell, J.T.'s mother, quickly reached them to wrap Mary Helen in a hug. "I saw you two coming down the path from my window and I simply could not believe it. Claire didn't tell me you were coming down from New Jersey."

"I came impulsively, only got here last night, and this morning I drove over to Beaufort to have lunch with Mother and Parker. I just got back and thought I'd pop by to see all of you." She pushed a swath of her hair behind her ear that the sea breeze had blown awry. "And if you don't mind I'm borrowing J.T. tonight to go to the Crabhouse on James Island."

J.T. watched his mother's eyes widen with surprise at that last comment. He knew he'd get the third degree later as to why Mary Helen wanted to spend any time alone with him. It certainly wasn't the norm. She'd spent the last ten years since he was eighteen trying her best to avoid him.

"Well, let's go find John. He'll want to see you, too."

After they visited with his mom and dad and toured the rest of the Mikell business, J.T. popped upstairs to his own office in the bike store to wash up and change into a clean shirt. Working with bicycles and other rentals, he always kept a few extras on hand.

He came back downstairs to find Mary Helen chatting with Leon's wife Vernita, a pretty black woman with warm brown eyes and curly hair.

"I had to come over to see Mary Helen for a minute when Leon called to tell me she'd come visiting," Vernita explained.

"It's good when old friends can get together," J.T. said.

"Can the two of you go to the Crabhouse with us to eat tonight?" Mary Helen asked.

"I wish we could say yes," Vernita answered. "But we've got a meeting to attend at the church tonight. If you're still here next weekend, though, maybe we can all get together then. You can come over to our place, and Leon and I will cook you some good Southern island food."

"I'd absolutely love that," Mary Helen said, surprising J.T. with her answer. "You call me this week and we'll make plans."

Deciding not to make any comment about this, J.T. let Mary Helen chat with Vernita for a few more minutes while he talked to Leon about store business before they left.

"If you'd like, you can drive your car back to Oleanders before we leave, Mary Helen. Then you won't have to pick it up here when we come back."

"That's a good idea."

She got into her little blue Camry parked out front while J.T. went around to the back parking lot to get his car. A short time later he pulled up in her driveway to find her locking up the Camry and watching for him. Strolling up to his car, she put a hand on her hip and studied him. "I expected to see you in that old battered work truck you used to drive with Mikell's Island Rentals painted on the side."

He shrugged. "It's been a while. I bought a new car."

"Yes, a cute black MG convertible. I love it, and I remember you always wanted one. You were such a car buff."

"It's a very economical little British car, rear wheel drive, good for getting around on the island."

She laughed. "You don't need to convince me it was a good choice, and it will be fun riding in this over to the Crabhouse." She sighed as she slid into the passenger seat beside him. "I could use a little fun."

"Still feeling depressed?"

"Maybe a little." She shrugged. "But mostly I'm feeling at loose ends with all the unexpected changes going on in my life right now."

"Sometimes change can be fun. Maybe you need to lighten up, get into the moment." He popped a CD into the player as he pulled out of the driveway. Sheryl Crowe's voice singing her hit "Soak Up the Sun" soon filled the car.

J.T. started singing along and he was glad to hear Mary Helen join in. They always sang in the car together when younger. It brought back good memories now to hear her voice once more, and he enjoyed seeing Mary Helen looking happy and obviously enjoying herself.

At the Crabhouse, they were able to get a table by the window. After ordering, they talked about random things while they waited for their food, caught up on news of friends they both knew—who'd moved, gotten married, had kids, or settled into an unexpected career. Mary Helen commented about boats on the river and nearby sights, and J.T. shared about local happenings. Easy, comfortable conversation, like two old friends. They ate seafood, dipped hush puppies in tartar sauce, and drank sweet tea, a Southern tradition.

Unfortunately, too, their cute little red-haired waitress kept flirting with him. He knew Mary Helen noticed it.

"The girls obviously still like you," she commented after their waitress actually dropped hints about where she lived while refilling their tea.

"This one seems to." J.T. rubbed his neck, uncomfortable and not sure what else to say.

Mary Helen nodded toward a couple of girls at the bar watching them.

One of them waved a few fingers when J.T. glanced her way.

"Girls plural," she added. "Surely you noticed."

He threaded a hand through his hair in annoyance. "It isn't

anything I do, Mary Helen."

She shook her head. "Basically I know that."

"But it's always bothered you." He looked across at her, gorgeous in her yellow sundress. "For myself, I always feel a little smug when guys look at you when we're out, because I know you're with me."

"You know it's not the same. You don't see guys waving their little fingers at me, swishing by the table, and writing their phone numbers on napkins."

He frowned. "No one's written their number on a napkin."

"Not tonight—at least not yet." She sent him a smug look. "But the night's young."

He winced at the familiar sarcasm.

"This probably isn't a good subject," she added, wrinkling her nose.

"No, it's not, because I've told you a million times I don't even notice other girls when I'm with you. You're all I see, Mary Helen."

"That's sweet. You always have been charming."

He decided not to reply this time. Instead he changed the subject. "You said you'd tell me why you're feeling better today and about what Isabel said to you this morning."

"That blessed woman." Mary Helen smiled then. "She came over early this morning, helped me see everything that happened more clearly without all the emotion layered in. She also helped me see that what happened wasn't the end of the world and, like you, she felt I'd done the right thing to leave. That was a really hard decision for me to make."

He chuckled. "You probably wanted to kick the man's teeth down his throat and make a stink. Keep reminding yourself though that you really did do the best thing you could."

She looked across at him. "Thanks. It helped me to hear both of you tell me that. Letting a wrong go unpunished, without consequence, has always bothered me."

J.T. felt like groaning. He certainly knew the truth of that last remark.

Mary Helen finished off her last few shrimp with relish and then sent him a sunny smile. "The good news is that Isabel offered me a temporary job at The Little Mermaid. The girl working for her this summer is going back to college this weekend and Isabel was dreading working the store full-time until she could find someone."

J.T. sat up with surprise. "And you're going to do that?"

"You sound surprised. What did you think I would do?"

"Go back to New Jersey, look for another job in the area. I know you have an apartment in Milburn and that you liked living there."

She made a face. "I don't think I'd want to stay in that area now. I might run into Wendell Hembree or others I worked with and it would be awkward. My apartment lease is up next month and I told them I wouldn't renew."

"What about all your furniture and stuff?"

She looked uncomfortable. "The place was furnished; working so much I accumulated little. I loaded everything up I wanted to keep and brought it with me. The rest I took to a mission store the day before I left."

He didn't say anything.

"It's sad to realize I had so little there except for my work."

"I'm sure you had friends."

She gave him a small smile. "I made a few good friends that I'm sure I'll stay in touch with. The others were simply acquaintances. You know."

"Like summer people we meet here."

"Exactly."

Seeing they were finished with dinner, the waitress came to clear plates and ask them about dessert.

"Let's get salted caramel cheesecake," J.T. suggested.

Mary Helen hesitated. "I don't know. I am *so* full."

"We'll split it."

She laughed. "Which means you'll eat most of it and I'll get maybe two bites."

"You can order your own."

"No, two bites is about right. And coffee would be good, too."

They lingered over dessert and coffee, watching darkness fall outside. Mary Helen told him more about her job and talked about companies she might apply to for future work, networking she might initiate to see what jobs were open she'd be qualified for. She asked him more about his work and they talked retail. They'd always had that love in common.

Back at the island, he pulled into her driveway and stopped the motor, turning to look at her. "I had a good time."

"So did I." She gave him an impish grin. "Is this where you're going to wonder whether you should kiss me goodnight or not?"

"No. I've never had to wonder whether I'd want to do that or not." And J.T. leaned over to settle his mouth on hers, putting his hand behind her neck to pull her closer.

To his amazement she didn't pull back, slap his face, or toss out one of her usual sarcastic comments. She kissed him right back. And kissing Mary Helen the woman was even more exciting than kissing Mary Helen the girl had ever been.

When she murmured a soft "ummm" under her breath, he moved closer, drawing her as near as possible in the MG, wanting to feel her against him. Wanting to hear her breathing escalate, her heartbeat kick up. He'd missed her so much. He hadn't even realized how much until he held her close like this, felt her mouth soft against his, felt their passion rise. He'd never lacked for female company, but there had never been anyone he cared for like Mary Helen. She was his other half, like the other side of an oyster shell. And the only time things ever felt perfect like this with a woman was with her. He'd tried to erase her memory, but he'd never been able to. He knew he'd probably lose her again soon, but, mercy, he was going to enjoy every second while she was here.

"J.T." she whispered. "I think I'm going to enjoy having a little time at Edisto."

"Me, too, Mary Helen. Me too." He murmured the words while running his lips down her neck and praying—probably irreverently—that it would take her a long time to find a new job.

CHAPTER 5

On Sunday morning, Mary Helen took her coffee out onto the screened porch of Oleanders where she could hear the peaceful sounds of the waves washing up on the beach not far away. Already the beauty and quiet of Edisto was spinning its magic in her soul.

With this being Sunday, she could have driven to Beaufort to attend church with her mother and Parker and enjoy lunch afterward at Waterview, their historic home downtown. But her parents had an early afternoon wedding to attend in Savannah. Claire's book illustrator, Vanessa Yardley, was getting married. She and Claire had grown close working together on Claire's six Polka Dot Kids books, and then on the Farnsworth Fairies books following, and Claire and Parker had accepted the invitation to attend her wedding over a month ago.

"You can drive down to Savannah with us," Parker suggested, but Mary Helen declined. She was glad for a little quiet time on her own. Working retail as a visual merchandiser often meant putting in long weekend hours when others were off.

The house phone rang and Mary Helen slipped inside for a minute to answer it. She'd avoided answering her cell, not wanting to respond to calls from associates at Adopt-Me-Dolls yet, but only family members and old Edisto friends had the number at Oleanders.

Mary Helen picked up the phone to hear J.T.'s voice.

"Hey. What are you doing?"

"Sitting out on the porch drinking coffee and enjoying a quiet morning."

"Sounds good," he said. "I need to work until six but I thought you might like to come over to my place to eat shrimp and crab cakes from Belle Buoy's tonight. I have salad makings at the house, too. We can hang out."

She hesitated a moment, but not for long. Time with J.T. had proved to be nice so far and helped her life feel more comfortable and normal. "Okay. I'll walk up to the house at about six thirty to give you time to stop at Belle Buoy's." She paused and then asked. "Is Leon at the shop today?"

"No. He and Vernita are really invested in their church. All the Heltons go to the same church if you remember, Olivet A.M.E., and the whole family go to Kizzy and Lewis's place for Sunday lunch after church. So I usually always work Sundays or Carlos does."

She nodded. All the Mikells worked long hours in retail, especially in summer. "I'm looking forward to going to Vernita and Leon's house one night next week," she said. "I'm enjoying seeing old friends again while here. Today I'm going to Jane's for lunch. I'll get to see her new house."

"Well, tell her and Barton hello for me."

Mary Helen heard voices in the background.

"Customers," J.T. said. "I've got to go."

"I'll see you later." She hung up the phone and then headed back out on the porch.

August was still a busy time on the island. Already Mary Helen could see tourists setting up chairs and umbrellas on the beach, walking in the early morning sunshine, and enjoying the ocean.

J.T.'s words about the Heltons caused her mind to drift back to Kizzy's words at the store on Friday when she'd stopped in for groceries—that she was a preacher's daughter but had slipped away from God. The words made her remember her father. Losing him at only nine had caused many memories to fade while others often popped back clear and strong at the oddest times. She had known a strong spiritual upbringing when her father was alive and afterward, as well, with her mother and Parker.

"But I have slipped away from the close relationship I once knew with God," she said out loud to herself. She knew Kizzy was right; she needed to try to recapture that.

She could almost hear her father's voice now, announcing as he often did from the pulpit, "Hold up your Bible. That's your Instructional Manual for life. It ought to be in your hands when you come to church. It ought to be in your hands and heart every day to guide you through life."

Her dad had been a wonderful man, so vibrant, so wise.

"I've certainly failed to use my Instructional Manual, Daddy," she said.

It seemed then as if the wind whispered, "It's never too late to come back to God."

Heeding that advice, Mary Helen went up to her room to dig out her Bible from one of the boxes she hadn't unpacked yet. Finding it, she carried it back to the porch. It was a beautiful navy blue leather Bible, thumb-indexed with ribbon markers, and with Mary Helen's name embossed on the cover in gold. She'd gotten it for high school graduation from her mother; Suki got an identical one in maroon when she graduated. Mary Helen had carried her Bible off to college with her, of course, and on to her first job later, but admittedly, little used it. Life got busy. College was full of academic reading, other types of study, and her work life grew busier and busier.

"Life is full of choices." She seemed to hear her father's words again. "Be sure you make the best ones. And be sure you talk with God before you make your choices."

Mary Helen shivered. Being back here at Edisto seemed to bring her father much closer again.

The rest of Kizzy's words floated back into her mind and using the concordance in the back of her Bible she looked for the scripture she remembered Kizzy quoting. It was a familiar one, inscribed on a plaque in her mother's office in their house in Beaufort. She soon found it in Proverbs: *'Trust in the Lord with all thine heart; and lean not unto thine own understanding. In all thy ways acknowledge Him and He shall direct thy paths.'"*

Well ouch. She couldn't remember the last time she'd inquired of God about anything. She'd been figuring out her own way for a pretty long time, and she thought she'd been doing a bang-up job of it. But maybe she hadn't been so smart after all. Here she was running back home to Edisto with everything a mess.

Sighing, she flipped to the front of her Bible where her mother had written a verse from James: *"Draw nigh to God and He will draw nigh to you."*

Well, she supposed that would make sense.

She made an effort then to pray, to talk to God, to take the first steps to get back into a close place. When she'd been a little girl she remembered simply talking to God like a friend, so confident He heard, so confident He cared. She wanted that back again, that sweet and trusting place.

"Lord, I haven't done a very good job of drawing nigh to You these years or in leaning to Your understanding," she prayed out loud. "I'd like to do better with that and to get close to You again. I'm asking You to help me with that journey back. And help show me the way I need to take in going forward, too."

She prayed some more, read several chapters in Proverbs in her Bible, and then realized she needed to get ready to head to Jane's or she'd be late. She ran upstairs, brushed her teeth and hair, zapped on a little make-up, and slipped into some lightweight black slacks, a simple white blouse, and her black leather flip-flops. Tossing her Chanel bag over her shoulder, she headed out of the house, remembering to take the directions to Jane's house she would need.

Jane Whaley Edings, Mary Helen's best friend since childhood, had grown up in the house next door to Oleanders on Point Street. Jane's parents Elaine and Pete Whaley still lived at Whaley House, but their four kids, Tom, Chuck, Jane, and Emma, were grown now. All worked in some capacity for the family business, Whaley's Realty, except for Emma, who taught college English in Beaufort.

Jane had married four years ago and recently moved to a new home off Oyster Factory Road up island from the beach. Following Jane's directions, Mary Helen soon pulled into the driveway of the cute pink house built on stilts, like most Edisto houses anywhere near water.

Barton waved to her from the porch where he'd obviously been watching for her. A very, *very* big dog on the porch began to bark at her as she got out of the car, but the dog quieted as Barton put a hand on its head.

Mary Helen hesitated at the bottom of the stairs, watching the dog warily—probably the largest dog she'd ever seen.

"Bear is big but he's as gentle as a lamb," Barton said to her. "Come on up and don't worry about him."

Surprisingly, Barton was right. After giving Barton a hug, Mary Helen reached down to pet the big dog's head. "What kind of dog is this? He looks like Nana, that huge dog in *Peter Pan*."

He laughed. "That dog in *Peter Pan* was a Newfoundland and Bear is a Newfoundland-Labrador mix. They do look alike." He opened the door of the house to let her in.

"Mary Helen's here," he called out.

Jane came into the room to grab Mary Helen and exclaim over her. "I'm so glad you're here. It's wonderful to see you again."

Tall and leggy like Mary Helen, Jane had long, reddish brown hair, hazel eyes, and a smattering of freckles across her sun-browned face. She wore a loose top, obviously pregnant again, and Mary Helen could feel the firm bulge of the baby when they hugged.

A small girl pranced around the corner into the room but then held back shyly, not recognizing Mary Helen.

"Elena, this is my best friend ever Mary Helen Avery. We grew up together." Jane grinned at Mary Helen as she said the words.

At almost three years old with a head of curly, red-brown hair and bright eyes, Elena was a darling.

"Mary Helen sent your favorite doll Phoebe to you," Jane said as the child still hesitated.

Elena skipped over to the couch to grab up her Adopt-Me-Doll to hug it. "I wuv Phoebe," she said, smiling at Mary Helen.

Jane glanced toward a table set with dinnerware, beyond the living room in the house's open-space floor plan. "Lunch is ready, so come and eat while everything's hot. We'll visit afterward. Barton is going fishing with one of his friends so we can enjoy a true girls' time."

Barton winked at her. "I figured you girls would like some time for just the two of you to catch up on all your news."

After they sat down, with Elena tucked into her toddler chair with her doll, Barton grinned across at Mary Helen. "Elena really loves that little doll. It was nice of you to send it to her for her birthday. She likes the book about it, too."

"Adopt-Me-Dolls likes to make girls feel they've adopted a real child that needs a loving home," Mary Helen explained. "Phoebe's story, in the book about her, is linked to an orphanage in Greece that the owners of Adopt-Me-Dolls, the McCrarys, help to support. I thought the coastal pictures of Greece might feel familiar to Elena living near the beach here."

"She loves Phoebe's story of growing up in Greece," Jane said, bringing food from the kitchen. "So do I. It makes me want to visit there."

Mary Helen's eyes moved over all the serving dishes now on the table. "Everything looks really good," she said, surprised at such a big Sunday meal.

Jane giggled, sitting down. "You know I didn't like to cook much growing up but I've really started to enjoy it now." She pointed at dishes, beginning to pass them around. "I made fried chicken— that's one of Barton's favorites, mashed potatoes, green beans, which Elena loves, and a cherry tomato salad as a fun extra. Elena loves cherry tomatoes, and I try to make vegetables she will eat when I can."

"And beans!" Elena held up a green bean in her hand.

"Use your fork, Elena," Barton prompted, reaching over to remind her how to spear green beans.

Lunch was a sweet family affair. Mary Helen spent so much

of her free time with single friends she'd forgotten most of the girlfriends she grew up with were married women now with husbands, children, and homes. It gave her a little twist in her heart watching how doting Barton acted with both Jane and Elena, even running a hand over Jane's belly and giving her a suggestive smile when he didn't realize Mary Helen was watching.

"I saw your dental office on the corner of the highway when I turned off toward your home earlier," Mary Helen said to him at one point.

"It's called Edisto Dental," he clarified. "The older dentist was retiring and I was looking for a small practice to buy. I'd been working in Walterboro, living in the garage apartment at mom and dad's to save money. I really liked the practice when I saw it and liked the idea of living on the island nearer the beach, too. My family often came down to Edisto when I was growing up. It's beautiful here and it gets in your blood."

Jane grinned. "I was working part time for mom and dad at Whaleys that summer, showing houses and answering phones in the office, besides helping with the books. Barton needed someone to take him around to show him available rentals on the island and I got the job." She leaned over to kiss him. "And I got the man."

He laughed. "Meeting Jane *did* influence my decision. Our former rental house worked for a while after we married, but with a second baby coming, we needed our own place. This area is growing and really close to my office."

"You chose a great house and I love the location." Mary Helen hesitated. "I have to ask about your dog, Bear. Not many people own a dog that big."

Barton finished a bite of chicken before answering. "I found Bear at the pound as a pup and brought him home to my apartment in Walterboro before Jane and I married." He shook his head. "He was so loveable and good-hearted, even as a pup, but I admit I was clueless about how big a dog like Bear would grow."

"We worried a little how Bear would do with kids when we had Elena," Jane added. "But he's incredibly sweet-natured and loving with her. Very protective, too."

Mary Helen glanced over at the big dog curled up in the corner. "I told Barton when I arrived I thought he looked like Nana in *Peter Pan*."

"He does," she agreed. "He eats a lot, too. It's a good thing Barton is a dentist. Bear goes through a bunch of dog food every month!"

After lunch, Barton took Bear out for a walk and then left to go fishing with his friend. Jane showed Mary Helen around the house, put Elena down for a nap, and then the two girls finally sat down to visit.

"Whew!" Jane put her feet up on an ottoman. "It's good to sit down. Carrying this baby around makes me tired sometimes."

"Are you all right?" Mary Helen asked in alarm.

She waved a hand. "Of course. I'm fine—just over six months pregnant." She pointed to her stomach. "Look. Even though I'm ready to rest, he's not."

Mary Helen's eyes lifted with surprise as she saw a ripple pass across Jane's stomach.

"Come over and feel," Jane said. "This one is a boy. I'll bet he's going to be a handful from all the jumping around he's doing."

Mary Helen, with a little wonder, laid her hand on Jane's stomach and almost immediately felt the baby move under her fingers. "Unbelievable, "she said, sitting down again across from Jane on the sofa. "I still can hardly believe you're a married woman, a mom, and a mother to be."

Jane smiled. "I never imagined how great it would be. It always looked kind of boring watching moms with their kids when I was growing up. But things happen to your heart and feelings when you marry and start raising your own children. I don't know how to explain it. My nesting urge has already hit and I've started getting John Jared's room set up—that's what we're planning to name this new baby, John Jared after Barton's dad John Edings and his older brother Jared."

She reached over to pick up her glass of tea on the table by her chair to take a sip. "Elena is sleeping in a little twin bed now and, blessedly, I've got her potty trained. Life will be easier with Elena out of diapers when the new baby comes."

"You'll be busy."

"I will." She frowned and changed the subject. "I hated so much hearing what happened with your job when we talked last night. That man was such a creep to act like that. I wouldn't want to stay anywhere near where he worked either. Bless your heart. I hope somehow his family and the company find out how awful he is before he tries to treat someone else like he did you."

She leaned forward. "Honestly, Mary Helen, what if he'd taken you on that trip and then come in your room or something. He might have raped you or really hurt you. It could have been much worse."

Mary Helen bit her lip. "I never really thought of that."

Jane shrugged. "Well, selfishly I'm thrilled you're going to stay at Edisto for a while so I can see you more. I've made a lot of friends over the years but none I love like you. I think we hit it off like two peas in a pod from the first day as toddlers playing on the beach."

Old memories rolled over in Mary Helen's mind at her words. "We've always been kindred spirits, you and me."

"Like Anne Shirley and Diana Barry in the *Anne of Green Gables* books. Didn't you love those? We read every one of them as girls."

They reminisced more and then Jane said, "Okay, I've been patient, but you've got to tell me what's going on with J.T. You said you'd gone out to dinner with him last night. I'm still in a state of shock you'd do that."

Mary Helen lifted a shoulder. "I told you. He came over Friday evening when I first got to the island, still upset and tired, and he pushed his way in when he was the last person I wanted to see." She spread her hands. "But then he got me to talk about all that happened. You know how pushy he is."

She leaned back against the sofa. "Despite that, he was surprisingly nice." She avoided adding more. "The next morning Isabel said I should thank him for being helpful. I thought she had a point, so I took him out to dinner. Like I told you we drove over to the Crabhouse. Had a good time."

Jane shook her head. "I simply can't believe you went out with J.T. Mikell. I still remember what a horrid fight you two had when you broke up. You've spent all the years since avoiding him whenever you came to Edisto. I know you didn't keep up after you went away to college either."

"So? Maybe we both grew up a little."

Jane leaned forward again, not ready to let this subject go so easily. "Is there still a spark there? I remember how you and J.T. were back then, how he used to look at you, find any excuse to touch you. The air simply simmered between you. I admit it used to make me a little jealous."

"That was a long time ago, Jane, and obviously you found a man who loves you unbelievably. I caught some of those simmering looks Barton gave you today."

Jane rubbed her belly thoughtfully and laughed. "I am lucky. Barton's a great guy."

"*And* tall and good looking," Mary Helen added. "I love that curly hair of his. He really is a dream." She felt glad to divert Jane's attention away from J.T. She wasn't ready to discuss the unexpected feelings that seemed to have reignited between them.

Thankfully Elena woke up, demanding Jane's attention.

Mary Helen stayed a little longer and then headed home.

Back at Oleanders, she finally answered some of her emails and started working on updating her resume. It helped to keep the odd little sadness at bay she felt after being in Jane's sweet little house today. She'd always thought in time she might get around to home, family, and all that but then she got so busy with work. And no one she met ever made her want to think about changing her life.

Later she headed toward J.T.'s house, taking the homemade cookies Jane insisted she bring home with her. She knew chocolate chip cookies a favorite of J.T.'s and it kept her from arriving empty handed.

CHAPTER 6

Monday morning at work, J.T. walked out the back door of Mikell's Island Rentals to head over to the Dock Store. People on the island generally called the Mikell's Dock Store simply John's Place since J.T.'s dad, John Mikell, could usually be found there. These days his dad basically ran the Dock Store on the Yacht Basin leaving J.T. to run the original bike rental store on Jungle Road. It worked well.

At the water's edge, he headed across the weathered, wooden walkway leading to the long building on high stilts on an inlet off Scott Creek. Already tourists fished from the side rails of the marina while others wandered around in the Dock Store checking out the nautical merchandise. Old fishnets and glass balls hung from the ceiling and weathered collectibles from the ocean lay scattered around the store, including shells, wooden mastheads, and dried coral. It gave the store a great beach feel.

"Ahoy mate," the big green parrot near the check out counter called out. "Say Hello to Billy Bob. Say Hello to Billy Bob." The parrot cocked his head and noticing the apple in J.T.'s hand, added, "Give Billy a bite. Give Billy a bite. Pretty bird. Pretty bird."

Chester Holloway, the manager at the Dock Store laughed from behind the counter. "You should have known if you came in here with that apple Billy Bob would hit you up for a bite."

"Yeah. Well, I've been busy and haven't had time to catch lunch yet. The apple was meant to tide me over until I can grab a sandwich." He broke off a chunk of apple and passed it to Billy

Bob in his huge cage.

When Chester retired from shrimping and started working at the Dock Store he asked if he could bring his parrot to the store to keep him company and to give the parrot companionship. J.T.'s dad said yes and Billy Bob was now a staple of Mikell's Dock Store. Many tourists stopped by year after year simply to see Billy Bob. Since Amazon parrots are amazingly long-lived, it seemed likely Billy Bob would be around for a long time, as well.

"Is Dad here?" J.T. asked.

Chester shook his head. "No. He took a group of tourists out on a boat tour of the marshes. You know how he loves any excuse to get out on the water."

"So do you." J.T. broke off another piece of apple to give to the parrot.

Chester chuckled. "Yeah, John and I about fight over who gets to do the tours or take folks deep sea fishing." He glanced at the papers tucked under J.T.'s arm. "You want me to give those to your dad?"

"Yeah. They're a listing of distributors and prices for some new items we've been looking at." He laid the papers on the counter beside Chester.

Although in his late seventies now, Chester was still a healthy, strong man from all his years of physical exercise on his shrimp boat. He knew the waters around the island like few others, and was a wealth of information about places to see, things to do, and problems to avoid when on the water.

Hearing the screened door to the marina shop open, J.T. saw his mother come in.

"Pretty girl. Pretty Lula," the parrot called out.

She laughed. "Honestly, that parrot can make a girl's day." She walked over to give J.T. a hug. Glancing at the apple in his hand, she asked, "Have you eaten lunch?"

He shook his head. "Too busy this morning."

"Good, then let's run down the street to the Sea Cow and get a bite together. I've been too busy to get out of the office, too, and the Sea Cow won't be crowded this time of day during the week."

J.T. hesitated. He knew his mother still hadn't had a chance to grill him about seeing him with Mary Helen.

As if reading his mind, she added, "Or I can just follow you on back to the store."

He rolled his eyes. "Okay." He turned to Chester. "Give Leon a call at the bike store and let him know I'm catching a bite of lunch with Mom."

"Sure," he said.

"Bye-bye. Come back soon," the parrot called after them.

The Sea Cow sat only a few blocks down Jungle Road from the Mikell stores, so J.T. and his mom snagged one of the store's golf carts to drive to the cute restaurant tucked among the Edisto Village Shops. They settled into one of the small tables on the screened porch with a paddle fan turning softly overhead. J.T. ordered one of the restaurant's classic burgers, called The Cow, with all the fixings and fries, while his mom ordered her favorite lunch item the Curry Chicken Salad plate with slaw, fruit, and a bagel.

They'd passed by The Little Mermaid store on their way down Jungle Road. His mother looked back in that direction now as they waited for their food. "I heard from Isabel that Mary Helen is going to work for her while she's here and I also heard what happened with her job in New Jersey. I hate she had an experience like that. It's always so disillusioning when people you trust prove to be a disappointment."

J.T. scowled. "I hate that happened to her, too." He sipped on his cola, trying to avoid his mother's eyes.

"You know we're not leaving here until you tell me what happened to link you up with Mary Helen Avery again. I've heard a condensed story from Isabel, of course, but I want to hear your version."

"I'm sure Isabel told you all there is to hear. I saw the lights at Oleanders, stopped by to check it out, found Mary Helen crying. I could hardly walk off and leave her like that. So I hung around, and eventually got her to talk to me about what happened."

"And?" she prompted.

"Isabel told Mary Helen the next day she ought to thank me for stopping by, so Mary Helen came to the shop and suggested we go for dinner at the Crabhouse. End of story."

Lula snorted. "Honestly, J.T. I may be your mother and you may not credit me with as much intelligence as I possess, but even I know that *isn't* all the story."

They stopped talking for a minute while the waitress brought their food, his mother catching up with the woman about a piece of local news. In a small place like Edisto Beach everyone who lived on the island full time tended to know each other.

J.T. and his mother dug into their lunch—both hungry—and then his mother picked up their conversation again. "I remember watching you and Mary Helen play together as children, always so competitive, often fighting, with both of you so strong willed. But the affection was always genuine between you. You had a young crush on Mary Helen even in grade school and I wasn't surprised to see it blossom into more later. We all loved seeing you and Mary Helen fall in love that summer when Mary Helen turned thirteen and you fifteen. It was so sweet."

She spread cream cheese on her bagel before speaking again. "I started to entertain hopes you and Mary Helen might marry later. It about broke my heart when you two quarreled and broke up your senior year of high school. I kept hoping you'd make up with her but it never happened."

He glared at his mother. "It wasn't for my lack of trying that we didn't get back together."

She reached across the table to put a hand on his arm, realizing she'd ticked him off. "I saw how hard you tried, J.T., not only then but through the years when Mary Helen came back to the beach for visits. I saw how it hurt you, too, that she all but brushed you off, would hardly say more than a few casual words to you, and wouldn't let you get close."

"So what's your point?" He didn't like this discussion or remembering those times.

"My point is that this girl, who would hardly speak to you and stayed stubbornly unforgiving all these years, suddenly went out with you." She put a hand on one hip. "Isabel says she's seen the two of you walking up the beach together. And I saw the way Mary Helen looked at you at the store the other day and the way you looked at her."

J.T. ate another bite of his hamburger before answering. "I would think you'd be pleased Mary Helen and I are cordial again. Our families have been friends for a lot of years. It's been awkward for everyone that we were at such outs with each other."

She gave an exasperated sigh. "I can see you're not going to tell me anything, which I think is mean-spirited of you. But here's the thing, I love both you and Mary Helen. Whether you talk to me about this or not, I know how much you loved Mary Helen in high school and I know you haven't had one single serious relationship since she left."

"I've dated, Mom. I've brought girls around." J.T scowled at her. "It's not like I've been a monk or anything."

She shook her head. "I'm certainly aware you haven't been a monk. You have that same enigmatic charisma with women your father had—and still has. When I was younger I used to hate the way the girls flocked after John, but over time I finally realized he only had eyes for me. The way I see it, you're that way about Mary Helen."

"So?" he asked with annoyance. "What good does it do me if I do like her, even now? She's only here for a short time until she finds another job off somewhere. Yes, I'm glad she's speaking to me again. Friendly again." He didn't add more to his mother. "But there's no point in me getting overly excited about it."

His mother studied him quietly for a moment. "I've never thought of you as someone who gives up without a fight, Son. If you want this girl, still love this girl, you fight for her."

Annoyed, J.T. hesitated before replying. "Mary Helen has made it clear she isn't staying, Mom. She doesn't want a life here on the island. She's always said that—no matter what else might be going on." He leaned closer to his mother. "What do you want me to do? Pack up and leave the island with her if I can even get her interested in me again? Would that make you happy?"

"You know it wouldn't," she snapped. "But she's at a turning point now. I know enough about girls to realize they start thinking about home and family in their mid to late twenties, even career women. She might be at a point to reconsider some of her stances. Especially for the right man."

He snorted. "And you think I'm the right man?"

She smiled then. "Yes I do. Of a certainty. So does Isabel, and she has a vested interest in wanting Mary Helen to stay here. She wants her at the Mermaid, loves her like a daughter, and wants to keep her here."

Finishing off her tea she added, "You take some time off from work to spend what days you can with Mary Helen. Court her, Son. And court her sweetly. When your father sets his mind to be sweet to me like that, it always breaks down any resistance I might be feeling toward him." She smiled as if with some secret thought. "God's given you a gift of charm, so use it. If you love Mary Helen Avery, fight for her with every weapon in your arsenal."

"And if she leaves again anyway?"

She reached out a hand to lay it on his cheek. "Then you'll know you gave everything you had to keep her and you won't hold regrets that you didn't try."

"Just end up with a broken heart."

She patted his cheek and then took it away. "You know you will anyway. I saw your eyes when you looked at her yesterday. It's obvious to me you still love her."

Reaching for the ticket on the table, she said, "I'll treat lunch since I all but blackmailed you to come. But I wanted to encourage you to go after your dreams. You know I've always encouraged both you and Ryder to do that, always wanted both of you to be happy."

He looked down at the table. "I know that, Mom."

"Well, just know that your father and I won't fault you for any time you need to be off. Sometimes other things take priority over work." She grinned at him as she got up from the table. "Remember that all's fair in love and war. You're a handsome, virile young man. Make the most of it."

The conversation with his mom surprised him, and J.T. found himself thinking about it often over the rest of the afternoon. Traffic in the store stayed busy all day but with the end of August not far ahead, tourism would drop off after Labor Day. He might find more time for a campaign, as his mother put it.

At the house later he actually looked up the word *campaign*— military operation to achieve a goal or objective. He laughed. It would take a campaign and a battle to win over Mary Helen Avery and to change her mind about staying on the island. But maybe it was worth giving it a try as his mother suggested.

With that in mind, he slipped upstairs and took a shower, shaved, put on a cologne he knew suited him, dressed in some good-fitting jeans, a T-shirt, and a button-up, open-front shirt, that would show a little physique. Then he went out on the deck to watch for Mary Helen, pulling up memories of the things she liked best to put in his new arsenal. He hated that it was his mom who provided such good advice about his love life, but she was right in one thing: Mary Helen was worth fighting for.

He realized this even more a short time later as he looked out toward the ocean to see her walking up the beach with Winifred Meggett, The Turtle Lady, laughing and animated as only Mary Helen could be. Beautiful too. He loved the way she walked with a little sway and long strides. He loved the shape and feel of her. She'd let her hair grow longer at one point in her college years, but he liked it better the way she wore it now, in a short pageboy hugging her cheeks, her bangs drawing attention to her rich, expressive, chocolate brown eyes.

She wasn't a busty woman but he loved her build, her shape, the way her body molded up against his, the way she smelled, that mix of her favorite cologne and some sort of lemon shampoo. In high school, she'd started wearing a citrusy, spicy, floral cologne by

Calvin Klein called Eternity and other scents like it. It was typical of Mary Helen that she wouldn't favor the usual popular perfumes most of the other girls used. He never passed the Calvin Klein counter in a store without thinking of Mary Helen, never caught a whiff of that scent she loved without thinking about her.

He watched her walk up the sandy pathway to the back porch of his beach house now, dressed in dark brown Bermuda shorts almost the color of her hair, her shirt the same brown with white stripes. Classy, clean in looks, never fussy. Meeting her at the top of the steps, he moved closer to her, smiling at her, tracing his fingers slowly down her bare arm.

"You look nice," he said, watching her flush at the words, hearing her quick intake of breath at how close he stood.

He stayed there studying her for a moment, letting his eyes trace over her face, looking into her eyes. Inwardly he grinned, too, as he watched her eyes dilate a little. Oh, yeah, she liked him. No matter what she said, she was attracted to him. He could work with that.

"Who was that woman?" she said, stepping away to break the tension and intensity between them. She pointed behind her toward the beach.

"That's Winifred Meggett or Wacky Winnie," he answered, leading her across the back porch and into the house.

"Why Wacky Winnie?" she asked, following him inside. "She seemed nice and very intelligent to me. She's really interested in the sea turtles, too."

"Yeah, she's more commonly called The Turtle Lady." He turned to wink at her. "Behind her back most of us call her Wacky Winnie though."

She frowned. "That's hardly nice."

He shook his head. "Well, you haven't gotten to know Winifred Meggett yet. She's odd, somewhat bossy and opinionated. She's also decided it's her personal responsibility to police the beach and rant at anyone who bothers the turtles."

"Maybe that's good," Mary Helen argued, typical of her.

"And maybe not."

She stopped arguing to glance around. "The house looks different."

"It does." He felt like adding: *And what did you expect after ten years?* She hadn't stepped foot in the house since then.

Instead he smiled, leading her inside. "I bought the house from my folks after they built their new place. That gave me liberty to make changes, to make the place more my own. Mom and Dad took most of their furniture with them so I bought things I liked to replace it." He gestured around. "More grays and neutrals, some navy and blue touches."

Her eyes traveled around the open living, dining, and kitchen area. "You've put some beautiful paintings on the walls. Large prints, too."

"A guy on the island paints those. I've collected his art as I could." He hadn't realized before how much he'd decorated with the idea of impressing her in the back of his mind. They'd always liked the same types of décor in homes, including big, lush landscapes to set a room's tone and color scheme. It pleased him to see her admiration as she walked around looking at things.

"Do you want to throw a salad together while I stick Mrs. Belle's crab cakes in the oven and start boiling water for the shrimp?"

"Sure," she replied, starting toward the kitchen. "And that bag I dropped on the table inside the door has chocolate chip cookies in it that Jane made. She's become very domestic. You should have seen the big spread she cooked for Sunday dinner."

"People change," he said, putting several crab cakes on a baking sheet and sliding them into the oven.

"Jane has certainly changed. She used to hate to cook and we both hated to babysit as girls, neither of us sure we even wanted to have a family." She frowned. "You know how awful some of the kids are that come down to the beach every summer."

"Elena is really cute, though, isn't she?" J.T. glanced toward Mary Helen as he asked the question and watched her expression soften.

"She's a sweetie." Mary Helen sighed. "Jane and Barton seem

really excited about the new baby coming, too. They've already picked a name."

He turned to hide a grin. "Parents tend to do that." His mom had been right that Mary Helen's biological clock was ticking strongly. He'd never heard her talk this wistfully of babies and family before.

"Tell me more about Winifred Meggett," she asked, wanting to change the subject. He knew Mary Helen well enough to recognize that tactic, too.

Before answering he pulled some plates from the shelf to put them on the table with the silverware. He'd set the table earlier with woven basket placemats, blue cloth napkins, candles with a touch of island scent, nice wine glasses, and a bottle of a favorite white wine, a Pinot Noir, cooling in a marble wine cooler. He'd also picked up a nice loaf of French bread from the market, which he'd buttered and warmed in the oven before Mary Helen arrived.

"Here's what I know," he said, turning to dump shrimp into the boiling water on the stove. "Winifred Meggett is from off island, from Boston, I think I heard. She taught biology and science in some private high school for most of her life and developed a huge interest in conservation. Maybe too much interest. You know how people can get about that sort of thing."

"What brought her to Edisto?" Mary Helen asked, putting the bowl of salad on the table, along with a bottle of Italian dressing.

"Mom said she has a family link to the Meggetts who used to own a plantation on Edisto. She visited the island and decided to buy a villa, one of those over in Fairfield." He leaned against the counter keeping an eye on the shrimp. "She's been here about two to three years now, enough time for her to get a reputation as a difficult woman who gets along with few people. Despite her interests in conservation and turtles, she couldn't even get along with the island protection group. She held fast to her own strong ideas about how to do everything. Wouldn't go along with any of the group's rules."

Mary Helen considered this. "I think she's experienced difficult times in her life from a few things she said. It might have colored her. I enjoyed talking with her though. She's so knowledgeable about the turtles." She sent him a smile. "I remember the first time I saw little sea turtles hatch. It was after we came to Edisto to stay when Daddy died."

"Dinner's ready," he announced, changing the subject as he dumped the shrimp into a strainer in the sink and pulled the crab cakes out of the oven.

They sat down to eat then, at a cozy table in an alcove looking out toward the ocean. They enjoyed their meal, laughing and catching up on their lives.

"So the beach house here on Point Street is yours now," she said at one point, as if thinking about that earlier statement of his again.

"Yes. Mom and Dad, and even Ryder, wanted the house to stay in the family." He got up to pour more wine in Mary Helen's glass, making sure to brush against her as he did, to put a hand on her shoulder.

Sitting back down, he added, "The Mikell Island Rental Store is in my name now, too. The Dock Store is in Dad's name but later when he passes, the Dock Store and marina will be mine, as well."

Her eyes widened. "What will Ryder think about that?"

"Ryder has his life in Savannah. I'm the one who's worked with the business since only a kid, all through college and after. Dad and I together made the decisions to enlarge and grow the business. He said, if he hadn't known I wanted to continue it, he probably wouldn't have expanded at all. So many on the island built businesses only to see their children walk away from them or sell them after their parents passed on."

She thought about that. "So you'll stay."

He sent her a thoughtful look. "You've always known that."

"People change."

"Sometimes they do. I have changed in many ways. College, working, and life experiences have a way of changing people. But I've always known what I love, what I wanted for my life. My big dreams haven't changed."

Mary Helen flushed as she looked up from her plate to find his eyes on her, moving over her. She'd never been the blushing sort, but a flush would surface when she felt moved about something.

He lifted his glass to her. "I'm glad you're here tonight. I've always thought you're the most beautiful woman I've ever known."

"Many women are more beautiful than I am, J.T., but thank you for the compliment."

"You carry more than just outward beauty, you hold inner beauty—an intelligence, energy, and creativity that radiate out of you. When anyone looks at you they see more than a beautiful woman; they see an interesting woman. That's more alluring than you might know."

She looked away. "You've always had a way with words."

He decided not to respond to that. "Want to sit out on the porch to eat our dessert?" he asked instead.

"What's for dessert besides Jane's cookies?"

"Ice Cream. Lemon custard for you and chocolate for me."

"Lemon custard?" Her eyes widened. "You remembered?"

"I remember more things than you might think," he answered, letting his eyes drift over her again. "You can take the rest of that carton of lemon custard home with you, too."

She laughed. "I'll do that." She got up to start clearing off the table.

They ate their ice cream out on the porch at a small table where they could watch the moon spread its glow over the ocean like a silvery sidewalk.

After taking their dessert dishes inside a little later, J.T. returned to find Mary Helen leaning on the railing of the porch, looking out toward the sea. He walked up behind her and put his arms around her. "I'm still crazy about you, Mary Helen. Spending time with you again has shown me that. You'd think after all this time the magic between us would be gone, but it's still there. I know you feel it. It's too strong to deny."

He heard her sigh. "Even if I admitted it, it wouldn't change anything would it?"

"It would make my heart feel better to hear you say it." He turned her around in his arms so he could look into her eyes, trace his fingers down her face and along her arms again. "There has never been anyone like you in my life. Never."

Hearing her breath catch at the words, he leaned closer to kiss her, beginning to release some of the tension and longing that had built gradually between them all night long. It was sweet holding her against him again, and J.T. reveled in it, in her scent and in her response after all the years of rebuff. He still didn't know why she'd softened to him after all this time but he loved it that she had.

The house phone rang, interrupting the moment.

He tried to ignore it, but Mary Helen pulled away and smiled at him. "You'd better get that. You know people get upset when you don't answer when they know you're home. Your mom or dad might come over or something."

He groaned at that idea and went in to answer the phone.

She met him at the door coming back. "What is it? I could tell by your tone of voice that something's happened."

He shook his head, dropping into a chair on the porch. "That was Leon. Someone killed their dog."

"What?" Mary Helen's mouth dropped open.

"They owned a big German Shepherd, a beautiful dog. They often brought him over to my house when they came to the beach or to have dinner. His name was Rinny." J.T. ran his hands through his hair. "Leon named him after Rin Tin Tin, the old television dog. He's kind of a sentimental guy like that. He and Vernita loved that dog. I did, too."

"I'm so sorry," Mary Helen said, sitting down in the chair beside him.

He shook his head. "Leon was crying when he called. They went out for dinner and came back and discovered Rinny. A friend of theirs in their church, who works with a vet's office, came over and found all the evidences of poison. Someone must have climbed the fence and put it in Rinny's food."

"Who would do that? That's awful."

"Yeah, it is, and I didn't know what to say to make Leon feel better. I loved Rinny, too. It makes me sick and angry to think about it."

"Should we go over?"

"No. The police asked them to take the dog to a vet they recommended to be examined." He turned toward her. "This isn't the first dog that's been poisoned on the island. It's been happening off and on over the last year. But most of the dogs that died didn't belong to people I know well. Some belonged to summer people who only come for vacations or seasonally."

"Why would anyone kill dogs?" Mary Helen asked. "And I still cannot wrap my mind around something like that happening here at Edisto."

"Well, the police can't find any clues or reasons why it's happening either. It's really troubling."

Talking about the loss of Leon's dog and absorbing the shock of it changed the mood of their evening. Their talk grew more serious and both tried to think of something they could do to comfort Leon and Vernita.

"They don't have kids yet so they loved that dog like a child," he said as he walked her back to Oleanders a little later.

"Anyone who has loved pets would be grieved over a loss like that, especially if the animal was poisoned." She paused at the steps leading up to the screened porch. "Let me know tomorrow if the police learn anything. I'll probably be at the Mermaid all day working."

He leaned over and kissed her. "Sorry our night ended sad."

"I'm sorry such an awful thing is happening on Edisto and that Leon and Vernita lost their pet."

J.T. started down the path, but then turned back. "Mary Helen."

"What?" She turned at the top of the steps.

"Remember what we used to say to each other in high school when we said good night?"

"Yes." He heard her voice soften.

"So think of me when you close your eyes," he said, reminding her of the words. "And know I'll be thinking of you."

CHAPTER 7

It felt lovingly comfortable and familiar to be back working in The Little Mermaid. It was where Mary Helen cut her teeth on retail long ago. She'd spent time in the small children's store with Isabel as a girl and later worked at the store every summer through her teen and college years. Isabel, a wise and astute businesswoman, had taught Mary Helen so many lessons about sales, promotion, marketing, store placement, and more.

"I can never thank you enough for all I learned here at this store," Mary Helen said, glancing up at Isabel from where she sat on the floor un-boxing and putting away a carton of small collectibles.

Isabel took off her glasses, letting them drop around her neck on the jeweled chain she wore. She frequently popped them off and on to read small labels and fine print. "Well, I'm glad it's you and not me down there on the floor unloading those boxes. Since I hit seventy some store tasks have become a little more challenging."

"You just let me know anything you want me to do while I'm here."

Isabel sat behind the register on a stool, sorting through store catalogs. The old wooden stool she sat on, with its latticed back and cushioned seat, had been in the store for as long as Mary Helen could remember, recovered in various colorful fabrics over the years.

"What do you think about all those little snow globes I ordered from Ships and Wharves Enterprises?" Isabel asked.

"They're absolutely charming." Mary Helen held one up, with

a pretty mermaid inside, and turned it over so the sparkling bits cascaded down. "Everyone will love these globes and the little mermaids and mermen in each are all different. I imagine some people might even start collecting them."

"Hmmm. We'll suggest that when we sell one and try to encourage buyers to pick up another one or two to start their collection."

Mary Helen smiled. These were the types of smart marketing tips she remembered so well. Isabel had a gift for sales and also for making customers happy with their purchases.

"You always used to say: *A happy customer comes back*," Mary Helen reminded her.

"Well, it's true. People are going to buy gifts or items at some store anyway, but if they have fun doing it in your store—and enjoy your company—they'll come back. Haven't you seen that to be true?"

"Absolutely." She pulled another globe from the box, unwrapped it, and placed it on the shelf.

"How do you like those new handsewn mermaid dolls I'm carrying?" She pointed to a display not far from Mary Helen.

"They're cute, small enough for little girls to tuck into a purse or pocket, and distinctive with their fanciful colors." She studied the dolls. "I still miss the old See Wees molded plastic dolls Kenner used to make, those two inch dolls with the long hair you could comb. Suki and I had several and we could take them into the swimming pool and play with them on the beach."

"Kenner stopped making those in 1985. It's a shame, too. They sold well here at Edisto." She pulled a catalog from a stack and took it over to Mary Helen. "Look at these I spotted in this catalog. These mermaid dolls are taller, five inches high, but they have the molded plastic bodies and long hair. Do you think girls would like these in the same way?"

Mary Helen studied the picture and read the product description. "I do, and I love that they each come in their own individual boxes. The company offers this nice display case with them, too." She flipped the page. "Oh, and look, Isabel, the company also makes a twelve inch mermaid doll. Girls could pretend these are teenage sisters or even mothers to the smaller dolls."

Smiling, Isabel carried the catalog back to the register again. "I do like them and I'll definitely order a selection for the store. They retail in the three to five dollar-range, too. Girls will love that. You know how they're always coming in here with five or ten dollars looking for something fun to buy."

"Well, I think they'll sell well." Finishing her shelving, Mary Helen pushed up off the floor and then took the box into the back storeroom.

She came back to find a group of women visiting with Isabel and exploring around the store. One was decorating a beach house she and her husband recently purchased on the island. Before she left, she bought a cute wooden sign saying "The Beach is My Happy Place," a whimsical brass mermaid lamp, a few fanciful pillows, a white spike coral to sit on a side table, and a big ship in a bottle. The other women bought gift items, as well, and all left happily loaded down, delighted with their purchases and the store.

"This is simply the cutest, happiest store," one said before she left. "I know we'll be back to pick up more items before we leave next week."

Her friend added. "I want to bring my little granddaughters here, too. The things in this store are so much nicer than those in the tourist gift shops."

"Come back soon," Mary Helen called after them, smiling.

"Well, that was a nice sale for a Monday," Isabel said with satisfaction when they left. "Those ship-in-a-bottle collectibles are expensive but when we sell even one it makes the sales week."

"Where do you get those?" Mary Helen asked, going over to look at several more in a glass display case.

"They're built by a man who lives near St. Simons in Georgia. He builds every ship by hand, constructing the little schooners bit by bit, stuffing them into the bottles somehow as he goes, and then hoisting up the sails after the ships are completed inside the bottle. It's a skilled and complicated art." She put her glasses on to look through some mail. "I read it's an old maritime art that sailors of the past often used to fill the long hours on board ship."

"Well, each of these is gorgeous and I see why they need to be kept locked up in this display case. They are pricey."

A few more customers came in to the shop throughout the morning and between times Isabel updated Mary Helen on the store. The growth of the island had continued to expand the bottom line of The Little Mermaid, and of course it helped that Isabel owned the property out right and paid no rent.

At noon Mary Helen's mother, Claire Avery, came in the door carrying several bags. "I've brought lunch for us. I knew Mary Helen would be working here today and hoped you two wouldn't have eaten yet." She sat her bags on the table at the front of the store by the window.

"Perfect timing, Claire. I was trying to decide what I might get for lunch for Mary Helen and myself." Isabel smiled. "What did you bring?"

"I stopped at McConkey's and picked up three of those wonderful Chicken Cordon Bleu Sandwiches they make because I remembered Mary Helen loves them."

Mary Helen's eyes widened. "The ones with chicken, melted Swiss, ham, lettuce, and their special sauce?"

"Yes, and those dreadfully fattening shack-chips." She gave Mary Helen a hug. "It's such a special day having you back again."

"And working for me," Isabel added. "I'll get three bottles of water from the refrigerator for us and some paper plates."

"Are you enjoying being at the Mermaid again?" Mary Helen's mother asked after Isabel left.

"Yes. It feels like coming home," Mary Helen said, sitting down in one of the chairs at the table.

"I enjoyed some happy times working here myself before Parker and I married," her mother said, joining her at the little table by the store window.

"Claire has graciously filled in for me a few times when I was sick or needed to travel, too," Isabel added coming back to bring water, plates, and some extra napkins. "I'm truly grateful for that."

"It's always a joy." Claire passed the bags around and for a time they were quiet, digging out their sandwiches and eating before more customers headed into the store.

Mary Helen studied her mother. She looked much the same as she always had, except a little fuller in figure and with a few more wrinkles. Today, her dark hair was pulled back in a neat bun behind her neck, a familiar style Claire adopted after she and Parker married. She wore navy slacks, a light blue blouse and sandals. Claire at five foot eight was tall but Mary Helen had outgrown her by an inch or two now.

"You look good, Mother," Mary Helen said between bites of her sandwich.

"So do you," she replied, reaching a hand across to pat one of Mary Helen's. "But I still can't get used to looking up at you. I always felt so tall growing up with Mother and my twin sisters, all three so short."

Isabel added, "I always liked being tall, although I'm only five seven. You two resemble each other with your height and dark hair. Parker is tall, too, and dark-headed. Then, in contrast, there's Suki, blond, blue-eyed, and fair-skinned."

"And truly beautiful," Mary Helen added. "She's so sweet and trusting. It worries me sometimes."

"She'll be fine," Isabel said.

A few customers popped into the store and Isabel jumped up to wait on them. "You two visit. I'll take care of things."

"Tell me more about what's going on with your books," Mary Helen said. "And about the new ones planned."

Claire shook her head. "Who would ever have believed there would be so many?"

"It's wonderful." Mary Helen glanced toward the store's cozy bookshelf section that held Claire's popular children's books. "There are six Polka Dot Kids books and ten Farnsworth Fairies books now."

"I still can't believe how well those little fairy books went.

Whittier started with two, about the fairy queen and king, but then decided to publish more featuring the other eight fairies."

"I like that each of the fairy books are pocket sized rather than big like the Polka Dot Kids books. Isabel sells a lot in sets." Mary Helen finished off her sandwich. "The artist did a wonderful job with the illustrations on the fairy books, too. So fanciful." She glanced toward her mother. "It was your illustrator, Vanessa, who got married yesterday, wasn't it?"

"Yes, and it was a lovely wedding. Her first husband was killed in the military and Parker and I felt pleased to see her find a new opportunity for happiness. Donald is such a nice man."

"Will Vanessa illustrate the new series?"

"No, Whittier thinks a different artist would do better with them. It will give Vanessa more time to honeymoon and settle into her marriage, too."

"Tell me about the new books."

"Whittier is calling them the Annabel Abroad Books. They're going to be about a young girl who goes traveling with her mother and father who both write travel books. Obviously, she'll have adventures in each of the places they visit, get to meet new people, experience new cultures. I'm really excited about them. The first will be *Annabel in London*, then *Annabel in Paris*, and if the first two books go well a third and fourth are planned for Rome and Madrid. I have notes and ideas about the storylines for each but I've never traveled abroad myself and feel that I really need to see those places, to experience them like Annabel does, to bring the books to life."

Mary Helen grinned. "Which explains the big trip abroad you and Parker have planned."

"At least we aren't leaving right away and I'll still have some time with you." Claire made a face. "I hate to leave at all with you here."

"I'll be fine. You know that. Besides, I think it's wonderfully exciting you're going abroad to all those cities."

"So do I," Isabel agreed, coming back to join them as the

customers left. "You and Parker will have a marvelous time. I'm also glad Drake and Nora convinced Parker he could take off for an extended vacation to go with you."

"Well, it is helpful that Nora's son Andrew is working full time in the business now. He always loved Westcott Antiques, worked for us part-time off and on through the years, and more in college. A few years ago he decided to work with us full-time. Parker was thrilled, of course. Drake too. Andrew is practically like a son to all of us. He has a wonderful way with people and a good eye for antiques. We were all so happy to welcome him into the business."

"I like Andrew," Mary Helen said, remembering many happy times shared with him growing up.

"I imagine you're enjoying seeing many of your old friends while here," Claire said, shifting topic. "Isabel said you'd gone to Jane's, seen Vernita Johnson, and even J.T." She hesitated over that last name.

Isabel chimed in. "You know your mother is tactfully trying to ask whether you and J.T. are reestablishing a relationship. I've been wondering about that, too."

"It's complicated," Mary Helen answered. "But I should think everyone would be glad we've patched up some of our differences. I know it was awkward for everyone to see us often rather hostile at gatherings."

Isabel snorted. "You mean *you* were hostile. I recall J.T. always trying to be the peacemaker but you'd have none of it."

Mary Helen stood up frowning. "I still don't know if it's wise for us to spend so much time together. I'm only here temporarily. There are a lot of unresolved differences between us."

Claire bit her lip. "Have you and J.T. been quarreling? I didn't mean to bring up a difficult subject after all you've gone through, Mary Helen."

"No, we *haven't* been quarreling." She walked over to the window. "That makes it even more complicated actually. I'd rather not talk about it."

Mary Helen saw Isabel lift an eyebrow at Claire.

"Well, then we'll chat about something else," Claire said in the sweet way Mary Helen remembered so well. She certainly hadn't inherited her argumentative spirit from her mother and that was a fact.

Changing the subject, Isabel started talking about Claire and Parker's upcoming trip again. Then they laughed about small stories, updated each other on happenings around the island.

Mary Helen waited on the next group of customers who came into the store and then walked her mother out to her car to say goodbye before she headed back to Beaufort.

"Thanks for coming over to the island for lunch," Mary Helen said as Claire opened the car door. "I'll try to come to Beaufort for church on Sunday."

"That would be lovely." Claire smiled and gave her a kiss on the cheek.

Mary Helen scraped a hand through her hair. "I'm sorry if I acted rude earlier." She leaned against the car. "It's just that I'm really confused about the feelings surging between J.T. and myself. I didn't expect them and it's hard to sort it out."

Her mother put a hand on her arm. "Feelings take time to sort out. And you've been through a harsh rush of emotions this last week with all that happened at your work." She paused. "Have you talked to anyone there yet?"

"I responded to a few emails sent to me." She looked out over the yard by the parking area, noticing flowers still in bloom. "And I talked to my friend Rita. I know you remember she's also the manager at the Adopt-Me-Dolls store at Short Hills where I worked. We're close friends so it was hard talking to Rita and not telling her the truth. I know she senses there is something I'm not telling her."

"People who know you well usually pick up on things like that." Claire glanced toward the yard, too. "It was such a hurtful thing you had to experience, Mary Helen. Those moments when innocence and trust are shattered are so difficult. It sort of turns everything in your world upside down for a time."

Mary Helen offered her mother a small smile. "Thanks for understanding that. I feel at such loose ends right now, my world sort of topsy-turvy, like that fairy of yours caught in the storm and blown to a world she didn't recognize, not sure how to get back home again."

"Ah, Loraleaf. She did endure a difficult time, but remember everything turned out well in the end."

Mary Helen grinned. "That's because you were writing the book. You always write happy endings."

"Surely this dark and unhappy time hasn't made you stop believing in happy endings, Mary Helen?"

She brushed a leaf off her mother's car. "I feel very confused right now, Mother. Like I don't know what I want." She bit her lip. "That's not like me at all. I'm usually very decisive."

"You'll sort it out. I'm sure of it." Claire patted her arm. "Remember, too, where the best help comes from."

"I've already had that lecture from Kizzy. You know how she picks up on things."

"Your father used to be like that, too."

Mary Helen twisted her hands. "In an odd way I've thought about Daddy a lot lately, often remembered his words." She hesitated. "I've even felt sometimes he might be speaking to me. I know that sounds weird."

Claire smiled. "No, that's not weird. I remember it was you and Suki who assured me, after your father died, that he would always go with us and watch over us wherever we went. Even to Edisto."

Mary Helen laughed. "He always did like Edisto. Maybe my difficult time with work gave him the perfect excuse to pop in for a while."

"Perhaps." Claire laughed, too. "But you stay open to all those leadings like that. Pray and you'll find your way."

Mary Helen reached out to hug her mother. "Thanks."

Claire put a hand to her face. "You know I believe in you, Mary Helen. You're a strong, capable, intelligent, and loving woman. You have a lot to give to life—and to someone—when you find the right person."

Mary Helen sighed.

"Are you thinking that someone might be J.T.? There was always a strong bond, a sweet love, and a deep understanding between you." Claire twisted a ring on her finger. "I do want you to know how much I love J.T. It would only gladden my heart if you two reunited."

"Thanks for that, I guess."

"I know you two had your quarrels and misunderstandings. Maybe this season will give you an opportunity to work them out, now that both of are you are older. You were so young when you quarreled, only sixteen, and J.T. only eighteen. I know you felt very mature and grown-up then but surely you can look back now with a different perspective on that time."

"Maybe. I'll think about it." She glanced at the store. "I'd better get back to help Isabel. I know she has a lot she wants to go over with me today."

"I'll see you Sunday," her mother said, getting in the car to leave.

Later than evening back at Oleanders, Mary Helen wasn't getting any more clarity about the direction for her life. J.T. had gone to Leon's tonight and planned to drop by to see Carlos's wife, too. She thought of J.T. as she walked up the beach past his house though. It was Edisto that brought peace and joy back to her after her father died, but now it didn't seem so easy to find the peace and answers she needed.

A short distance ahead she saw the Turtle Lady, standing by the dunes near a roped off area to protect a turtle nest. Mary Helen waved at her.

"I see someone else likes to stroll on the beach in the evening," she said, walking up to her.

Winifred turned to look at her, frowning. "I walk the beaches at night and check on the turtle nests." She pointed. "See those tracks. They're raccoon tracks. Sometimes they dig into the nests to get the eggs. Seabirds and crabs often dig into the nests, too."

Mary Helen smiled. "Nature can be harsh as well as beautiful.

When the little turtles hatch, they face more problems and predators as they swim out into the deep sea, too. The little hatchlings are still so small. They make a nice lunch for larger sea creatures."

Winifred walked around the nest studying the tracks. "Little can be done once they swim out to sea, but we can try to see that as many as possible get the chance to try. We don't want the sea turtles to become extinct."

"No, and I know groups, at Edisto and on other islands, try to increase the chances of the turtles getting to sea." Mary Helen put a hand on one of the wooden stakes. "They put the stakes and orange ties around the nests to keep people from harming them. They encourage people not to keep bright lights on at night by the beach and to carry in plastic, fishing lines, and garbage so little turtles won't get tangled in them. They admonish people to keep pets on leash that might dig into nests, too, and to watch chemicals and sprays they might use in turtle areas."

Winifred turned on her, an angry look on her face. "Do you think I don't know those things? And do you think people pay any attention to those rules posted inside their beach houses or to the programs and talks groups give or the ordinances passed?"

Surprised, Mary Helen put her hands on her hips. "Well, everything helps. I learned the things I know from their educational efforts. I've watched the good they've done here at Edisto ever since I was a girl, too." She leaned toward Winifred, annoyed. "What do *you* think they should do, Ms. Megget? Nothing?"

Winifred laughed then. "You've got spunk, girl. I like that." She studied Mary Helen. "How did you know my name though? I don't think we've been introduced."

"Someone mentioned it to me."

"You asked about me?"

"I did after we talked the other day."

Winifred snorted. "I'll bet they didn't have anything good to say about me." She started down the beach and Mary Helen walked along with her.

"I'm Mary Helen Avery," she said, introducing herself.

"Winifred Lurlene Meggett," the older lady answered.

They strolled along in silence, enjoying the evening, the sounds of the waves and the quiet.

Mary Helen studied Winifred out of the corner of her eye as they walked. She was tall, too, white haired with an intelligent face, tan and fit, her clothes neutrals, a little baggy, her shoes made for comfort. She wore a fisherman's vest, and Mary Helen could see a flashlight in one pocket, the bulge of a pocketknife in another, maybe other items. She couldn't tell.

As if reading her mind, Winifred said, "Sometimes I need to cut a line that one of the sea creatures has gotten wrapped up in. I've been known to clip a fishing line untended, too. I don't like that sort of thing, leaving lines untended like that. One night I found a seagull caught in a line and managed to get him out. I try to look out for the wildlife." She stopped to use her walking stick to push a landed jellyfish back out to sea.

Mary Helen smiled. "A quote on one of the signs we sell at The Little Mermaid says: 'Each and every animal on earth has as much right to be here as you and me.' It's an Anthony Douglas Williams quote."

"I've always had a heart for the sea creatures." Winifred glanced out to sea. "I try to help them. I try to protect them."

"That seems a good goal," Mary Helen said, and she wondered later after she went back home why people thought so poorly of Winifred Meggett.

CHAPTER 8

After a busy week at work, J.T. really looked forward to this Friday night. Most of the old summer gang of Edisto kids, who all used to live on The Point and play together at the beach, were coming to his house for a potluck dinner. He'd planned the evening mainly for Mary Helen, to gather their old friends for a good time. Everyone was excited Mary Helen was back in town and eager to see her. Coming were J.T.'s best friend Chuck Whaley and Chuck's sisters Jane and Emma, Andrew Cavanaugh from Beaufort, and Mary Helen. He hadn't asked his brother Ryder or Tom Whaley to come, as they were so much older than the others and had their own group of friends.

Mary Helen came over early to help him get ready for company and to set things up on the back porch of his house.

"I'm so glad it's a clear night with no rain in the forecast," she commented, stacking plates on a long buffet table they'd set up to hold all the food. "I'm really excited about seeing everyone, too. Chuck stopped by the The Little Mermaid one day to say hello for a minute but I haven't seen Emma or Andrew since I got here."

"I think they're driving up together since they both live in Beaufort."

"Are they seeing each other?"

"No, they're just friends and don't live far from each other." J.T. put a pile of silverware at the end of the table beside the plates. "Andrew worked today so he's picking up a big bucket of Kentucky Fried Chicken." He laughed. "Emma said she's bringing potato salad, Jane is making a green bean dish, Chuck's bringing slaw—borrowed his mom's recipe—and I've got a shrimp casserole in the oven, one of my mother's recipes and a good one, too. And you brought dessert."

"Yes. I made a key lime pie and a lemon pie for dessert—Kizzy Helton's recipes." Mary Helen dropped into a chair for a minute. "She brought me a lemon pie when she came to clean for Isabel earlier in the week—sweet woman—so when you planned this get-together I called her and wheedled two pie recipes out of her."

"Kizzy does make good pie. You're lucky to get her recipes; I hear she doesn't give them out readily. We're all going to eat well tonight."

She smiled at him. "Thanks for planning this, J.T. It will be nice to get together with everyone again."

He nodded, thinking how nice it would be to have her speaking to him at a get-together and not ignoring him all evening. He still couldn't believe how well things were going between them.

His mom shrugged it off lightly when he stopped by to get her casserole recipe. "You've both grown and changed," she said, as if it was a natural thing anyone would have expected.

J.T. hoped her words true, because he was tumbling head over heels back in love with Mary Helen Avery—as if he'd ever stopped.

Mary Helen got up from her chair and started toward the tables they'd pushed together to eat on. "I'm going to arrange these candles on the table if it's okay," she said, shifting the assortment of candles he'd gathered from the house into an artful pattern around a bowl of seashells.

He studied her while she worked creating a pretty display. She wore white slacks and a loose, royal blue blouse—always so simple and elegant. Blue was a fantastic color for her, too, and every time she passed J.T. caught a whiff of her trademark scent. He'd probably remember that smell into eternity, just like the cologne's name.

Chuck and Jane came clomping up the back stairs of the deck.

"Hi, you two," Jane called out. "I'm so excited about our night." She turned to grin at Chuck, behind her. "Since I'm so pregnant now, Chuck came over to pick me up. Wasn't that a nice brotherly thing for him to do?"

"Isn't Barton coming?" Mary Helen asked, giving Jane a welcome hug.

"No." She wrinkled her nose. "He's keeping Elena since she caught a cold. He thought she'd be happier with him than with a sitter, not feeling well."

"You tell him we missed him," Mary Helen said. She took Chuck's dish of slaw to put on the table and gave him a hug, too.

J.T. noticed Chuck's face flush over her gesture and noted, too, the way he hugged Mary Helen back more tightly than necessary, even kissing her on the cheek.

"Honey, you sure do look good," he said, running his eyes over her after she pulled back.

"Thanks." She breezed over to the buffet table to help Jane find a place for the green bean casserole she'd brought.

Chuck sidled closer to J.T. "Man, I can't believe you and Mary Helen are speaking again. How did that happen?"

J.T. recalled his mother's words and repeated them casually. "People grow up and they change."

Emma and Andrew arrived next, laughing and calling out greetings, and the atmosphere shifted to a fun, party gathering, full of remember-when memories and catching up, as they all six filled their plates and shared dinner together.

Nobody made any direct comments about how drastically his and Mary Helen's relationship had changed, but he watched their old friends follow his and Mary Helen's conversation with interest. They all noticed her smiles his way, her warm friendliness. It was far different from the scornful, haughty looks and words she'd directed to him in the past—even when she deigned to show up at any of their gatherings at all.

In a lull in the conversation, Emma asked about Suki and then said, "Jane told me what happened at your job, Mary Helen. I am so sorry about that. We all hate you had such a dreadful experience. It must have been awful."

"It was. Thanks, Emma," Mary Helen said.

"I hope karma brings that awful man a heap of ugliness back." Jane looked across the table at Mary Helen. "But it's marvelous having you back with us for a while again. Maybe you'll get to stay until my baby comes."

"Mary Helen might still be here in November," Andrew added. "It takes time to find a good professional position, and I know she wants to take her time and find a company to work with she'll really enjoy."

"I do, Andrew, and thanks for that." Mary Helen lifted her glass of tea toward him. "I've started sending out resumes and making calls, but no positions I'm really interested in have opened up yet."

Hearing laughter, they all looked toward the beach to see J.T.'s brother Ryder and Tom Whaley coming up the deck stairs.

Ryder, tall and dark-haired like J.T., waved at the group. "I hope you don't mind us dropping by. Tom, his wife Nola, and their kids invited me and my wife Jennifer, and our two kids, for dinner tonight. Before we head over to Mom and Dad's for a quick visit and home to Savannah again, Tom and I wanted to run over to say hi to Mary Helen."

Mary Helen stood with pleasure to hug Ryder and then Tom. "You two are so sweet to come by to see me." She stepped back to look them over with a grin. "And look what fine, mature, good-looking men you've both become. Both daddies now, too. I can hardly believe it. You two were such scamps when I was a girl."

Ryder and Tom pulled up chairs to the table for a minute to catch up with Mary Helen and the others. Ryder was thirty-three now, five years older than J.T., and Tom thirty-four. Savannah life seemed to suit Ryder, while Tom loved working at the family realty company on the island, his passion handling sales in the larger Edisto area and helping with the growing rental business.

Ryder and Tom answered questions from Mary Helen about their jobs, wives, and kids, and then Tom said, "Look, I hate to bring up an ugly subject, but our neighbor's little dog got poisoned and died yesterday." He frowned. "Rascal was a Jack Russell Terrier and a bit of a nuisance, always burrowing out from under the Trenton's fence, digging up flower beds, causing problems, and barking a lot, but nobody wanted to see the little guy killed. Pamela and Neil Trenton are pretty torn up about it. If the ongoing problems with dogs around the island weren't already in play, they probably would have thought one of us who lived nearby took the dog out." He waved a hand. "Not that we'd ever do anything like that. But we've had words with the Trentons on more than one occasion over that dog."

"I remember their dog always got out and ran loose a lot," Chuck added. "Barked like the very dickens, too. He was a bit of a pest."

Emma put a hand to her mouth. "But he was still only an innocent little dog. Poor little thing. He certainly didn't deserve to be poisoned. That's an ugly death for any animal to endure." She sighed. "Do you think someone is killing dogs because they're a problem on the island?"

J.T. shook his head. "Leon's dog Rinny wasn't a problem."

Chuck frowned. "Yeah, but Leon often let him off leash to run when he was down here. He was a big shepherd and did cause problems sometimes. Dad had a skirmish with him one night."

"That was an isolated incident." J.T. frowned. "Rinny wandered into the Whaley's yard next door while Leon and Vernita were visiting with me. Pete came around the corner of the house unexpectedly and Rinny acted a little aggressive—rare for him. Mostly he was even-tempered, smart, and sociable."

"That's true," Jane agreed. "I do remember, too, how Rinny loved to run on the beach. Big dogs like that need to run a lot. We let Bear run on the beach sometimes when there aren't many tourists around."

"Well, it's sad to think of dogs being hurt for any reason," Andrew put in. "There are better ways to handle things. And killing is wrong."

"I totally agree," said Mary Helen. "It might be good if we speak to people we see with dogs off the leash to be watchful with these problems going on." She paused. "How many dogs have been killed now?"

Tom lifted a shoulder. "No one really knows for sure. I think there are five or six documented deaths, but there could be more."

"That is so sad," Emma said. "You better watch Zella carefully, Tom. We all love your big spaniel." She turned to Mary Helen. "Tom and Nola have the prettiest brown and white Springer Spaniel. She's the best dog. "

"I'm watching out for Zella, you can be sure," Tom added. "We keep her on leash and she stays inside most of the time, too."

Ryder shifted the subject. "Tom told me the house next door was put up for sale today. Did you know that yet, J.T.?"

"No I didn't." He glanced toward the familiar house to his right with surprise.

"I was going to tell you about it but I forgot," Chuck put in.

"The Sandpiper is for sale?" Emma asked. "I love that house."

They all glanced in the direction of the house to the right of J.T.'s place. All the houses on Point Street were familiar to them and they'd cut through the yards and ridden their bikes by all of them as kids. The Sandpiper was an older beach house, weathered tan with a soft barn red roof and a somewhat distinctive hexagonal screen porch on back.

"What are they asking for the house?" Andrew queried, walking over to the edge of J.T.'s porch to study it more carefully.

Tom named a figure. "Why? You interested?"

"I might be. I've been thinking about buying a place at the beach. With Mom divorced and single, I stayed on with her in Beaufort through college until my dad died. Then I inherited his house—a huge surprise—so the money I'd saved for a house in Beaufort can go toward a place at the beach now." He grinned, a handsome blond man.

"That's great, " Tom said. "The Sandpiper, as one of the older houses on the island, has a cottage look and a lot of interesting architectural details the new homes don't have," he offered. "Being in the antiques business, you'd love that, Andrew. It only has three bedrooms but that's enough for you. It has a metal roof, old plantation shutters, nine-foot ceilings, original hardwood floors throughout, a screened porch on the back plus a lot of other special touches. It needs to be renovated and updated in some ways, but it's a wonderful house. The Landers, now in their eighties, are tired of renting it and seldom come to the island anymore."

"I've always liked that house," Andrew said, still studying it.

"It would be wonderful if you got a place at the beach," Emma added, virtually starry-eyed.

J.T. had noticed Emma watching Andrew often through the evening. It looked like she might have a little crush on him.

Andrew didn't seem to notice. "Although it's an hour and a half's drive to Edisto from Beaufort it's only about twenty to thirty minutes to Edisto by boat. The commute wouldn't be bad by water, and I own a boat now. I bought Drake's old cruiser when he got a new model this spring."

"It's a super boat," Chuck put in. "And it would be great if you could swing buying the Sandpiper. I know people who could help you with renovations and we could all pitch in a little."

J.T. grinned. "Well, I'd love having you as a neighbor, Andrew. See what you can work out. We'll throw a party when you move in to welcome you as an official island resident."

Tom pulled a realty card from his pocket to hand to Andrew. "You let me know if you want to see the house sometime."

"We need to get going," Ryder added, standing to leave. "It's two hours back to Savannah and Jennifer and I still need to make a quick stop to see the folks. Mom always comes up with a present for them when we visit."

Mary Helen laughed. "I can guarantee you there will be presents. Lula stopped by the store earlier today and left with several bags."

Ryder grinned. "More reason for us to head over to their place. Peyton and Eric would never forgive me if they found out I cheated them out of gifts. Treats like that are still a big deal to them at five and seven."

Tom and Ryder said their goodbyes, and then Mary Helen sliced pie for everyone for dessert while J.T. made coffee to go with it.

Andrew didn't drink alcohol of any kind, even wine, so J.T. hadn't served wine with dinner. Andrew's dad, Hayden Cavanaugh, had been an alcoholic before his death and Andrew's memories of times around his father when he drank lingered heavily. His mother Nora divorced Andrew's father when Andrew was a baby, but the man came around often enough through the years to make Andrew avoid any kind of alcohol. Knowing Andrew's strong feelings on the subject, J.T. and the others didn't drink when Andrew visited as a friendly form of respect.

The group broke up shortly after Tom and Ryder left. Emma had a Saturday morning meeting at the college and Andrew had to work at Westcott's. Jane needed to head home to check on Elena, and Chuck had an early tee time, being an avid golfer around his work schedule at Whaley's.

As they all gathered up dishes to leave, Andrew said to Mary Helen, "I'm so glad you and J.T. made up."

Leave it to Andrew to be the only one bold enough to mention it.

A small silence fell, and after a moment Mary Helen shrugged casually. "The night I arrived J.T. acted nice to me and was a good friend when I needed one." She didn't add more, although J.T. could tell they all wondered about the rest of the story.

"Old friends are the best friends," Andrew said, trying to bring closure to an awkward moment.

Jane smiled knowingly at Mary Helen. "I agree with Andrew that old friends are the best, and if I remember right you and J.T. were always very special old friends, too." She giggled. "Nice to see some of those old sparks still flying around."

Chuck grabbed Jane's arm. "I'd better take you home before you get us in trouble." He sent J.T. and Mary Helen a knowing smirk.

After they left J.T. tried to keep a straight face as he went over to the buffet table to get the remains of his casserole to carry into the kitchen.

"If you laugh, I swear I'll throw something at you." Mary Helen stomped over to glare at him.

He leaned toward her and kissed her, although she jerked away, still annoyed. "You're lucky they didn't grill us from the minute they arrived. You know they were all curious after hearing bits and pieces to pique their curiosity. I thought they acted very gracious overall."

"I suppose."

She walked to the deck railing to look out toward the ocean.

"It was bound to be awkward, Mary Helen. We've hardly spoken to each other in years."

"You might as well say it," she snapped. "They all had to tiptoe around our quarrel all these years."

"I suppose they did." He didn't want to push this issue, obviously getting her riled up. He changed the subject instead. "Let's take the food into the kitchen that needs to be put away and then take a walk on the beach. It's a nice night. I'll take care of the dishes later."

J.T. heard her sigh after a few minutes.

"That's a good idea," she said, deciding to let her anger go.

A short time later they strolled down the beach, the sound of the waves soothing away the tense emotions remaining. J.T. picked up shells, avoiding conversation until he saw Mary Helen relax, slow her pace, and quit frowning.

"I was sorry to hear about another dog," she said finally as they rounded the point and turned to start back. "It's really hard to imagine why anyone would want to hurt animals."

"Many people have a cruel side. Watching the news and reading the newspapers shows you that every day." He tossed a seashell out to sea. "Some people are afraid of dogs; some don't like dogs. And some people are just crazy wackos. It's hard to know what's behind this."

"Tom said the terrier was a pest. I wonder if the other dogs were."

"I don't know." He paused to look up at the moon, only a wisp behind the clouds tonight. "Rinny certainly wasn't. He could be hyperactive, prone to bark at strangers and a little temperamental sometimes, but mostly he was even-tempered, smart, and sociable."

"There's got to be an answer, some reason why someone is targeting dogs," Mary Helen said.

Ahead they saw Winifred Meggett with a friend, stopping to check a turtle nest.

J.T. walked over to the women. "Good evening, Winifred and Evelyn." He paused. "Mary Helen, I think you've met Winifred, but have you met Evelyn Dalton, Winifred's neighbor?"

"No. Nice to meet you." She gave Evelyn a small wave. "I'm Mary Helen Avery."

"Nice to meet you, too." The older lady, small and a little plump with short graying hair, smiled at Mary Helen.

With Evelyn holding a small dog on a leash, at a good distance from the turtle nest, Mary Helen didn't reach out a hand to her.

Evelyn gestured to the dog. "This is my dog Putney, just a mutt, mostly beagle with a little terrier and possibly dachshund mixed in. I've never been sure, but he's a sweet old boy. You needn't worry about him biting or barking at you." She laughed as the dog swung his tail in welcome. "He's as friendly as can be."

Mary Helen walked closer to squat down to pet the dog. It fondly licked her hand.

"He's a cutie," she said.

J.T. watched Winifred pull some trash off the turtle nest against the dunes and frown over tracks around the area. The marks looked like dog tracks instead of raccoon tracks.

"Some dogs can cause some real damage to turtle nests, can't they, Winifred?" he asked.

"They can, just like raccoons and other animals that like to dig." She moved some more debris and a few empty cola cans away from the nest. "People are sometimes almost as bad. They throw their trash on the beach, forgetting that the wind blows it up against the dunes. I chased off some little boys tonight digging into a nest looking for turtle eggs. Not even a thought to the damage they might cause. I'd have paddled their behinds if they were mine."

She pointed at the home above the dunes behind them. "I had to go up and tell the folks in that house to turn off their lights, too. They had the entire house lit up like a Christmas tree, inside and out, not even thinking about how light could confuse the turtles if they should they hatch tonight or disconcert a mother turtle if she swam in to lay. It makes me so mad."

"People do a lot of things when they're mad." He walked closer to Winifred. "Do you know anything about all these dogs being poisoned?"

She stood up, crossed her arms and glared at him over the words.

Evelyn answered before Winifred could. "Oh, Winnie and I've been reading about that in the newspapers. Such an awful thing. I can't imagine who would try to hurt dogs. Winnie and I both love dogs." She reached down to pat Putney. "Winnie used to have a dog of her own before she moved here, a Cairn terrier, but the little thing died. She was so cute, too. I've seen her picture. What was her name, Winnie?"

"Her name was Gretchen." To J.T.'s surprise, Winifred smiled, her face growing soft. He couldn't remember ever seeing the woman smile before.

Mary Helen cleared her throat. "I'm sure J.T. didn't mean to imply you two might know anything about the dogs that were poisoned."

Winifred's face hardened. "Oh, I think J.T. was *more* than implying I knew something about it. I think he was specifically asking if I did it. You were asking that, weren't you, J.T.?"

"I did wonder, Winifred," J.T. answered candidly. "You're often rather overly zealous about protecting the turtles."

"You need to form a better opinion of me." She shook her head. "I'm an intelligent woman. I have three degrees. I've taught high school and college classes. Spoken for many groups. Do you really think I'm the sort of woman who would poison dogs? It is usually backwoods raffle that do that sort of thing. People that don't like dogs, who think the world would be a better place without them. The same sort of people who shoot eagles, drown cats, and kill endangered species in our world without a thought. I'd say you could probably find a few of those types around here if you looked hard enough, don't you?"

Evelyn piped in. "There are a lot of mean people out there, but Winnie isn't one of them. You should see all the things she does to help animals and birds on the island. I can't imagine her going around poisoning people's beloved pets." She lifted her chin, offended at the very idea.

"I'm sure J.T. is sorry he even mentioned it," Mary Helen said, linking an arm into his firmly. "We'll let you enjoy your evening and get on with our walk now." She all but dragged him away.

Out of earshot down the beach, she punched at him. "What were you thinking to ask that women outright if she'd been poisoning dogs? That was so rude and I was really embarrassed."

He shrugged. "The idea just came to me. I figured if it were true Winifred would be the type to come out and admit it, to even brag about it if she was responsible. She'd see it as a feather in her cap to be solving a problem and saving more turtles."

Mary Helen shook her head. "You do have a low opinion of her. It doesn't seem founded either. You saw her out walking with her friend, and her friend's dog, and then saw her face when she remembered her own pet. People like that—intelligent people— don't poison dogs. Besides, isn't it illegal or something? And wouldn't Winifred be smart enough to know that?"

"Maybe, I don't know." He hated to back off the idea. "Somebody is behind this. An environmental wacko would be exactly the type to be behind it, too."

"Honestly." Mary Helen stalked off ahead of him up the beach.

He quickly caught up with her. "Listen, even if she isn't the one, Winifred gets around. She watches; she listens. She may know who is doing this but doesn't want to say. Or she might have seen something but didn't connect the dots before. Now she'll be thinking about it."

"I doubt that. She'll probably be thinking about how crazy you are. And how rude." Mary Helen glared at him. "She'll probably avoid me again in future, too."

"If we don't start asking questions, we won't find out who's doing this. The police aren't learning anything. Besides, I don't like the idea of more dogs dying. I like dogs." J.T. looked out to sea.

After a few moments he said more quietly, "I'd like to have a dog, too."

"You got really fond of Rinny, didn't you?"

"I did." He sighed. "I love Tom and Nola's dog Zella, too. I'd hate to think of anything happening to her."

"Why don't you get a dog?"

"I work all the time. You know that. Probably the same reason you haven't gotten a pet."

"That is a point." She took his arm, then stopped, turning him toward her. "Listen. From now on, if you want to ask people if they know anything about what's happening to the dogs at Edisto, just ask them politely to keep a look out, to report if they see anything suspicious." She shook her head. "Don't come out and say: Hey, have you been killing dogs around here?"

He scowled. "I wasn't that direct."

"No, you were worse!" She laughed.

She started walking again. "Come on. Let's get back and I'll help you clean up. Then I need to head home. We both have to work tomorrow."

CHAPTER 9

The rest of August flew by. Mary Helen settled into life at Edisto again more easily than she could have imagined. She glanced around The Little Mermaid today with fondness. She'd forgotten how much she loved working at the store, spending time with Isabel, hanging out with old friends she'd grown up with.

Isabel came out from the back of the store with a big box, sitting it down on the floor beside the counter. "Here's that box of sparklers, flags, and other paraphernalia to make a Labor Day display with for the store. Edisto's last hurrah is coming up this weekend. We'll be busy."

"I'll work on making a cute display and I'll put some holiday trappings in the window and out on the porch," Mary Helen said, beginning to sift through the box.

"What kind of display would you have set up at Adopt-Me-Dolls for Labor Day?"

She shrugged. "Whatever corporate sent to me, built around the dolls they wanted to feature with the display."

Isabel sat down behind the register, watching Mary Helen start to clean off an area near the front of the store for the new display. "It's fun having all the decisional power, don't you think?"

Mary Helen glanced up. "What do you mean?"

"An old quote says life's too short to be working for someone else's dream. I did that for a time, worked in retail, often setting up store displays."

"I didn't know that." Mary Helen came over to get the box Isabel had brought out to move it closer to the display.

"Yes. When we lived closer to Charleston I worked a number of little jobs in the retail stores downtown to keep busy. They all quickly realized I had some moxie and gave me more responsibilities, but of course without any additional pay or an increase in title. I was always coming up with ideas to improve business, to set up the store in a way to bring in more customers."

Mary Helen grinned at her. "I can imagine that."

"It lost me several jobs from jealous people. A few store managers stole my ideas and took credit for them, too. Often I was patronized as though a lowly clerk shouldn't possess a sharp mind or a creative concept worth considering." She picked up a catalog on the desk to thumb through it while she talked. "After a time I began wishing for a store of my own where I didn't have to kowtow to those above me whose ideas were no better than my own."

"That sounds like you." Mary Helen hung a flag tablecloth over the cleared area she'd emptied to start her display.

"Then my grandmother passed and left her little cottage at Edisto to me. She was always fond of me and knew I loved the house." She hesitated, cocking her head, thinking back. "Ezra and I came down to look at it, and he said, 'Why don't you convert this place into a little store? You keep saying you want one.'" Isabel looked up and smiled. "And so I did. I studied what was here on the island, what seemed to be needed, and decided on a children's shop. Ezra always liked the beach here at Edisto, so we sold our place in town and bought our house on Point Street. We've been here ever since."

"I didn't know all that," Mary Helen said. "I keep learning new things about you."

"And I you." Isabel's eyes met her. "In your weeks here I've heard enough snippets of your conversation to know you haven't been given the liberty you yearn for working corporate. I've watched you thrive on having all the decisional power here."

"It's your store, Isabel. I hardly have all the decisional power."

"Nonsense. I've given you free reign to do whatever you want here at The Little Mermaid, in ordering new items, reorganizing the store, its displays, and more." She gestured around. "Look how you've rearranged the store since you've been here, changed out the window, put displays on the porch—even in the yard—and ordered all sorts of new merchandise. Can you recall me once saying your ideas weren't good?"

Mary Helen thought back. "Actually, no. Looking back further you've given me a free reign here for more years than only this summer."

Isabel smiled. "I go to a lot of these buyers' conferences and events, sit in on meetings, share lunch with people in a variety of retail positions. They all envy me owning my own business. Someone said a wise thing once: Unless you're the lead dog, the scenery never changes."

Mary Helen doubled over laughing. "You're so funny, Isabel."

"The truth is what it is." She reached under the counter to get her purse. "I'm going to head over to the house to get some things done. We invited Elaine and Pete Whaley over to cook out and talk about our upcoming cruise together. Then we might drive over to Folly Beach to watch the fireworks."

"That sounds like fun." Mary Helen smiled. "Mother and I still can't believe you talked Elaine and Pete into going on a cruise with you. It's rare they'll leave their business for even a weekend getaway."

"I told Elaine that since she and Pete raised four smart children and now have her boys working full time at Whaleys, and Jane working part-time, that she and Pete should take advantage of that and travel while they can. None of us are getting any younger."

"Well, I think it's wonderful you will get to share a trip together." She dumped out the box to start sorting through the things in it. "Our block on The Point will seem really quiet after Labor Day. Your house, on one side of me, and Pete and Elaine's on the other, will be empty—with all four of you gone and cruising the ocean."

"Don't forget your mother and Parker are leaving for their

wonderful trip abroad, too."

"Yes. They'll be gone for over eight weeks. Isn't that fabulous?"

"It is. I'm so excited for them." Isabel started toward the door and then looked back, wiggling her eyebrows. "You'll need to get J.T. Mikell to keep you company so you won't get lonesome." She laughed over the words and let herself out.

Mary Helen wrinkled her nose. On a small island like Edisto there were few secrets, and she and J.T. had become somewhat of an item again.

Working on the new display, Mary Helen thought about the truth of some of Isabel's words. She had relished the freedom here at The Little Mermaid to order for the store, arrange things as she wanted, carry more leadership and responsibility. It was powerful. She wondered if it was better to be a big fish in a little pond or a little fish in a big pond. She had to admit she could see plusses in both.

None of her networking and job searching had netted any new offers so far, but yesterday she'd received an email from American Girl wanting to schedule an interview next week. It was a coveted opportunity with a big company, much like Adopt-Me-Dolls. She'd be foolish not to consider it. It would hurt to leave Isabel and the Mermaid but it would hurt even worse now to leave J.T. Mikell.

She picked up a Mermaid pillow from a nearby shelf and hugged it to herself. "J.T. is really getting to me again, and I don't know what to do about it. There are so many things we've never talked out and we still want different things from life."

A few customers came into the store then, and Mary Helen put conflicting thoughts aside to wait on them.

She finished the Labor Day display after lunch and was starting to carry the empty box to the storage room, when Gracie Byrd walked into the store. Shocked, but not wanting to show it, Mary Helen managed to walk behind the counter, drop the box to the floor, and then turn toward Gracie with a welcoming smile. *Hadn't she heard Gracie had married and moved off island? Was she simply back visiting for the Labor Day weekend?* The thoughts chased through her mind.

"Well, hello, Gracie," Mary Helen said. "What can I help you with today?"

"I heard you were working here since you came back," Gracie replied, wandering around the store as she talked. "I admit I was surprised. I thought you'd moved on to bigger things. Left this little island."

Mary Helen bit back a retort. She was working, and this was Isabel's store. "I heard you married and left, too. Are you back for Labor Day visiting with your parents?" She studied her old nemesis, still a pretty blond, more shapely than in her young teens, her complexion flawless, makeup perfect, eyes still baby blue. Her long ago perm was gone, but natural curl still showed in her hair, which fell to her shoulders. Mary Helen had always envied Gracie's blond curly hair. Her own was as straight as a stick, thick and rich, but plain, in her eyes, compared to Gracie's.

Gracie paused, fingering a paperweight before turning to look at Mary Helen more directly. "That marriage ended unhappily and I'm back on the island, working at Daddy's business now. I assumed you'd heard. I also assumed you heard J.T. and I were dating, but I guess not. People keep mentioning to me they've seen you two together."

She picked up the paperweight again and turned it around in her hand. "J.T. always was one to flirt with the girls. He is so good, too, in the romantic area—difficult to resist when he sets his mind to be sweet. I'm sure you know what I mean." She sent Mary Helen a smug smile. "No one can kiss quite like J.T. Mikell. It always thrills me right down to my toes."

Mary Helen sat down on the bench behind the register to keep Gracie from seeing how shaky she'd become from her words. And how shocked. Was J.T. dating Gracie Byrd? Had he simply not bothered to tell her?

"I'm invited to a little baby shower at the church next week," Gracie continued. "I thought I'd pick up something cute here for a gift." She walked over to a shelf filled with dolls and selected a pink and white rag doll, perfect for a small baby. "This should do, don't you think? They know it's going to be a little girl."

Keeping her professionalism to the forefront, Mary Helen answered with a calm, smooth voice. "That's a perfect choice. We sell a lot of those dolls for baby showers. I think your friend will love it." She forced a smile. "We sell cute pink gift bags you might like for the gift, too. They're on the wall there." Mary Helen pointed.

While Gracie turned her back to select a gift bag, Mary Helen drew in a deep breath. Fortunately, before Gracie turned around again, a couple of talkative tourists came into the store, filling up the space with chatter and laughter, exclaiming over most everything they saw.

Mary Helen rang up Gracie's purchases while talking to a couple of the visitors at the same time.

"I expect to stay here on Edisto now," Gracie said before she left. "So does J.T. We're neither one from "off" like you. This is our home."

She turned at the door and sent Mary Helen a pointed look. "You enjoy a nice visit, you hear? I know J.T. has been pleased to see you again. It's always nice to play 'remember when,' don't you think?"

Biting back any comeback, Mary Helen watched her leave and turned back to help the other customers. It wasn't until they, and a sweep of customers following them, left that Mary Helen felt tears dripping down her face at last. Tears of shock and tears of anger.

She closed the store at 6:00, drove home, and then set out walking up the beach toward J.T.'s place. How dare he not even tell her Gracie Byrd was back on the island? And how dare he not bother to mention he'd been seeing her and, obviously, from Gracie's words not casually?

To make the day even worse, she saw Miles Lawrence walking down the beach toward her. Much older now, but still handsome and distinguished. Still walking with that smooth, confident air Mary Helen remembered so well. Carrying that alluring draw around him. A draw much like J.T.'s.

"Hello, Mary Helen," he said as he came closer to her. "I heard you were visiting on the island."

She pasted another plastic smile on her face. "Hello, Miles. Are you here for the Labor Day weekend?'

His eyes moved over her in a slow accessing way, making Mary Helen want to kick him. How dare he look at her like that?

"Mother and I are down for the weekend." Miles put a hand out and cupped her chin. "And you've turned into a beautiful woman."

She jerked away from him. "Don't touch me, Miles Lawrence. We are not friends."

"Still holding old grudges, Mary Helen? Don't you know unforgiveness is unhealthy? Bitterness imprisons, too. You shouldn't cling to past negative experiences; doing so closes doors to possibilities in the future."

She started walking on. "I don't need psychological advice from you."

"You may not like the source, but the advice is good. And that anger you carry is unhealthy for you."

Mary Helen walked away, not looking back. What an insufferable man. Were all men so two-faced? Saying one thing but doing another? Never repentant for hurting people? Putting forth one image but living out another behind everyone's back? She was beginning to wonder.

CHAPTER 10

Home from the shop a little early, J.T. was relaxing on the back porch finishing up dinner, when he spotted Mary Helen coming up the beach. He saw her stop to talk to Miles Lawrence—obviously not a happy moment—before walking on. From her angry expression as she stalked up the beach pathway to his house a few minutes later, he could tell she was irritated about something. Miles must have really set her off.

"Hey," he said as she stomped up the back stairs. "You look upset. I saw you stop and talk to Miles. Did he say something to tick you off?"

She stood glaring at him for a minute, not answering.

"Have you had dinner?" he asked. "There's another chicken pot pie in the freezer I can stick in the oven for you."

Her eyes narrowed. "I am so mad at you I hardly know what to say."

He spread his hands. "What have I done?"

"You've been seeing Gracie Byrd but didn't bother to tell me," she blurted out. "You also didn't bother to even mention that Gracie Byrd had moved back to Edisto again." She gave him a murderous look. "Exactly when were you planning to mention these things to me?"

J.T. groaned, knowing he was in for it now. "First, I assumed you knew Gracie Byrd moved back to the island, that Jane or someone else already told you. Second, although I went out with Gracie a couple of times when she first moved back here, I realized quickly she saw it as more than two old friends getting together again. So I backed off." He gestured to the chair beside him. "Why don't you sit down so we can talk about this?"

"I'm too mad to sit down." She paced closer to him and punched a finger practically in his face. "Gracie came by the Mermaid today and made it quite clear to me that you and she were a couple. She also subtly suggested I was only someone you were filling a little time with."

He stood up to be on the same level with her, his own anger rising. "And you believed that? You should know by now that Gracie's middle name ought to be Liar or Troublemaker. I quickly saw she hadn't changed much as soon as I spent time with her again, despite her going away to college, getting married and everything."

"Why would you even want to spend time with her, knowing what she's like?" Mary Helen's eyes flashed. "And how do I know you're not still seeing her? She seemed to indicate you were."

"Watch it, Mary Helen." His fists clenched. "You're tiptoeing around calling me a liar and I don't like that."

She stomped her foot. "Well I don't like finding out today you've been seeing Gracie Byrd again. You know how I feel about her. You should have told me she'd come back to Edisto, and you should have told me you've been dating her." She sent him an anguished look. "Are you still seeing her?"

"No, I'm not. I haven't gone out with anyone else since you came back to the island. I haven't wanted to be with anyone else."

He saw tears pool in her eyes.

"I hate that you've been seeing her again at all. It makes me feel sick."

J.T. blew out a long breath. "You've always blown any friendship or relationship I've had with Gracie Byrd totally out of proportion. Can't you get over that Mary Helen? You're twenty-six years old now, not a kid any more. Couldn't you have simply come over here tonight and calmly told me what happened today with Gracie, and what she said to upset you, without throwing out accusations at me?" He ran his hands through his hair in exasperation. "I told you when we were kids and when we had that giant fight in high school that I have no romantic interest in Gracie. I never have." He paused for emphasis. "I still don't."

"Then why did you go out with her?" she asked, sniffling.

He paced across the deck. "I felt sort of sorry for her. Her marriage had broken up; she was unhappy. She came by the shop a few times and seemed at loose ends. When she suggested doing something together, it didn't seem like a big deal to say yes. We'd grown up together, gone through school together, graduated in the same class. I didn't think anything about going out to dinner a few times and to a movie with her. Until word began to filter back to me later that she'd started telling people we were dating and getting serious. So I backed off. I told her I saw us as only friends, but as you well know, Gracie creates her own realities and sees things as she wants to."

He tried to put a hand on Mary Helen's arm but she jerked away from his touch.

Irritated, he scowled at her. "Can't you see that Gracie is one of those people who has trouble with the truth? Ezra says she's borderline to being a compulsive liar, that lying has become a routine to her. She bends the truth, large or small, to create the reality she wants to see. Then after telling it for a while, she starts believing it herself. Even back in high school, most of us saw, and came to know, that about Gracie so we never paid much attention to whatever story she started spreading. Some kids develop problems with alcohol, cheating, truancy, or vandalism. Gracie had trouble telling the truth. Obviously she still does."

She bit her lip studying him. "Did you kiss her?"

He rolled his eyes. "Guys do that when they go out with girls."

Tears welled in her eyes again and she turned away.

"Be realistic, Mary Helen." J.T. made an effort to speak calmly. "The two of us fought over Gracie Byrd and other issues we couldn't agree about when in high school. We didn't even date again after that last giant quarrel over Gracie. We seldom talked without strain or argument."

He tried to think what else to say. "Time moved on after those years. It always does. I graduated high school, went on to college while working at the store. You graduated from high school two years later, went away to college in North Carolina and then moved to New Jersey to work. You rarely even came back to Edisto. Even if I missed you and still carried feelings for you, I had to go on with my life. So, yeah, I dated and kissed a lot of girls these ten years. I didn't sit at home staring at the wall." J.T. took a deep breath. "Kissing Gracie wasn't a big deal, Mary Helen. You shouldn't see it as a big deal."

She walked over to look out toward the sea again, and J.T. followed to stand beside her.

He was tempted to put a hand on hers on the deck rail but resisted. "What you should focus on is that since you came back, since we started seeing each other, I haven't gone out with anyone else. I'm crazy about you. I realized as soon as we started spending time together again that I'd never stopped loving you. I've never told another woman I love her. I've liked and even lusted after a lot of women but you're the only woman I've ever thought I could live my whole life with, that I'd want to have kids with. I tried to tell you that after we fought in high school a long time ago. I'm telling you that again. I guess it's up to you, though, whether you believe me—or whether you even feel the same way."

She eyed him warily. "I don't know what I feel."

His heart sunk. "I know you care for me, Mary Helen."

"I'm afraid of caring about someone too much. You always get hurt when you do."

He saw her looking toward the beach at the place where she'd stopped to talk with Miles.

"It didn't help things for you to run into Miles Lawrence tonight when you were upset, to be reminded of how he led your mother—and you and Suki—on after your father died. I know you still remember how the three of you saw him with someone else in Charleston. I know that hurt you."

"I hate it when people don't tell you the truth. That hurts." She sucked in a shaky breath before turning to look at him. "It hurts that you didn't tell me about Gracie, that I had to find out from her today and get all torn apart, shocked, and upset by all she said."

Warm tears slid down her cheeks.

J.T. tried to think what to say. "I'm sorry I didn't tell you. Maybe I should have. The one time I considered mentioning it, I visualized you getting upset like this, seeing it as more than it was. So I didn't bring it up."

She glowered at him. "That decision set me up to be a victim today, J.T. If I'd known the truth, I could have handled the situation differently."

"Well, you know the truth now. I went out with Gracie a few times, but we don't have a relationship." Feeling irritated, he added. "And just for the record, you may run into other women around the area I've gone out with in the past. They might mention something about our times together or even something about their feelings then or now. I haven't been a monk these last years. But you'll have to make a decision to realize that was in the past. As long as we're together, Mary Helen, there won't be other women."

She turned to him with unsure eyes. "I wish I could believe that."

He shook his head, exasperated. "Our biggest problem has always been that you don't trust me."

She lifted her chin and looked away. "That wasn't our only problem."

"Yeah, I know. You always wanted me to yearn after bigger and better things than a life here on the island, pushed me to go away to school somewhere, to test my wings, try new things." He ran a hand along his neck. "I could never get you to realize that what I wanted and loved was right here. This is my home, where I belong. I didn't need to go off searching for myself, trying to find my way. I've always known, since I was a little kid, that I wanted to live and work here, make my life here."

He paced across the deck, his emotions churning, and then

turned to walk back toward her. "I've never told you how much it hurt me that you never believed in my dreams, made snide little remarks about my family's business here on the island, insinuated with random comments that I'd never amount to much, always discounting my hopes and plans."

Her mouth dropped open. "I did not."

"You did, whether you'll admit it or not." He leaned closer. "You've been surprised, too, at how well our business has done, how well I've done. I have a happy life, Mary Helen. Most of the unhappiness I've known in life has been quite honestly due to you."

"That's a mean thing to say." Two spots of red appeared in her cheeks now.

"Over and over again I tried to apologize to you about what happened with Gracie Byrd back in high school, tried to convince you that she was lying when she said we were a couple and that I was taking her to senior prom."

"I saw you kiss her!" She shouted the words at him.

"You saw her kiss me and she staged it."

Mary Helen turned away.

"Even now you still don't want to believe me."

"It didn't look like you were trying to get away."

He came up behind her and put his hands on her arms, even though she flinched. "You saw what you wanted to see. Ever since that episode with Miles when you were a girl, you've carried this idea around in your head that men aren't trustworthy. You're wrong, Mary Helen."

She pulled away. "I want to go home now."

"Okay. You do that." He watched her walk down the steps. "I'll talk to Gracie if you want me to. But with Gracie, even if I call her to talk, she'll see it as more than it is. Construe it as interest."

She looked up at him with unhappy eyes. "There are always so many girls mixed up in your life. I've always hated that."

"I know, but I've always tried to tell you that you're the only one for me. The real question is whether you will ever believe it."

J.T. watched her walk away down the path to the beach, never once looking back.

He slumped into a chair on the porch, trying to think if there was any way to convince her his heart was reliable. Or if any man on earth could convince her he was worth trusting.

"Well, that may be the last I'll see of her," he said to himself. "But I knew we had to talk all this out sometime."

Glancing toward the darkening sky, he offered a little prayer. "Lord, if you mean for Mary Helen and me to get together, I think you're going to have to orchestrate a little miracle to work it out. Until then, it sure seems like an uphill battle for me to keep trying to win her over, but like mom encouraged, I'll try. I do think she's worth the fight." He paused, closing his eyes. "But I sure don't have any idea what to do now, and that's a fact."

A little later, J.T. picked up the phone and dialed a familiar number.

"Ezra?" he said, hearing Ezra Compton answer. "You remember that time I fixed your golf cart and you said you'd owe me a favor later? Well I could use one." He glanced at the clock. "I know it's a little late but I could really use some of your psychiatric counseling help." He tried making an effort to laugh.

"Sounds like you could use it right now from the strain in your voice."

"Yeah, I guess I could."

"Are you at the house?"

"I am."

"I'll walk up. We'll talk a little."

"Thanks," J.T. said, hanging up.

Ezra's name had come to him in the quiet as he sat staring out at the ocean. It was Ezra who'd given him counsel about Gracie Byrd before. Maybe he could help again.

CHAPTER 11

Mary Helen cried all the way back to Oleanders. J.T. had made her so mad with the things he said. She felt hurt and angry, too, every time she remembered Gracie Byrd's smug little smile as she left the store earlier.

"I should have known not to get involved with J.T. Mikell again," she mumbled to herself as she stomped up the back steps into the house.

Slumping into her favorite chair in the living room, Mary Helen tried to quiet her mind. She realized one thing for certain now: staying at Edisto would only continue to put her into proximity with J.T. and Gracie—both people she distinctly wanted to avoid.

Resigned to this understanding, and the same dilemma she'd faced before, Mary Helen went upstairs to her computer and replied to the email she received yesterday from American Girl. They'd responded positively to her resume about the Visual Merchandiser position opening at their store in Chicago and wanted to set a phone interview time. She confirmed one of the times they suggested for next week after the Labor Day weekend, knowing if she passed this stage, she might need to fly to Chicago for an in-person interview. The store's current Visual Merchandiser had been promoted and they wanted to fill the position before October.

Mary Helen glanced at her work schedule for The Little Mermaid posted on her bulletin board with a sigh of relief. She was off tomorrow. Good.

She pulled a small duffle bag from the closet and started tossing a few clothes into it. Knowing J.T. as she did, she felt sure he would soon head this way to try to talk with her more, either tonight or tomorrow. He didn't give up easily in an argument and he was always persistent in going after what he wanted. Not in the mood for more discussion now, she fully intended not to be here when he came knocking on the door.

Picking up her phone, she called her mother.

"Hi, Mom," she said when Claire answered. "I just realized I'm off tomorrow and thought I'd come and spend the night with you since you and Parker are leaving right after Labor Day for your trip. I have to work on Labor Day weekend at The Little Mermaid, with all the tourist traffic coming in, so would it be okay if I come?"

"We'd be delighted," her mother replied. "I'll run up and put fresh sheets on your bed while you're driving over."

"Thanks." Hearing the love in her mother's voice made her want to cry again.

"Is everything all right, Mary Helen?" she asked.

"I've had a fight with J.T.," she said, deciding to be honest. "But other than that everything is fine. I even have a job prospect to tell you about. I really want some time with you and Parker before you leave, too. If I get this job I might be gone before you get back to South Carolina."

"Well, you drive safely, and we will see you soon."

They hung up and Mary Helen finished her packing. Realizing she'd skipped dinner she grabbed a banana to eat in the car, loaded her duffle into the back seat, and headed for Beaufort.

The trip, only twenty to thirty minutes by boat, took over an hour and a half by car, winding its way along a circuitous route from Edisto to Hwy 17 south and then back toward the coast again to Beaufort. Mary Helen followed the familiar roads to the old downtown neighborhood where Parker and Claire's historic two-storied home, Waterview, sat looking out on the Beaufort River at the end of River Street.

She always felt a second nostalgic sense of home as she pulled into the driveway of the gracious plantation style house. When

Parker and her mother married, after her father's death, this house had become their home through all the rest of her elementary and high school years. She loved the old house and had a heart full of happy memories of her early life here.

She saw Parker rising from a chair on the back porch as she stopped the car in front of the garage.

"I've been watching for you," he called, coming to wrap her in one of his big hugs. Such a good man, so kind, thoughtful, and loving. How fortunate for she, Suki, and her mother Claire that her father's brother fell in love with Claire and that they united as a warm and happy family.

"You and Mother both still look wonderful," Mary Helen said as Parker reached into the back seat to get her duffle and a tote bag of toiletries. She glanced around. "I still miss Congress running over to greet me in all his doggy friendliness."

"So do we," Parker said, starting into the house. "That black Lab was a big part of our lives."

"You could get another dog," Mary Helen said, following him in the back door of Waterview and into the main hall, spanning from the front to the back of the house.

"We might later, but right now we travel so much it isn't practical." He started down the hall toward the stairs. "I'll take your bags up to your room. You run on into the kitchen. Your mother is puttering around in there fixing something."

Mary Helen soon joined Claire in Waterview's spacious, welcoming kitchen. The sunny room opened onto a small, comfortable dining and sitting area and to a broad, inviting covered porch on the side of the house. Waterview's kitchen had always been one of Mary Helen's favorite places in the home and where the family inevitably gathered.

Her mother gave her a quick peck on the cheek and then, grabbing a potholder, turned to pull a long baking sheet out of the oven. "I made some of those oatmeal raisin cookies you love while you were on your way over."

The smell of hot cookies wafted into the room as she sat the pan on the stove.

"Those look wonderful," Mary Helen said, settling onto a stool at the big island in the kitchen.

"Did you eat dinner?"

"No." She shook her head. "I got into it with J.T. and lost my appetite, but I did eat a banana on my way over."

"That's not dinner. I fixed a tuna pasta casserole for our supper tonight. The rest is still sitting by the stove there." She pointed. "Dish out some and heat it in the microwave. I'll cut you a slice or two of fresh tomato to go with it and pour you a glass of tea."

Parker came back in the room while Claire was setting a place for Mary Helen at the table.

"Make us some coffee, would you?" Claire asked him. "You and I can drink a cup of coffee with Mary Helen while she has dinner. She hasn't eaten."

They sat down at the small, familiar kitchen table a few minutes later. And Mary Helen eagerly dug into the casserole on her plate.

"Ummm. I haven't had this casserole in a long time. It's good."

"I gave you the recipe," Claire said, stirring milk into her coffee. "It's easy to make, just cooked pasta, tuna, onion, mushrooms, cheese, and canned soup stirred together with crushed chips and a little cheese on the top."

"I should take more time to cook," Mary Helen said, smiling at her.

"Tell us about this new job prospect." Claire propped her elbows on the table and leaned forward to put her chin on one hand.

"Well, I passed the first stage for a possible Visual Merchandiser job with American Girl. I have a phone interview scheduled next week."

"That's a big company and similar to the Adopt-Me-Dolls company that you enjoyed." Parker reached to get a fresh cookie from the plate Claire had placed in the middle of the table. "Where is the position located?"

"In downtown Chicago in a huge store on the street level of a seventy-four story skyscraper called Water Tower Place. It's right next to a big Macy's at the corner of Michigan Avenue and Chestnut Street. It's the company's flagship store, and it's a plum job."

Claire's smile waned. "Chicago is a big city."

"Yes," Mary Helen agreed. "It should be an adventure to live and work there."

"Do you want the job?" Parker asked, studying her.

"It looks like a very good opportunity." She lifted her chin. "I definitely think it's time for me to move on, too."

"Are you going to tell us about the fight with J.T.?" he asked.

"Yes, but remember I was already looking for a job before J.T. and I quarreled," Mary Helen reminded them. "Besides it was inevitable, I guess, that J.T. and I would get into it again."

"You didn't always quarrel," Claire put in.

"Maybe not always, but often enough."

"Tell us what happened," Claire said then.

Mary Helen reviewed the events of the day, leaving out some of the ugly accusations she and J.T. hurled at each other.

"I hate that you quarreled." Her mother sighed. "And frankly you and Suki always cared too much about what Gracie Byrd thought and did. It used to bother me."

Parker chuckled. "I remember Gracie Byrd, too. We once bought a pile of jelly bracelets in Beaufort when you and Suki were girls, because Gracie Byrd had started a fashion trend with them. If I remember right Gracie was always rivalrous about J.T's interest in you, Mary Helen, even when you were only kids. She caused a stink at Claire's first book launch and more problems later in yours and J.T's relationship when you grew older."

"Gracie always was a pain," Mary Helen agreed with a frown. "But despite that, I still don't like it that J.T. is seeing her again. I especially don't like it that he didn't tell me about it—or even tell me she was back at Edisto."

"You said he told you he thought that you knew," Claire reminded her. "He also said he only dated her a few times and then realized it a mistake."

Parker sat his coffee cup down, looking thoughtful. "The man also told you he loved you, basically said he wanted to spend his life with you." He looked across at Mary Helen. "A man has to get up a lot of nerve to say those kinds of words to a woman. Have you really thought about what that means?"

She fidgeted. "Even if he did say them, how can I know if I can really trust in those words at all or in J.T.?"

"Oh, Mary Helen," her mother put in. "Deep in your heart you know J.T. wouldn't say things like that to you if he didn't mean them. Parker and I have known him since he was a boy and I've *never* known him to lie, even though he and Chuck could be scamps sometimes. He was a sweet boy and I believe he has become a good man—with a wonderful family, too. You know that."

Parker tapped a finger on the table thoughtfully. "Mary Helen, ever since Miles hurt you, and your sister and mother long ago, you've held on to the idea that men aren't trustworthy. Surely you realize now it's not an accurate generalization to paint all men with the same condemning brush because of one old instance."

Mary Helen glared at him. "I've seen a lot of instances of untrustworthiness in men since then, even if I haven't talked about them. You can add this last scenario with Wendell Hembree to the mix. One thing I've seen for a certainty is that good-looking, charismatic men who like the ladies—to put it nicely—tend to have trouble giving up those run-around ways to settle down and be faithful husbands."

Parker shook his head. "Many men and women play the field a lot before marriage, but when they find the right one—the one they really love—they settle down and are faithful partners."

Mary Helen bit back her temper. "I'm sure your implication is that this would be true with J.T., but remember it was *after* J.T. told me he loved me the first time and *after* he started talking about us getting married the first time, that all the problems with Gracie happened. That doesn't seem to me like a good sign of future faithfulness, especially when I learned today he's been seeing Gracie Byrd again, the same girl who caused all our problems before. She certainly made it clear she views their relationship as meaningful, too."

Claire got up to take Mary Helen's plate to the sink and then came to sit down again. "Here's something for you to think long and hard about, Mary Helen. Gracie has always tried to stir up problems between you and J.T. Many times I can remember Lula, Elaine, and Isabel talking about how Stanley and Eunice Byrd spoiled that child, gave her too much all her life, and excused her problems. Not all only children are spoiled, but Gracie Byrd definitely was. I saw in field trips I took with the Edisto school children how Gracie always wanted what she couldn't have. She was a very pretty child, and popular because she was so confident, but she would do rather nasty things to gain her way and to get things she wanted. I hoped she would outgrow some of those selfish, childish ways, but apparently she has not."

Parker put a hand to his chin thoughtfully. "Claire, do you think Gracie deliberately came to the store and lied to Mary Helen to try to break her and J.T. up? The same way J.T. says she lied to break them up in high school?"

"I do," Claire said emphatically. She sent a pointed look at Mary Helen. "But the important thing is whether Mary Helen will be able to see that fact or whether she will continue to paint J.T. with a villain's brush that he doesn't really deserve."

"That's not the only factor in this scenario." Mary Helen's mouth tightened.

"No, it isn't." Parker agreed. "The other big factor is whether you love the man or not. He obviously loves you."

"And if I did, what purpose would it serve?" She snapped out the words. "He'd want me to stay at Edisto, and I'm not sure that's what I want."

Claire smiled. "Well, then that's something you'll have to pray about, isn't it? We know God has the best answers to all this no matter what our different opinions are."

"Claire is right," Parker added, getting up from the table to walk around to kiss Mary Helen's cheek. "I'm very confident a smart girl like you will figure out what is the happiest course for her life."

They moved into the den then and talked about other things, Parker and Claire deliberately shifting the conversational topic. The two talked about their upcoming trip, showed Mary Helen their itinerary and photos of places they planned to stay, things they wanted to see. They soon got Mary Helen into some humorous discussions imagining the upsets and problems Claire's new book character Annabel would get into along the way.

The three called Suki to talk and check on her. Claire and Parker chatted to Suki about their trip, and Mary Helen shared about her job opportunity.

"Well, pooh," Suki said. "If you move to Chicago, I won't see you as often. I loved that we lived close."

"You're hardly ever in New York and we both work so much, we rarely saw each other anyway." Mary Helen laughed. "Besides, there are lots of direct flights running between Chicago and New York all the time. We can plan some long weekend visits together. If I get the job you can come over to see my new place. We'll explore the city. Maybe you'll come to play with the Chicago Symphony and get to stay longer."

"Maybe. I'll try to get Jonah to schedule it later if he can."

After their phone call to Suki, they watched an Agatha Christie *Poirot* episode on a local television channel, each trying to guess the murderer before the end of the show. When it ended, they all headed to bed.

Claire and Parker had kept Mary Helen's and Suki's bedrooms much the same as when they last lived at home. Mary Helen had redecorated her room several times over the years as she grew older. When home from college one summer, she'd turned the room into more of a suite, decorated in a cerulean blue and white color scheme, with a new queen size bed, a sofa and sitting area with a television, and a big desk with a computer. The blue-green color scheme reminded Mary Helen of the ocean and she'd mixed in basket gold tones, like the color of sea grasses that waved on the dunes.

After glancing around her old room with fondness, Mary Helen dug her nightshirt out of her duffle bag, changed clothes, brushed her teeth, washed her face in the little bathroom next door, and then climbed into bed, propping herself up against the headboard.

"Your room has such restful colors, like the colors at the beach," Claire commented, coming in to check if she needed anything before going to bed. She carried a book with her and handed it to Mary Helen. "I thought you might like a mystery to read before going to sleep. I finished this one yesterday and loved it."

"Do you want to talk for a minute?" Mary Helen asked, patting the bed beside her.

"I'd love that." Claire climbed onto the big bed beside her, propping up against the headboard and tucking some pillows behind her back. "We used to sit in bed and talk when you were a little girl."

"This is such a confusing time for me, Mother," Mary Helen said, sighing and leaning her head back.

Claire pulled up a cover over their legs. "Life is full of confusing times. I think they are especially hurtful when we're younger. We're still so innocent then in many ways, so idealistic, so emotional. You remember how very disappointed Meadowlark was when she found herself caught up in all those hurtful events away from home. She was so grieved, too, at the behavior of the ones she thought she trusted in the Forest of Mim."

Mary Helen smiled. Her mother often talked of her book characters as through they all were real people.

"Well, I can hardly fly away home on the wings of a giant moth as Meadowlark did," she said.

"But you did fly home already." Claire patted her knee. "Some of us wish you'd stay. I'm sure you know that."

"Well, I came home to find other problems."

Claire traced her finger over the embroidered design on an accent pillow. "Or perhaps you came home to resolve those problems finally."

Mary Helen looked away, not sure she wanted to have this conversation.

"I'm remembering our talk outside The Little Mermaid one day, where you admitted you might be falling in love with J.T. again." Claire set the pillow aside. "Perhaps because you have fallen in love, this misunderstanding feels even more hurtful."

Mary Helen crossed her arms. "Do you really think, as you and Parker said, that it's a misunderstanding? That Gracie tried to orchestrate this event to hurt me and to break J.T. and me up?"

"Can't you look back through the years and remember all the other times Gracie did similar things? Do you think people change that much?"

Mary Helen wrinkled her nose. "Why would anyone, even Gracie, want another person to like them that desperately when they don't?"

"With Gracie I think it's simply a matter of always wanting what she can't have. J.T. has never been interested in Gracie and so, like the forbidden fruit, that very fact has made him irresistible to her." She hesitated. "Ezra says a person can get obsessed with the idea of someone not interested in them."

Mary Helen's eyes widened. "You talked to Ezra about this?"

"Heavens no." She acted shocked. "I overheard Ezra and Isabel talking about it one day. They'd evidently been at J.T.'s store when Gracie came in simpering and flirting with him. They watched how embarrassed J.T. acted and how he diplomatically tried to say no to all Gracie's pushy invitations. They felt rather sorry for him."

"Why didn't you or Isabel tell me Gracie was back or that J.T. and Gracie had been dating?"

"Like J.T., I really assumed you knew Gracie came back home, that you'd heard about her divorce through Jane. She's been back over a year now. It's hardly news anymore." She straightened a pillow behind her back. "I didn't even know Gracie and J.T went out together and I don't think Isabel knew either. If she had, she certainly would have told me. Frankly, I don't think anyone thought much of J.T. and Gracie dating a few times even if they knew. It never went anywhere."

"I just wish J.T. had told me."

"Mary Helen, be honest. Don't you think some of the reason you're so angry is because Gracie caught you off guard in this, embarrassed and humiliated you? I'm sure your pride is smarting. I'm sure, too, she picked up on the fact that you didn't already know about her dating J.T." Claire laughed. "Probably she knew you wouldn't know either because she was making most of it up as she went along anyway."

"J.T. did admit that he kissed her, Mom. Gracie bragged about it, too."

"People kiss when they date. You know they do." She shook her head. "You need to remember, too, that J.T. went out with Gracie when you were in New Jersey. When he didn't know if he would ever see you again. Be realistic, Mary Helen. J.T. didn't cheat on you when you were a couple. You weren't dating and the two of you had hardly spoken to each other since high school. J.T. had no reason to be loyal to you at that time."

Mary Helen closed her eyes. "I hate it when people are reasonable when I'm upset."

Claire laughed. "Well, at least you're seeing that you possibly might have been a little unreasonable."

Mary Helen sighed.

"Let's do a little suppose game," Claire said, clasping her hands in front of her. "Suppose you suddenly realized tomorrow that you loved J.T., despite all, like Fleuradew realized she loved Cloverdan in the first Farnsworth Fairies book. You always loved their story, even as a girl."

"I did," she admitted, smiling and settling into one of her mother's lovely fantasies.

"Let's say J.T. rescued you when you had drifted out to sea on a raft one day and you knew suddenly without a doubt he was the one. Then of course, you faced the dilemma of realizing the very next day that you planned to leave for your new job in Paris, France, all the way across the ocean. What in the world should you do?" She put a hand to her heart. "You had a little job on the island working at a lovely shop, of course. Perhaps you could open a store yourself. But where would you get the money? Suddenly LilaRose, your dear grandmother, comes to remind you that you have a little family chest of gold hidden away in a hollow tree behind the castle. You had forgotten."

Claire paused, considering her ending. "When your grandmother leaves, you go outside to sit on a high wall, looking across the Farnsworth Forest. Do you love the forest and Cloverdan enough to stay? Enough to give up Paris and all its adventures? You search your heart." She paused. "Then you see Cloverdan walking through the forest, striding in that old familiar way. And you know exactly what to do."

Mary Helen hugged her mother's arm. "You are such a romantic, Mother. But love isn't always that fanciful and simple."

"My point is that only your heart will tell you whether you love J.T. enough to stay at Edisto with him. If you do, an answer for any other dilemmas you face will find their way to you, as well." She leaned over to kiss Mary Helen's cheek. "I do believe in happy endings. Especially for my girls."

"I'm not sure yet that my road to happiness is with J.T."

"Then that is the answer you most need to search your heart for. Despite our fondness for J.T., Parker and I certainly wouldn't want you to consider marrying him unless your heart is as sure as his."

"Thanks for that."

"You are welcome." Claire climbed out of the bed. "We both need to get some sleep now."

"Good night, Mom," she said, as her mother slipped out of the room and shut the door behind her.

Tired herself, Mary Helen turned out the light and climbed under the covers. As she lay quietly drifting off to sleep, she realized something. J.T. had said he loved her. She'd basically overlooked the words, dismissing them in her anger. She also remembered J.T. told her she was the only woman he'd ever said those words to. Was that true? It spread a warm and comforting glow in her heart to think about it. But unlike Fleuradew in her mother's story, she still didn't know her own heart with certainty about J.T. She certainly didn't know either if she could be happy spending her life in the quiet Farnsworth Forestland of small Edisto Island.

CHAPTER 12

Later, after his fight with Mary Helen and his talk with Ezra, J.T. headed over to Oleanders to look for Mary Helen. She'd had time to calm down now, like he had ... and as Ezra said, their talk over the past was long overdue.

"Thanks for the free psychiatric advice," J.T. said to Ezra as he got up to leave. "It's nice occasionally having a shrink living nearby."

"It's my business. Glad it can help a friend now and then." Ezra leaned over to lay a hand on J.T.'s shoulder. "You and Mary Helen tiptoed around the old problems and issues that broke you up, when she returned to Edisto this time, obviously both dreading and avoiding bringing them up—even when they still lurked in the closet." He shook his head. "It's unfortunate a heated quarrel finally flung open the closet door and let everything come howling out. But maybe it's for the best. You've heard each other out now—although there are preferable ways to resolve difficult issues."

"What should I do now?"

"Talk calmly to her again soon. Tell her you're sorry you quarreled. Don't let this fester. The old counsel of not letting the sun go down on your anger is a wise one."

"Thanks. I'll remember the other things you told me, too."

Ezra smoothed a hand over his head, nearly bald now. He wasn't a handsome man but he had wise eyes. He'd offered good counsel to J.T. in many matters in his life, too. Ezra tapped his chin now, obviously still thinking over the issues J.T. had talked to him about.

"A difficult person with emotional problems can create havoc, J.T., even among healthy individuals. You and Mary Helen need to come to terms with who and what Gracie is, with how you've allowed her to play and manipulate you over the years—and put a stop to it."

J.T. sat quietly thinking over Ezra's words for a time after he left. Then glancing at the clock to check the time, he let himself out of the house and walked down the beach to Oleanders. It was time to talk with Mary Helen again. Drawing close to the house, he found it quiet and dark, Mary Helen's car gone. Great.

The next day after work, she still hadn't come back. He learned from Isabel she'd gone to Parker and Claire's in Beaufort.

"Ezra told me about the fight," Isabel said when he stopped by the store. "He saw the dark house, too, when he came back from talking with you. Concerned, I called Parker and Claire. Parker said Mary Helen was on her way to their place, planned to spend the night and share time with them. They're leaving after the Labor Day weekend on their trip."

"Thanks for telling me that Isabel."

She glanced at a desk calendar by the register. "She'll be back either late tonight or in the morning. She's working tomorrow and all Labor Day weekend. We'll be busy. You know how it is on the island then."

Thankful Isabel didn't grill him about the quarrel, J.T. headed back to work. On the way home later he stopped by Mary Helen's again, still finding her not home.

At his house, as he looked around in the kitchen trying to decide what to fix for dinner, the phone rang. He picked it up. "Hey. This is J.T."

"What are you doing?" Chuck asked.

"Scrounging around in the kitchen for something to eat for dinner."

"Want some company? Andrew is with me. He put in an offer on the house next door to you. Tom just told us the owners accepted.

I thought we could celebrate. Andrew and I will pick up steaks and some fries to stick in the oven if you'll fire up the grill while we're on the way over. Your place is bigger than my villa in Fairfield for a get-together."

J.T. grinned. "Sounds great. I'll get some charcoal started. Pick up one of those Caesar salad bags, too. I've already got bread here."

Still brooding about Mary Helen, J.T. felt glad for some company.

His house soon filled with the laughter, jokes, and the easy talk of three long time friends. They caught up on their lives and then discussed the major league baseball playoffs coming up and the University of South Carolina's chances of having a good football team this fall.

"The Gamecocks stomped Ohio State in the 2002 Outback Bowl in Tampa in January and they're looking good this fall, too," Chuck said. "They're playing their first game Saturday night." The biggest sports lover of the three, Chuck was an avid football fan of the South Carolina Gamecocks. "I think Lou Holtz has recruited some good new players, too. Tom and I have tickets to the game at seven and we're driving up to Columbia."

The three young men sat draped across the sofa and chairs in J.T.'s living room, relaxing after a big dinner.

Andrew shifted the subject. "Tom was a great help to me negotiating a good sale on The Sandpiper next door. He saved me over ten thousand on the price. That gives me more for renovations."

"Does it need a lot of work?" J.T. asked. "I haven't been inside the place in years, probably not since I was a kid."

"It mostly needs the floors refinished, new paint, upgrades in the kitchen and baths. New ceiling fans, furniture, paintings, and lamps. The outdoor furniture could use replacing, too, and landscaping needs to be done around the grounds."

Chuck tipped up a bottled cola to take a long drink. "Being in the antiques business, you ought to enjoy fixing up the place and decorating." He laughed. "Mom did most of the buying for my villa in Fairfield. I possess zero vision for that sort of thing. I thought my place looked great when I bought it. It had a sofa, a bed, a good television. What more does a guy need?" He shook his head. "Mom and Jane threw a fit when they saw it. Thought it wasn't aesthetically pleasing." He emphasized the word aesthetically with a big grin.

"Your place looks good now," J.T. said.

"No thanks to me." Chuck laughed again.

J.T. glanced across at both of his long-time friends with affection. Chuck had grown into a tall, fit young man with the red-brown hair and hazel eyes characteristic of the Whaley family. Chuck and his brother Tom both went off island to college to the University of South Carolina in Columbia and stayed in the dorm. They came home weekends and holidays to work in the family realty company, with Columbia only a two and a half hour drive away, and they worked full-time in the business in summers.

Chuck was laid back and fun loving in personality with an easy, comfortable way with people. Likeable, but smart too, he fit into the family realty business like a hand in a well-worn baseball glove. He and J.T. spent a lot of time together, boating and fishing around the island, hanging out at the beach, sharing dinner, or going into Charleston for a little nightlife. Both Chuck and J.T. had a way with the girls, too, while Andrew showed little interest for the party or social life.

"I think maybe Emma has a little crush on you, Andrew," J.T. said now.

Andrew glanced up with surprise.

"I've noticed that, too, "Chuck added. "You'd better be nice to my little sister."

"I think you must be wrong." Andrew frowned.

"The guy's clueless," Chuck said. He threw a bottle cap at Andrew. "Man, you need to start dusting off your antenna about women. You're missing out on some good times."

J.T. watched Andrew's discomfort with their conversation. As his dad often said of Andrew, his wire was wound a little too tight. A serious guy, Andrew had trouble letting down and really relaxing.

"I wouldn't want to encourage Emma's interest," Andrew said after a few moments, troubled over their words. He glanced at Chuck. "I haven't encouraged it either. Not that Emma isn't a sweet and wonderful girl, of course. Everyone I talk to says she's a fine teacher at the college. She's well liked." He hesitated. "But I see her more as a younger sister."

Chuck laughed. "Hey, you don't have to tiptoe around not having the hots for Emma. She and Suki always looked up to all of us older guys in the group, thought we were cool, I guess."

J.T. noticed Andrew's face change a little at the mention of Suki. He'd always carried a special fondness for her.

"Jane and Mary Helen never tagged after us much though," Chuck continued. "We mostly fought or competed with them all the time, except when Claire made us be *nice*."

Chuck laughed as he got up to snag a handful of peanuts from a dish on the coffee table. He turned to J.T. then. "I remember Tom, Ryder, and I were really surprised when you and Mary Helen got serious in high school. Although I guess I noticed you sort of liked her before." He lounged back on the couch again. "I know you've been seeing her now that she's back. How's that going?"

J.T. gave his friends a condensed guy-version of their quarrel.

"Man, that's a bummer," Chuck said.

"You should talk to her like Ezra suggested," Andrew added. "It sounds like you could build a good relationship if you can get the issue with Gracie Byrd resolved." Andrew stopped, thinking for a minute. "I remember that girl always caused trouble. Mary Helen and Suki often talked about her and the things she did." He looked at J.T. "Why did you go out with her anyway, knowing what she is like?"

Chuck hooted and rolled his eyes. "Man, have you looked at her? She's a babe. I'd go out with her if she was interested in me."

Andrew shook his head, obviously not following that logic.

"You're clearly a wiser man than I am, Andrew," J.T. said, clapping him on the shoulder as he got up to get another cold drink from the refrigerator. "Maybe you'll prove a good influence on me, living here on the island more."

"Maybe we can find him some girls, too," Chuck said, finishing off the last of his cola. "He's a good looking guy—girls like that, even with the glasses he wears sometimes. I'll start looking around."

Andrew looked somewhat alarmed.

"Don't worry, Andrew," J.T. said. "We won't set you up with any girls you aren't interested in. We're only glad you're going to be hanging out at Edisto with us more often now."

After his friends left, J.T. walked down the beach again to see if Mary Helen was back. This time he saw house lights on. He started up the beach path to the house and found Mary Helen along the way, sitting in the cabana in one of the weathered Adirondack chairs. The cabana, with its worn, wooden floors and thatched roof, sat midway between Oleanders and the beach. It had always been one of their favorite play spots as kids.

"Hey," he said, taking the steps into the old wood shelter.

She glanced up at him with a small scowl.

He stopped, studying her face. "You still mad at me?"

She sighed and sent him a churlish look. "We had a huge fight and said ugly things, J.T. What do you think?"

He came and slumped into the chair beside her. "I'm really sorry we quarreled."

She pushed her hair back out of her face. The sea breeze was strong here, wafting softly through the cabana. You could smell the ocean, too. He'd always loved the old structure. He propped his feet up on a bench, stretching his legs out, waiting for her to answer.

"Okay. I'm sorry we fought, too," she said at last.

Relieved, J.T. decided to shift topic a little. "Did you enjoy your visit at your folks?"

"Yes. They helped me see things with more perspective, like they always do." She wrinkled her nose. "I hate sometimes how reasonable they are."

J.T. laughed. "Yeah, my folks are like that, too. Takes the sails right out of a good mad."

He saw her lips twitch in a smile.

J.T. kept his voice steady. "We said some hateful things you and me, hollered and stuff, but maybe we needed to talk, Mary Helen. We'd put off talking about the past since you came back. Both avoided it. I wished we'd talked calmly about everything earlier but I'm glad we talked. It was like having a monster in the closet, knowing it was always there, maybe ready to spring out at any time."

He watched another faint smile play over her lips.

"Well the monster's out now," she said.

"*And* the monster has a specific name. You ready to talk about that more?"

J.T. watched her think about it for a minute. "There are few people in my life who have annoyed me more than Graciella Adeleine Byrd. Ever since I was a girl she's caused difficulties for me, provoked me, and made me mad more times than I can count. You can be sure I was *not* sad to see the last of her—or so I hoped—when I left home for college."

"Gracie has some genuine problems. I've even talked to Ezra about it, trying to figure out how to handle it."

She lifted an eyebrow.

"You weren't the only one glad to see her move off island. She caused me a lot of problems, too—besides the ones she caused between us."

Mary Helen turned toward him, putting a hand on one hip. "Then why in heavens name did you go out with her when she came back? I know, as Mother said, we weren't a couple then—weren't even communicating—but I still fail to understand why you would even want to date her, much less be more intimate...." Her words trailed off.

J.T. thought of Chuck's words about Gracie being hot and decided Mary Helen wouldn't relate to that logic. Instead, he reverted to his old argument. "She worked on me, made me feel sorry for her.

Gracie's a master with manipulation sometimes. She's done a work on you now and then, too—you know it's true—getting you to believe things she makes up. We both need to find a way to put a stop to Gracie interfering in our lives. To not let her play and manipulate us."

"Do you have any plans for that?" Mary Helen asked with a touch of sarcasm. "Besides avoiding her as much as possible?"

He shook his head. "Yeah, I'm going to tell her straight out that I want her out of my life, let her know I made a mistake going out with her, that I hold zero feelings for her, and that she needs to get on with her life without imagining any place in it for me."

"Wow, that's pretty strong." Mary Helen's eyes widened.

He crossed his arms. "She broke us up in high school with her plotting and lies. You cancelled your date with me to my senior prom because of her lies and schemes. I always hated that. Then I couldn't get you to believe afterward, or through all the years since, what she'd done, that she lied and made all that stuff up. We lost those years, Mary Helen. Now she's playing the same scams with us again." He ran a hand through his hair. "I've had it with her, with her lies and manipulations, even if she does carry emotional issues."

He got up and squatted down on his knees in front of Mary Helen. "I don't want to lose any more time with you, have any more quarrels with you over Gracie Byrd." He took both her hands and kissed them. "I love you Mary Helen Avery."

Tears welled in her eyes. "Oh, J.T. I wondered after I calmed down if I dreamed you said those words."

He smiled at her. "I was afraid to say them before, afraid you'd laugh at me, but getting mad brought them out."

"If I told you I loved you back you'd want things I don't know if I can give you. I'm not totally sure of my feelings yet anyway." She reached out a hand to touch his face, tracing a finger over his lips. "But you will always hold a place in my heart. I can tell you that."

He moved between her knees to get close enough to kiss her. "I'll take that for now," he said settling his mouth over hers, pulling her face down with his hands, savoring the taste and smell of her, loving her soft little moans as he took the kiss deeper, slid his hands into her hair.

They walked up the beach afterward, stopping often to kiss and to talk, baring their hearts about things they'd neither one shared before. Especially their regrets over the time lost through the years and how neither of them had found anyone else they cared for more than the other.

J.T. wasn't sure yet if he'd won the campaign to win Mary Helen, won the fight to gain her heart, but at least he was further along than before. And tonight, things were looking really good.

CHAPTER 13

September 2002

Nearly a week had slipped away since Mary Helen and J.T. made up. Over the Labor Day weekend, Isabel and Mary Helen put in long busy hours at The Little Mermaid and then on Tuesday, after the holiday, they started training Nancy Palmer in the store. Isabel met Nancy at church. Nancy and her husband Gill had bought a house in Fairfield and retired to Edisto in the spring. After fixing up their new home and entertaining her grown children and grandchildren over the summer, Nancy told Isabel she felt restless and a little bored and might look for a part-time job. When Isabel learned Nancy had a strong background in retail, even managing a Hallmark store, she offered her a part-time job at the Mermaid.

"I'm really glad Isabel hired you to help at the Mermaid," Mary Helen told Nancy as they worked in the store this Thursday together. "The store is really too much for Isabel to run alone and I'm only here full-time until I find another merchandising job."

"How did that phone interview go?" Nancy asked, glancing up from the low stool she sat on, un-boxing merchandise for several store shelves.

"It went well. They called back to set a conference call by speakerphone to interview again, so I'm in the running."

"That's good. It sounds like a wonderful opportunity." She smiled at Mary Helen. "One of my daughters lived near Chicago for a season before coming back south again. It's vicious cold there in the winter. I imagine you'll miss Edisto as the ice and cold settle in around the Lake Michigan area."

"I'm sure I will." Admittedly, Mary Helen shivered at the thought. She hated even the New Jersey winters and had read enough to know Chicago would be even colder.

She jotted notes on items they needed to order for The Little Mermaid while observing Nancy. Isabel had made a good choice. Nancy was a hard worker, capable, and congenial with the customers. She didn't need constant supervision and had quickly learned the small store this week. Pleasant in appearance, with almost silvery hair, blue-gray eyes and a good Edisto tan from the summer, she dressed tastefully and always presented an upbeat, positive attitude.

"Feel free to leave for lunch with your friend," Nancy said, glancing at her wristwatch. "I can take care of things here. It's quieter today than this weekend."

Mary Helen smiled. "I'm glad you dropped by to see how hectic the store can get on holidays. Off-season days can be quiet, but our weekends will still stay busy throughout the year."

"I'm happy to be busy again. Gill and I were excited about retiring and knew we wanted to move here from Charlotte, but after settling in we both quickly wanted more to do. Gill's a fine electrician, owned his own company in Charlotte before selling out. He's already started taking odd jobs on the island, around playing golf as much as possible. I needed something, too, and I love working here." She looked thoughtful then. "I wonder how Isabel is enjoying her cruise?"

Mary Helen smiled. "I think Isabel, Ezra, Pete, and Elaine couldn't help but have a wonderful time. They're doing an eleven-day Carnival Sunshine cruise. They left Charleston this morning and are going to St Thomas, Aruba, Bonaire, Grand Turk, and Half Moon Cay before heading back home. I look forward to hearing about it and seeing photos, don't you?"

"I do." Nancy smiled. "Maybe Gill and I will plan a trip like theirs after hearing how they enjoy it. We haven't ever taken a Caribbean cruise."

"Me neither," Mary Helen said, reaching for her purse under the register. "I'll try to check in with you a time or two this afternoon to see if you have any questions. Jane and I are going to eat lunch on the beach and visit while her little daughter Elena plays."

"Well, you girls enjoy yourself."

Jane had insisted on bringing sandwiches and lunch for the three of them, so Mary Helen headed home to put on a swimsuit and a cover-up. Then she carried a big beach umbrella and a couple of chairs down to set them up not far from the pathway to Oleanders.

"Hi!" Jane called out to her a short time later. "Isn't this just like old times, hanging out on the beach behind our houses?" Jane grew up at Whaley House, her family's home, right next door to Oleanders.

"It is." Mary Helen went back to Jane's car to bring out the cooler, a blanket, and some sand toys for Elena—adding to the items Jane already hauled down to their beach camp.

She and Jane set up a second umbrella, leaning it close to the first and spread a large play quilt under it for Elena. Jane soon settled the child there on the big quilt with a sandwich, chips, and grapes for her lunch.

"Look! Birds!" Elena pointed to several seagulls on the beach.

"Those are seagulls," Jane told her.

"Seagulls," Elena repeated, separating the words as she tried it out. "And big ocean." She pointed toward the water.

"She's learning more and more words every day now," Jane said, sitting down in the beach chair beside Mary Helen. "At home I read to her all the time and she wants to know what everything is now."

"You're a good mom."

"Thanks. I try."

"What's for lunch?" Mary Helen asked.

"I made chicken salad sandwiches on croissants for us," Jane said, taking a lunch sack out of her beach tote. "There are grapes in the Ziploc bag, too, and two yogurts tucked in the cooler."

Mary Helen pulled a diet cola from Jane's cooler and then dug into the lunch sack to get a sandwich. She glanced at Jane's belly as she started eating. "Wow, you're getting big now."

"Thanks for noticing." Jane stuck out her tongue at her. "I feel like a giant whale, you can be sure. I'm seven months with only about two more months to go now." She glanced down at her stomach. "I thought the black maternity suit helped to camouflage things a little, but it is what it is." She grinned. "Wait till it's your turn. I am so going to laugh at you."

Mary Helen's eyes widened. She glanced down at her well-tanned—and very flat—belly, still slim between the top and bottom of her sapphire blue two-piece swimsuit.

Jane watched her and then said in a softer voice. "It's really a sweet time, Mary Helen, despite a little discomfort. You know you're creating a new life and your own baby." She glanced at Elena smiling. "And then you get a beautiful child."

As if sensing them watching her, Elena pointed toward the ocean. "Play water, Mommy."

"We'll play in the water in a minute after Mary Helen and I finish our lunch. Do you want a cookie now, sweet girl?" Jane handed Elena a cookie.

"I brought you a little present, Elena, that you can play with while your mother and I finish eating," Mary Helen offered, remembering the gift she'd chosen earlier at The Little Mermaid. She reached into her beach bag to pull out the small box containing one of the new dolls she and Isabel had ordered for the store. "It's a little mermaid doll. Do you like it?"

"Mer-mer!" Elena said, reaching for the box with a huge smile.

"Well, that's a hit," Jane said, helping Elena take the little doll out of the packaging. She grinned at Mary Helen. "This mermaid doll looks a lot like the Sea Wees we used to play with down at the beach."

"I thought of that when I picked it out."

"What do you say to Mary Helen for your gift?" Jane prompted.

"Tank you, Mary He-wen. I like my mer-mer." Elena held the little doll up with another smile. She looked so cute today in a red polka dot swimsuit and a little white sunhat.

When they finished their lunch, Mary Helen and Jane took their chairs closer to the waves so Elena could play in the edge of the water and dig in the sand with the bucket of sand toys Jane brought. The two women stretched out their legs to catch some sun while Elena played.

"How did your phone interview go?" Jane asked.

"Good. They called back to schedule a second conference call early next week. If I pass that stage, I'll need to go to Chicago for a final interview. If they ask me to come to Chicago—and they like me—they'll probably offer me a job while I'm there."

"I looked up Chicago on our realty search at the office," Jane said as she daubed sun lotion on Elena's shoulders. "Nice apartments in the city are *really* expensive near the store where you told me you wanted to live."

"That's true. The cost of living is higher but the salaries are higher to compensate, and downtown Chicago has marvelous restaurants, incredible cultural attractions, and lots of entertainment. Chicago offers good city transportation, too, like the L or elevated trains and the pedestrian walkway system, plus a great biking trail along the lake."

Jane stretched her toes out into the water so an incoming wave could wash over her feet. "I'd like to visit Chicago some day but I don't think I could handle the winters there. Temperatures can drop to zero degrees with wind chills to twenty below. I read Chicago gets about forty inches of snow every winter, too. The first snows usually come in November and it can snow even in April there, with some snows dumping twelve inches at a time." She shook her head. "I can't even imagine that."

Mary Helen smiled. "You've always lived at Edisto. But when you live other places, you adjust, and you see the beauty each place has to offer."

"My grandmother says your blood changes when your family has lived in the Deep South for generations. I definitely have Southern blood; I complain about winters here at Edisto. I feel like I'm freezing if the temperatures falls below forty."

Mary Helen punched her with her elbow. "Okay. I admit I'm going to miss this gorgeous weather."

Jane looked at her over her sunglasses. "Is that all you're going to miss? Seems like you and J.T. are getting thick again."

Mary Helen leaned her head back. "I don't know what to do about that, Jane. It's really bad timing for J.T. and me to fall for each other again when I'm only here for an interim visit."

"Maybe it doesn't have to be an interim visit."

"You sound like Mother and Isabel."

"Would it be so bad to live at Edisto? You have family and friends here. It's certainly a more desirable place to live to my way of thinking than Chicago."

"There aren't job opportunities like I want here." She pulled out her sun lotion to smooth it over her arms and legs.

Jane grew quiet for a moment. "Have you told J.T. you're getting close to getting a job offer?"

Mary Helen looked away. "No, but I need to. I'm off work tomorrow and we're spending the day doing something together. I'm not sure what yet. I'll talk to him then. He knows I'm looking, but he doesn't know I'm getting close to a possible offer now."

"If you get this job in Chicago when would you move?" Jane leaned over to give Elena a kiss as the child brought her a shell to look at.

"I know they want someone by the end of September or the first of October, possibly sooner. They realize the candidates they are interviewing need to give their current employers notice, make moving arrangements...." She shrugged. "I'd need to move soon if I get an offer."

"Isabel will be disappointed to lose you again."

"She has Nancy now. I'm sure Nancy will work more hours if Isabel asks her to." She pushed her bangs back off her face, hoping to get sun on her forehead. "Knowing Isabel has Nancy makes me feel less bad about leaving. Isabel will be back from her cruise before I need to travel to Chicago for another interview, too."

As promised, Jane and Mary Helen played in the ocean with

Elena after lunch, holding her hands to lift her out of the waves. Then they took a short walk up the beach, helping Elena load her sand bucket with shells.

When they returned, they settled under the umbrellas again to get out of the sun for a time. Elena, sitting on her blanket and playing with her mermaid doll, suddenly stood up, pointing behind them. "It's Tee," she called out, as J.T. came walking down the beach pathway.

"Hi, sweet girl," J.T. said, swinging Elena up and around, making her laugh.

"She always calls J.T. just Tee," Jane explained.

"It works," he said. "I saw you girls down on the beach and thought I'd come down and join you. I got off early today."

He played with Elena for a while, then persuaded her to lie down while he read her a story. When she fell asleep, he settled on a corner of the blanket where he could talk, putting his arms around his knees.

Mary Helen watched his eyes rove over her with appreciation, before turning to Jane. "Girl, you are getting large with child. But you really glow, too. I've always thought pregnant women are incredibly beautiful."

Jane leaned over to give him a little kiss. "You lovely man. That just made my day. Thank you."

"I meant it."

"You look good, too." Her eyes wandered over him. "Have you been working out?"

He laughed. "Just working, period. My job's pretty physical sometimes."

Mary Helen couldn't help noticing he did look good in his dark green swim trunks, his skin tanned from the summer months outdoors, his white smile flashing in the sunshine.

He hunched his shoulders. "There's been another dog death," he said. "I didn't want to talk about it in front of Elena, but since she's asleep now I thought you'd both want to know."

Jane put a hand to her mouth. "Another poisoning?"

"No. This time the dog was shot." J.T. shook his head. "It happened up island near the causeway. A neighbor heard the gunshot, called the police, described the truck. They caught two men not long after. They'd robbed the house next door to where the dog lived."

He shifted his position. "From what I heard, the dog started barking when they broke into the house, so they shot him to shut him up. The police found stolen goods in their truck, figured out the likely story of what happened from that. The police believe this is the answer to the dog deaths that have been going on."

Mary Helen frowned. "But this dog was shot, not poisoned."

"Yeah, well, evidently they started looking at records of random thefts over the last year and found many occurred at houses near where the dogs died. The links fit and one of the men admitted he'd poisoned a dog—right before his partner told him to shut up. Despite further questioning, the police couldn't get more out of the two men, but catching them seems to be the answer to the poisonings."

"I'm so glad to hear that," said Jane. "It makes sense, too, that crooks willing to steal wouldn't think anything of killing a dog in their way—especially a dog trying to give them away by barking."

Mary Helen's eyes met J.T.'s. "Well, I guess you might owe Winifred Meggett an apology for suspecting her."

Jane looked confused. "What?"

"J.T. practically accused Winifred of poisoning the dogs one night when we were walking on the beach."

Jane tried not to laugh. "You didn't!"

J.T. looked uncomfortable. "With her over-zealous love for turtles and with that anger she carries, it wouldn't have been out of the question for her to poison a few dogs to save some turtles. Most of the dogs poisoned have run loose on the beach, too. They probably dug up a few turtle nests here and there. Dogs, like raccoons, can smell the eggs. They'll eat turtle eggs and the turtle hatchlings, too. Some dogs will even attack adult female turtles when they nest. For someone who loves turtles, it's an upsetting idea."

Mary Helen reached into the cooler to hunt for a cold bottle of water. She passed one to J.T. "Well, despite some of Winifred's slightly odd ways, I'm glad she's not the one behind this. I sort of like her. It's nice too that someone cares about turtles, birds, and other animal life here at the beach. So many people are careless about things like that. They trash up the beach, do needless things to hurt the wildlife, don't think about the impact of their ways on the environment. We could all probably learn from people like Winnie who care about those things more. I've learned a lot on the subject from conservation groups in the past."

Elena woke up then and, after giving her a hug, Jane said, "I need to head home. Elena's had enough sun and fun for one day."

J.T. and Mary Helen helped her pack up. While J.T. loaded Jane's cooler, bags, and umbrella into the car, Mary Helen slipped into the house to call the store to see if Nancy had any questions.

"I'm doing fine," Nancy told her. "Isabel showed me how to close, so you don't need to come by later unless you want to. I can open tomorrow easily, too. It's your day off. You should enjoy it."

After hanging up, Mary Helen walked back down to the beach to join J.T. He'd left her umbrella out and the two beach chairs she'd brought down to the beach earlier. They pulled the chairs out into the afternoon sun and then talked more about the theft and the dog that was killed.

"Did you know the family that owned the dog?"

"No." He shook his head. "They lived up near Helton's store. Kizzy and Lewis probably know them. Leon had heard of them but he didn't know them personally. The house the two guys robbed was a vacation rental looking out over the marsh on the Intracoastal Waterway. Swanky place. I heard the dog, a big hound mix, belonged to locals who lived in a small place next door. That's all I know."

They talked about other things after a time, playing in the ocean and enjoying the afternoon. While taking a walk up the beach later, J.T. told her that Andrew was closing on The Sandpiper soon and had already gotten estimates for renovations.

"It's nice he'll own a place here on the island," Mary Helen commented, as they stopped to sit on a bench along the way.

"He worried that his mother might be upset, but she was excited for him." J.T grinned. "He'll probably use the beach house mostly for weekends or days off. I told Andrew I'd watch the house for him in between."

"That was nice of you."

"I'm a nice guy," he said, winking at her. He leaned over and kissed her long and well then. No one sat on the beach near them, giving them privacy. Often during the off-seasons at the island a whole stretch of beach would be completely deserted of tourists and even locals.

Mary Helen sighed, when he drew back. "I agree. You are a nice guy."

He smiled. "It was on this bench that I told you I wanted to marry you for the first time. Do you remember?"

She looked around in surprise, realizing he was right. "It was." She shifted her eyes away from him as her heart filled with old memories.

"I was only eighteen, just a kid. I realize that now." He laughed softly. "You think you know so much at eighteen."

"I was sixteen, not even driving yet."

"Yeah, we were only kids." His voice dropped to a husky tone. "But I knew then I loved you just as I do now. That hasn't changed. Now, like then, I think about living with you, having kids with you, spending my life with you."

She didn't know how to answer, what to say. She'd be lying to say she didn't think many of the same thoughts, but to tell him that might encourage him to say more. To put those thoughts into a question she couldn't say yes to.

Mary Helen looked out over the ocean, thinking. In all honesty, she knew, too, that it still bothered her that girls flirted with J.T. whenever she went out with him. She knew he was a man that women would always notice. Could she deal with that? And could J.T. be faithful through the years? Over and over she'd seen and heard stories of that sort of man straying. Could she really trust J.T. with her full heart? She simply wasn't sure. Going away was probably the best answer, given his feelings and hers. She knew she loved him but simply wasn't sure they belonged together for the long term.

As if sensing she wasn't ready to commit to more, J.T. said, "Hey, I'm getting hungry. Let's drive up to Po Pigs Bo-B-Q restaurant, BoBo Lee's place, and eat buffet for dinner. I haven't been there for a while and they're open tonight."

Grateful for the diversion, Mary Helen stood up. "That's a great idea. I love Po Pigs. They serve incredible home-cooked Southern food on their buffet—barbeque, fried okra, great slaw, creamed corn, field peas, macaroni and cheese, squash casserole..."

"And great hushpuppies and fried chicken." J.T. got up, too, and started back down the beach with her. "I'll help you haul in the umbrella and chairs, then I'll walk over to my place, get dressed, and pick you up in about twenty minutes. Will that give you enough time?'

She smiled at him. "Make it thirty minutes. I need to wash my hair and get the salt and sand out of it."

"Okay."

They made quick work of carrying beach items to the house, and then J.T. headed across the well-worn path next door, in back of the Whaley's house, toward his own place beyond it.

Mary Helen stood inside the screen door of the porch at Oleanders watching him walk toward his house. It felt like being in a sweet dream having all this time with J.T. Mikell again. She knew the memories would keep her warm on cold Chicago nights later if she got her new job.

CHAPTER 14

"**I** see you're up and dressed," J.T. said the next morning on Friday as he walked up the back steps onto the screened porch at Oleanders.

"Yes and enjoying my second cup of coffee here on the porch." Her eyes flicked over J.T., dressed casually in khaki shorts with a marine blue, button-up sport shirt, tucked neatly into his shorts. "You look sharp."

"Thanks." He dropped into the chair across from her at the porch table. "I thought we might go into Charleston and poke around, eat lunch downtown, maybe even catch a movie, if you'd like."

"That sounds good, but I'll need to change clothes." She glanced down at her wrinkled shorts and old T-shirt.

He grinned. "There's a catch to my invitation. We need to stop by my grandparents on the way off island."

"Your Mikell grandparents?"

"Yeah. Grandad and Grams are upset about all these break-ins and the dog deaths. Grandad wants me to walk around the old Mikell plantation, check it carefully, see if there are any signs of someone trying to break in or any traces of vagrants. I promised him I would. It won't take long. When Grams found out you'd be with me, she made me promise to stop by their house first. I hope you don't mind."

She took another sip of her coffee. "No. I don't mind. I haven't seen your grandparents since I've been back and I don't think I've seen the old plantation since my school years. Does your family still allow people to tour it sometimes?"

"The house was on the island tour until last year, but Grandad took it off until repairs can be made."

"So no one lives there anymore, right?"

"That's right. After my great grandparents died, Grandad and Grams built a more modern place nearby, where they live today and where my dad grew up. The plantation house was too expensive to keep up."

"Your full name, Jenkins Townsend—that was your great grandfather's name, also, wasn't it? I think I remember you telling me that."

"Yeah, that's right. He and his wife Callie had three sons, including Emmett Townsend Mikell, who is my Grandad. Their two older boys Sterling and Bailey died in the war, which left Grandad the only heir—good in some ways, problematic in others."

He picked up a shell from the table to study it. "Grandad and Grams lived with my great grandparents at the plantation house after they first married. It's a big place, if you recall, but I know from stories I heard they squabbled a lot. Grandad could never get his parents to move out of the old house over the years, even though he tried. They lived there until they died."

"Was your dad born at that house?"

"Yes. Grams had trouble in childbirth, too, and she couldn't have any more kids. So my dad grew up an only child."

Mary Helen propped her chin on her hand listening to him. "Who built Point Place, your house on the beach?"

"My dad did. My great grandfather bought the beachfront property and a lot of other island property back when land was cheap. Grandad later developed some of it for the Mikell rental business he started on Jungle Road, where dad and I still work. With farming on the wane, the family needed a new way to make a living." He paused. "Grandad was smart to see that tourism on Edisto was growing and to develop a business when he did. After my dad and mom got married, Grandad gave them the beachfront lot on Point Street and they built the house there, where I grew up and where I live now."

"I feel like I'm catching up on your family history." Mary Helen smiled at him. "Didn't you say your Mom and Dad's new house is near your grandparents' place and the old plantation house?"

He leaned back in his chair. "Yeah, they built on family land on a little side road on St. Pierre Creek. You sure are asking a lot of questions."

"I'm interested, and I know there are other Mikell homes around the island."

J.T. nodded, pleased with her questions about his family. "There's another family house called Peter's Point Plantation that Isaac Jenkins Mikell built in the 1840s. It's on the National Register of Historic Places, like the Mikell Plantation is. There were a lot of Mikells on the island at one time. Ephraim Mikell Seabrook was one of the early owners of land on Botany Bay that the Meyers family owns now. Ephriam's old place Sea Cloud Plantation was torn down in the 1930s, but I've heard the land at Botany Bay— over 4,500 acres—will be deeded to the state of South Carolina as a wildlife preserve when Mrs. Meyers dies."

"That's wonderful." She finished her coffee and pushed her cup back. "It must feel good to know your family's roots reach back to Edisto's earliest days, to have these stories to tell, and to be able to visit old relatives' homes and graves nearby."

"Roots grow deep where generations of your family have always lived," he said, hoping this conversation helped her understand his love for the island and why he'd never wanted to leave.

She reached to retrieve a book from a side table. "I was looking through this little book about Edisto's history last night. It got me to thinking about the past. There were some Mikell family photos in it. I enjoyed seeing all the gracious old homes, reading about the early families."

"Their lives weren't always gracious and easy," J.T. said, flipping through the book. "They experienced losses through the Civil War, hurricanes and disease, the massive destruction of the boll weevil. The boll weevil pretty much destroyed the cotton industry."

He laid the book down, thinking of the stories he'd heard as a boy. "Many old families left over time, but others stayed. Those that stayed found new ways to sustain themselves, to make a life here. We still do a little farming on our land, but not much. Grandad has investments and rental properties that bring in a more reliable income. The family's in good shape, mostly thanks to him. He's seen to it that the old plantation house is kept up and he likes letting people tour it. After the repairs and renovations are completed next month, the house will be safe to walk through again."

"There isn't furniture in the house now?"

"No. Grandad took the remaining pieces out long ago. It encourages squatters if he keeps anything there." J.T. smiled at her. "If you want to see a furnished place, still lived in, you can go to Sunnyside Plantation on Store Creek, constructed by some more Mikell kin. "

"I read that a lot of the old families are interlinked by kinship."

"Yes. It makes sense if you think about it." He opened the book again, glancing at the old photos. "There weren't many families on Edisto in the early days so they all socialized together. Transportation was limited. They tended to intermarry."

"Well, I love all the old stories like the ones you've told me this morning." She smoothed back her hair. "Isabel, Elaine, and your mother Lula shared stories with me, too, when I was younger."

He glanced at his watch. "It might be good if we head on over to Grams and Grandad's place. After stopping to visit them, and after I check on the plantation house, we'll head to Charleston. We should get there in time for lunch and an afternoon to do whatever you'd like."

She sent him a bright smile. "I think I'd like to simply walk around the old streets downtown, go to the market, White Point Garden and the Battery. The temperature is cooler now than when I came earlier this summer. It should be a perfect afternoon for a walking tour."

"Sounds good to me." He reached across the table to get her

coffee cup to carry into the kitchen. "Put some comfortable walking shoes on when you run upstairs to change."

She did and they soon headed out in J.T.'s sporty MG. After following the highway away from the beach, they turned on Peters Point Road not far beyond the Old Post Office Restaurant. The two-lane road wound back through shaded woods and past marshy vistas to make its way to the Mikell property. Mary Helen pointed out white herons sitting on trees along the way and asked questions about homes they could see tucked off the road, many with long docks reaching out into the marshes and the creek.

J.T. drove Mary Helen past his parents' new place so she could see it, and then turned down a quiet lane nearby to reach his grandparents' large white, two-storied home. Built above ground, in a classic, Lowcountry plantation style, it had a broad covered front porch and long shuttered windows.

J.T.'s grandparents sat on the front porch watching for them. As the older couple rose to greet them, their two dogs scrambled down the steps to offer greetings, too. The dogs, knowing J.T. well, were excited to see him, barking, wagging their tails, and weaving around his legs.

J.T. squatted to pet them. "They're both friendly, Mary Helen— even if excited. The black lab is Beauregard and the blond cocker Maisie."

She greeted the dogs, too.

"Come on up on the porch," his grandmother called. "I made fresh-squeezed lemonade and a lovely tea cake."

White haired and in her late seventies, Frances Mikell was still spry with an easy Southern style and grace.

J.T.'s grandfather, Emmett, in his eighties now, limped as he rose from his chair and walked to greet them. A mild stroke a few years ago left him with a bad leg.

"Bring that pretty girl on up here," he said, grinning a charming smile. He reached out to hug Mary Helen as she walked up the steps onto the porch. "Lord, girl, you've made a fine-looking woman." He winked at J.T. "No wonder J.T.'s been seeing so much of you."

Mary Helen blushed. "It's good to see you Mr. Mikell."

"Sit down. Sit down." J.T.'s grandmother gestured to a comfortable grouping of black wicker furniture on the porch.

"Frances, you can cut that cake now. Finally," J.T.'s grandad said, as they settled into their chairs. "She baked an Apple Butter Cinnamon Cake this morning when she knew you were coming, but she wouldn't even give me a sample until you arrived."

"Emmett eats too much sugar," she fussed. "I have to watch his sweets." She pulled a tiered cake stand toward her and began cutting into a rich-looking teacake, drizzled with white icing.

"That cake looks wonderful," Mary Helen said.

"It's an old island recipe ... flour, white and brown sugar, cinnamon, homemade apple butter, a little buttermilk, an egg, a touch of baking power and soda, and some chopped pecans from the tree in our back yard. I love a company excuse to make it." She put four thick slices on pretty floral china plates and passed them around, along with glasses of fresh, cold lemonade.

J.T. noted the ease with which she handled every gesture, reflecting the easy Southern charm so inbred in island women. He wondered if Mary Helen had missed these gracious gestures living up north—wished for comfortable get-togethers on old porches with the whisper of a paddle fan overhead.

They chatted and caught up, with J.T. aware of his grandparents' speculative glances toward Mary Helen.

Seeing the dogs start to wander too far from the house, J.T.'s grandfather pushed himself up from his chair to whistle and call to them. "Beauregard, Maisie, get on back up here."

Both came immediately, climbing the porch steps, eager for pets and approval.

"We've been worried sick thinking about someone poisoning dogs around the island," his grandmother said. "Beau and Maisie love to get out and run around our yard and property, but we watch them like a hawk now." She leaned over to scratch the cocker's long ears.

Beauregard came to settle himself contently across J.T.'s feet.

"That dog has always loved you," his grandfather noted. "I bred him to the Houston's pretty female lab not long ago. Charlie said he'd give me pick of the litter. Why don't you take the pup? You've been wanting a dog."

J.T. looked down at Beauregard with longing. "I don't know, Grandad. I work so much. It doesn't seem fair to leave a dog alone so often."

"Take the dog down to the shop with you. If your dad and Chester can keep a dang parrot at the Dock Store like they do, running its mouth all the time, you ought to be able to bring a dog to the store."

J.T. laughed. "Billy Bob certainly is vocal but he spends the day in a cage. He doesn't chew up shoes or get underfoot like a dog would."

His grandfather scowled. "Well, you could figure something out—smart boy like you." He turned to Mary Helen. "Our grandson's a catch if he hasn't told you. Since Ryder chose to run off with that girl to Savannah, it's J.T. who will inherit all the businesses, the farm, the land, and the houses in time. We may live modest but we've got old island money."

"Emmett," his wife cautioned. "Watch your manners. Women don't care to hear about those things."

He shook a finger at her. "A smart woman thinks about security, Frances. Your daddy sure did talk to me about it."

J.T.'s grandmother got up to add more lemonade to their glasses. "Well, those were different times."

Changing the subject, J.T.'s grandfather asked, "J.T. do you think those two men the police arrested are the only ones thieving the area and killing dogs? Often there are more than just the ones caught. It worries me. I'm still a good shot if I need to be—if anyone tried to break in on us here—but I don't like the idea of them killing our dogs. You know Beau and Maisie will bark and get protective if they think there's a threat to us. It's quiet on our little street here. Thieves might target us for that reason, or try to break in at the old plantation house to strip out valuables, pipes, and such."

Mary Helen leaned forward. "I doubt you have anything to worry about, Mr. Mikell. The police caught the thieves. If they suspected a ring of thieves operating I assume they would have said so."

He frowned at her. "I've learned over my lifetime to never *assume* anything about a matter, large or small. You might want to keep that in mind."

J.T. set down his plate after finishing his cake. "I'll go over to the old place, Grandad, walk around, see if I notice any tracks around the property or signs of break-in."

His grandad nodded. "You do that. I can't get around to see about things like I once did with this gimp leg. Provokes me to be so limited. The old woman fusses at me, too, if I try to do too much."

J.T.'s grandmother crossed her arms with annoyance. "I don't want you tripping in some hole and falling in one of our fields, in the marsh, or somewhere else." She shook a finger at him. "And don't you be calling me an old woman. People are living longer and stronger than ever before now. It's a bad confession to be speaking different."

"Humph." His grandad rolled his eyes. "Time marches on whether you like it or not." He pushed up from his seat. "We'd best let these young folks go on now. I know they want to drive to Charleston today, both of them off work. We'll invite them to dinner later on and visit more another time."

"Let's definitely plan to do that," his grandmother said, rising. "We're so delighted you both stopped by for a little visit today."

A few minutes later, as he and Mary Helen headed down the road toward the old Mikell plantation, she smiled at him. "I'd forgotten how nice your grandparents are."

"Grandad's a bit opinionated, stubborn, and outspoken, but he and Grams are good people." He draped his left arm over the door of the convertible, driving easily with his right arm along the quiet two-lane road.

Turning into a dirt lane a few minutes later, they soon arrived at the old home-place, a classic two-storied tabby yellow plantation house with tall brick chimneys. Even old and faded, it was grand to see, whispering of another era and time and of the families of the past who'd made their homes in it. Arching live oaks formed a canopy over the driveway closest to the house and several barns, cabins, and structures could be seen scattered around the grounds.

"If you look beyond the house, Mary Helen, you can see the edge of the marsh, sweeping out to the creek behind it." J.T. pointed. "The waterways were the travel routes the plantation owners used in past to take their goods to market. You can see a weathered dock reaching out through the marshlands connecting the land and water."

"It is a beautiful place," Mary Helen said, getting out of the car as they stopped. She shaded her eyes from the sun to gaze up at the gracious old home with its tall pillars and wide double porches across the front.

J.T.'s glance followed hers. "Ryder calls the place 'the old albatross.'"

She looked surprised. "He sees it as only a burden?"

He grinned. "Ryder is an accountant, remember? A practical numbers man. And the upkeep of this place doesn't come cheap."

J.T. glanced around. "I'm going to walk around the house, check for problems, stick my head into some dirty old holes and buildings. Why don't you wait for me here?" He pointed to a worn bench under a tree. "You can sit there, if you want, or walk around a little."

"Okay."

He looked toward the marsh. "Don't go exploring out on the dock though. The boards aren't stable. With no one living here now, critters and snakes have settled in, too." He glanced toward the farm fields to one side. "I wouldn't go walking in the fields or too far from the house for the same reasons."

"I'll just hang around here then." She glanced toward the house.

"Is the house open?"

"No, it's locked up. I'd take you inside but some of the floorboards are rotten and the stair rails are loose. The wood floors on the porches need replacing, too." He looked toward the second-tired porch. "That upper porch is especially rickety. It's why we stopped the tours for a time until we can get repairs made." He paused. "You can walk around with me if you'd prefer."

"No, I'll be fine here. I can look at the flower beds." She pointed to a little garden area not far from the house. "I still see flowers in bloom."

"We pay to keep the grounds up, to a degree," he said. "In some of the flower beds you might see salvia or gazanias, like at the beach, but it's too late for the azaleas, gardenias, or camellias that plantation homes are famous for."

She waved a hand at him. "Go on. I'll be fine."

"It won't take me more than twenty minutes to check things out. I'll be in hollering range the whole time. Call out if you need anything or get lonesome." He flashed a grin at her with those last words, leaning over to give her a kiss, and then headed off.

J.T. followed a familiar route inspecting around the house, outbuildings, and grounds. As expected, he didn't find any problems or any human tracks except near the water, where fishermen had probably pulled up a boat to fish off the bank or from the dock. The only other tracks he spotted were the usual raccoon or rodent tracks you'd expect at an empty place.

He was checking the old stable when he heard Mary Helen's high-pitched scream fill the air. He turned and raced back toward the house, his heart hammering, following her voice.

"Mary Helen?" he called as he neared the house. "Where are you?"

"At the porch." Her muffled voice answered.

He rounded the corner of the house, started up the steps, and spotted the big broken gap in the porch floor. Working his way over to the area cautiously, he leaned over to look into the gap and saw Mary Helen piled in a heap on the rough ground below amid a pile of broken boards.

"Please don't say 'I told you so.'" She glanced up at him, rolling her eyes. "I know you warned me about the porch. But I wanted to look in the windows of the house since I couldn't go inside. I checked the porch at the top of the steps, and thought it would be okay to walk across with care. Everything was okay until I started over this section coming back."

J.T. felt a sweep of relief. For Mary Helen to be talking this much, she couldn't be hurt too badly. He squatted down with care on a joist near the spot where the boards had broken through. With the porch only four feet or so off the ground, she hadn't fallen far. "Are you okay?"

She looked herself over. "Scratched up, filthy, and humiliated," she answered sarcastically. "But otherwise okay, I think."

J.T. smiled at her words. "See if you can stand up so I can help you get out of there."

Pushing up with her left arm, she got to her knees, then reached down with her right arm to push herself to her feet.

"Ouch!" she cried, grabbing her right arm and holding it against her. "I think I hurt my arm or something."

"Can you move it?" he asked.

She tried and winced. "Not without it hurting." She held it tightly against her. "Maybe I sprained it or something."

J.T. accessed the situation. "If you can push to your feet using your left arm, I can still reach down and help you out."

"Okay. I'll try." She struggled and finally got to her feet.

After some maneuvering, J.T. was able to lean into the hole and pull Mary Helen out, holding her under her arms and then seating her beside him on one of the floor joists supporting the porch.

The way she gritted her teeth throughout the process let him know she'd really banged her arm up good.

"We'll need to scoot carefully over to the steps now," he told her. "It's only a few feet from here. Let me try it first to check if any other boards are rotted out. I don't want you falling through again."

"Neither do I," she said, hugging her arm.

After he reached the steps, he looked back at her. "See if you can work your way over now following the same path you saw me take, okay?"

She scooted her way carefully, using her left arm to help her along. J.T. watched her wince with pain every time she moved.

Reaching the top of the porch stairs, Mary Helen shifted to sit beside him, holding her right arm tight against her side and rubbing it.

"Your arm really hurts, doesn't it?"

"It doesn't hurt as much when I hold it really still," she said with a sigh. "I must have sprained it."

He examined her, looking for cuts or splinters. "I see some skinned up places on your arms and legs and on your face." J.T. wiped a smudge off her cheek with his finger and gave her a small kiss. "I can't tell you how scared I was when I heard you scream."

"You weren't the only one." She wrinkled her nose. "I was walking back, after looking in the windows, and the floor simply broke through right under my feet, tumbling me down with the boards into that hole where you found me." She shook her head. "I was so stupid not to pay attention to what you told me about the porch. I'm sorry."

"I'm simply glad you're okay." He gave her a smirk. "I'm also glad you didn't run into one of those big snakes that likes to nap under that dark old porch."

"Ewww." Her eyes popped wide.

"I need to take you to the clinic, Mary Helen. It's out on the highway, not far from here beside Barton's dental office. I want the doctor to check your arm, and you have a lot of bad scratches. You picked up some dirt and spider webs, too." He pulled a spider web out of her hair and off the back of her shirt.

"Yuk." She shuddered. "Check for spiders, okay?"

"I don't see any." He looked her over. "But all these scratches need to be cleaned and bandaged. A few, like the one on your knee, look nasty."

She rubbed her arm, obviously still hurting.

"Do you think you can walk to the car?" J.T. asked.

"I think I can walk all right. I stood up so you could help me out of the hole, and I don't think I sprained my ankle or anything." She rubbed her arm again. "Do you know the doctor over at the clinic?"

"I do. Her name's Ainsley Boone. She's an island girl who went off to school, practiced in the city, and then came back home. She's a good doctor. She can look you over, see what you've done to your arm."

"Maybe I simply need to go home and rest," Mary Helen said.

"Not when you can't lift your arm and with that pain you're having. You need to get it checked."

Moving around to her left side, J.T. helped Mary Helen stand up and then walk to the driveway. She winced most of the way, especially when getting into the car.

Fortunately, it wasn't far to the clinic. Once there, J.T. helped her inside and explained the situation to the receptionist, a friendly older woman.

She smiled as she handed J.T. a clipboard with paperwork on it. "The doctor's not busy today. I don't think you'll need to wait long. See if you can help your friend to fill this out."

"Okay." J.T. took the clipboard from her. "Tell the doc that J.T. Mikell is here, too." He grinned at her. "She and I went to school together."

The doctor came out to the waiting room a short time later. She greeted J.T. with warmth, and he introduced her to Mary Helen. Then she took both of them back to the examining room, after he insisted on going along.

CHAPTER 15

Mary Helen stopped in the bathroom on the way back for her exam and got a first good look at herself. Yikes! She looked awful.

"You idiot." She scowled at herself in the mirror while making an effort to tidy her hair and wipe dirt smears off her face. "Why didn't you listen to J.T. about that porch? It's your own fault you're in this mess right now."

Coming out of the bathroom, she followed the sounds of J.T.'s and Dr. Boone's voices down the short hall.

"Sorry to meet you in these circumstances," Dr. Boone said, smiling, as Mary Helen climbed onto the examining table.

"Me, too," she answered.

Ainsley Boone, closer to Ryder's age than J.T.'s, leafed through Mary Helen's paper work and then asked her a few questions before beginning an exam. She checked Mary Helen's temperature and vital signs and cleaned visible cuts and scratches, usually things a nurse would do in a larger practice.

When Dr. Boone began to examine her arm, Mary Helen winced and pulled back. "Ouch, my arm really hurts."

"Can you lift it at all?"

"No." Mary Helen hugged it against her.

"I think you might have dislocated your shoulder," she said after asking a few more questions. "There's swelling, pain, and inability to move the shoulder joint. I can do an x-ray and reset the shoulder if needed, but this is only a small rural clinic. I'm limited here."

She turned to J.T. "I'd feel better if Mary Helen went to the emergency room at the hospital in Charleston. Do you know where Bon Secours St. Francis Hospital is in West Ashley? I'll get some paperwork ready for you to carry with you and call ahead if you can drive Mary Helen over there."

"I know right where it is," J.T. answered.

"Is this really necessary?" Mary Helen asked. "Couldn't I just go home and rest?"

"Not with that arm." The doctor shook her head. "If it's dislocated, they'll take care of you at the hospital. I'm going to give you a shot for pain here so you'll be more comfortable on the drive over. We'll give you a sling for your arm, too, to keep it still." She paused. "I know that old plantation house. Falling through that porch and onto that dirt and rock foundation underneath, you're lucky you weren't hurt worse."

A little later, with her arm in a sling, a shot in her hip, and a prescription for pain meds in her purse, Mary Helen headed to the hospital outside of Charleston with J.T. Surprisingly when they got there, she didn't have to wait long. A nurse soon zapped an ID bracelet on her, cleaned her arm, helped her into a hospital gown, and sent her to x-ray. Back in the examining room afterward, Dr. Bridges, the orthopedic doctor, called J.T. in to join them, after Mary Helen suggested it might be a good idea.

"The shoulder isn't dislocated; the arm is broken." He put an x-ray up for them to see. "It's a proximal humerus fracture in the upper arm, not too far from the shoulder, as you can see." He pointed at the break line on the x-ray. "The good news is that it's a partial non-displaced break, versus a full break, with the bones separated. That means if all goes well with the healing, you won't need surgery."

Mary Helen felt stunned. "I've broken my arm?"

The doctor looked over her medical record. "I don't see mention of a broken bone on your record before."

"I've never broken a bone. I'm hardly ever sick, in excellent health. I've never been in a hospital before, except to visit someone else."

The doctor laid the clipboard on a side table. "I'm going to put an arm brace on your upper arm to keep that area still and quiet, then give you a better and more supportive sling than the one you got at the clinic." He reached for packages a nurse had laid on a side table containing an arm brace and sling.

"How long will I have to wear these?"

He glanced at the x-ray. "Healing time for a break in the arm like this will probably take eight to twelve weeks, four to six weeks in the brace and sling, depending on how quickly the break heals. Gentle range motion exercises are usually started after three to four weeks with a physical therapist if all goes well. Usually at four to six weeks patients can begin more ongoing physiotherapy to restore normal range of movement. Therapy and strengthening continue to about eight to twelve weeks, possibly longer."

Stunned Mary Helen knew her mouth dropped open. "That's two to three months!"

"It takes time for bones to heal. You'll need to rest, avoid movement, and be careful to avoid falls while healing. The nurse will give you an ice pack and you'll want to apply that to the injured area several times a day to decrease any swelling. Do know that you will have swelling, bruising, and pain, however, and severely restricted movement of the shoulder for a time. You might experience numbness and tingling in your arm, forearm, or hand." He continued talking, but Mary Helen couldn't seem to take in the words.

He came over and began to wrap her upper arm into the light brace, which she noticed had Velcro attachments to hold it close around her arm.

"Can I take this off to go to work and to sleep?"

"Not for a time. I'll see you again in two weeks and every two weeks after to x-ray and check on the healing process. If the bone doesn't heal in good alignment, we'll have to consider surgery to correct the problem." He helped her into the sling and adjusted it. "Do you work Mary Helen?'

"I'm a Visual Merchandiser between jobs right now. I've been working in retail sales at a small shop on Edisto Island called The Little Mermaid."

The doctor actually smiled then. "That's Isabel Compton's shop. My wife and I know the Comptons and the store well. After you start to heal a little, you should be able to work there if you're careful to do no lifting." He paused. "Are you right-handed?"

"Yes." Mary Helen looked down at her arm, snuggly encased in the sling, with her arm pulled slightly upward.

"That may prove a problem. You'll need to rely on your left hand for any tasks for a time. You'll probably need help dressing and bathing. Eating will be a little awkward. You won't be able to drive a car." He paused. "Do you have family in the area to bring you to doctor appointments and take you to physical therapy later? Or anyone to pick up medication and groceries? To help with cleaning in your home and other personal tasks?"

Mary Helen felt tears prick her eyes. "My mother and father live in Beaufort but they are abroad right now and won't be back until early November. I'm staying at their beach house."

"She has good friends on the island," J.T. put in. "I'll bring her to doctor appointments and therapy later. I live two doors away from her. Isabel and Ezra live right next-door and good neighbors live on the other side, too. A lady on the island cleans the house. Mary Helen's best girlfriend isn't far away either. She'll be okay."

Businesslike, the doctor nodded. "Mary Helen, you may find sleeping difficult for a time. You might want to elevate with extra pillows or a bolster in the bed or try sleeping in a recliner. I'll write you a prescription for pain medication. It's a narcotic, but using it for a short time, as needed, is all right. An instructional sheet will note all this information and more you might need. Call the office if you experience any unexpected problems like …"

His voice droned on, but Mary Helen hardly heard the words. Whatever she'd expected, it hadn't been this. However would she manage?

In a haze, she left the hospital with J.T.

"I'm so sorry about all this," J.T. said as they started the drive home. "I shouldn't have taken you to that old house or left you alone while I checked on things. I knew the place was dangerous."

Mary Helen looked across at J.T.'s hands clenched on the steering wheel, his face set. "This isn't your fault. Stop blaming yourself."

"It feels like my fault." He glanced at her for a minute, before turning his eyes back to the road. "And I feel so bad for you."

"Well, join the club. I feel bad for me, too." She snapped out the words, knowing them sarcastic.

A grin touched the corner of his mouth then.

Mary Helen leaned her head back against the car seat. "I can't believe this has happened. Isabel is gone; she won't be back until Tuesday. Elaine's gone, too, on the same cruise. Both my neighbors on either side gone. Plus Mother and Parker just left the country and Suki's off to play in Texas somewhere. What luck is that! What am I going to do?"

"I said I'd help you and I meant it." She saw his jaw clench in a stubborn way.

"Well, that's sweet, and I appreciate it. But be realistic." She scowled at him. "You can hardly help me pull my up panties in the bathroom. I had a dickens of a time doing that at the clinic and at the ER. You can hardly help me bathe or dress either. The nurse at the hospital had to help me get my bra on!"

She saw him smirk.

"I think I might like helping you get your panties and bra on."

Mary Helen punched him with her left arm. "Leave it to you to find something funny in this situation."

He drummed his fingers on the steering wheel. "On the positive, this might have happened at a worse time, like on your job in New Jersey with heavy physical work demands. As it is now, you can probably handle limited work at the Mermaid until you feel better. Isabel and Nancy can easily cover what you can't do."

She lost her temper. "And who's going to answer my ongoing job emails? I'll need to peck out replies with my left hand! And if I pass this next phone interview stage with American Girl, they'll want me to fly or drive to Chicago next. How am I going to do that?" She gave a disgusted snort. "Plus if I can even get there, they're not likely to hire me in a sling, knowing I won't be able to do my job well for months to come. If I'd been with their company a long time already, they'd have worked with me. But they won't hire me over another candidate now."

J.T. grew very quiet. "I didn't know you'd been interviewing for a job in Chicago."

"I hadn't mentioned it yet." She looked away from him, already regretting her outburst. "I only just passed the first interview stage. There's nothing definite yet."

"I'm sure you had a sense about whether you might get an offer though."

She sighed, deciding to be honest. "I did feel good from the responses I got in the early emails and at the first interview. The human resource director who interviewed me said I was the most qualified candidate they'd interviewed so far."

The quiet in the car lengthened for too long, making Mary Helen nervous. She'd meant to talk to J.T. about this later today.

He spoke at last. "If you really want this job, I'll drive you to Chicago to interview if you make the next stage. Maybe they'll be more accommodating than you think if they really want you for the position."

Mary Helen felt tears dribble down her cheeks. She swiped at her face. "I can't believe you offered to do that. I thought you'd be mad at me, that you wouldn't want me to go."

He swore under his breath, surprising her. "You know I don't want you to go, but I want you to be happy. I'd started to hope you might want to be happy with me, that's all."

Mary Helen felt like a heel then, her conscience smarting as badly as her arm. "I'm sorry, J.T."

"Yeah. Well, life is what it is. You'll get better in time, and if you don't get this job, you'll get another. For now you should focus on healing." He paused. "Ryder broke an arm playing football in high school. I remember the time well. You're in for some discomfort and major exercises in patience."

She rubbed her hand down her right arm over the sling, which was throbbing despite the pain meds. "I've never been very good with patience."

He grinned. "Neither have I. I guess we'll learn together."

"You're being really nice to me again."

A faint smile played over his lips. "I told you I was a nice guy, remember?"

She heaved a sigh. "I remember."

On the way into the island, J.T. stopped at the pharmacy to pick up her prescription and then at The Little Mermaid so Mary Helen could ask Nancy to cover for her until Isabel came back.

"Of course, I'll work the weekend until Isabel comes back. Don't worry," Nancy said without hesitation, fluttering over her with sympathy. "Bless your heart, child. You simply rest at home, you hear? I am so sorry this happened to you. I'll be fine in this little store by myself, and I'll call if I have any problems. I promise."

While Mary Helen talked to Nancy, J.T ran over to the Sea Cow nearby and ordered a couple of lunches to go. Between their trips to the clinic and the ER, they'd neither had a chance to eat.

Back in the car, J.T. managed a smile. "See? I told you Nancy would cover the store for you. Things are quieter now in September on the island. She'll be fine, and she can call you if she has questions."

He drove down the street and parked at the Mikell Island Rental store.

"Why are we stopping here?" Mary Helen asked.

"I need to check at the store about something."

She sent him a suspicious look. "You're not planning to take off to hang around with me, are you?"

He hopped out of the car. "It's my business if I want to."

Mary Helen sat in the car, annoyed until he got back. "I don't want you sacrificing work time for me, J.T. Mikell."

"Maybe I want to sacrifice some time. I have weeks and weeks of vacation time accumulated. Maybe I'd like a little break myself."

"Well, think how that will look to everyone." She felt herself flush.

"It will look like I'm crazy in love with you and want to take care of you when you've been hurt. So what? It's true." He slowed for a stop sign. "Word will get around quickly that you broke your arm out at my family's old plantation house. They'll figure I felt guilty about it, and they'll be right."

He leaned over to trace a hand down her cheek. "What do you care what people think anyway? I don't. All I care about is you, and helping you get well. I hate seeing that pain on your face, those scratches, that sling, and knowing the discomfort you're going to deal with for a long time. Let me be sweet, Mary Helen, and don't mess with me. I'm going to do what I'm going to do anyway. You might as well make up your mind to enjoy it."

"You're a stubborn man." She frowned at him.

"So I've been told." He grinned. "I might also mention I've heard you described the same way. Looks like we make a good pair."

When they pulled up in her driveway, she turned to look at him. "You need to know I am not an easy patient to spend time with. Ask my mother. Ask Suki or Parker. I hate being sick. I hate being limited or inactive. I get restless and bored and irritable. Sometimes I get morose and feel sorry for myself. You'll regret quickly this idea of yours to act as a nursemaid to me."

He got out of the car to come around and help her out. "You're not talking me out of this, Mary Helen." He gave her a kiss despite her trying to turn away. "You can think of me as a home health companion. I like that term better. Maybe we'll even have some fun—or some laughs—between you being crabby and cross."

Giving up for a time, Mary Helen made her way into the house. It looked like for a season, at least, she'd have to cope with more of J.T.'s company than she really wanted around dealing with her broken arm. Just realizing this even happened at all still stunned her and didn't feel real.

In the house, Mary Helen cleaned up, letting J.T. help her put ointment and band-aids on some of her scratches. Upstairs in her bedroom on her own, she sponge bathed the dirt and dried blood off herself and then started struggling to get her soiled clothes off.

Finally, frustrated from the effort and getting nowhere, she called out. "Hey, J.T. ... can you come up here a minute and help me?"

She heard him take the steps and open her bedroom door.

Slumped on the bed, she looked up at him in anguish. "I can't get my shirt off. It's a pullover knit top. What am I going to do? Cut it off?"

He studied the situation. "Maybe if we slip your arm out of the sling for a minute, then take your shirt off your left side, then over your head, we can slide it down your right arm carefully."

She considered it. "I'm only wearing a bra under this shirt."

He smirked. "I've seen bras before, Mary Helen."

"I'll bet you have."

He glowered at her. "This isn't a time to be petty. I've also seen you in skimpy two-piece bathing suits. There's no difference."

"Yes, there is. Bathing suits aren't underwear."

She saw his dimples flash in another grin. "I'll just imagine you're wearing a white bathing suit then."

"My bra is black."

"Black?" He rolled his eyes. "Don't paint me visuals and get me excited. I really need to help you do this."

He paused for a minute glancing at Mary Helen's fresh clothes on the bed. "That outfit you laid out to put on isn't a good choice. You need a shirt that buttons up in the front so you can get it off and on by yourself and you need elastic-waist shorts you can pull up and down easily. How do you think you're going to manage a zipper and a button like on those shorts?"

She studied the clothes she'd laid out. "All I thought about was getting out of these filthy clothes and into something clean."

He rubbed his neck. "Well you're going to need to think out clothes you can wear that will be easy for you to get off and on."

"I hate this." She stomped her foot.

"A nasty attitude doesn't help." He cocked an eyebrow at her. "Get up and find some clothes to change into. Then we'll do this, Mary Helen."

J.T.'s idea proved a good one and with a little patience she changed into clean clothes. Feeling better now, she went downstairs to join him on the screened porch to eat some lunch.

"I put a straw in your glass to make handling your drink easier and I cut your sandwich in little pieces."

"Thanks," she said, feeling like crying now that the adrenalin of the day was wearing off.

Sensing her mood change, he entertained her with some light banter while they ate, even making her laugh a little.

When the pain kicked up in her arm as they finished lunch, J.T. found pain meds for her. "Why don't you take a little nap? You've had a really rough day."

"That's a good idea." She sent him a feigned smile, glad to escape his company to curl up in bed by herself.

She quickly found the doctor was right that getting comfortable in bed to sleep would be hard. She propped three pillows together and wedged one pillow under her sling trying to get comfortable but still every movement hurt. Only when the pain meds kicked in did she finally drift off.

When she woke later, she managed to get to the bathroom by herself—awkwardly—and then went downstairs to find something to drink. She found a note from J.T. on the table, saying he'd gone home to get more clothes for himself and to check on things at the store.

"Maybe he won't come back for a while if I'm lucky," she said pettishly, getting a canned cola out of the refrigerator. She struggled to pop it open with her left hand, soon giving up and banging it down on the table in irritation.

Frustrated and ready to cry, she heard someone coming up the back steps and turned to see Kizzy Helton let herself in the back door. Kizzy carried a cardboard box with several dishes in it.

"I brought dinner, honey child," she said, sitting the box on the table and starting to take the dishes out to put in the refrigerator. "Leon called Vernita and then Vernita called me to tell me what happened. God bless your heart. We're all so sorry." She came over to check out Mary Helen's arm, giving her a careful hug, and then opened the soda for her and poured it into a glass of ice.

"I brought you a lemon pie, along with a chicken and rice casserole, good homemade green beans, fresh corn cut right off the cob, and a few other things." Kizzy put the dishes in the refrigerator and then set the pie out on the counter. "I'll cut you a nice piece of this pie right now."

She did, bringing it over to the table to Mary Helen, along with a fork, and then sat down across from her. "Now, while you're eating, you tell me all of what happened."

Mary Helen did, sniffling and crying before it was over, grumbling about J.T., telling Kizzy how this accident had ruined her chances for the job she hoped for. "Why have all these awful things happened to me?" she asked Kizzy. "That horrible man groping me and forcing me to leave my job in New Jersey and now breaking my arm here. Is God punishing me or something, trying to teach me something?"

Kizzy clucked her tongue. "What kind of faith talk is that and you a preacher's daughter? You know only good gifts come down from our Lord and the bad from God's enemy or because of our own faults or ignorance. Don't be assigning blame to God for things He didn't do, girl."

She put a hand on one hip. "It seems to me your whole attitude over this could use adjusting ... mad at this, mad at that, mad at J.T. and with him being so good to you, showing himself a friend and more. Where's your gratitude? Where's your thankfulness you weren't hurt worse? I've seen accidents around here on this island that left a man or woman crippled or permanently disabled, a family impoverished. Will your injury permanently cripple you? Are you impoverished? Think of all your blessings, child."

Mary Helen hung her head, well chastised. "You sound like Mother."

"Well since she's off traveling, I'm filling in for her." Her dark eyes met Mary Helen's. "Like the old song says, the God of the good times is still God of the bad, and He'll see you though this like he has everything else. It might help Him do His job a little better if you reached out to Him in some prayer though. You tried that yet? You or J.T.?"

"Have we tried what?" J.T. said, coming in the kitchen, carrying a small duffle bag.

"You come over here and give me a big hug, boy," she said. "I hear you've been real good to my girl today, taking her to the hospital and looking after her real sweet."

J.T. leaned over to give Kizzy a hug, then spotted the pie on the table. "Lord in heaven," he said. "Is that one of your lemon pies? Can I have a piece?"

"Go and cut yourself a piece but quit using the Lord's name unless you use it respectfully or in prayer. I was just now telling Mary Helen she needed to be doing more praying, thanking God for things not being worse and for the old enemy not getting further in the door to bring more damage than he did. You need to keep that in mind, too."

"Yes, ma'am," J.T. answered, sitting down at the table with them to eat a big slice of Kizzy's lemon pie.

"How are you doing, Mary Helen?" J.T. asked, looking across at her.

She sighed. "I'm all right."

"Good." His eyes moved over her.

They all sat in silence, Kizzy watching them for a minute.

"Hmmm." She looked at J.T. "You're in love with this girl, aren't you?" Then she looked at Mary Helen. "But you're fighting your heart, not wanting to open it up to love and trust. What you want to be that way for? I've always seen you two well suited. Never could figure out why you squabbled so with each other, except because the both of you are so ornery and stubborn."

Mary Helen was wise enough to keep her mouth shut. So was J.T.

Kizzy got up to pour some more cola in Mary Helen's glass. "You know what I do when the devil gets a lick in at me? I make him sorry he messed with me. I tell him, 'well, devil, you know it's real stupid of you to try to lay me up, cause when you do, you know what I'll do with all my extra time while I'm down for a while? I'll just get strengthened up reading the Word, praying and having lots more time for it. I'll come out stronger and better.' That's what I tell him."

Mary Helen couldn't help grinning.

J.T. laughed out loud. "Dang, if that isn't a good idea, Kizzy. I like the idea of fighting back."

"Both you young people need to be learning more about God's ways and about His Word and His promises so you can fight back better, get through hard times easier, and get on the offensive to protect yourselves more. Don't you know we're living in a war zone all the days we're down here on this earth with an old enemy wanting to kill us, steal from us, and destroy us if he can? Both you young folks need to be suiting up in your spiritual armor more daily, getting stronger in your faith walk. You may be nearly grown up in body now but you two are still weak and small in your faith. It's a shame. It's getting in the way of everything God's wanting to work out for you."

She stood up. "I need to be getting on back." She looked at J.T. "I reckon you're gonna stay here and look after Mary Helen whether she likes it or not. Or whether I do. But I'll be knowing if you don't act as you should and you'll see me coming. You understand that, boy?"

"Yes, ma'am. I'm not looking to take advantage of Mary Helen when she's sick, Kizzy."

"Well, that's good to hear." She glanced toward the empty box. "I brought some food over in that box and put it in the refrigerator. It's food you only need to heat up. It'll give you both dinner tonight and more again for tomorrow. Vernita's bringing dinner over after church on Sunday afternoon. I'd say others will come by soon with more."

"That's really nice," Mary Helen said. "Thank you, Kizzy."

"It was my pleasure." She paused, her eyes moving from one to the other. "Will you two do me a little favor?"

"Sure," they both said at once.

"Read the book of Ephesians together tonight, especially that part in the sixth chapter about putting on the armor of God. You'll learn from that. I want you both to determine, too, that in this bad time you'll build your faith up and give the devil a black eye for messing in your lives. You should pray together, too. Couples that pray together stay together." She gave J.T. a stern look. "You remember that, boy."

"Yes, ma'am," he said, glancing at the box she'd brought in. "Do you need to keep that box? I can carry it out for you."

"No." She shook her head. "We have boxes aplenty at the grocery. Just break it down and put it out for the trash."

She came over to give Mary Helen a kiss. "I'm so sorry you've been hurt in this season—in several hard ways, too. But God will work all for good. You just watch Him do it."

Kizzy went over and kissed J.T. on the cheek, too. "I'll be praying for Mary Helen and for you. We all will. Keep that in mind."

After a little more talk, she left.

"Well," Mary Helen said after Kizzy let herself out the back door, not knowing what else to say.

J.T. looked after Kizzy and then turned to grin at her. "She's right about everything, you know."

Mary Helen lifted an eyebrow. "You think so? I didn't know you were a big man of faith."

He chuckled. "Honey, there's a whole lot you don't know about me. You've been running too hard from me to really see me at all."

Mary Helen wondered about those words much of the evening.

To her surprise, J.T. got out her Bible and read the scriptures Kizzy asked them to read later, offering a rather heartfelt prayer, too. If he was uncomfortable doing it, she couldn't tell.

He'd brought a movie back with him for entertainment and they laughed through *Crocodile Dundee*, even though they'd seen it before. He heated up dinner for them after the movie, like a pro, and kindly helped Mary Helen settle into bed later.

Without counsel, he put a glass of water with a straw by her bed, helped her layer several pillows to sleep on, propped another under her arm to elevate it, filled her ice pack and even tucked her covers around her.

That done, he backed off, moving toward the door. "I'm not kissing you goodnight this close to a bed, Mary Helen Avery."

She watched his eyes move over her in the thin button-front gown they'd chosen for her to sleep in. The raw desire she saw made her pull the covers up tight.

"Thanks for all your help," she managed to say.

"Sure. You call me if you need me. I'm going to sleep across the hall in Suki's room so I'll be nearby tonight."

He left, shutting the door behind him. In the quiet of the dark room now, remembering all J.T.'s kindness of the day, Mary Helen wondered how much she really did know about J.T. Mikell after all.

What had he said: *You've been running too hard from me to really see me at all.* Had she? And was Kizzy right that she'd been too ornery and stubborn to open her heart to love and trust again? Mary Helen sighed and then winced as a flash of pain sliced down her arm. Who knew what was right after a day like today anyway?

CHAPTER 16

J.T. didn't get much sleep that night, not that he expected to. Thinking back over the day made him toss and turn. So much had happened and it played through his mind over and over again. Throughout the night he got up often to check on Mary Helen, too, once when she knocked over her water, mad about it, another time he heard crying, trying to get to the bathroom by herself, frustrated and in pain.

Toward morning he heard her weeping again, this time mostly feeling sorry for herself. Not that he could blame her. He'd held her, offering comfort, trying not to think about the feel of her against him with nothing on but that thin, flimsy, little nightgown. He hated himself for feeling lust at a time like this and for remembering, as he tried to settle back into sleep, how she'd looked in that black bra earlier.

When Mary Helen listed all the reasons she'd be a difficult patient for him, he doubted she realized how being close to her would be the biggest difficulty for him. Andrew might be a little obtuse about the physical pleasures women could offer, but J.T. had never known that problem.

He was up early fixing coffee Saturday morning when his mother came in the back door. "How's Mary Helen doing?" she asked. "I know Kizzy brought food last night, but I got up early today to make a breakfast casserole to bring over before I head to work."

"I think she's still sleeping. She had a rough night," J.T. said, lifting the cover on the Pyrex dish to sniff his mother's sausage and egg casserole, a favorite dish of his.

"Poor little thing. Your dad told me what happened to her yesterday and how she broke her arm out at the old plantation house. I thought of coming by last night but decided this morning might be better."

They heard a voice call from upstairs. "J.T., could you come up for a minute? I need help."

Lula put a hand on his arm. "Let me go. I'll help her wash up and dress. It can't be easy for you to help her with that." She gave him a pointed look, making him turn away, embarrassed.

She smiled and kissed his cheek then. "I've always been proud of having very red-blooded boys, so much like their father." She started toward the stairs. "You set the table, pour juice, and make some toast while I'm helping Mary Helen. Then I'll bring her downstairs to eat some breakfast."

About thirty minutes later, Mary Helen sat across from J.T. at the kitchen table, clean, dressed in a fresh outfit, her hair brushed and even with a little makeup on. She still hugged her arm close, letting him know it hurt her, but she looked better than she had last night. Thank goodness, there were no signs of tears this morning.

"J.T. had to deal with a really bad time with me last night," she informed his mother. "I tried to talk him out of staying here. I told him it wasn't appropriate and that I was a horrible patient."

Lula glanced across at Mary Helen, who was struggling to eat with her left hand. "Honey, you fell while on J.T.'s watch," she stated. "He feels responsible for that. Men are funny that way. I doubt either of us will be able to talk him out of putting in time to take care of you." She shook her head. "Actually, all the Mikell family simply hate that you broke your arm out at the old plantation house. People often ask me why John and I didn't move into the place and fix it up rather than building another house nearby. Their romantic ideas about that old albatross and the reality of it are two entirely different things. I'm sure you've seen that for yourself now."

J.T. saw Mary Helen smile, relieved his mother wasn't putting guilt and shame on them for spending the night alone together. "I should have never left Mary Helen alone with time on her hands while I checked out the property. I knew all too well the problems lurking at that run-down place."

"Creaky old floors, rotten wood, drafts, basically no closets, no central heat or air, termites setting up housekeeping every time we turn our backs." Lula checked off the items on her fingers. "Spiders, cockroaches as long as your finger—ugh!—mosquitoes, and snakes. You couldn't pay me to live in that place."

Mary Helen grinned. "J.T. did mention after I fell through the porch that he was glad I hadn't fallen on a snake."

Lula looked shocked. "Well, honey, we're simply so sorry this even happened. I hate, too, that it possibly dashed your chances at that nice job you wanted in Chicago. But I'm sure another opportunity will open later."

J.T. heard her words while knowing full well his mother was delighted Mary Helen would be staying around longer, even if not for a happy reason. She was glad for him to garner more time for his campaign to succeed.

Lula leaned toward Mary Helen now. "I want you to know that Isabel, Elaine, and I will be stopping in often to help you out with Claire overseas. You can call on us any time you need us, too, you hear? We'll fill in like three little Southern mothers." She smiled at her own turn of phrase and then added with a lift of her eyebrow. "There are a number of things J.T. doesn't need to be helping you with. You know what I mean."

He saw Mary Helen smirk at her words. "Yes, I do, Lula, and thanks for helping me get dressed and cleaned up this morning. I feel so helpless and awkward trying to do things in this brace and sling. I am *not* used to doing things with my left hand either." She looked down at her plate, frowning. "I've dropped food all over the place trying to feed myself this morning, like a little toddler or something."

"That's the least of your worries, cleaning up a little food here and there." Lula waved a hand. "Tell me what the doctor said about your break and what he said about the recovery time to expect before I head to the office."

Mary Helen did, J.T. listening in while he drank another cup of coffee and wolfed down a second helping of his mother's casserole.

After Lula left, J.T. cleaned up the kitchen and then suggested a walk up the beach. They didn't walk as far as usual, Mary Helen needing to keep her pace slow, careful not to trip or fall. He knew it provoked her doing so.

The pain in Mary Helen's arm came and went in sweeps and spurts that day and into the night. His mother dropped by the next morning to help Mary Helen bathe and dress again and then she popped in as J.T. was making coffee on Sunday morning, too. J.T. knew it a blessing he didn't have to help with too much with Mary Helen's intimate dressing and undressing. Just being with her all the time was hard enough for him.

After his mother left, J.T. said, "Since it's Sunday, Mary Helen, do you want to pull on a skirt over your shorts and go to Kizzy's church?"

She looked across the table at him in surprise. "Are you serious?"

"Of course I'm serious." He shrugged. "We could go somewhere else if you'd prefer, but I thought it would be nice to pop in at Kizzy's church. She was nice to bring all that food on Friday and, remember, she said Vernita would bring food later today, too."

"That's an AME church they go to. You're Baptist and I'm basically Presbyterian turned Baptist after we moved to Beaufort. You know the service will be really different at Olivet AME than what we're used to."

"Different isn't bad. I've been there before with Leon and Vernita."

"What was it like?" She leaned forward, curious now.

"Lively. Zealous. Great music. Good message. Kizzy's son Farlin Helton is a strong charismatic pastor."

"Were you the only white man there?"

He shrugged. "There might have been one or two more besides

me. I can't remember, but I was definitely in the minority. Leon had to teach me how to clap on the offbeat and he pushed me to even clap at all. The singing is more like the Bible schools I used to go to as a kid on the island. More fun and interactive."

He watched her face and could tell she was considering it.

"Come on," he said. "It will be an adventure. You'll get to see all the Helton family, too."

She glanced down at her outfit.

"You can pull on that black skirt hanging in your closet. It will go great with that raspberry blouse you're wearing. Add some flats and you'll be dressy enough for Edisto." He looked down at his own shorts. "I'll run over to the house, pull on a pair of slacks and a dress shirt and come get you in about fifteen minutes. What do you say?"

"Okay." Her eyes lit up with some of the old spirit he remembered. "Let's do it."

Despite how lively the church was—and the fact that they were the only two white faces in the congregation—they enjoyed the service at AME. Both J.T. and Mary Helen were well known to most of the members and lovingly welcomed. Many in the church expressed regret about Mary Helen's fall, but better—to J.T.'s way of thinking—they gathered around to pray for her, not an event that would have happened in either of their churches.

"That prayer was powerful," Mary Helen admitted to him on their way home. "I really felt something when they prayed; I almost fell over it was so strong." She rubbed a hand over her sling. "Farlin told me when I left that he'd seen I would experience a total and quick healing."

"I'd hold fast to that. All the Heltons walk close to God."

She flashed him a smile. "He told me to repeat those words in faith to myself and to others, and to not speak anything oppositional."

"Then we'll do that."

She looked surprised. "I thought you might laugh."

"Why? Do I look like a fool? Farlin Helton has God's ear. Why would I laugh? I respect the close place he walks in with the

Lord."

She grew quiet for a minute. "You sound a lot like my father."

"Parker?"

"No my natural father, Charles Avery. He lived in a close place to God, too, and he respected that in others, regardless of their denominational preferences."

"Well, thank you for that compliment. I know your father was an admirable man."

She sighed. "I've really seen a different side of you in the last few days."

He laughed. "Meaning I've showed you my soft side, that I pray and try to live right."

"Yes."

"We all went to Bible school together on the island as kids, and you know my family well. Didn't you think of us as good people?"

"I suppose."

"Look. Boys and men don't always go around talking faith and righteousness and stuff most of the time, even if they count it as important." He tried to think how to explain. "It's kind of ingrained in us, a guy thing. Not to show you're soft, not to be a wuss, or cry, or act like a girl."

She snorted. "You could have left out that last one."

He laughed. "Well, you were never a girly sort of girl, all silly, whiney, and weepy."

Mary Helen looked out the window. "I've shown some of that side to you these last days."

"It's all right." He patted her knee. "Maybe it's good we're getting to know each other a little better. I think we often put on a self we want others to see and aren't as genuine as we should be. Perhaps it's protective. We're afraid that softer side won't be appreciated. That someone will laugh at us."

She didn't answer.

J.T. pulled into the driveway at Oleanders. "I'm glad to have seen your softer side. I've liked having you lean on me, needing my help. You're so dang independent, never wanting to let me take care of

you most of the time. Always pushing me back if I get too close."
He leaned over and slid his hand over her leg, letting his voice drop.
"I've liked you needing me, Mary Helen. Actually, I've loved it."

She turned to him in surprise, starting to protest—he could tell—
so he leaned over and kissed her. Kissed her well, being careful of
her arm, and then pulled her closer, kissing her again, feeling her
soften and sweeten as he did.

He drew back and traced a hand down her cheek. "Don't say
anything and mess it up, Mary Helen. I've loved you being needy.
I've loved wiping away your tears, helping you with things, brushing
your hair." He threaded his hand through her hair. "It's been a
huge ego boost and a big turn on for me."

Her mouth dropped open. "A turn on?"

He chuckled at her surprise. "Maybe you need to be a guy to
understand."

"Is this a Me Tarzan, You Jane thing?" she asked, her lips
twitching.

"Maybe so." He pushed open the car door and got out. "Enough
philosophizing. Let's go eat some of the food Vernita sent home
with us—fried chicken, red potato salad, fresh slaw, tomatoes,
and chocolate cake. Your accident sure has brought us some fine
food."

Mary Helen reached across to open her door. "Do you think it
hurt everyone's feelings that we didn't want to go join them for
lunch at Kizzy's?"

"No. They understand you still don't feel very good, that you
needed to come home, take your meds, and rest." He reached into
the back seat to pick up the box filled with food dishes that Vernita
sent with them.

Mary Helen tried to reach in to get the cake box.

"Don't try to carry that. Okay? You need your free hand to hold
on to the rail climbing up the stairs. I've noticed you're still a little
unsteady on your feet. We don't want you to fall again. I'll come
back and get the cake."

"You sound like my mother now."

He turned around to move closer to her, his voice dropping. "I doubt your mother would have kissed you like I did."

J.T. watched her blush and head for the stairs.

"You know what I mean, J.T.," she said lifting her chin.

He followed her with a grin.

They ate lunch and Mary Helen rested after. Later in the day, Jane, Barton, and Elena came by to visit. Jane brought an enchilada casserole for them to eat tomorrow, a chess pie, and a stack of mystery books for Mary Helen to read.

J.T. left Mary Helen curled up and reading one of the new books while he went over to the shop for a few hours. When he came back, he found her asleep on the couch, the book open across her chest.

He stood and looked at her for a few minutes. It was sweet to see the strong-willed, outspoken, stubborn girl he knew lying so quiet, still, and vulnerable. Granted, he loved that strong, independent nature of hers, a good match to his own personality. Mary Helen had always been a daredevil—adventurous and willing to try practically anything when they were kids together.

She opened her eyes. "I didn't know you were back."

"I just came in the door." He watched her shift her position, wincing as she tried to sit up. "Want some help?" He held out a hand.

"No, I've got it, but thanks." She pulled into a sitting position.

"Come help me make dinner," he said, seeing that despondent look flash in her eyes.

She snorted. "Yeah, right. I'm a lot of help."

"You can set the table, pour tea, and make an attempt at slicing one of those tomatoes Vernita gave us. You need to work at getting your left hand to do more. I don't care if the tomato slices are a little uneven." He opened the refrigerator. "I'm going to get out the slaw and potato salad and maybe heat up the rest of the chicken a little." He paused. "You don't mind having the same thing for dinner that we did for lunch, do you?"

"No." She leaned against the counter. "We sound like an old

married couple, bantering over dinner preparations."

He smiled, liking the idea of her picturing them that way. "How do we rank on a scale of one to ten as a an old married couple?"

Regretting her comment, she replied saucily. "I really can't say."

After dinner J.T. suggested they play Scrabble out on the screened porch, where they could enjoy the evening air and hear the ocean.

"That sounds fun, but remember I *always* play to win," she reminded him. "Your little Tarzan ego might get a hit."

He grinned at her as he dug out the game from a shelf in the living room. "Seems to me I recall winning as many games with you in past as I lost."

"Maybe, but we seldom won any time with Emma playing. Even if younger than most all of us, she knew so many clever words to play." She headed out to the porch. "I'm not surprised she got a masters in English and is teaching at the college now."

After they set the game board up and settled into play, J.T. asked, "Have you told Suki, your mom, and Parker about your accident?"

"No. Suki was performing this weekend. I never tell her troubling things before she plays; you remember how sensitive she is. I hated to worry Mother and Parker about this either. You know Mother will think they should come home. I think I'll wait to tell her until I'm healing more."

"Which we know will happen *soon* from what Farlin said today," he said.

"Yes." She smiled at him. "I do admit I like thinking that way."

He played the word "quail" on the board, starting it on a double letter space, trying not to gloat over the points he racked up.

She glanced at the board. "Good word." Then she played a high scoring word of her own.

A few minutes later, he asked, "Have you talked to any of your friends back in New Jersey? Or to anyone where you worked?"

"I've talked to Rita Sacco a few times. She was the manager at my store and a good friend, probably the best friend I had in New Jersey. We hung out a lot, went to shows, shopping, out to eat and stuff. She pushed on me to tell her why I left so suddenly, and I flat out told her I could not talk to her about it." She paused to place a word on the board, snagging a triple score space. "I told her if she couldn't respect that, I was sorry."

"What did she say?"

"She said that she, Lila Arquette—she's our assistant store manager—and even Meredith Kessler, the HR at corporate who hired me, said they felt sure something happened to make me leave with so little notice and without talking to anyone before I left. Rita encouraged me to share, saying maybe it could be resolved so I could come back."

"Will you?" he asked, trying to figure out how to create a word using the "z" he'd drawn.

"Oh course not. But I admit I'd be pushing Rita for answers, too, if the situation was reversed. They all know me well enough to realize I wouldn't walk off without a very good reason."

"Do you think they'll figure it out?"

She shook her head. "No. I was totally blindsided by Wendell Hembree. He's a longtime employee, well thought of in the community, a family man, married to the owners' daughter with two boys in college. I'd never have suspected in a million years he might act as he did."

"I still say it's probably not the first time."

"You could be right." She put a hand on her hip in irritation. "You know, the entire incident doesn't help me feel good about the general world of men and their trustworthiness."

"Listen. Just because one man thieves, one man lies, one man kills, one man cheats on his wife doesn't mean most men do those things. Be reasonable." He found a spot for the word "zoom," using his "z" to advantage.

She scowled. "You're racking up the points tonight."

He flashed her a grin. "I'm loving it, too."

"I thought you were supposed to cater to me while I'm injured, be sweet and gracious toward me."

"Not with games."

She laughed. "Well, since I'm going to be staying longer at Edisto now, we'll have time for more games in future and a chance for me to get even if I don't win tonight."

They played a few more words and then she asked, "Will you take me out in your boat one day? I still remember how excited you were to get your boating license as a teenager, even more than when you got your driver's license."

"Sure. I'll take you." He considered the idea. "We'll explore and do some fishing. I love any excuse to get out on the water. I own a great boat, too. It's a Carolina Skiff. "

"What did you name your boat?"

"Wanna guess?"

She gave him an annoyed look. "How would I know?"

"It's the name you thought of."

She wrinkled her nose, trying to remember.

"The name is from a song in the old musical *Meet Me In St. Louis* sung by Judy Garland."

She thought for a minute or two. "The Silver Lining?"

He nodded. "You'll see the words Silver Lining painted on the bow."

Her face brightened. "I loved that classic movie. We all watched it on television as kids one day on some old movie channel. Mother knew all the songs in it and she kept singing them with us afterward." Mary Helen propped her chin on one hand thinking. "You and I watched that movie again as teenagers. You were talking about boats then and dreaming of the day when you could afford to buy one."

He smiled. "And you said you thought Silver Lining would be a great name for a boat if I ever got one. You told me a name like that would remind me to always look on the sunny side of life. I think of those words—and I think of you—every time I take the boat out. It's my happy place for sure."

She sighed. "You romantic thing. It almost makes me want to cry when you remember things like that."

He leaned closer, across the Scrabble board. "I remember a lot of things about those days when we were young and falling in love. I remember you always loved lemon custard ice cream, that you wore Eternity cologne—and still do—that you kept a book of quotes by people you admired, that you loved to read mysteries, and that your eyes always widened and lit up when you smiled."

She looked away, her eyes not meeting his.

"I also remember you always looked away when your emotions surfaced, not wanting anyone to see how much things affect you sometimes."

Mary Helen looked back at him then and reached out to touch his face. "You're not the only one who remembers things. I remember how I loved seeing those dimples flash in your cheeks every time you smiled, how I could hear your laugh even far down the beach. It always made me want to laugh simply hearing it." Her voice softened. "I remember how you always carried shells and sharks' teeth in your pockets, how you could ride a paddleboard on top of an ocean wave as smooth as a fish, how cute and handsome you always were, striding down the beach." She paused and her face clouded. "And how the girls always watched you."

J.T. tried to think what to say to that last remark. "I noticed the girls sometimes, but my eyes were most always on you. In your heart you know that, Mary Helen. You and Jane ogled the boys, too, and flirted with them. Kids do those things. Even now, my eyes might notice a pretty girl, a lovely shell, or a beautiful sunset, but you will always hold my heart. It's important that you know that."

A few tears trickled down her face. "You're making me cry, J.T."

"Good. I want you to see how much I love you, to stop doubting it or doubting my heart."

She reached out her left hand to lay it over his on the table. "There is a part of me that has always loved you, J.T. Mikell, that is yielding more and more every day to those sweet feelings, even though a stubborn side of me tries desperately to hold those feelings back."

His heart kicked up at her words. He wanted to move around the table, take her in his arms and make her never doubt for a minute that he cared. But with them here alone, he worried how much further he'd take it if he did.

She studied him and laughed. "I know exactly what you're thinking right now." She got up and walked around the table. "But you'd better stand up and kiss me, you handsome thing. I feel confident you won't take advantage of me with this arm in a sling. And if you try, I'll call your mother."

Mary Helen wrapped him in her good arm before he'd barely stood to his feet, kissing him soundly. "You've been my silver lining through all this horrible time with my arm and after the terrible time with my boss, too. You've made my days, even when difficult and disappointing for me, more bearable. And special."

She kissed him again and he reveled in it, taking care about her arm as he pulled her closer against him.

"We've always fit together perfectly, you and me." He whispered the words against her ear.

"Do you think so?" she said with a little teasing note in her voice.

He pulled her closer. "I know so." J.T. was losing himself in her, his heartbeat kicking up and his mind clouding, when the phone rang.

Of course, she needed to answer it and she let herself in the house to pick up the phone. It was Suki, her sister. Mary Helen waved her fingers at him through the sliding glass door and then settled down on the couch in the living room to talk to her.

While Mary Helen visited on the phone, J.T. walked down the back steps and out to the beach, thinking over her words, beginning to hope at last he had a chance to talk Mary Helen into staying.

"Time will tell," he said, looking out over the ocean. She might be acting soft and vulnerable now with all that happened to her with this broken arm, but he well knew how she could change in a moment.

CHAPTER 17

Late October 2002

September and October slipped by quickly, with Mary Helen's six-week checkup coming up on Friday. It seemed unbelievable six weeks had passed since she fell through the porch at the old Mikell house.

"You're moving your arm more freely every day now," Isabel commented as they worked together on Monday at The Little Mermaid. "I know you're glad to be out of that brace and sling, too."

"I'm glad to be driving more than anything," Mary Helen said. "I hated it that everyone needed to drive me around everywhere like an old lady—to therapy sessions, to doctor appointments, to the grocery, to go anywhere."

"Be careful about that old lady talk." Isabel gave a disgusted snort. "Some of us might be sensitive about that term."

"You're not old," Mary Helen said, smiling at her.

"I may be young at heart, and expect to stay that way, but I am well into my seventies now."

Mary Helen stopped dusting to look across at Isabel, who sat at the little table by the front window. "You're all right aren't you, Isabel?"

"I'm absolutely fine, but I notice the passage of time more occasionally. It sneaks up and surprises you." She lifted an eyebrow. "You won't understand that until it bites you one day. Age is a pesky little thing."

"You'll never be old to me."

"Hmmph. Sweet words. Why don't you quit that dusting and come over here and talk to me for a few minutes?" She pointed at the chair across from her at the table. "The store is dead today anyway."

"It was busy this weekend, though, even for late October."

"The October festivals around Charleston and Beaufort bring folks down to the island, plus it's a good time for golfing with the weather cooler. More area events before the month ends will bring in traffic, too." She tapped a nail on the table, thinking. "With Halloween at the end of next week, we need to decorate the store and pick up some trick-or-treat candy to keep on hand for the kids."

"I already found the box of Halloween decorations in the storage room and put it out on the kitchen table in back. I'll start working on decorating the store between customers today." Mary Helen retrieved her bottle of spring water from the counter and settled down across from Isabel. "What did you want to talk about?"

The older woman studied her. "I want to know if you've fallen back in love with J.T. Mikell. It seems obvious the two of you are more than an item, and I watch the way you both look at each other."

"He's growing on me."

"That's an evasive answer."

Mary Helen sighed. "I fell in love with J.T. when we were in our teens. I'll always remember that initial sweet awareness, those young feelings, our fervent stolen kisses." She smiled at Isabel. "It's sort of special when love for someone goes back to an early first love. All the new feelings get mixed in with the old, and yet the new feelings are stronger and richer."

"That sounds like a yes."

She shook her head at Isabel's directness. "I can't say that these months haven't spun into a relationship I never expected when I came running back here to Edisto from New Jersey."

"I see." Isabel hesitated. "I also notice you haven't been talking about job interviews and prospects for a long time. I've seen a warm, comfortable little happiness growing in you since I got back from my cruise in early September, despite your arm and all the difficulties you've experienced with it."

"It has been a sweet season despite the problems with my arm."

Isabel sat watching her, twisting the rings on her fingers.

"What are you really wanting to know Isabel?"

"Probably things that are none of my business to ask as your employer." She rearranged a few of the artificial flowers in a small vase on the table. "But I have reasons for wanting to know if you and J.T. might be thinking of marriage and if you might be considering staying on the island. We both know J.T.'s life is solidly built here."

"I well know that. Edisto and J.T. come as a package deal," Mary Helen admitted. "I understand, too, that if I consider responding to his ongoing hints for marriage—and his outright proposals— that I'll need to decide if I can be content to stay on the island."

Isabel smirked. "I felt sure the boy had asked. I'm glad to hear that." She paused. "But you're still a little uncertain. What is holding you back from saying yes, your own heart or something else?"

Mary Helen leaned her head back. "Oh, I'd be lying to say my heart is not sure any longer but my ambitious head still struggles with the idea of giving up some of its loftier dreams for my future. Back in early September, after I broke my arm, I told the American Girl store it wouldn't be fair for me to interview further with them. They were gracious about it and honest enough to tell me I'd been their top pick in consideration. They asked if they could keep my name on file if another position opened in another store."

Isabel twisted at her rings again and looked away.

"Are you upset at me for having ambitions, for wanting more? It isn't as thought I don't love the Mermaid or love working with you…" She let her words trail off, not sure what else to say.

"I'm not upset with you. I'm simply having difficulty finding the words I want to say to you today."

"That's unusual for you." Mary Helen grinned at her. "You usually tell me to just spit it out when I'm skirting around a topic."

"A point well made." Isabel lifted her chin. "Well here it is then. I'd like you to think about partnering with me at the Mermaid, gradually taking on more responsibility, and eventually buying the store. I can't think of better hands to leave my little store in, and I'd like to think this legacy I've built here will live on."

Mary Helen knew her mouth dropped open.

Isabel crossed her arms. "Don't look so surprised. You know I have no children and surely you know you've been practically like a daughter to me. I've told you so often enough. It shouldn't be such a shock to you that I'd like you to own the store one day."

"Well, it is a shock."

"Hmmm." She shrugged, picking at one of her fingernails. "The idea came to me after you returned, when I saw how well you ran the store and made things easier for me. Then I watched you and J.T. growing close—saw that obvious look of love in his eyes—and listened to your discontents with the corporate world that slipped out while we worked together. You're strong and independent like I am, more of an entrepreneur than you may realize. I think— like me—you'd be happy having your own place." She paused, running a hand through her hair. "If you think about this and like the idea, I'd like to give more of the store over to you in time. Ezra is wanting to cut back his practice, give more of the business to a young intern he's working with. We'd like to travel some."

Mary Helen opened her mouth to reply, but Isabel held up a hand to stop her.

"Ezra and I are terribly rich," she added, surprising Mary Helen with her candor. "You may not know that. Both of us come from old money and we've made a lot of money. I could give the store to you easily and it wouldn't even be a problem for me. However, I know from working with your mother that you and Suki have money saved. I also know that Claire put money back for you from her book sales and that Parker created accounts for you. Knowing that—and knowing you, as I do—I think you would feel better contributing toward a partnership."

Mary Helen bit her lip. "You wouldn't make this offer just to try to get J.T. and me together, would you?"

Isabel snorted. "Have you seen me to be the sentimental and foolish type of woman who would do something based on emotion and not reason?"

Mary Helen laughed at her answer. "No. That's why this offer has thrown me for a loop. You love this store. You built it from scratch. I simply can't imagine you wanting to sell even a part of it."

She shrugged. "I'm not expecting to walk away. I think of this as a good business venture—securing the future of something I love. It's like writing a solid life insurance policy for the store. I rather like the idea of the store continuing on after I'm gone some day, too, and I like the idea of it continuing on in your hands." She smiled. "I did train you from the time you were only a little girl, you remember. That's special to me. I also know you hold special feelings about the store."

"I really do. And I'm stunned about your offer."

Isabel put a hand across the table and laid it on Mary Helen's. "You think this over in the next week or two. I don't expect you to give me any sort of solid answer now, or until you talk to Parker and your mother. They'll be home at the first of November. Perhaps by then you'll know if you even want them to learn about this offer at all." She hesitated. "Maybe by then, too, you'll know if you want to say yes to J.T.'s requests."

Mary Helen nodded, still shocked.

Isabel's eyes found hers again in that searching way of hers. "Would it seen too humble to your ambitions to own a little store on Edisto? You could expand the store if you wished later on or open another branch in Beaufort or Charleston one day."

She smiled, looking around her store. "You actually might find that a slightly low key business like this, quiet for much of the year, could work well around raising children if you were so inclined. You've seen how Jane works only part time now, with the new baby coming and with Elena still small, but you also know she plans to add hours back later when she wants to work more again.

Perhaps you remember, too, how you and Suki came to the store after school when your mother worked here." She glanced around the store again thoughtfully and then smiled. "I think adding a playpen and a resident baby in the store might fit in very nicely with the ambience, don't you?"

Mary Helen couldn't help giggling. "You have given this a lot of thought, Isabel. Why were you so nervous about talking to me about this?"

"Because this business is *my* child. I worried you might laugh at the idea of taking on such a modest opportunity. But I can see you're considering it."

"Silly woman." Mary Helen shook her head. "Surely you know how much I love this *child* of yours, too. Even if I wanted to return to a corporate opportunity I'd always cherish the memory that you offered such a gift to me."

"Hmmph. Well, let's not get overly sentimental." She stood up, returning to her more businesslike self. "You give this a little thought. If you're going to stay on the island, it might be a good opportunity for you to consider."

Isabel glanced at her watch. "I need to run to the bank and make a deposit." She headed across the room to get her purse from under the register. "I can pick up two salads at the Sea Cow on my way back. Do you want a Caesar or Garden Salad? We usually get them with a little chicken on top, too. Do you want that?"

"A Caesar with chicken sounds good today. We still have tea in the refrigerator; we won't need drinks."

"That will do us then." She draped her purse over her shoulder. "I'm going to run to the Edisto Island Bookstore up the highway to find a new book to read, too. Do you want anything there?"

Mary Helen smiled. "No, I'm good. I bought a stack of used paperback mysteries last week. I'm working my way through a Sue Grafton one now."

"Oh, which one?" Isabel's eyes brightened.

"I think this one is *M* is for *Malice*. I've been reading them in order."

Isabel smiled. "Aren't they delightful? I'll pick up the next one in the series if I see it on the shelf." She paused at the door. "By the way, if the librarian comes by while I'm gone, give her a dozen of those little wooden tops for her children's story hour. They only cost us about fifty cents each to order. The preschoolers will love them."

"I'll do that," Mary Helen said as Isabel let herself out the door and started down the sidewalk to her car.

Mary Helen sat at the window looking after her with a big smile for a long time. "Who would ever have believed Isabel Compton would offer me a chance to buy into the Mermaid?" she said out loud. "Wow."

Letting her eyes move around the familiar children's store, Mary Helen had to admit she felt better about the idea of possibly staying at the island, knowing she could partner with Isabel and later own The Little Mermaid. It was a dream she'd held in her heart since she first fell in love with the store as a girl.

She felt flattered too, that Isabel would trust her with the Mermaid. Mary Helen knew it had been hard for her to bring up the subject, to even talk to her about it. She also recognized the change of conversation back to normal topics very intentional on Isabel's part to cover over any emotions she'd been feeling. Isabel didn't show affection easily.

Mary Helen glanced at the clock behind the register. It was only eleven in the morning, still early in the day. Suki was home in New York for a few days. Probably practicing, but Mary Helen didn't care. She walked over to sit behind the register, picked up the phone, and dialed her sister's number.

"Yes?" Suki answered after a few minutes, sounding distracted.

"Are you practicing?"

"Well, I *was*," she replied with that touch of irritation Suki always got when interrupted.

"Guess what?"

"What?" Suki asked, picking up on the tone of Mary Helen's voice now.

"Isabel Compton just offered me the opportunity to buy into The Little Mermaid and to eventually take full ownership of it."

Suki squealed. "Are you serious? I can't believe that? You used to wish for that when we were little." She paused. "But is it what you want now? You said before you didn't want to live in a small place like Edisto."

"I think there might be *someone* at Edisto now who is making me want to change my mind."

"Oh, Mary Helen, you're falling back in love with J.T." Suki's voice rose with excitement. "I knew it the last few times we talked. And he's been so sweet to you through all this time while you've been recovering."

Suki sniffed audibly and Mary Helen heard her snatch a tissue from nearby. "I'm already starting to cry I'm so happy for you both," she said. "I always knew J.T. had never stopped loving you. I could just tell. This is so wonderful. Has he proposed already?"

Mary Helen grinned, enjoying Suki's responses. She'd known it would be fun to call and share this news with her sister. "J.T. has proposed, actually more than once, but I haven't felt sure of my own feelings until lately. I think, though, I'm about ready to say yes now. I don't think I could leave him, Suki. My life and heart are all wrapped up in him. I haven't talked to Mother or Parker about this yet, or to anyone else, either. Only to you. So don't tell anyone yet. Okay?"

"I promise. You know I always keep your secrets."

"That's true, and I love that about you."

"You always keep mine, too." Suki sighed. "I guess this means you won't be moving back north near me. But at least whenever I can get time off I'll know you, Mother, and Parker all live in the same place now. That will be wonderful. I get a long break in December at the holidays this year, since I'm off tour for several weeks. I plan to come home, and I can't wait to see all of you." She grew quiet for a moment. "This is a lonely life even if exciting. You and I used to talk about that, how working at what we loved was wonderful but also time consuming and hard."

"Where are you traveling next?"

"To play with the Cincinnati Symphony Orchestra, then at a music festival in Hot Springs, Arkansas, then to Texas to play with the Dallas Symphony. Then there's an early holiday concert somewhere. I forget where. Then I get a long break for the holidays."

"You'll be busy. Bring home lots of pictures to show us at Christmas."

"I will. And promise you'll call me if you and J.T. get engaged. You tell him I said he'd better be romantic about proposing, too. A girl should always have a special story to tell about getting engaged."

Mary Helen hung up after a few minutes, realizing suddenly as she did that she was amazingly happy. She smiled at the new realization. How had that happened after all her earlier problems, sorrows, and disappointments?

The door opened, interrupting her thoughts and bringing in a group of customers, and Mary Helen put her thoughts away to get back to work.

The rest of the day kept her surprisingly busy, but after work she made her way up the familiar beach path to J.T.'s house. She and J.T. had fallen into a pattern of sharing dinner every evening, either at her place or his, when they didn't work late hours. They'd been learning to cook together, trying out some of Lula and Claire's favorite recipes and experimenting with others from cookbooks, borrowed from the library or bought on trips into Beaufort when they drove over to check on her parents' home.

Tonight they planned to grill shish kabobs with instructions they'd found in her mother's recipe box in Beaufort. J.T. had gotten off earlier than Mary Helen today and stopped by the Piggly Wiggly for all the needed ingredients, plus rice for a side. Knowing J.T., he'd probably picked up some calorie-laden rich dessert, too.

She found him in the kitchen, after letting herself in the back door, stirring up something on the stove.

"Hey," he said, turning to grin at her. "I've started heating the teriyaki sauce for the kabobs—soy sauce, ketchup, a little garlic powder, and ground ginger. It smells good."

She stopped in the kitchen door to watch him, a little twist coming to her heart at the sight of him. He wore old jeans and a golf shirt with Mikell's Island Rental embroidered on the front, his feet bare, without socks, in a pair of worn dock shoes—typical of him.

He turned the stove heat off, moving the saucepan to the side, and then turned to glance at her. "You're quiet. Are you okay?"

"I'm good." She smiled at him, letting go—at that very moment—of the last piece of her heart she'd held back for so long.

J.T. studied her as if sensing some change. "You look good, too." His eyes drifted over her and she felt the heat in his glance.

He always made her feel beautiful. "You are a very special man, J.T. Mikell."

"Glad to hear you acknowledge that." He winked at her. "Not every guy gives this much time learning to be a decent cook. How did you talk me into this anyway?"

"Mostly because neither of us knew how to make anything in the kitchen and we got tired of TV dinners."

He laughed and moved over to wrap her easily in his arms, kissing her in fun and then with that sizzling passion that always gave her a shiver right down to her toes. She closed her eyes, moving closer against him, letting all her senses open up to the taste, smell, and feel of him. How had she ever left him before? And what a blessing life had brought her back.

J.T. pulled back to look into her eyes. "You're really tempting me to abandon our idea of grilling shish kabobs tonight, you know."

She stepped away, pushing at him playfully. "Well, we can't have that. I'm hungry. Tell me what I need to do."

He studied her again, as if trying to figure out what was different with her tonight, and then shrugged. "Help me chop up the vegetables we need to thread onto the kabobs. Then I'll go put them on the grill outside while you make some rice, set the table, get some drinks out, and cut the apple pie I bought at the store.

How does that sound?"

"That sounds great." She sniffed the air. "That sauce really smells wonderful, doesn't it? I think we're going to like this recipe." She got a knife out of the drawer and started chopping up peppers and zucchini while J.T. rinsed off fresh mushrooms and cut up onion.

They loaded skewers with beef chunks, vegetables, fresh pineapple, and then lavishly basted sauce over each one. J.T. headed to the grill outside then, carrying extra sauce along to baste on the kabobs as he cooked them. While he was gone, Mary Helen got everything else ready, finding herself humming contentedly in the kitchen while she did.

They ate dinner a little later, J.T. chatting about his day and both of them catching up on island news. Over dessert, they finalized plans for the potluck dinner J.T. was hosting Friday night for a bunch of their friends.

"It's probably one of the last parties Jane will be able to attend with the baby due at the first of November," Mary Helen commented as they cleaned up after finishing dessert. "Are you dressing up for Halloween at your store?"

"Yeah. We all dress up as pirates every year. It fits with the dock store and water sports theme." He loaded the last of their dishes into the dishwasher. "What about you? Will you dress up?"

She put the last of the leftovers into the refrigerator. "We got some cute little black cat ears in at the Mermaid, so I thought I'd dress all in black, paint on some whiskers and a black nose, and add extra eyeliner around my eyes. It's an easy, cute look for a kids' store."

"Come by the rental store on Halloween if you can. We'll get Leon to take a photo of us together." He glanced around as he finished that thought. "With the kitchen cleaned up, do you want to take a walk?"

"Yes, I could use one. I always seem to eat too much with these great dinners we've been creating. You always buy desserts to tempt me, too. I try to stay away from those most of the time."

He swatted at her. "Well I know. At dinner at your house, you buy fruit or sherbet or some kind of diet ice cream for dessert."

"Quit fussing." She hung up the dishtowel she'd wiped the counter with. "You know you always bring a dessert with you that you like."

"It's a defensive action."

Still bantering, they walked up the beach together, enjoying the sight of the sun beginning to drop over the ocean, savoring the sounds of the waves lapping onto the beach. They caught the hum of voices and laughter drifting down from the beach houses and heard a few crickets and night frogs starting to sing. The beach in late October offered a quiet walk, with only a few others out enjoying the evening, all watching the full moon hanging over the water, leaving a golden pathway before it.

"It's nice to swing my arm again while I walk," Mary Helen commented, moving her arm in gratitude. "And to raise my arm over my head again."

"Your six-week check is Friday. I can drive you to Charleston to the doctor's office that day. I'd like to go with you."

"Okay. We can catch lunch after and celebrate six weeks being past. The doctor said I'd healed fast the last time I visited. I'll need to keep physical therapy going for a little longer, I guess, but the worst is over now." She caught his hand in hers as they walked. "Thanks for putting up with me through this hard time, J.T. I owe you for all the patience and kindness you've given me."

"It's what you do for someone you love, Mary Helen."

She sighed. "I know."

A little silence fell as they walked on.

Glancing ahead, Mary Helen said, "Let's go sit on that bench for a minute and watch the full moon."

J.T. laughed. "You know that's my proposal bench. Are you sure you want to pick that bench to watch the moon from? My mind tends to drift to subjects you'd rather avoid on that particular bench."

"I'll risk it," she said lightly.

They settled on the old bench not far from their beach homes, chatting for a few minutes and then growing silent as they watched the light from the moon sparkle across the water, creating a shimmering white highway across the waves.

"I love a full moon over the ocean," Mary Helen said, her voice soft.

J.T. drew in a long, deep breath. "I know your arm is almost healed now, Mary Helen. I'm sorry you broke your arm, but I've loved the extra time it's given me with you. I'm glad life brought you back here to Edisto, even if for a cruel reason." He leaned his head over, growing quiet. "I think I'll die when you leave me."

"Maybe you should ask me to stay."

He sat up and turned anguished eyes towards her. "Don't mess with me about this, Mary Helen."

She tucked a strand of hair back behind her ear the sea breeze had blown into her face. "I talked to Suki today. She said to tell you that when a girl gets a proposal it ought to be romantic and memorable."

He studied her face, trying to read her.

After looking out at the ocean for a few minutes he said, "When you were a saucy little kid and first came to Edisto, I started liking you for reasons I couldn't understand, even when I didn't want to. You argued with me about everything. You competed with me. You gloated when you beat me out at anything. You weren't like any girl I'd ever known. You were smart, but funny, stubborn and serious, but you could laugh with me until both our sides ached. No one was more fun to create crazy games with, to play hide-n-seek with, to ride bikes around the island with, singing at the top of our lungs. No one was more fun to take long walks on the beach with, to explore everything with. You made my life more vivid, more exciting."

He turned, moving closer and touching her face with one hand. "Then one day when we came up out of the waves, laughing, your hair wet, both of us drenched from a slap from a really huge breaker, I looked at you and my heart dropped to my knees. I knew from that minute on I was crazy about you in a new way. After that

I watched and waited for a chance to kiss you for the first time. I couldn't wait to see what it would be like and I wasn't disappointed. I think I fell in love with you that very minute."

J.T. looked back toward the ocean again. "My brother Ryder teased me about it. He said, 'How come when all the girls are crazy about you and run after you like they do, you're so crazy about Mary Helen Avery? Half the time she doesn't even like you.'" J.T. shook his head. "It was true, but you've always been the one for me, Mary Helen. I don't know if I can ever love anyone else. I honestly tried to in the years while you've been gone. I needed to forget, but I couldn't. I think I'm just a one-girl sort of guy."

His words had tears pooling in Mary Helen's eyes.

"Can you not decide to love me?" he asked, stroking his fingers down her arm, studying her with those rich dark eyes of his.

"I do love you," she answered quietly. "With all my heart."

His mouth dropped open, making her smile.

He touched her face. "That's the first time you've ever said that to me. Ever. Can you say it again, just so I can be sure I really heard you?"

"I love you, J.T. Mikell. I really do. I think, in a way, I always have."

He took her hands and kissed them one after another. "Will you stay with me, then, and not leave me?"

She grinned at him. "I've been thinking about staying at Edisto but I'd like a better reason to do so. Perhaps something more permanent."

His eyes widened in surprise and then he grinned back at her. "Never let it be said I'm not a romantic man." He dropped to one knee in the sand in front of her. "Beautiful woman, love of my life, will you consider spending your entire life with me here on Edisto, loving me always—and I do mean in every way—and sharing your life with me. I would count it a joy and a blessing if you would marry me. I will do all I can to make you happy."

She put her hands on either side of his face. "My answer is yes, J.T. Mikell." She gave him a saucy look. "But you had better get a nice ring for me if you want us to announce we've gotten engaged."

"I have that with me." He pulled the dog tag from out of his shirt, showing her the ring hanging on it. "I've been carrying it around just in case some miracle like this happened."

While she caught her breath in shock, he got up and sat down on the bench beside her again. Then he pulled the dog tag chain off his neck to get the ring off. "I got this ring in Charleston after one of those days when you dragged me shopping in one store after another. We went in Croghan's Jewelry so you could look for a gift for Isabel."

"I remember." Mary Helen smiled. "Isabel still collects silver charms for her charm bracelets. I think she wears three of them sometimes. I wanted to get her a new charm for her birthday in late September."

He nodded. "You got her a seahorse or something to add to her bracelet, but your eyes kept roving over the rings. You kept looking at this ring in particular. The lady asked if you wanted to try it on. You said no and sort of blushed then, saying it looked too much like an engagement ring even if it was gorgeous."

She took the ring he handed to her. "And you remembered that and went back to get this? It's beautiful—silver-white platinum, with this lovely square diamond and a timeless, European look." She slipped it on to find it fit perfectly. "How did you know what size to get?"

"You tried on other rings that day. I paid attention."

She studied the ring, holding her hand up to admire it. "You shouldn't have gotten something so expensive. This is not a tiny diamond."

"It wasn't a problem, Mary Helen."

She looked at him, smiling. "And you've worn it around your neck on your dog tag all this time, hoping I would say yes?"

He nodded. "I asked once not long after I bought the ring, but you said you were still trying to know your heart and what you wanted to do."

"But you kept wearing the ring anyway."

"I never gave up hope. How could I?"

Mary Helen touched his face. "I don't deserve such love and kindness. I haven't always been fair or kind to you, J.T. Instead, I've often been suspicious and selfish. Frequently sarcastic and never as encouraging as I should have been about your dreams and goals."

He shrugged. "We were kids when love caught us somewhat unaware. Despite our feelings, we had different dreams, too. Mine here, yours bigger, somewhere else." He paused, leaning over to trace his fingers down her cheek. "I hope you won't have regrets, staying on Edisto. That you won't feel unfulfilled here. I know you wanted more."

She leaned over to give him a kiss, which, of course, progressed into more kissing for a time. Then she pulled back when his hands began to wander places they didn't need to go.

"I'm a preacher's girl and the wait-until-you-get-married-type," she told him, scooting a little further away from him.

"I know," he said, moving back. "I just got a little excited."

She smiled at him. "Well, you hang onto that excitement. We've waited this long. We can wait a little longer."

"Not too long though, okay?"

She looked out to sea, thinking. "How about over the Christmas holidays? Mother and Parker will be back. Suki is coming home for a few weeks in December. Who knows when she'll get a holiday to come home again with her busy schedule. And I want her to be our maid-of-honor."

J.T.'s eyes lit. "Christmas would be great!" He hesitated. "Can we tell our family and friends about this? Or do you need more time to think about it. Whatever you decide is best."

She ran her hands through his dark hair, pushing back that piece that always drifted down over his forehead, before kissing him again. "If you think about it, you'll remember I am generally a very decisive person. I may be slow to make up my mind on occasions, but once I do, the issue is settled. I won't be changing my mind, J.T."

He stood up then, pulling her from the bench to swing her around, making her laugh. "You've made me a happy man tonight, Mary Helen Avery."

They kissed, giggled, and goofed around in their joy, celebrating, until a family walking down the beach interrupted them, making them both draw back.

"I guess we should walk back now," Mary Helen said, looking at her watch. "We both have to work tomorrow."

"Will you keep working at the Mermaid?" J.T. asked as they started down the beach. "We could find a place for you in the business if you want. Your retail skills would be an asset. I know you'll want to stay busy."

She smiled at him. "As it happens, Isabel has offered to let me buy into the Mermaid. We'll partner at first and later the little store will be mine. I think that might be enough to satisfy me and keep me busy. You know I've always loved The Little Mermaid, and I love working with Isabel."

He stopped to look at her, his mouth dropping open again. "That's terrific. When did this happen?"

"Today," she admitted. "Isabel asked me some pointed questions about our relationship first and as she did I realized my own feelings had moved past the holding point where I'd kept them stalled. That helped Isabel realize she could make the offer to me. She knew one of the reasons I ran away before was because we had problems."

They walked on as Mary Helen finished her thoughts. "I think I needed to leave for a time, J.T., to grow up and to learn, to see what I could do."

"I knew you wanted that chance to leave the island, even before our other problems."

She smiled at him. "I was never as certain as you about my direction, about what I wanted most to be happy and fulfilled. You were lucky that you knew early what you wanted. Most people don't."

"Will you be content with island life, working at the Mermaid, living here, raising our kids at Edisto?"

"I wasn't sure I would be at first, but staying here these months has made me realize how happy I am on the island. Suki always called it her happy place, but it took me a while to see it's mine, too."

She paused and started to tell him then that somewhat like Floraleaf in one of her mother's books, she felt certain now she'd be content to live her life in the Farnsworth Forest that was Edisto, but she doubted J.T. would remember the fanciful story. She'd save that thought to share with her mother later on.

CHAPTER 18

J.T. often hosted get-togethers for his friends at his house on the beach with its spacious broad porches, but this Friday's event was especially exciting since everyone knew he and Mary Helen were officially engaged.

"I thought we'd announce our engagement tonight, but word got out and everybody already knows," Mary Helen grumbled Friday afternoon as they set up extra tables and folding chairs before their friends arrived.

"The island is small. It's almost impossible to keep secrets here. And if you remember, we did run into Isabel and Elaine taking a walk on the beach the other night on our way back to your house."

Mary Helen sent him a small smile, her mood shifting. "They said we were both glowing, and of course I had on my ring." She held it up to admire it. "I'll be a Sadie soon."

"A what?" J.T. turned to her in question.

She giggled. "It's from the movie *Funny Girl*. You remember—when Barbra Streisand sang about Sadie, Sadie the married lady."

"That's another of those musicals your mother loved so much, but I remember that old movie, too." He set up the last folding chair and then moved over to wrap her up in a warm hug and kiss her. "I'm really looking forward to you being a Sadie and to enjoying new adventures with you." He nibbled at her ear and then let his lips trail down her neck.

"I think I'm looking forward to those adventures myself." She gave him a quick kiss but then pulled away with a little grin. "We need to quit playing around and finish setting up. We have friends coming any time."

"The night is young." He winked at her.

Ignoring him, she spread tablecloths and an embroidered table runner over the two long tables they'd set up for everyone to eat on tonight and began to decorate. She always had a way of making everything look special.

"It was nice of you to invite Farlin and Yvonne to come tonight," he said watching her. "Leon and Vernita have visited our get-togethers many times, but I hadn't thought to invite Farlin and Yvonne."

She paused to look at him. "You're all right with that aren't you? Farlin is Vernita's brother, both of them Kizzy and Lewis's kids. We've known them forever. You work with Leon, and we've gotten to know Farlin popping in at the AME church every once in a while when we're off on Sunday."

"It was a great idea to include them. I hope they'll come to our wedding."

"Are you okay with having the wedding at my home church in Beaufort? It will make it easier for Mother and Parker. We know a lot of people in Beaufort and at the church there."

"The wedding should be in your home church. We haven't settled into a church here on the island yet, always working so many Sundays. You've visited my family's church, the Edisto Island Presbyterian Church, once or twice with me. I know my parents' and grandparents' friends will drive over to Beaufort for the wedding though. No problem."

"I think all our friends on the island will come, too, if they can," Mary Helen added.

"Everything will be awesome," he assured her. "Mom says everyone loves a holiday wedding." J.T. began to set out paper plates, tucking the plates into wicker holders. Beside each he added a Mason jar glass with plastic cutlery tucked inside. He liked to go simple for parties, with throwaway plates and plastic silverware.

"I love those Mason jar drinking glasses with the handles. Where did you get those?"

"I ordered a case of them through work, about sixty for eight dollars, I think. A great deal. We sold some at the store but I brought home about a dozen to use for get-togethers. I like them better than plastic cups."

"Me, too, and they look great with the wicker plate holders and the blue tablecloths I found on a shelf in the kitchen closet."

"Mom left those behind when she moved, along with the matching napkins and that runner with the seashells on it."

"Lula is so excited about us getting married." Mary Helen finished arranging the seagrass basket of shells she'd put together for a centerpiece and began to set a couple of candles around it, each tucked into shiny votive candle holders she'd brought with her from Oleanders.

J.T. looked at the nice table arrangement she'd created. "Marrying a visual merchandiser, I can always be assured of great decorations for every event." He watched her fold the cloth napkins into artful shapes, putting one on each plate.

She smiled at him. "I like things to look nice."

"You look nice tonight, too." His eyes moved over her trim brown slacks, long, creamy white blouse with small tucks at the top, silver hoop earrings, and strappy sandals.

"Thanks." She glanced toward the beach. "This will probably be the last outdoor event we can host for a time. We're lucky for the warm temperatures this weekend so we can still eat outside. It went up to seventy today."

"It has been warm lately. Good weather helps tourism, too. Our Mikell shops stayed busy last weekend, and I know the Mermaid did, too."

Their friends began to arrive. J.T. and Mary Helen had made a big pot of shrimp, crab, and sausage gumbo to serve over grits. Vernita was bringing a corn casserole, Yvonne a bean salad, Andrew bread, Emma jugs of peach tea, Chuck a few bags of ice, and Jane a carrot cake for dessert. When everyone helped with food and drinks, it made the evening more fun and J.T.'s preparation load lighter. In the past Chuck used to come to help him set up, but now Mary Helen helped. And tonight Chuck asked to bring someone.

"This is Antonia, or Toni, Legare." He introduced J.T. to a pretty girl with reddish shoulder-length hair, grayish-green eyes and a warm, friendly smile—a nicer, more intelligent type than Chuck usually hung around with.

"Glad to meet you." J. T. shook her hand. "Are you kin to any of the Legares around here?"

"My family are from Johns Island but I know Legares also lived here on Edisto and in Charleston as far back as the 1700s. They're probably all interrelated somewhere." She laughed. "My grandmother is in the Daughters of the American Revolution and she tells me family stories all the time."

Chuck moved in closer as if worrying about competition from J.T. "Toni is working in the golf shop over at Fairfield," he added. "We met there."

"Chuck is a great golfer." Toni flashed him one of her smiles.

"You're pretty good yourself," he said back.

Chuck introduced Toni to Mary Helen and then took Toni around to begin introducing her to others.

"She seems nice," Mary Helen said, watching them.

J.T. nodded. "Yes, and not the norm for Chuck to date. He's acting rather territorial about this one, too."

Mary Helen snorted. "Don't make women sound like possessions."

He shrugged. "You know what I mean."

"Yes, all too well." She swatted at him, before wandering away to mingle and help Vernita and Jane arrange food on the side buffet table.

J.T. soon brought out the big shrimp pot, filled with hot gumbo, and a deep pan of buttered grits he and Mary Helen had kept warm on the stove. Everyone soon piled their plates with gumbo over grits, corn casserole, bean salad, cheesy garlic bread, and poured themselves cold glasses of peach tea.

"I love this bean salad," Mary Helen said. "What's in it?

Yvonne smiled. "Green beans, black-eyed peas, and lima beans that Mama and I picked from the garden this summer and froze. You cook them a little, toss all the beans in a bowl and add chopped onion, lemon juice, fresh dill, some olive oil, and black pepper. It's simple to make."

"The simple things are usually the best." Mary Helen took another bite of the salad. "It helps that the beans are from your garden, too."

Emma interrupted their talk of food with a question. "Yvonne, don't you and Vernita both teach over at Jane Edwards Elementary?"

"We do," she answered. "I teach first grade and Vernita teaches fourth. That's where Vernita and I met and that's how I met her brother Farlin, too. Vernita brought me to church and then to one of her family's Sunday dinners."

"I was smitten immediately," Farlin put in.

Yvonne winked at him. "We did hit it off well from the first."

They all visited and caught up over dinner. Toni joined in as if she'd always been one of their group, and even Bear enjoyed a good time.

"I'm sorry we had to bring Bear," Jane apologized, glancing toward the big dog. "The new babysitter we found is wonderful with Elena but she is terrified of Bear."

"She had some sort of traumatic experience with a dog as a small child," Barton explained. "We didn't realize she feared dogs so much until she got to our place tonight. Even when we promised to put Bear out in the fenced back yard, she didn't want to stay. It was too late to find another sitter, so we decided to bring Bear with us."

"I'm glad you brought Bear," Leon said. "Vernita and I sure miss our dog Rinny. We've liked having Bear here."

Chuck piped in. "Dad said the police let those two guys out on bail until their trial comes up. They only found proof for one burglary and it was a first offense for both."

"Well, they'd be stupid to try anything else while out on bail,"

Leon said. "But I heard the police aren't even pressing charges for them killing the dog."

"That doesn't seem right," Andrew said. "A lot of nice dogs got poisoned."

"Yes, but there were no witnesses or evidence to any of those deaths and the links between the poisonings to the other burglaries are sketchy at best," Chuck explained. "The men probably won't get more than a fine and a slap on the wrist tacked on in relation to any of the dog deaths."

They were all quiet for a minute, upset over this news.

"Let's talk about something happier," Jane said.

"Yes," agreed Farlin, his eyes moving to J.T. and Mary Helen. "Let's talk about your wedding. Tell us your plans so far. We're all so happy the Lord brought you two together."

J.T. tried to hide a smirk, thinking the Lord hadn't faced an easy time of it getting the two of them together.

Mary Helen glanced at him with a warning look, as if reading his thoughts, and then turned a bright smile toward Farlin. "You are sweet to ask, Farlin, and J.T. and I hope you and Yvonne will both come to our wedding. Right now our plans are to get married on the Saturday before Christmas week when my sister can be home. The service will be in my parents and my church in Beaufort in the afternoon at 3:00 pm. After the service we hope to have a reception and a small buffet dinner in the fellowship hall behind the church. Neither of us want a fancy event with drinking or dancing, but we do want to have a receiving line to greet everyone who comes. We also want to cut the cake together and provide dinner for everyone and a time to visit."

She paused, thinking. "J.T. and I thought we might get the church organist and pianist, Morgan Dillon, who was Suki's old piano teacher and is in the Beaufort Symphony, to locate a chamber group to play soft music at the reception. We only want something simple. However, we can't finalize the date or any other plans exactly until my parents come home next week."

"Your plans sound lovely," Vernita said. "We'll come if we can."

J.T. got up to pour more tea from a big pitcher on the side table. "Ryder will be my best man and I'm hoping Chuck, Tom, and Andrew will be groomsmen. Suki will be Mary Helen's maid of honor, of course, and she wants Jane and Emma as bridesmaids, along with her best friend from school years, Chelsey Mitchell Berle."

"I remember Chelsey," Jane put in. "Mary Helen used to bring her down to the beach sometimes. When I went to Waterview to spend the night we ran around with her, too. Chelsey moved when she married, didn't she?"

"She and her husband Wyatt, and two little girls, live at St. Simons, Georgia, now," Mary Helen answered. "He's an administrator with the Chamber of Commerce. I was in Chelsey's wedding and her parents still live near Parker and Mother—and are friends of theirs. I think Chelsey will come for the wedding and be happy to do so. We've stayed in touch. I had hoped to drive down to see her before I broke my arm this fall."

"I'll take you down one day," J.T. offered. "It's only a three hour drive. We can go and come back on one of our days off."

"I'd like that. Thanks." She beamed at him, and as J.T. smiled back at her with pleasure, he wondered if he'd ever get used to being back in her favor again. Or get used to the fact that she loved him and had agreed to marry him. It still totally blew him away and sometimes felt unreal.

They all laughed and talked as darkness fell. Mary Helen lit the candles on the table and turned on a lamp inside, careful not to use too many outdoor lights because of the turtles. Jane passed around slices of the rich carrot cake she'd brought, each topped with a big dollop of whipped cream.

Later on, while Farlin was telling a funny story, J.T. noticed out of the side of his eye that Winifred Meggett was starting up the beach path to his house. *Wonder what she wants?* he thought. Then he saw that she dragged Bear along behind her with a rope tied to his collar.

J.T. stood and so did Barton, spotting his dog.

"Does this dog—or whatever this beast is—belong to any of you?" Winifred called out, stopping at the bottom of the porch steps. Her face, blotched and angry, moved over the group of friends as if looking for the guilty party.

"That's our dog," Barton said, walking down the steps toward Winifred. "He must have slipped away while we were eating and visiting. I thought he was sleeping in the corner of the porch." He glanced back toward the spot. "I'm sorry if he bothered you."

"*If* he bothered me?" She glared at him. "He bothered me, all right. I came walking down the beach and found him digging up a turtle nest and eating the eggs like a big glutton. He ruined the nest, tore down the tape around it, and trampled on everything. The eggs he didn't eat he stomped all over with his big feet."

"We're really sorry Bear slipped away and caused a little problem with the turtle nest," Jane said, coming down the steps, to stand by Barton, and leaning over to pet Bear.

Winifred's face flamed. "A *little* problem, you say? Do you know how many turtles that dog killed? There were over one hundred eggs in that nest. One hundred." She glared at Jane. "You as a mother-to-be, heavy with child like you are, ought to see those lives as precious. Would you see it as a little problem if someone destroyed your baby before it could see life?"

"Now listen here," Barton said, his voice growing steely. "You've gone far enough with this. You don't need to attack Jane. We said we're sorry."

J.T. frowned. "You need to back off from this, Winnie. The dog slipped away while we visited. We are sorry about it. I assume you're talking about the turtle nest five or six yards up the beach, so Bear hadn't gone far from the house. And dogs will be dogs sometimes."

"Dogs will be dogs!" She almost hollered the words. "Is that all you have to say about this? What about those turtles?"

Mary Helen came down the stairs, too. "Winifred, I know how upset you must be, as much as you watch over the turtles. All of us truly regret that Bear got away and caused damage to the nest."

She paused, thinking. "Can J.T. and I help you clean up the area, put back the stakes or the tape? Is there anything we can do?"

"No." She glared at Bear, her eyes narrowed. "There's nothing anyone can do now. But you can see to it that this dog isn't allowed on this beach again anytime soon and, hopefully, *never* on this beach again off his leash."

"Winifred, I can promise you won't see Bear this weekend while you're so upset," Mary Helen assured her. "Barton and Jane are going away this weekend for some time together before the baby comes, and I'm sure from now on they will try to watch Bear more closely whenever they come down to the beach."

Jane stepped forward. "I can assure you we will, Ms. Meggett, and, again, we are so sorry this happened. Barton and I love the sea turtles, too, and regret Bear dug up the nest like he did."

Winnie glared at the dog, sitting beside Barton, as she turned to leave. Bear wagged his tail at her with doggy friendliness, not seeming to realize how upset she was with him at all.

"You call your dog Bear." Winnie all but hissed the comment as she left. "That's certainly an appropriate name for him; he's practically the size of a bear." She glared at Barton. "A dog that big doesn't have any place on the beach any time. He can dig up dunes and cause destruction to other sea animals and birds."

J.T. stepped forward. "A dog doesn't cause any more trouble than people, Winnie, and you well know it," he added, annoyed. "People cause far more problems to the environment here at Edisto than any *one* dog ever could."

Winnie shook her head and walked off, still grumbling.

"Boy, she was really upset," Mary Helen said, watching Winifred stomp off down the beach.

"I so regret this," Barton said, running his hand over his neck. "I'm not sure when Bear slipped off the porch. I should have kept a better eye on him."

J. T. slapped Barton on the back fondly. "We were all eating and talking, and forgot about him. Don't beat yourself up too badly over this. My guess is that Bear went down the steps to take a leak, walked around a little, and then picked up the scent of the turtles. Instinct kicked in then. It's the way animals are made. They don't think things out like we do."

"I do feel awful about this though." Jane rubbed her belly as she spoke. "Winifred will probably never speak to us again and I imagine she'll tell everyone Bear is a horrible dog."

J.T. shook his head, leading the way back up the steps to the porch again. "Don't worry about that either. Everyone calls her Wacky Winnie, and no one pays much attention to her ongoing theatrics. She's always irritated at someone and mad about something."

Barton glanced at his watch as they walked back up to the porch to join the others. "I think we'll go on home now. We enjoyed the evening, but Elena is with the new babysitter tonight, and I know Jane is tired. Her due date is only two weeks away now."

Cleaning up later after everyone left, Mary Helen said, "Winifred really put a damper on the evening, didn't she?"

"Yes and you can see more easily now why Winnie isn't better loved around here. She seldom handles anything diplomatically— just attacks and blames. It isn't like we weren't all sorry about the turtle eggs, too," J.T. replied, pausing to look with regret toward where the nest had been. He'd walked down the beach with Leon before he and Vernita left to see that the turtle nest had been completely annihilated.

CHAPTER 19

On Saturday after work, Mary Helen walked over to J.T.'s for dinner to share leftovers from the night before.

"I hope you don't mind eating gumbo again tonight," J.T. said, as they each carried a plate loaded with food out to the porch.

"No. The recipe turned out great, and Vernita and Yvonne insisted on leaving the last of their corn and bean dishes behind, too." Mary Helen sat down in her favorite spot at the table on the porch. The slatted wood outdoor table, weathered gray with a driftwood finish, had matching chairs with comfortable cushioned seats.

Mary Helen loved this beautiful beach house, named Point Place—a deep, gray two-storied home trimmed in crisp white, raised high off the ground to protect it from the ocean washing in during harsh storms. The home sat two doors away from Oleanders, tucked among palms, shrubs, and yucca with a pretty stairway leading to the front porch and dark green ivy trailing around the garage doors. On the back of the house J.T.'s parents had built a wide covered porch, open to the sea breezes, but sheltered from the fiercer winds and blazing sun—a lovely oasis looking out across the dunes and the wide beach to the Atlantic Ocean.

J.T. settled into a chair beside Mary Helen's. They'd already brought out bread, bottles of water, and glasses of wine to make the evening special.

"Here's to us." J.T. lifted his glass to click hers.

"Sometimes this doesn't feel real, does it?" She smiled at him.

"No, it doesn't, but I'm sure happy about it. I'm getting real comfortable spending my evenings with you, sharing dinner like this. I'm a fortunate man."

They ate for a time, chatting about their day.

"I'm glad Farlin encouraged us to call the minister to tentatively schedule the church in Beaufort, even thought Mother and Parker aren't back yet," Mary Helen said. "The date and time we wanted were still open. So we're good to go. He suggested we come by later to talk more."

J.T. nodded. "Yeah. You said we needed to set a counseling appointment with him. That's pretty standard I think."

"The minister is nice. You'll like him."

J.T. dug into his meal for a few minutes and then paused. "We're both off tomorrow on Sunday. Do you want to take the boat over to Beaufort to check on your parents' place?"

"That's probably a good idea. Andrew pops in to check on the house occasionally, since Parker gave him a key. I still like to check myself though, and assure Mother and Parker all is well when they call."

"They usually call on Sunday night. Will you tell them we got engaged when you talk with them tomorrow?"

She wrinkled her nose. "I think I'll need to. Mother would be unhappy to learn later I hadn't told her right away."

"Do you think she'll be glad?"

"Yes." She lowered her eyes. "She already told me she and Parker both love you and would be pleased if we got back together again."

"Nice to know." He grinned at her. "My family are thrilled, too, so at least we won't have to worry about in-law problems."

She laughed. "No, and that's a relief."

When they finished dinner, Mary Helen went in the house to bring out two generous slices of carrot cake from the dessert Jane left behind. "Jane insisted on leaving this since she and Barton would be gone through Sunday for their little trip. Barton's parents in Walterboro are keeping Elena."

"It's nice they could snag a private weekend together before the new baby comes," J.T said, forking into his cake.

"Yes. Their lives will get busy with two little ones," Mary Helen agreed.

"This cake is fantastic," J.T shifted the subject.

"It is, isn't it?" Mary Helen licked creamed frosting off her fork. "Jane said the recipe was passed down to her mother from her grandmother. Those old family recipes are always the best, don't you think?"

"Yeah." J.T. glanced out toward the beach to see a small woman shading her eyes and looking up the path toward them. "Who's that?"

"Hmmm." Mary Helen said, "I think that's Winifred's friend Evelyn Dalton. Remember, we met her on the beach one day?"

"Yeah, I think you're right. She has that little dog with her again. Putney, I think she called him."

Mary Helen waved at the woman, and she started up the pathway toward them.

"Wonder what she wants?" J.T. asked.

"I don't know." Mary Helen stood to welcome Evelyn, inviting her to come up on the porch.

"I hate to be a bother," she said, climbing the stairs, the little dog trotting beside her.

"You're no bother at all," Mary Helen assured her. "It's nice of you to drop by to say hello. We're just finishing dinner." She reached down to pet Putney who was wagging his tail like a flag. "Would you like some iced tea or a piece of carrot cake?" She gestured toward the remnants of cake on their plates.

"No, no." She sat in the chair Mary Helen indicated, and J.T. noticed she kept twisting her hands, obviously uncomfortable.

"Is anything wrong, Evelyn?" J.T. asked, deciding to help her along.

"Well, I don't know." She bit her lip. "I'll admit I asked around to find out where you lived and walked over here hoping to find you."

"How can we help you?" Mary Helen asked, offering an encouraging smile.

"It's Winnie. I'm worried about her."

Mary Helen stiffened. "I'm sure you heard about the dog getting into the turtle nest. We're sorry about that. It really was an accident."

J.T. grinned. "Did Winnie send you to fuss at us about it?"

Evelyn's eyes widened. "Oh, heavens, no. She'd be really upset if she even knew I was here." She rubbed her hands together, anxious.

"Why don't you tell us what you're worried about," J.T. said in a steady voice. "You obviously have something on your mind."

She took a breath. "Winnie was really upset about that dog. She's been angry ever since, too, keeps talking about it. Today she carried on and on over it when we had lunch together. She kept saying something needed to be done, that this island didn't need a dog like that around. It made me uncomfortable."

J.T. leaned forward, alert to the undertones in Evelyn's words now. "Do you think she'll try to harm Bear, Evelyn?"

"I'm not sure." She twisted her hands again. "She kept talking about where the dog lived, said she'd driven by the house, that its owners were out of town. How could she know those things? And why would she drive way up island to someone's house like that? It's worried me all afternoon."

"Oh, my." Mary Helen put a hand to her mouth. "I did mention to Winifred that Jane and Barton were going on a trip this weekend. I meant to reassure her that she wouldn't see Bear on the beach any time soon."

J.T. interrupted. "Mary Helen, your comments didn't tell Winnie where Jane and Barton lived. And like Evelyn said, what business would Winnie have hunting up their address and driving to their neighborhood?" He stopped to think. "Did Winnie say anything else that made you think she might try to hurt Bear?"

Evelyn sighed. "I feel bad even talking about this, but little comments from the past kept coming into my mind. Like times she said it was a good thing certain dogs were gone, when we read of another death in the paper, or times she didn't seem upset when I felt heartbroken for the owners." She reached down to pet the little dog at her feet. "I remember wondering out loud, after we read a news article, how someone could even poison a dog. She said you could put rat poison, antifreeze, chemicals, or even toxic plants in a dog's food and that they would just wolf it right down, greedy and stupid. I didn't like her saying that."

Evelyn rubbed her neck. "I know Winnie is a teacher, and smarter than me, but all of it together started to make me worry. Then I remembered what you asked her on the beach that day, if she'd poisoned those dogs. I thought it awful you asked her that, but the way she acted and talked today made me remember it. That's why I came here. Do you think I'm being silly?"

"No, you are right to be concerned." J.T. crossed his arms, tensing. "People like Winifred who get so involved in causes often lose sight of right and wrong when they believe their actions benefit a cause."

"She is strong-minded on the subject..." Evelyn's voice trailed off.

Mary Helen's mouth tightened. "Do you two really believe Winnie might try to kill Bear over this?"

"It's possible," J.T answered. He turned to Evelyn. "Is there anything else you remember her saying?"

Evelyn sighed. "She canceled our plans to go to a movie in Charleston tonight, one she really wanted to see. She said something had come up, something important she needed to take care of." She shivered. "Winnie was acting odd and animated, even for her. I didn't know what to do. I felt so awful imagining Winnie might hurt someone's pet. In some ways I felt it wasn't any of my business at all, but then I remembered what you said—to let you know if we learned anything." She reached down to stroke a hand over her dog's head again. "I kept thinking how I'd feel if someone wanted to hurt Putney. So I came to you. I thought you might not think me awful, like someone else would."

"I don't think you're awful." A muscle in J.T.'s jaw bunched. "I'm really glad you came to warn me that Bear might be in trouble, too."

"What do you think we should do?" Mary Helen asked, biting her lip. "Should we call the police? Or call Barton and Jane and ask them to come home? I know they always leave Bear in their fenced yard when they go away for a night or two. Barton and Jane live on a quiet little street. It's never been a problem, and Jane says he's much happier at home than at the vet's. Barton made a big dog door leading into their garage so Bear can go inside to eat and sleep. Jane told me Barton's friend stops over every day to check on Bear, too."

"Will you call the police?" Evelyn asked.

J.T. shook his head. "No, and I don't want to call Barton or Jane. She's due a baby soon, and this would upset her. I know Barton's friend Isaac who looks after Bear. I've gone fishing with him and Barton before. I'll call Isaac and one of us will go over and stay at Barton and Jane's house tonight, and maybe tomorrow if needed, to be sure Bear is safe. My guess is that if Winnie has plans to try to hurt Bear, she'll do it at night—and possibly tonight since she told you something had come up she needed to do."

Evelyn sighed. "Thank you. I'm so glad I came to see you. Winnie said one day not long ago it was a shame those men got caught who shot that dog. Can you believe she would say that?" She looked shocked. "Her comments here and there have really troubled me lately. I hate to believe she would hurt a dog, but she's been very angry about that turtle nest."

"Someone staying at the house will keep Winnie from hurting Bear if she really planned to," Mary Helen assured her. "So don't worry, Evelyn, and thank you for coming to talk to us. I know it wasn't easy when Winnie is your friend."

Evelyn stood up. "Winnie is an odd friend, if you know what I mean. But she's smart and interesting when she isn't on one of her bandwagons. We've enjoyed some nice times together." She picked up Putney's leash. "Maybe Winnie will calm down after a few days go by. She might simply have been making idle threats while angry."

"I hope so," J.T. said. "Thanks again for coming to talk with us. We appreciate it. Barton and Jane are good friends of ours."

"Will you let me know if there is anything else I can do?" Evelyn asked.

"Absolutely," Mary Helen told her. "And you and Putney will both sleep better tonight knowing Bear will be safe."

They stood by the porch rail watching Evelyn walk back down the beach. Mary Helen waved at her as she turned to look back at them.

"Oh, my gosh," she said then. "Do you really think Winifred will try to hurt Bear tonight?"

"Yes, I do."

She ran a hand through her hair. "Are you going to call Barton's friend Isaac to tell him about this?"

"I could, but Isaac Pope staying at the house tonight or keeping Bear inside won't keep Winnie from trying to hurt him another day in future."

Her eyes met his, suspicious now. "What are you planning to do, J.T. Mikell? I can see that mind of yours ticking away."

"I'm going to do a stakeout near the house and hopefully catch her."

"You're what?" Her mouth dropped open. "That might be dangerous!"

His lips twitched. "No, it won't. The danger is to Bear. The danger is also to other dogs on this island if Winnie is poisoning dogs she thinks are a threat to the turtles and the island's wildlife. She needs to be caught and stopped."

Mary Helen put her hands on her hips. "So you've decided you're the one to do that?"

"Why not? Someone needs to."

"I don't like this idea." She put a hand on his arm. "What exactly are you planning to do on this stakeout?"

"Like you said, Bear will be out in the fence or in the garage.

You can see both areas clearly from that hill that sits between their house and the new construction home two lots over. Barton walked me all around the property when he and Jane bought the house. I remember I could see the yard and the back of the house from that hill, and I can be down that hill to the house in less than five minutes. It's time Winifred Megget was stopped."

"So you're going to sit over there on that hill all night in the dark watching the house?"

"If I have to, but I think she'll come early, just waiting until it's good and dark. I don't think I'll have to stay all night."

"Maybe you should call Isaac and get him to go with you."

"He's a nice guy, but I don't know him very well. He might offer different ideas about how to handle this. He might not even believe Evelyn's warning. He might call Barton—which I don't want, or he might call the police."

"Maybe *you* should call the police."

He looked at her in irritation. "And tell them what? Do you think they'll believe Evelyn's supposition? If they did, which is unlikely, they might contact Winnie and alert her. I don't want that."

"What will you do to be safe out there in the dark?"

He grinned at her. "Haven't you ever done a stakeout? Grandad, Dad, and I have done a few to catch vagrants or petty thieves on our property. You dress in dark clothes, put on a lot of bug spray, take a backpack with a few things you might need, find a good vantage spot, and then watch and wait. It's boring but it works."

She gave him a mulish look. "Then if you won't take Isaac, I'm going with you."

He rolled his eyes. "That's not a good idea."

"Because it's a man's job?" she said sarcastically.

"I didn't say that. But most people wouldn't like it." He began to pile up the plates and glasses left on the table. "You'd be happier at home, getting a good night's rest." He glanced toward the darkening sky. "However, I need to get on my way; it will be dark soon."

"Tell me what to put on and what to bring. I'm going with you."

He walked over and kissed her. "Honey, it's not going to be an easy night. You'll soon regret coming along, and I won't be able to leave the stakeout to bring you back."

"I won't expect you to, and two sets of eyes are better than one. I'll bring my cell phone and if there's more trouble than you expect, I can call someone. Besides, Winnie will be more intimidated with both of us there—if she even comes—and it will be two individuals' words against hers if she denies trying to harm Bear later."

He studied her for a minute. "You're a stubborn woman, but if you insist on coming, go put on jeans, dark clothes, dark shoes or boots, nothing white that can be seen in the dark. I've got a black backpack you can throw a few personal things in. I don't know how long we'll be out there. There's a side street I know of nearby where I can park the car and leave it. We'll walk in by a back path I know. I don't want my car visible."

"Why don't we drive my dark blue Camry? Your sporty little MG stands out, even on a side road. Someone might recognize it, too."

"Smart thinking." He picked up the dishes from the table to carry inside. "I'll be over in about fifteen minutes. It's getting dark. I don't have extra time."

She followed him inside to get her purse to drape over her shoulder. "I get the message. I'll be ready." She hesitated starting out the door. "Are you planning to take a gun, J.T.?"

He turned to look at her. "I plan to put my snake gun in my backpack and a good knife. The gun is a lightweight revolver. I know how to use it if I have to. We'll be outdoors at night. You wouldn't want me not to take it."

She considered his words. "All right then."

Mary Helen walked back to Oleanders, wishing she could think of a way to talk J.T. out of this stakeout idea. But she'd known J.T. Mikell most all her life. If he was determined to go, he'd go. Resigned and shaking her head, she headed into the house to throw on some old clothes and get ready.

A little later, after they parked her car on a side road that led to a marsh pond and dead end, J.T. led them on a trail winding up and over the hill to come out behind Barton and Jane's house.

"There's their house." Mary Helen pointed down the hill. "You're right. You can see all the back yard clearly from here with the outdoor lights on."

J.T. looked around until he found a good spot where they could lean their backs against two trees with some brush cover in front of them. "This will be a good stakeout spot," he said. He pulled a worn vinyl cloth from his backpack, doubling it and spreading it on the ground in front of the trees. "We can sit on this to keep the damp from seeping up through the ground and lean back against those tree trunks."

"Smart." She settled down on the cloth. "Were you a Boy Scout?"

"No. We didn't have a troop here on the island. Dad took us to one beyond Hollywood, near Charleston, for a while, but it was too far to attend regularly. We learned our scouting lessons with Dad, Grandad, or other men on the island, like Pete Whaley. Because we grew up in the outdoors and spent time hunting in the woods or fishing on the back creeks in the marshes, we had to know how to take care of ourselves."

"What do we do now?" she asked as J.T. sat down beside her, leaning back against the other tree.

"We watch and wait and talk very quietly. Sound carries. Keep your eyes scanning the property and the woods behind it. Scan the fence every few minutes, the sides of the house, along the garage, under the deck. I remember Leon said someone must have found a way into their fence to put out poisoned food for Rinny."

"Oh, my, I hate to think Winnie was the one who poisoned Leon and Vernita's shepherd." She zipped her jacket against the night air. "Wouldn't Rinny have barked, tried to attack an intruder?"

"Leon and I always wondered about that." He crossed his legs, trying to get comfortable. "If it was Winnie though, a woman Rinny often saw on the beach, and a woman with a gift with animals, he might have viewed her as a friend."

"Don't you remember Winnie hauled Bear back with a rope around his neck the other night though? Bear might not see her as a friend."

J.T. laughed softly. "Although Winnie was glaring daggers at Bear before she left, Bear just wagged his tail and grinned his doggy grin at her. He didn't seem to realize she was even mad at him."

"Ah, I see," she said. "So even if Bear recognizes Winnie—if she comes tonight—he might not view her as a possible threat."

He nodded. "I doubt that he would. I'm sure she'll sweet talk Bear, act friendly, and she'll be carrying food, too—probably something rich and meaty with a good smell. Never let it be said that Winifred Meggett is stupid."

Mary Helen closed her eyes and leaned her head back. "I'm still having such a hard time thinking of her poisoning little dogs, people's loved pets. It's so heartless."

"Remember, she justifies it in her mind. Most people who commit criminal acts do that. The guys who stole from the wealthy home up island, decided the owners of the house had too much property and money, that it wasn't fair they owned a second house they let sit empty half the time while others struggled." He reached into his backpack to take out a flashlight to keep handy if needed. "People who kill often justify murder by deciding the victim needed killing."

"I guess." She searched in J.T.'s backpack to take out a bottle of water. "This just seems like sort of bad movie or something to me."

"Well, life's like that sometimes. Stranger than fiction."

CHAPTER 20

"**W**ell, I've decided I'm not a rustic camp-out type of girl," Mary Helen admitted in a quiet voice as the hours crawled by. Dark had fallen three hours ago and they'd sat on the hill watching the house for four hours now.

J.T. continued whittling a small stick to pass the time, deciding not to mention he advised her not to come. She'd worn out most topics of conversation while they watched and waited, and now had become, quite frankly, bored. He could tell by her continual fidgeting. She was also tired and cramped from sitting in the same spot for so long.

"Do you think Chuck is getting serious about Toni Legare?" she asked at last, searching for something to talk about.

"He likes her, that's obvious." He kept his voice low answering. "I guess we'll have to watch and see. Time will tell. She comes from a good family line. The Legares were a prominent family in the area's early days. Branches of the family owned big plantation homes here on Edisto, on Johns Island, and up at Charles Town Landing. There's even a Legare Street in downtown Charleston."

She rubbed her neck. "I think I remember seeing a crypt with the name Legare on it in the old cemetery behind the Edisto Island Presbyterian Church. Is that the same family?"

He eyed her thoughtfully. "Don't you know the old story about that crypt?"

"No, I don't think I've heard it."

He grinned. "It might not be one you want to hear out here in the dark."

Her eyebrows went up a notch. "I doubt that. Tell me about it."

He shrugged. "Back in the 1800s, a little girl named Julia Legare came down with diphtheria at Edisto." He kept his voice hushed and low as he talked. "Some stories say her immediate family lived on Edisto; some say she only visited family here. Either way, diphtheria was an awful and usually deadly disease in that time. It progressed to the point where Julia fell into a coma and was pronounced dead by the family physician. Burials weren't delayed long then with no embalming fluids or anything. The family put her little body in the family's crypt or mausoleum, held a short service, grieved, and then closed and locked the big marble door. Afterwards, they went on as well as they could I'm sure."

"How sad. It's always hard when a child dies." She glanced over at him. "Why did you think that story might scare me?"

He grinned. "That's not the end of the story." J.T. straightened his legs out, stiff now from sitting so long. "Fifteen years after the child's death one of Julia's brothers was killed in the Civil War, and the family gathered again to put his body in the family crypt. They unhooked the heavy locks and several of the men pulled the big marble door open. Inside they ran into a horrible sight. Bones lay scattered around the floor of the old mausoleum along with remnants of little Julia Legare's white burial dress."

He paused. "Dead girls don't get off a marble slab to wander around in a tomb. On examining the bones, they could see the child's fingers worn away and broken from where she'd tried to claw on the door to get out. She'd obviously been buried alive and came out of the coma only to find herself locked in a dark, musty crypt full of dead bones. She either died of suffocation or starvation, possibly both. The family was horrified, of course. But everyone thought the child dead."

Mary Helen shivered. "How awful. I think it will give me the creeps to walk in that church cemetery after this. Is that old crypt still there?"

"Yes, and there's more to the tale. The family secured the heavy mausoleum door again after the second burial of the brother. Still grieving, several in the family went to the crypt shortly afterward to pay their respects. They found the door wide open."

J.T. scanned his eyes over Barton and Jane's property before continuing. He could still see Bear lying asleep under the deck on the back patio.

"So what did they do when they found the door open?" Mary Helen prompted, keeping her voice low.

"They secured it more tightly this time, thinking maybe they hadn't locked it well before. However, a few weeks later a clergyman at the church found the door open again. He shut and locked it once more, but this kept happening over and over. It went on for years no matter what type of chains and locks were put on the door to seal it tight."

"Ewww, what a story." Mary Helen made a face.

J.T.'s eyes moved across the yard, noticing Bear still quiet and asleep, everything still.

"That's my family's church, if you remember," he added. "Grandad said even fifty or sixty years ago, after they put locks on the crypt that only machinery could remove, they still found the door open again. This time they discovered the door not only open but unhinged from the mausoleum, with the broken door lying in the grass in front of the tomb. After that they never tried to close the door again. The bones of any family members still in the crypt were carried away and buried elsewhere and the remains of the old door buried in the floor of the crypt. Today there is no door on the J.B. Legare mausoleum. It's an open crypt now."

Mary Helen's eyes shifted around warily in the darkness. "What is the explanation?"

J.T.'s lips twitched. "Storytellers say Julia Legare's ghost purposed to never be locked in that tomb again and kept taking down the door."

"Do you believe that?" she whispered, conscious of the need to stay quiet as they watched Jane and Barton's yard.

"No. I don't believe in ghosts. However, those that do continue to tell the story and bring visitors on ghost tours to the church cemetery." He shifted to get more comfortable. "My grandmother always said she believed God's angels kept coming to open the door, like the angels opened Jesus tomb by rolling away the stone. She said they wanted little Julia to rest in peace and to provide a warning for others to be sure a person was truly dead before burial."

Mary Helen hugged herself. "You did warn me the story about that crypt would be a creepy one."

"I did." A shadow below caught his attention. J.T. leaned forward, putting a hand on Mary Helen's knee and a finger to his lips. He pointed toward Jane and Barton's backyard. A woman in dark clothes stood by the fence calling to Bear, who after a few barks began to wag his tail, starting toward the woman at the fence. Even with her back toward them it seemed obvious the woman was Winnie.

"We move out quietly now. Don't talk. Follow me down the route I told you, circling around to come out behind her. We need to move fast."

Stealthily they moved down the hillside to come out behind Winnie, J.T. popping on his flashlight then.

Winnie whirled around in surprise. To J.T.'s astonishment Mary Helen immediately pulled out a little camera from her pocket and snapped several quick photos of Winnie with her hands raised and her eyes shocked. Never let it be said he hadn't chosen a smart woman. He hadn't even thought to bring a camera.

"We know why you're here, Winnie." J.T.'s eyes moved to the plastic bag of food in her hand. "And I want you to hand me that bag of food. You'll not be feeding that to Bear tonight."

She looked around, obviously trying to determine if anyone else was here and if she could make a run for it.

J.T. watched her look back toward the dog, too, standing near the fence now, wagging his tail in recognition of people he knew stopping by.

"Don't consider for a minute tossing that bag of poisoned food over the fence to that dog, either," J.T. warned. "Bear belongs to friends of ours, and even though he did something wrong in your eyes, he is a good dog and greatly loved." J.T. paused. "I also have a revolver in my back pocket. I do know how to use it."

Winnie studied him, her eyes moving to the bulge in his back pocket, where the top of his gun stuck out.

"Have you called the police?" she finally said in a low resigned voice, handing the plastic bag of food to J.T.

"No, not yet."

Winnie, dressed, as they were, in dark clothes, pulled the knit hat off her head that covered her white hair. "You both know what that dog did." Her voice rose in anger now. "He should pay for destroying all those innocent lives. Even in court, murderers pay."

"Yes, but it's not your place to decide that." J.T. stuffed the bag of poisoned food into the backpack hanging over his shoulder.

Mary Helen added, "You can't appoint yourself judge and jury in matters like these, Winifred."

She frowned defiantly at them. "So *who* will see that justice is done? I've watched dogs time and again tear up turtle nests, eat the eggs, destroy any chance for the baby turtles to hatch and swim to sea. Loggerhead turtles are listed under the Endangered Species Act. Less and less of them exist in the world. Someone has to take care of them."

"So you've obviously appointed yourself guardian of Edisto's turtles. How many of those dead dogs did you poison, Winnie? Did you kill Rinny, Leon and Vernita's German Shepherd? He was a great dog."

Mary Helen's voice hardened. "Killing dogs you think endanger the turtles isn't the way to handle this problem, Winnie. Surely you know that? You must know it is wrong and also *illegal* to kill dogs."

"The fines are minimal and it's hard to prove the cause of animal deaths," she said flippantly, making J.T.'s anger rise.

He held on to his temper. "Actually, I believe the police might be very interested in talking to anyone guilty of poisoning dogs around Edisto. It isn't good for tourism. The police have been harassed for almost a year with complaints and pressured repeatedly to find the person who would do something so cruel. People are fond of their pets, Winifred."

"They are, and I am horrified by your actions," Mary Helen added, shaking her head. "How could you do something so cruel, when you love animals as you do, when you had a loved little dog of your own in past?"

"My dog never cruelly killed wildlife." She spit the words out at Mary Helen. "And I seem to remember you were the one who quoted words to me that all animals deserve life."

Mary Helen sent her a mutinous look. "The term all animals *includes* dogs, Winnie, even dogs you don't particularly like."

Tired of the conversation now, J.T. decided to bring it to a close. "Mary Helen and I talked about this, and you have two options tonight, Winifred. We can call the police, give them our evidence, including the photos and the poisoned food. Or you can pack up and leave the island. Immediately."

"What?" her eyes widened. "You're threatening me and suggesting I pack and leave my home?"

"It's an option."

"What if I don't agree to leave?"

He began to lose patience. "We'll contact the police. Mary Helen brought her phone and the contact information needed. Even if the police don't deal harshly with you and, as you suggest, only give you a slap on the wrist and a fine, word will get out all over Edisto and the surrounding area about what you've done. It won't be a happy place for you to live anymore. No one will think you justified in what you chose to do. Some people might even decide you should pay. I'm sure you'll get harassed and it could be worse. A few of the people who lost dogs are very angry."

Mary Helen crossed to the fence to reach through to pet Bear. "Another old quote I remember says 'Hell hath no fury like a long-tongued woman.' I personally will help to see to it that everyone knows what you tried to do tonight and what you've done before. I'm sure others, like Vernita, who lost her sweet dog, will enjoy spreading the word, too."

Winifred scowled. "Those burglars who shot and killed that dog are out on bail. How do you know they didn't poison the other dogs? There's no proof about what happened to any of the dogs."

"It doesn't take proof for talk to spread, Winifred." J.T. scowled. "This won't be a happy place for you to live anymore."

She bristled and then snapped, "No one has ever liked me here anyway."

"Then you won't miss Edisto very much when you leave will you?" J.T. asked, without sympathy. "What will it be, Winifred? Mary Helen and I are tired after a long night outside watching Bear. We'd both like to head home."

"What made you two know to come at all?" she asked, suspicious.

He chose not to mention Evelyn. "The way you acted last night, how angry you were, the things you said about Bear." He paused. "I remembered, too, that Mary Helen mentioned Jane and Barton would be out of town tonight. It worried me."

Mary Helen, obviously tired and annoyed, moved the topic back on subject. "It really would be smarter if you simply left the island, Winnie. Do you have friends or family where you lived before that you could stay with?"

Winifred fingered the knit cap in her hands, silent for a few moments. Then she lifted her chin as if making up her mind. "I have a friend back in Boston I could stay with for a time, until my condo sells."

J.T. nodded. "Good. Speak to the Whaleys tomorrow morning. They'll work to sell your condo quickly." He shifted his backpack on his shoulder. "It's Saturday now. I will expect to see you gone from the island by midweek. And if anything happens to Bear or any another dog before you leave, this deal's off. Do you understand?"

She glared at him. "I have never liked you, J.T. Mikell."

"The feeling's mutual. Don't come back to visit either. I'd also advise you to stop taking the law into your own hands. There are better ways to handle things." He looked out toward the street. "Where is your car?"

"Down the road, pulled up by an empty lot."

"Well, I'll let you head that way."

"Where's your car?" She snapped back, looking around.

"Nearby. And be aware a friend of Barton's is coming to stay at the house until they get back. Mary Helen and I will stay here until he arrives."

Winifred glanced toward Bear again and then turned to stalk away, not saying another word to either of them.

After she moved out of sight, Mary Helen said, "Are you really going to call Isaac to come over to stay?"

"I think it might be a good idea. I don't trust that woman not to come back. I'll be glad, too, when I know she's left the island."

Mary Helen came over to lean her head against his shoulder. "You handled all this beautifully, stayed calm, stayed solid. I was proud of you." Her voice softened. "I didn't believe Evelyn at first about her suspicions and got angry at yours earlier, too. But you were spot on that she might be poisoning the dogs. You have good intuition, J.T. I'll remember that in the future."

"Thanks." He kissed her forehead. "I didn't want you to come with me tonight, but I was glad for your company. While we waited, you helped me solidify my plans for dealing with Winnie, and you were really smart to bring a camera."

She moved over to pet Bear again through the fence. "At the last minute before leaving the house I remembered I'd picked up one of those little disposable cameras, so I stuck it in my pocket." She glanced back at him. "You do think she'll really leave the island, don't you?"

He nodded. "Yeah, I think she knows her number is up. She knows if we report her the police might begin to ask questions, look for other evidence, and they might find more to submit in court."

"What will you tell Evelyn? And Jane and Barton?"

"The truth," he said. "I intend to tell everyone the truth. People who lost their dogs need to know what happened. They need closure." He put out a hand. "Give me your cell phone and I'll call Isaac. I know his number. It's after midnight, but he'll understand me calling late when I explain. He doesn't live far and he has the keys to the house. If he can't come to stay over, I'll stay if he'll unlock the house for me. I'd like for Bear to spend the night inside tonight and stay inside for the next few days until Winifred is gone."

J.T. called Isaac while Mary Helen petted and talked to Bear. Alarmed and concerned, Isaac readily agreed to stay at the house. After Isaac arrived and they filled him in on the situation, J.T. and Mary Helen walked back to their stakeout spot to get the items they'd left behind before heading home.

"Are you going to be all right by yourself tonight after all this?" J.T. asked as he pulled into her driveway.

"Yeah," she answered. "It may take me a while to get to sleep after all the adrenalin rush of this evening, but I'll be okay."

"I can stay over," he offered.

"I don't think that's a good idea anymore." She gave him a small smile. "I'm not injured and a patient now. I might find it difficult to be *nice* if you stayed."

He grinned. "Yeah, I can relate to that," he added in a husky voice, pulling her close for a long kiss before he started home.

CHAPTER 21

Mary Helen headed into her kitchen a week later on Saturday morning to start coffee, still yawning and waking up. A whole week had passed since she and J.T. staked out at Jane and Barton's. Winnie left Edisto by mid-week, with no further problems. Halloween on Thursday brought busy hours at the Mermaid, and on Friday evening, Mary Helen, J.T., Chuck, and Toni drove into Charleston for dinner and a movie.

Waiting for her coffee to brew now, Mary Helen flipped the calendar on the kitchen wall to November. With a pen she circled Jane's due date, coming up November sixth, and the date her parents would arrive home on the tenth. She smiled remembering the last time she'd talked with them, her mother and Parker so excited about the wedding in December. The next two months promised to be hectic with wedding plans.

When the phone rang, Mary Helen walked over to pick up the wall phone with a smile. J.T. often called her before heading to work.

"Hi and good morning," she said, beginning to pull eggs from the refrigerator to start breakfast.

A voice, not J.T.'s, responded in an odd muffled tone. "This is a well-meaning friend. You need to go to J.T. Mikell's house right now. Hurry. It's important." The voice sounded urgent. "Don't call him first, either."

Before she could answer, the line went dead.

"What was that all about?" Mary Helen looked at the phone in her hand, shaking her head. She immediately started to punch in J.T.'s number, but then paused, remembering the urgency of the word *Hurry*.

"Oh, well. I'll just walk over to see what's going on. It's probably a prank call or something." She glanced at the clock. "J.T.'s probably already up and getting ready for work anyway."

She slipped her feet into flip-flops and headed out the screen door. The sky looked a little gray and gloomy, like it might rain later.

As she started up the pathway to J.T.'s house from the beach, she glanced toward the back porch and stopped dead in her tracks as a cold chill flashed through her. In the doorway, she saw Gracie Byrd plastered against J.T., her arms around his neck, the two kissing.

Hesitating a moment, struggling to take the scene in, she noticed Gracie seemed to be dressed in what looked like skimpy white underwear and J.T. wore only his boxers, his chest bare. Shocked and horrified, Mary Helen whirled to run back down the beach path, not wanting them to notice her. Obviously someone knew the two were still seeing each other and wanted to warn her. She wondered if it might have been Evelyn Dalton. Had Evelyn seen J.T. and Gracie? She often stopped by Mary Helen's on her early morning walks with Putney.

Mary Helen glanced behind her as she ran home, hoping J.T. hadn't seen her and followed. She felt sure he'd create an excuse and explanation of some kind for what she saw. He always did.

Inside the house at last, she leaned against the wall, her heart racing. Then she started crying. She sobbed for a while, before moving into the kitchen, banging pots and pans with anger, trying to pull herself together while she scrambled an egg.

"What am I going to do?" She wept while she stomped around the kitchen. "I knew things were going too well between us. Didn't we say last week it didn't seem real?" She choked on the words. "That's because it wasn't!"

She picked at her scrambled egg after cooking it, too upset to eat much and trying to decide what to do. Should she walk back over and confront J.T.? Have this out with him once and for all?

While she mulled over her options, the phone rang again.

"Great." Mary Helen snapped out the word, her voice laced with sarcasm. "I'll bet that's J.T. now." She snatched the phone off the hook in a fury, ready to vent her anger and disappointment on him.

"Hello," she said in a stiff voice, waiting to pounce.

An unfamiliar voice surprised her. "Is this Mary Helen Avery?"

"Yes, it is," she answered back, trying to calm down.

"This is Donna Hembree with Adopt-Me-Dolls."

Stunned at the name, Mary Helen sat down on the kitchen stool by the wall phone.

"I hope you remember me," she continued. "Your friend Rita Sacco—our manager at the mall store—gave me this home phone number for you." She paused. "Do you have a moment to talk? I hoped to catch you before you went to work this morning. Rita said you managed a store on the island."

"I'm off today, Mrs. Hembree, and of course I remember you. What can I do for you?"

A small silence ensued. "This is a very difficult call for me to make. I discovered recently my husband Wendell has been involved in an extramarital affair. A private investigator I hired also uncovered evidence that this is not the first of Wendell's indiscretions." She heaved a deep sigh. "People say the wife is always the last to know and I guess, like the old saying, love is blind to facts like this." She hesitated. "I doubt you would understand that, being so young."

Mary Helen winced. "Actually I understand more than you might imagine. I'm truly sorry, Mrs. Hembree."

Waiting, Mary Helen heard the tap of the woman's fingers on her desk before she continued. "The most recent indiscretion was with the new Assistant Merchandise Buyer hired in August after you left. Her name doesn't matter and, obviously, she—and Wendell— are no longer with the company."

"This must be such a painful time for you."

"It is," she admitted. "Additionally, Kimberly Harding, who held the assistant buyer position before you did, admitted Wendell tried to compromise her on a business trip. She also acknowledged she left the company with no notice for that reason. She didn't seem to think anyone would believe Wendell would stoop so low as to try to rape a company associate."

Stunned, Mary Helen tried to think what to say. "I'm so sorry about this, Mrs. Hembree. I don't know what to say."

She heard the woman's fingers drumming the table again. "Our family never understood why you left the company the way you did, Mary Helen, not even giving notice. You were one of our best employees. Meredith Kessler, our Human Resource Director, who hired you, along with Rita at the Adopt-Me-Dolls store, all believe something happened to cause you to leave as you did. Rita said you wouldn't even tell her why you left."

"That's true." Mary Helen waited.

Mrs. Hembree continued. "I can't help but wonder now if Wendell might have acted inappropriately with you. Bea Hardy, our receptionist at the corporate office, says she saw you slipping out the side door crying the Monday after you met with Wendell before leaving your job. We know you were scheduled to go on a buyers' trip with Wendell the following week, but that you left before the week was out. I recall Wendell acted provoked when you quit suddenly, but I never put two and two together that there might be a connection between those events until now. Can I ask you candidly if there was a connection? You don't need to give me details."

Mary Helen took a deep breath. "There was a connection, Mrs. Hembree. I hate to add to your hurt to say so."

"Well, I'm very sorry to hear that. I hope your situation wasn't as shocking as Kimberly's. She felt terrified, out of town and alone with Wendell in a strange city."

Mary Helen tried to think what to say. "Mr. Hembree suggested at our Monday meeting what I could expect on our trip the following week, and I realized I couldn't stay at the company after that. I loved and respected everyone at Adopt-Me-Dolls, your parents, your brother and sister in the business, and yourself. I hated the idea of even suggesting anything that might cause trouble in your marriage. You had been married so many years, seemed happy, had children." She hesitated. "I also admit your husband threatened to spread a defaming story about me, if I reported him to anyone."

"Don't feel bad to admit that, Mary Helen. Kimberly told us the same thing. So have others who worked with the company and left. One of the most grievous parts of this whole horrible situation is that Wendell used his position in the company to try to compromise young girls. I'm sure you can imagine what a shock this has been to our family and to our business." She hesitated. "Now the story has hit the media, too, and we're working our way through that as well."

"I'm really sorry, Mrs. Hembree."

"I wish you'd call me Donna." She offered a strained laugh. "I'm not fond of my married name at this particular moment. I'm sure you can understand why."

Mary Helen thought over their conversation so far. "I have little information to offer in a lawsuit action if that's why you called. Your husband only verbally laid out his expectations to me. Even though shocked to hear them, I knew I couldn't continue to work under him after our meeting. He didn't attack me as he did Kimberly. I was lucky in that." She decided not to mention the fact that he'd run his hand up her skirt.

"Well, thank you for your honesty."

"I wish I could help more."

Donna hesitated. "You might be able to help in another way. I've been forced to pick up Wendell's job and his assistant's workload, with all that has happened. I know Wendell's job well, so I can cover it for a time, along with my other duties at corporate. However, as you probably recall, Wendell handled most of the decisions about the creative displays to be used year-round in our stores, made most of the buying decisions, traveled to the trade shows..." Her voice trailed off. "I was told you were interested in assuming more of those responsibilities. Is that correct?"

"Yes. I was flattered with the opportunity to move into a new area of the company with more responsibility." She couldn't imagine why this mattered at this point.

"Thank you for answering that. At this point, Wendell is out of the company—and I might add out of the city. He has moved temporarily to a beach condo we own at the Jersey shore until the divorce proceedings are completed. Obviously he will not be returning to Adopt-Me-Dolls."

She paused. "Anyway, two key people are gone now. I need someone to train in the corporate buying area of the company. I wondered if you would consider coming back to work with us. Quite frankly, I'd like to train you as my Assistant Merchandise Buyer, and if things go well, eventually move you into the corporate position Wendell held. Both jobs, as you know, involve quite a bit of travel but also offer a lot of creative responsibility that I think you might enjoy. We're prepared to offer you a strong starting salary."

She named a figure that raised Mary Helen's eyebrows.

"To sweeten the offer, since we know you left with a bad taste in your mouth, you'll gain a large office at corporate in our headquarters building in Milburn and we want to offer you free housing for the first year in a nearby condo complex we own. You can continue renting the condo after the first year if you like it or find a place elsewhere." She sighed. "To be frank, we're in a bit of a pinch with all this, as you can well imagine. We would prefer not to do a full search for a candidate right now but to hire someone we know and trust. We all agreed you would be ideal."

"I don't know what to say," Mary Helen said, stunned.

Donna laughed. "I hope you'll say yes. You and I always got along well and I think we could work easily together. Everyone at corporate likes you and respects your work. We all believed originally you would be an asset to the company and we still hold that same belief. I thought of having Meredith, our HR, call to give you this offer, but I decided I wanted to call you myself. I feel awful Wendell used his position so despicably and caused you to leave your job with us. I hope we didn't cause you financial hardship, as well."

"No, fortunately I have a very supportive family here in South Carolina." Mary Helen decided to be honest. "I am also fortunate a family friend needed a manager at her shop here at the beach when I needed a job. I've been working at The Little Mermaid at Edisto since I left New Jersey and I'm living in our family's beach house."

"That's good to hear." Donna Hembree hesitated. "Again, we are in a very difficult spot here with two employee losses in the same division. If you think you might be willing to come back, we'd love to have you as soon as possible. The condo is furnished. Rita told us your rental apartment was furnished, too. However, we are prepared to take care of any moving expenses you might need. In addition, we want to offer a signing bonus."

She named another figure that almost made Mary Helen whistle out loud. "That's very generous."

"Think of it as partial compensation for being humiliated as you must have been by my husband. Our family deeply regrets that Mary Helen."

"I'm sure this has been a harder time for you than for me."

"Well, it's never fun to find out you're linked up with a cheater."

Mary Helen felt like saying, *how well I know*.

Donna spoke again after a moment. "Rita says she thinks you've met someone you care about while there. Will that be a problem? And will you need to give much notice to the shop where you've been working?"

"Actually, neither of those things will be a problem," Mary Helen said, making her decision as she considered the questions. "The relationship I formed hasn't proved to be what I hoped and the shop is in off-season now. The store owner and another employee can handle everything easily." She glanced at the calendar, suddenly eager to leave. "I could tie things up and come next week."

"Wonderful!" Donna Hembree clapped her hands. "I'm simply delighted and I know everyone at Adopt-Me-Dolls will be. Thank you for saying yes, and welcome back to the company, Mary Helen. We'll start getting the paperwork ready, the condo and your office cleaned up for you."

"I admit I was surprised when you called this morning," Mary Helen admitted. "But I'm really glad you did. My job search for another corporate position got postponed because I fell and broke my arm in early September. I want to be upfront about that fact. The break is fully healed now, but I might need to be watchful about heavy lifting for a season until the healing is totally complete."

Mary Helen took a breath before continuing. "I finished physical therapy at a center in the area, although I'm still doing follow-up exercises at home. I'll talk with my doctor specifically about temporary limitations I might experience and have him send you a letter if you like."

"A letter won't be necessary. It's that sort of honesty and integrity we've always respected about you. We can work around that easily."

"Thanks." She sighed. "An old friend told me that problems in life always work to the good, even bad things. I hope this will be true for you. It must be such a hurtful time for you and your sons."

"We're strong. We'll get through this. It's been a shock to the boys, but having a loving and supportive family network helps. It helps, too, that both boys are away at college in other cities and not living in town. It provides distance for them."

They talked a little longer, catching up on some company business, discussing work ahead, getting to know each other.

Mary Helen felt like her head was spinning by the time she hung up. But she knew, too, deep in her heart, she couldn't stay at Edisto after what she'd seen this morning. She simply could not continue to encounter these kinds of heartbreaking scenes with J.T. all of her life. Donna Hembree had actually offered her the perfect answer to the situation today.

"It seems like providence, Lord," she said out loud, sitting down at the table to drink a freshly poured cup of coffee. Her first had grown cold during her talk with Donna.

Mary Helen doodled on a notepad on the table as she drank her coffee, trying not to focus on the hurt in her heart. Adopt-Me-Dolls had offered her an enviable salary, excellent benefits, a lovely signing bonus, and the additional perk of free housing for a year in one of the corporate condos. She knew how nice those condos were, the building within walking distance of the corporate offices downtown and near a nice park. Mary Helen also knew everyone at corporate in New Jersey, knew and liked them, and she loved the company. Nothing nicer could have happened to her than this after having her heart broken today.

"Thank you, God," she said out loud. "Thanks for vindicating me and for this lovely offer at this perfect time. I'll be very busy with all this new work responsibility, but I won't crowd you out of my life again. I promise. I've learned through this season that Your love is a true love and one I can always count on. I'll move past all this other hurt with Your help."

As she prayed and finished her coffee, Mary Helen realized her anger at J.T. had fizzled into a dull, slow hurt. Glancing at the clock, she realized she'd talked with Donna for over an hour. She also realized she simply did not want to see J.T. Mikell today.

With that thought in mind, she went upstairs to change clothes and pack her duffle. She'd go to Waterview in Beaufort to spend the night and to check on the house for her parents. She had a few things there she wanted to pick up to take with her to New Jersey, anyway. She'd also need to call and talk to her parents, call Suki and several others. Looking around, she realized she wanted very badly right now to get away from the sweeps of memories of J.T. here at this place. Everywhere she looked, she could see and remember sweet loving scenes—memories she didn't need crowding her mind right now.

Before leaving for Beaufort, she'd stop and talk to Isabel. That would be hard after the loving and generous offer Isabel made to her, but it had to be done. She couldn't stay now. She hoped Isabel would understand.

She'd spend this weekend at Beaufort, settle herself, and then come back on Monday to pack. If she could manage it, Mary Helen hoped to leave for New Jersey on Tuesday.

It had been a bittersweet time since returning to Edisto and now it would be a bittersweet time to leave again. Funny, how life turned out. Never like you expected.

A short time later at The Little Mermaid, Isabel fixed her gaze on Mary Helen in astonishment, "What do you mean, you're leaving the island?"

"Just what I said," Mary Helen answered. She'd been glad to find Isabel working alone without Nancy in the store when she stopped by. "Donna Hembree with Adopt-Me-Dolls called to tell me she learned of her husband's indiscretions, realized why I quit unexpectedly, and she offered me a job back with the company in a higher position. I thought I explained all that."

Isabel studied her across the counter from where she sat on the old stool writing out bills. "I got that part, Mary Helen. It's a fine opportunity."

Mary Helen shifted, finding it hard to meet Isabel's eyes. "I realize you offered me a beautiful opportunity with the store, but I need to do this."

"Fie on that." Isabel leaned forward. "That isn't what I'm talking about and you well know it. You're engaged to be married, the last I heard. And you haven't even *mentioned* talking to J.T. about this at all."

She looked away. "There's nothing to say to J.T."

Isabel crossed her arms in annoyance. "Your eyes are red, your face is blotched. You've obviously had a fight and a break-up, and then this opportunity surfaced this morning. Is that right?"

"It seemed like the perfect answer when I realized I couldn't stay here."

Mary Helen lifted her face to look at Isabel more directly now. "I don't want to talk about this further, Isabel. But you know me well. You know I wouldn't break an engagement and leave without just cause. Trust me that I have a good reason to leave, would you?"

She felt tears start in her eyes. "It's hard enough for me to say goodbye to you without you giving me a difficult time."

Isabel walked around the counter and wrapped Mary Helen in a surprising hug. She was not the hugging sort. "Dear girl, I am sorry about whatever has happened to hurt your heart. It must have been a serious issue for you to make a decision like this. I won't probe now while you're still upset and hurting, but I hope you will come and tell me what happened before you leave next week."

Mary Helen nodded, trying not to burst into tears at Isabel's surprising touch of affection and sweet words. "I plan to come back on Monday to start packing and I hope to leave Tuesday morning. I promise I will come see you and say goodbye before I leave."

Isabel walked over to reach into an open shipping box sitting on the floor by the counter. "Here," she said, reaching in to pull out a T-shirt. "You wear this and know it's the truth."

Mary Helen looked at the emerald green shirt. It read: *Mermaids are Strong* across the front.

"You are a strong, bright, wonderful girl," Isabel said. "You wear that shirt and think of me when you do. And remember I believe in you and I always will."

"Thank you. Surely you know you're like a second mother to me and will always be a part of my life."

"Good. I'll be expecting you to stay in touch," she said in a more business-like tone, as a group of ladies came into the store.

Mary Helen managed to say goodbye and get to her car before she burst into tears. And she cried most of the way to Beaufort.

CHAPTER 22

Saturdays in early November were always a little busier in the store than weekdays. Mikell's Island Rentals carried items in their store inventory that locals needed year round and visitors came to Edisto all year, too. Tourism never really stopped near the beach.

J.T. snagged a couple of fried flounder sandwiches at The Waterfront Restaurant and headed to Mary Helen's house for a lunch break. He knew she was off today and he'd told her he'd try to stop by if he could. Not finding her at the house, he drove over to the Mermaid, figuring she must have gone into the shop to help Isabel.

"She's not here as you see," Isabel informed him curtly, studying him over the top of her glasses.

Seeing his scowl, she added, "I figured you would know why."

"What does that mean?" he asked, annoyed at her tone.

"She came in here earlier today to announce she'd taken a job back at Adopt-Me-Dolls in New Jersey. It seems Wendell Hembree's indiscretions were even more widespread than we imagined and his wife finally discovered them. I'm sure the entire debacle proved a local stink. It led the company to realize why Mary Helen must have left."

J.T staggered at her words, his head swimming.

"Sit down in that chair at the table, son, before you faint on me." She got up to usher him over to the chair and then sat down across from him. "I gather you didn't know anything about this."

He shook his head. "How could she suddenly decide to leave

me, Isabel? She said she'd be happy staying here. This doesn't make sense. Not now. We talked about this often. She was going to buy into the store with you. We'd started making plans for a wedding, for our future." J.T. knew he was babbling.

Isabel scratched her chin. "Well, this is odd indeed. I hoped to get from you what I didn't get from her in explanation."

"What did she tell you?"

Isabel repeated the story Mary Helen told her about the call from Donna Hembree, the revelations she revealed, and the job offer. "I asked her what you thought about all this and she all but snapped my head off. 'There's nothing to say to J.T.' she said. When I tried to question her further, she insisted she didn't want to talk about it any more at all. "

"That doesn't make any sense," he said again.

"Well, the girl had red eyes, a blotched face, acted stiff and formal, and was unable to talk without tears leaking out, which means she was deeply upset and hurt about something. I know that girl. Something happened." She leaned forward giving him a tight-lipped look. "You two must have had a fight or disagreement about something."

He scratched his head. "We didn't, Isabel. We went to Charleston last night, to a movie and out to dinner with friends, and shared a happy time. Mary Helen and I laughed, necked a little saying goodnight. This doesn't make any sense to me at all."

"Did you see her this morning or talk to her? Something must have happened. Mary Helen wouldn't suddenly have a change of heart like this without cause."

"I didn't see her this morning at all." His mouth dropped open as a new thought hit him. "Surely not," he muttered.

"Surely not what?" Isabel probed, leaning toward him. "You've thought of something."

He closed his eyes and leaned his head back. "Gracie Byrd stopped by my back porch this morning, beating on the door, claiming some man tried to accost her while she was on the beach taking a morning swim. She was crying and all upset. I tried to calm her down and even walked her back to her car. She kept clinging to me, claiming she felt afraid the man might still be lurking around out there. She was really upset."

Isabel lifted an eyebrow. "How upset was she? And how deeply did your comforting go on the porch?"

His frown became a grimace. "She threw herself on me and kissed me. Held onto me like a vice. I thought I'd never pull back from her."

Isabel blew out a long breath. "My guess is Mary Helen saw that."

J. T. shook his head. "How could she have? I didn't see her."

"Sounds to me like you were busy." She emphasized the last word.

"This wasn't my fault." J.T. bit back, angry at her insinuation. "You don't know how Gracie is when she's upset like that. She was acting all crazy, crying and everything."

"Notice the word *acting* you used." Isabel crossed her arms and gave him a steady look. "If even I can imagine that Gracie would stage a scene to get your attention, why couldn't you see that?"

"I don't know." He rubbed his arm. "It never dawned on me she'd stage something like that."

"Hmmm. Well if she did, my guess is she either saw Mary Helen coming up the beach and staged it to cause trouble or she set it up entirely." Isabel paused in thought. "For Mary Helen to show up at the opportune moment when Gracie was there tends to suggest the timing wasn't a coincidence. Haven't you said she's staged situations like this in the past?"

J.T. barely suppressed a groan. "Surely this can't be happening."

"Remember the old quote: *Fool me once, shame on you. Fool me twice, shame on me.*" Her mouth twisted in irritation. "I've never thought you a fool, J.T. Mikell. But I could change my mind now. Aren't you ever going to get that girl's number?"

"But Gracie *knows* Mary Helen and I are engaged now, that I'm no longer available."

"Well, you really are a fool if you think that would deter her.

That doesn't mean anything to a person selfishly determined to get what she wants. Think of the story of Wendell Hembree. Did he consider the consequences of his actions or the people he might hurt? Really, son, your life has been too limited, if you haven't figured out yet that you need to carefully protect yourself in all areas of affection. It appears Gracie has taken delight in messing up your love life in the past and that you're still allowing her to do it."

He stood up, angry. "That's overly harsh, Isabel."

She crossed her arms. "Well I won't apologize. You've hurt my girl through this, and I'm losing her because of your actions, as well."

"Do you think I'm not torn up over this, too?" He gritted his teeth. "My heart feels like someone shredded it up with a meat grinder. And then I get to hear you call me an idiot."

"We're both obviously upset." She stood up and headed over to the register. "I doubt talking any more will help either of us right now. The point is: what do you plan to do about this? I can tell you Mary Helen went to Waterview in Beaufort if that might help."

"It does. Thanks." He let out a long slow breath. "I'm going to talk to her right now. Maybe she'll listen."

"Keep in mind the fault isn't all Gracie's."

"You've made that very clear." His jaw clenched.

"I hope so," she said. "Keep in mind, too, that the world is full of problematic people but our task is to live in such a way that they *don't* create problems for us as well as for themselves." She paused, giving him a pointed look. "And certainly not time after time."

J.T. bit his tongue not to smart back and headed out the door.

With the rental store quiet, he was able to get Carlos to cover for the afternoon for him. And to save time getting to Beaufort, he decided to take his boat instead of driving. He could get there faster by boat anyway, and getting out on the water would help him clear his head and think. He still couldn't wrap his mind around the fact that Gracie Byrd might have initiated a way, yet again, to break him and Mary Helen up. Why would she do that? What did she hope to gain from it? It wasn't as though her maneuverings, if they were that, could cause him to care for her? In fact, right now, if he learned she'd manipulated this whole scenario, like Isabel thought, it would be hard not to hate her.

He backed his boat out of the dock and started down Big Bay Creek heading for the Saint Helena Sound. He remembered Isabel said she could see Mary Helen had been crying. What might she have thought if she saw Gracie kissing him? The woman had held on to him like a vise when he tried to pull away. But even if standing on the beach or the path to his house, wouldn't Mary Helen have been able to see that he wasn't encouraging her? He tried to picture the scene she might have witnessed and winced remembering he'd been padding around the kitchen in only his sleep boxers when Gracie came banging on the door. What should he have done? Not answered the door? Not even cared she was crying and claiming some man had been after her? How could he know she was making it all up?

"She's really some actress if this was all fake," he said out loud as he steered into the Sound and started inland toward Beaufort. "Is Isabel right? Was I a fool not to have seen through her?"

It was a crazy situation. Nuttier than the old movie *Crazy About Bob* where Bill Murray gradually drove Richard Dreyfuss crazy with his neurotic compulsions. J.T. could feel sympathetic with that shrink right now. How did a person even deal with someone like Gracie? Her actions made no sense.

In the time it took J.T. to travel to Beaufort, he gradually calmed down a little. Surely, after all this time, and now that he and Mary Helen had become so close, she would understand when he explained what she must have seen. He couldn't imagine anything else that could have upset her this much since last night. She wouldn't simply jump on a job opportunity either, no matter how good, and plan to take it and leave town without talking to him. Seeing him with Gracie seemed the only reason he could imagine she'd break up with him and leave. She'd done it before. Mary Helen had always harbored a distrust for men since that incident with Miles Lawrence when only a girl.

He pulled his boat up to the dock behind Waterview a short time later, snagging the bag of sandwiches he bought earlier. Tying off the boat securely, he walked up the pathway from the marsh to the back of the house. He could see a light on in the kitchen and he let himself in the back door.

J.T. found Mary Helen curled up on one of the dark green sofas in the den off the kitchen. She'd always loved that room with its big windows looking out over the yard, its cozy feel with the sofas facing each other across a table always piled with magazines and books.

She looked up at him, her eyes red. "I locked the front door, but I forgot to lock the back. Go home, J.T. I don't want to talk to you."

"We have to talk, Mary Helen. People who love each other need to talk when bad things upset their relationship. It's a part of loving and caring."

"I don't love you right now."

Her words sliced across his heart. "I know you're upset about something. I went to your house at lunch to bring sandwiches." He set the bag on the table. "When you weren't there, I figured you might have gone over to the Mermaid. So I went there next."

"I'm sure Isabel told you I'm going back to New Jersey. That's all there is to say."

He took a breath. "No, that isn't all there is to say. You wouldn't take a job and break our engagement without talking with me first. Nor would you cry over it and run off to your parents, obviously upset, if something hadn't happened. Tell me what happened."

"I don't want to talk about it." She picked up an accent pillow from the couch and hugged it to herself.

"Then I'll talk," he said. "Last night, we had a good time. I sat at dinner looking across at you and realized I would be looking at you over dinner for the rest of my life. That was a great thought. I've loved you for a long time. For me that love only keeps growing deeper and deeper. Every time we're together, I think about how much I look forward to spending my whole life with you."

She blinked back tears. "I don't want to hear this kind of talk. A lot more matters than *talk* in life."

Realizing she wasn't going to discuss what was troubling her, he finally said, "I guess you must have seen Gracie throwing a fit on my porch early this morning, claiming someone was following her, trying to hurt her, throwing herself all over me and carrying on."

She raised her chin. "You left out that she was kissing you, too."

"Yes, and the wording is important here. *She* was kissing *me*; she grabbed on to me like a vise. That girl is strong. I thought I'd never pull away." He leaned toward her. "Did you hang around long enough to see me pull away, to see me push her away? To hear me tell her if she wanted my help she'd better get a grip on herself? To stop acting like an idiot?"

Mary Helen looked away. "Gracie had on underwear and you had on sleep boxers, your hair still tousled with sleep."

He shook his head, leaning back against the couch. "No. Gracie had on a white bikini. I did have on my boxers though. I'd just gotten out of bed and was starting coffee in my own kitchen. There was nothing wrong with that."

"Why did you open the door to her at all if that's the truth?"

"She came up and started beating on it, crying and hollering, saying someone was after her. What would you have done? Told her to bug off?"

She glared at him. "Actually I probably would have. I don't like Gracie Byrd."

"Neither do I, but I find it hard to be heartless to anyone in trouble. What if she'd been telling the truth? How would I have faced her father later if I'd left her out there crying and everything? If someone hurt her?"

She hugged the pillow tighter. "You just admitted she *wasn't* telling the truth. When did you figure that out?"

He sucked in a breath. "I didn't until I talked to Isabel and she presented the idea that something must have happened this morning to upset you. She called me a fool, too. I admit after the big kiss Gracie Byrd tried to put on me, I looked around the beach with suspicion to see if I actually saw anyone watching or following her. Gracie is known for making up tales. But when I walked her to her car, she still seemed upset. So I wasn't sure. Gracie is a great actress. If that whole scene was contrived, I think the woman missed her career calling in life. She should have been on the stage."

Mary Helen looked at him, tight lipped. "The point is why would she keep doing these things if you don't encourage her in some way? Doesn't she know you're engaged? Doesn't she realize you're the kind of man who doesn't fool around, who isn't available anymore?" She leaned toward him focusing her eyes on his. "Or do you keep giving her reasons to think you still hold some interest in her?"

He bristled and tried to hold his annoyance in check. "I have never given Gracie Byrd any reason to think I was interested in her."

"Actually, that's not true. You dated her after she divorced. That had to send a message to her that you were interested."

"All right," he admitted, slumping over. "Maybe that was a mistake. But you were out of the picture then. It didn't seem to matter until I recognized she felt more than I did. I stopped seeing her after that. Keep in mind, too, all this occurred before you came back."

She closed her eyes, leaning back against the couch.

He looked at her, trying to think what else to say next. "What caused you to come over to my house this morning at that particular time?"

"I got a phone call saying I ought to go to your house."

He sat up in surprise. "What? Who called you?"

"I don't know." She shrugged. "A muffled voice I didn't recognize. I started to call you right after, but the caller specifically urged me to come without calling and to hurry."

"This gets worse and worse. She set us up, don't you see that?" J.T. felt his temper rise.

"Maybe, but I simply can't keep dealing with things like this all my life. I can't, J.T." Tears dripped out of the edges of her eyes. "Also knowing Gracie as you do, I still think you never should have gone out with her when she moved back after her divorce. You knew she broke us up in high school by creating a fake romantic scene and spreading lies. Yet you gullibly walk back into scenes like this with her time after time, knowing what she's like, knowing you should be wary of her, knowing she is emotionally unstable at the least, and at the worst malicious and mean-spirited." Mary Helen was practically hollering now. "I simply can't keep dealing with this anymore. Running into these things, even if Gracie sets them up. Even if you see yourself every time as only the innocent dupe in this."

"I was *innocent* in this."

"You were *duped*, too, and all too easily. I'm not comfortable with that."

"Do you think I am?" His temper flared.

"I don't know, but the situation is what it is. To me it's like a third strike, a third time. I just can't keep playing."

"Do you realize how unreasonable you're being?" he asked, annoyed now. "I'd like you to trust me enough to always realize there might be a good explanation for anything out of the ordinary you see or hear about me. I'd always be like that for you. If someone said you did something that I knew out of character for you, or if I saw you with someone else—even kissing—I'd assume there was some reasonable explanation. I'd assume the best of you."

She gave him a small smile. "You say that, but you've never had to experience it. My guess is if the situation were reversed, you would feel no differently than I do now."

He ran his hand through his hair. "Remember that we said we weren't going to let Gracie play us anymore, break us up again."

"And yet she has played us once again. And broken us up once again." She took a deep breath. "I'm not interested in staying around to see how many more times she might do that."

"That's harsh, Mary Helen."

"Maybe, but I don't like going through these things. I think perhaps the call I got this morning and the opportunity to go back to New Jersey is the best answer for me. Perhaps for you, too."

"No, not for me; definitely, not for me. I feel like someone put a knife through my heart and I can't believe you could walk away from me like you're doing." He felt his voice rise. "What does that say about your reliability? About the truth of the words and promises you made to me? You question my ethics. What about yours? Trust is a decision, Mary Helen. You decide to love and trust and you stay steadfast in it."

"Stand by your man and all that kind of thing?" Her voice took on a sarcastic tone. "Seems like I read the woman who wrote that song got divorced five times."

"I don't know what else to say to you." J.T. sighed. "What can I do to make this right?"

"Let me go, J.T." She wiped another sweep of tears away. "I feel beaten and hurt. My trust is shattered, my heart broken. I can't move on to Step Two right now feeling like I do. Maybe time and space will help me feel differently, but I need that time and space right now."

J.T. laced his fingers together, letting his eyes run over her. "I don't understand you, Mary Helen. You know clearly now that Gracie set us up. That she, for some perverted reason, wants to break us up and has for a long time. We've exposed her plot, but you still want to believe the worst about me. To believe I somehow caused this or wanted this, when instead I'm sick at heart about it. I hate that Gracie was crafty and devious enough to design and plan this whole thing. I'm as confused as you as to why she does things like this. We are neither one at fault in this situation. Can't you see that?"

She shook her head.

"Well, then I don't know what else to say or do." He stood up. "I guess I'll head on back home and let you think about it." He paused. "Have you called your parents yet? Your sister?"

She sniffed. "I haven't been able to."

"Good. Well, give it some time and thought before you do." He reached over to touch her face. "And prayer. I love you with all my heart Mary Helen but I want you to love me the same way. I want you to believe in me through thick or thin. To stand with me when others try to hurt us and not to turn against me. To stay faithful to me in times of trouble, believing in me, knowing I am a good person. It hurts to always have my integrity questioned. It hurts when you always run instead of coming to talk to me."

She lifted her chin. "You always offer nice words, but we're known by our actions and not just by our words. You and I have been reading that in our Bible studies."

He willed himself not to smart back. "The Scripture I'm remembering is one from Corinthians that Farlin talked about in church the last time we visited. 'Love bears all things, believes all things, hopes all things, endures all things, and love never ends.' That's the way it is for me, Mary Helen."

With that said, J.T. couldn't think of any reason to stay longer. Despite his long campaign to win Mary Helen, he guessed he'd lost after all.

All the way home on the water, J.T. tried to think of what he might do to change Mary Helen's heart, to get her to see things differently. He also tried to think what he should do about the ongoing situation with Gracie Byrd. He didn't want to keep living his days worrying about what that woman would do next to mess up his life and relationships. Should he go and talk to her? He'd tried it before and it hadn't accomplished much.

He prayed a lot going back to the island. He definitely needed some divine intervention on this one. Surely God had an answer for all this mess, even if he didn't. Back at the island, J.T. tried to think who he might talk to. Who might help him. He'd never had trouble realizing when he was in a situation over his head and needed help.

After docking the boat, he went back to the rental store to finish out the day at work, letting Carlos pick up rental bikes, raking leaves and cleaning up around the business. After work, J.T. ate a little supper and then walked the beach, still trying to think what to do. Seeing lights on at Ezra and Isabel's house as he walked by their place, he turned up the beach path to their home. They loved Mary Helen as he did. And Ezra had helped him with Gracie before. Maybe he'd have some ideas and advice to help him again.

CHAPTER 23

Mary Helen slept little Saturday night after crying most of the day. J.T. offered some strong words that hurt her to remember them. She had to admit it did matter knowing Gracie obviously orchestrated a situation once again to try breaking them up, to get J.T. to like her when he supposedly didn't. That had never made any sense to Mary Helen.

Why would anyone keep pursuing someone who didn't like them? She could remember being embarrassed a few times in the past when she realized someone she'd started to like made it clear they didn't like her in return. She'd avoided them afterward, a little humiliated. Why would Gracie keep pushing to gain J.T.'s affection if he hadn't encouraged her in some way? And why did he keep letting himself get involved in these situations with her over and over again? He had no problem making it clear to Winifred Meggett he didn't care for her, that he hoped he never saw her again. Mary Helen also remembered how firmly, and with little softness or compassion, J.T. had handled his encounters with Winifred. He could be tough when he needed to.

By Sunday morning, despite all J.T.'s words and all her thinking since Saturday about the situation, Mary Helen decided to continue the plans she'd made, to pack and go back to New Jersey. It simply seemed the best option right now. At Oleanders, she pulled out all her suitcases and began unloading the drawers in her bedroom. She popped downstairs after a time to retrieve some of her other things and froze in shock as she looked up to see Gracie Byrd knocking on her back door.

Mary Helen mouthed the words "go away" and shook her head at the woman, turning to start back upstairs, but Gracie pushed open the sliding door and let herself in. "I need to talk to you," she said.

"I have nothing to say to you." Mary Helen paused by the stairway. "You have caused enough trouble in my life already. I don't need any more today."

Gracie ran a hand through her hair, pushing it behind her ear. "I need to say a few things." A few tears dribbled down her cheeks. "It's important."

"Is this another of your acts? I'm really tired of them, you know."

She sniffed. "I don't blame you for being mad at me. I know you probably hate me."

Mary Helen sighed. "If you have something you need to say, say it quickly Gracie. I have a lot of packing to do. I'm leaving Edisto to go back to New Jersey Tuesday morning. You ought to be pleased to hear that."

"Could we sit down?" Gracie asked, moving to perch on the sofa.

Mary Helen edged over to a chair across from her and sat on it. She studied Gracie, so pretty in a peach dress, her eyelashes long and thick around big blue eyes, her blond hair lush and wavy, her figure model-perfect. Why would a girl this beautiful need to chase after anyone?

Gracie nibbled at her lip. "Ezra Compton and J.T. came to our house to see me last night, with my parents there." Her glance fell to her lap. "It was really embarrassing."

Mary Helen rolled her eyes. "I gather your folks didn't realize you get your kicks showing up at men's houses early in the morning in your bikini, trying to put the make on them."

"That's mean." Tears gathered in Gracie's eyes again.

"No, it's the truth." Mary Helen crossed her leg impatiently. "Gracie, why have you kept pursuing J.T. all these years when he obviously isn't interested in you? I've never understood that. Look at you. You're a beautiful woman. It should be easy for you to interest men and to attract plenty of boyfriends. I remember boys always chased after you in school. Why wasn't that enough?"

Gracie twisted her hands. "Well, I think I have some problems. Ezra says unavailability holds great sway with some people. That some people want what they can't have and it can become like an obsession, almost like a sickness. But he said that they don't see it that way." She looked away again.

Mary Helen wondered where this conversation was heading.

"As an only child, I got a lot of what I wanted at home," she continued. "It wasn't hard to talk my parents into things. At school, it was easy, too. I was pretty and popular and everyone liked me. I don't know why I always started wanting things and people I couldn't have, like J.T. But I hated not getting what I wanted." She shrugged. "Then a lot of times after I got something I wanted, I didn't really want it that much anymore. All the excitement went out of it somehow." She wrinkled her nose. "The fun was in the chase, in figuring out how to win. Ezra says I didn't see things realistically."

Mary Helen snorted. "Meaning you didn't mind lying, manipulating, or doing anything needed to in order to get what you wanted?"

She sniffed again. "You make me sound horrible."

"Aren't you? Your happiness is *not* more important than others' happiness. There is never anything right about lying and manipulating and hurting other people. You've been doing that for a long time."

"Maybe, but I didn't see it that way." She shrugged again. "Ezra said I would tell things like I wanted to see them and soon believed that's the way it really was."

"Textbooks call that problem compulsive lying, Gracie. That's a psychological sickness."

She winced. "I told you that Ezra thinks I have some little problems. He's talked to me about them before."

"Evidently he hasn't talked enough."

Gracie made a face. "J.T. is so cute. I always liked him at school. I just knew I could get him to like me if I kept trying. Then you came. I could tell he liked you more than he did me. And I hated you for that."

"You made that obvious enough."

"I felt sure in time I could get him to like me. Other boys liked me easily enough. They would call me all the time, want to go out with me; they'd give me moon-eyes and all that, buy things for me. But never J.T. I always wanted him to like me, too." She looked away. "After I broke you two up in high school, I thought I would get him. But he really hated me after that. I could tell."

"What did you expect?" Mary Helen asked, her voice laced with sarcasm.

"Don't be so smart-assy with me." Gracie leaned forward, frowning. "You've been more stupid than I have. J.T always liked you and you never appreciated it. When I did silly things to break you up, you never even believed in him. You were too stupid to figure out I was only playing little games. So I never thought you deserved him. I thought you would make J.T. unhappy and that I would be better for him."

Mary Helen sat back in surprise.

Gracie lifted her chin. "Maybe we're both silly in a way. Me wanting what I can't have. And you being too stupid to figure out what you do have in your hand but never appreciated. Maybe you have some psychological problems, too. Ezra and J.T. kept talking about how bad I was, breaking you two up so that you're leaving town again. Saying you broke your engagement with J.T., and that it was ruining his life and all."

She paused as if choosing her words. "I just wanted to try one more time to see if I could win him. I guess it was silly, but I've been real lonely and unhappy since Tommy and I broke up. Here on the island again, seeing J.T. all the time, I sort of fell back into wanting him, into trying things to get him to like me. You'd dumped him and moved away, and my marriage had broken up.

I got to imagining us together as a couple. I really thought I'd be good for J.T., but that he just hadn't seen that yet."

"Why are you here, Gracie?"

She twisted her hands in her lap again. "For two reasons. Because J.T. cried last night and I realized how much he loved you. He actually cried right in front of me and Ezra and my parents. Can you believe that? I've never seen J.T. Mikell cry in my whole life. That's when I knew he really loved you, and Ezra said nothing I could do was going to be able to change that." Gracie picked at her dress. "While we were all talking, Daddy reminded me that Tommy cried when I left him. Tommy works with a similar heat and air company to Daddy's over in Charleston. The two of them do a lot of work together. That's how I met Tommy originally. He was crazy about me from the first. Daddy says he still is." She shifted on the sofa. "After Ezra and J.T. left I got to thinking that maybe Tommy loved me like J.T. loved you and that maybe, like you, because I didn't have to work hard for it, because it was just always there, that I didn't really appreciate him like I should. So I got in my car last night and went over to see Tommy."

"And?" Despite the fact that it was Gracie, Mary Helen found herself caught up in the story.

Gracie gave her a little smile. "We sort of made up. I stayed over and I'm packing my things today to move back with Tommy. Ezra is going to counsel with both of us to help us with our marriage relationship." She glanced down at her lap. "And to help me with my little problems."

Mary Helen tried to think what to say.

"J.T. said last night, when he was real mad at me and hollering, that I'd ruined his life and that he couldn't convince you I'd made up all these little things over the years. I only wanted him to see I was nice and maybe nicer than you." She looked directly at Mary Helen now. "But you would be really stupid if you walked away from him again over me. I'm not going to ever get him. I know that now, and you already have him if you'd just figure it out. So unless you don't want him anymore, I came to advise you not to leave him again. J.T. has always been nice to me and I don't like to think of him unhappy forevermore because of me."

"How do I know he didn't put you up to this? Or that this little visit isn't just another of your phony acts?"

She tossed her head and stood up. "I guess you'll have to figure that one out for yourself, Mary Helen. Or decide to believe J.T. for a change. I've never known him to tell a lie. Ever." She paused, her voice dropping. "Unlike me."

She moved toward the door, but then hesitated, looking back. "I don't think we'll ever be friends. You need to know that. I've always been too jealous of you."

"Of me?"

"Yes, you were always so smart, so confident. I knew you were going to accomplish things I never would. But I don't want you and J.T. to hate me forever. So I did this hard thing for me and came to see you. But I did it mostly for J.T.," she couldn't help adding at the end.

Mary Helen smiled as Gracie let herself out the door. What a morning. Despite all her grudges against Gracie, she kind of admired her for coming by like she did. And she hoped Gracie might work things out with Tommy.

Mary Helen sat down on the sofa to think after Gracie left. A lot of revelations had come out.

The phone rang while she sat thinking.

"Hello?" Mary Helen picked up her cell phone by the sofa.

"Oh, Mary Helen, I need help." Jane's anxious voice came over the line.

"My water broke and I'm here with Elena by myself. I can't reach Barton. He went out to do errands and to shop for groceries. He should be back soon, but he isn't back now, and I don't know where to call to find him. He must have turned his cell phone off or something or left it in his car. I need you to take me to the hospital and to keep Elena until I can track my mother down. Everybody seems to be out doing something today with it Sunday and all. Can you come?"

"Of course. I'll be right there." Other problems forgotten, Mary Helen grabbed her purse, raced down to her car and headed to Jane's.

A short time later, she tucked Jane and Elena into Jane's little car, with Jane's labor pains already starting, and headed to the hospital in Charleston. They'd decided to take Jane's car for expediency since Elena's child seat was already in it.

"Are you all right?" Mary Helen asked, setting her own problems aside as they drove over the causeway toward the city. Jane knew nothing about Mary Helen's ongoing problems with J.T. and now certainly wasn't the time to bring them up.

"Yes, but thank you for coming. I'm not due until next week, so I saw no reason why Barton shouldn't go to the store to get some things we needed and to run errands. As big as I am now, I hate waddling around in the stores. I didn't want to go with him, and I was fine when he left." She put her hand on her belly as another pain came. "Owww. I don't think this one is going to wait around as long as Elena did to come."

A thread of panic slid over Mary Helen's nerves.

Jane turned to glance over into the back seat to Elena, strapped into her car seat. "Are you okay, honey?" she asked.

Elena held up her doll. "Me and Phoebe get to go with you to have our new baby."

"That's right," Jane said, trying to get comfortable as another pain hit.

Mary Helen sent her a worried look. "Are you sure you're going to be okay until we get to Charleston?"

"Yes, but it might have been a problem if I'd waited around for Barton to come back or for Mother and Daddy to return from lunch. I couldn't even find Chuck or Tom. Tom and his family are down at Ryder's in Savannah doing something today and Chuck is playing golf somewhere." She reached over to put a hand on Mary Helen's leg. "I'm so glad you were at home."

"Me, too," Mary Helen said. "I'm sure Barton will be heading straight to the hospital when he gets back and finds your note."

Jane giggled. "He'll probably freak out. I hope he gets to the hospital before the baby comes, but if not I'll be fine. It's not like this is my first time."

An hour later, Mary Helen had checked Jane in through the hospital's emergency area and sat now with Elena in the waiting room, reading one of the books Jane tucked into a bag for her. Amazingly, Jane had quickly packed a bag for Elena, written a note for Barton, and packed a travel case for herself while waiting for Mary Helen to arrive.

Barton came storming into the waiting room then. "Where's Jane? Is she in delivery?"

"Daddy!" Elena got up to wrap her arms around his legs. He picked her up to hug her.

"I'm not sure where Jane is now," Mary Helen told him honestly. "I needed to stay here with Elena."

"Thanks, Mary Helen." He sat Elena back down in the chair, and then dropped to one knee to speak to her. "I need to go check on Mommy. So you stay here with Mary Helen and be good, okay? Your Gramma Edings will be here soon and she plans to take you home with her to spend the night in Walterboro. That will be fun."

He stood, turning to Mary Helen. "I imagine Jane's mother and father will arrive soon, too. Jane's note said she left a message for them at the office. They'd gone to lunch with friends."

Mary Helen smiled at him. "Elena and I will be fine. We have lots of books to read and I found some children's magazines in the waiting room, too."

He left and Mary Helen watched the time tick by afterwards as she entertained Elena, hoping all was going well for Jane.

After Jane and Barton's families arrived, time seemed to move along more rapidly, the waiting room filled with the chatter of two sets of anxious parents. Chuck, the last to arrive, had been golfing at Stono Ferry. A friend drove him from the golf course to the hospital, and he told Mary Helen he'd drive her back to the island later in Jane's car.

With Jane and Barton's family here, Mary Helen took a break to walk to the cafeteria to get a cola and a snack. It gave her a few quiet minutes to herself. Afterward, she went outside into the afternoon sunshine to sit in one of the hospital's courtyards. She knew from the doctor's report it would be another hour or so before the baby arrived. Jane's delivery was moving along quickly but babies took time to make their way into the world.

Mary Helen wore a light sweater, but the day was mild and the sun felt good on her shoulders. "What a day this has been," she said to herself, glad for this time alone. She'd hardly had time to process the stress of Gracie's visit before Jane's panicked call came.

Sitting quietly for a few moments, she watched the fall leaves toss under the trees and listened to the birds chatter. As she did Mary Helen finally felt a little peace seep back in. She'd needed this time to think.

An older lady came walking by slowly, leaning a bit on a cane. She paused by the bench where Mary Helen sat. "It's nice to get outside for a few minutes, isn't it?"

"Yes, it is." Mary Helen smiled at her. "Are you here with someone who is ill?"

She paused by Mary Helen's bench, pushing back a strand of gray hair caught by the breeze. "Yes, my Paul suffered a little heart attack, but he's going to be all right. And you?"

"A friend is having a baby."

"That's nice. Family is everything, you know. Paul and I had five children and we've enjoyed such a long, rich life." She smiled wistfully. "When we met I was an airline stewardess, flying and seeing the world. I hesitated when Paul asked me to marry him, not eager to give up that glamorous life, but I've never regretted for a minute making that decision. He's my life. All the other things in life are nice, but having someone special to love and raising children together, that's what life is really all about. The rest is only gravy." She laughed at her little joke. "I hope your friend has a fine, healthy baby. Is her husband with her?"

"Yes, and much of her family."

"All will be well then." She smiled and looked toward the hospital. "I'd better go back in. My Paul was napping but he'll be looking for me when he wakes."

She walked on and Mary Helen suddenly found tears in her eyes.

"The rest is only gravy," she repeated to herself, and then she dug her cell phone out of her purse to dial a familiar number.

"Mikell's Island Rental. This is J.T.," a voice answered.

"This is Mary Helen. What are you doing?"

She heard him hesitate, and then he said, "Just working. How about you?"

"I'm at the Bon Secours St. Francis hospital again, this time waiting for Jane's baby to be born."

"Is she all right?"

"I think she's fine, just in labor. Barton's here, and most all the family are here now, too. Jane called earlier this morning when her water broke. Barton was gone and she needed a way to the hospital."

"It's good to have friends."

"Yes, it is." She hesitated. "Would you like to be a good friend and come and get me at the hospital? I drove Jane's car over because it had Elena's car seat in it. Chuck plans to drive it back. He can bring me back, too, but I thought you'd like to come and see the baby with me. Maybe we could go out to eat afterward. I have a special place in mind."

She heard only silence for a moment.

"Leon and I are both working this afternoon," he said then in reply. "I think he can cover things until close. Tell me where to find you."

Mary Helen smiled. That was J.T. Always someone you could count on.

CHAPTER 24

J.T. was shocked to pick up the phone at work and to hear Mary Helen's voice. Casual, nonchalant, like nothing had happened. Mary Helen had never been predictable and that was a fact. When she asked him to come to the hospital to pick her up, he only hesitated a minute. He wanted every second possible with her until she left.

Parking at the hospital about an hour later, he made his way to the waiting area where Mary Helen said he'd find her. He also found most all of Jane and Barton's family there, talking and excited. Jane's baby had come.

"We've got a new baby," Elena said, running to meet him.

He picked her up for a hug. "So, I heard."

"A fine little boy," Pete Whaley announced. "Eight pounds, five ounces. I'm a Grandpa again."

"Congratulations," J.T. said. He put Elena down to walk across the room to shake Pete's hand, his eyes finding Mary Helen as he did, sitting in a corner with Pete's wife Elaine.

J.T. moved around the waiting area, congratulating the different family members. Since no one knew he and Mary Helen had broken up, it seemed natural for him to show up. Isabel hadn't quickly hit the phones broadcasting their break-up news after he talked to her on Saturday, and she and Ezra had kept the couple's problems to themselves since. Isabel probably hoped things might yet work out between them. But J.T. held little hope for that. Once Mary Helen stubbornly made up her mind, it practically took dynamite to change it.

"Where's Barton?" he asked Mary Helen, dropping into the empty seat on her other side.

"With Jane and the new baby, I'm sure," she answered.

Elaine smiled. "Jane's in recovery now. Doing well and so is the baby. They'll have a little bonding time and then the baby will go to the maternity ward and Jane will go to a room. We'll all be able to see Jane then and to pop over to the nursery to see the baby."

"They've named him John Jared Edings. You probably knew that," Mary Helen reminded him.

"Yeah. That's a good name." He felt a little awkward with Mary Helen, their situation looming between them like a big dark cloud no one else knew anything about. And what had she meant earlier, saying she wanted to take him out to eat somewhere special after he picked her up? The last he remembered she didn't ever want to see him again, couldn't wait to escape and leave Edisto. She sure was a woman hard to read.

The family trotted off to see Jane and the baby not long after, taking turns in doing so. He and Mary Helen made a quick visit to see Jane and then headed to the maternity ward to see the baby.

"There he is." Mary Helen pointed to an incubator pushed near the window. "Awww. How sweet. He has a lot of dark hair, doesn't he?"

"Yeah." J.T. felt an odd lump in his throat standing with Mary Helen looking through the glass at all the little newborns.

She sighed. "Kind of makes you want one, doesn't it?" she said in a soft voice, shocking him. He decided not to answer.

"I think we can leave now," she said after a few minutes. "Elena is going home with her Edings grandparents for a night or two until Jane and the baby come home. Elaine and Pete, and probably Chuck, will hang around for a while. Barton will stay with Jane, of course, and one of the nurses will bring the baby out to Jane and Barton later on. We don't need to stay longer."

"Okay." His eyes moved again over the tiny new baby, wrapped snugly in blankets with a little knit hat on his head. Cute little guy.

They headed out into the warm, early November afternoon. The sky was blue and clear with white clouds scattered across it. A fine day for this time of year, if his life wasn't a mess.

"You don't have to take me to eat for coming to pick you up, Mary Helen," he said as they made their way into the hospital lot to where he'd parked his MG.

"I said I wanted to take you somewhere special." She slipped into the car after he opened the door.

He walked around to get in the other side. "Where do you want to go then?" he asked, going along.

She flashed a smile at him, one of those bright warm smiles of hers that always took his breath away and lingered in his memory. "I thought we'd go to Bowen's Island Restaurant."

His eyebrows lifted in surprise. "Great idea. I love that place."

She gave him a smirk. "Did you think I'd take you to one of those swanky restaurants in downtown Charleston, like Michael's Alley, where steaks are forty dollars or more each and side salads ten bucks?"

"It crossed my mind. You've been a city girl for a while now. I wasn't sure you'd still like a place like Bowen's."

"It holds a lot of good memories." Her voice softened.

J.T. leaned his head back against the seat before starting the car. "You're killing me with this game, Mary Helen. What's going on?"

She put a hand on his leg. "I think I might stay around if it's still okay with you."

He turned to study her face, a little thrill starting to spread through him. "Do you think so?" he managed to say.

She put a hand to his face. "I don't think I can leave you, J.T. We're just going to have to work this out."

He snatched her to him and kissed her. "We will work it out, Mary Helen," he said against her neck. It felt like a giant weight had been lifted off his heart. "What changed your mind?"

"A lot of things. I thought we might talk about it over dinner." She glanced at her watch. "I know it's not even five yet, but you know how busy Bowen's can get. We should head on down to the island, find a place to park and get in line."

"It won't be as busy in November as during the heavy tourist season." He started the car, backing out of the parking space.

"It's always busier on Saturday and Sunday nights any time, though." Her voice dropped. "That's usually when we boated over to the restaurant when we were in high school, remember?"

"I do remember." He wanted to reach over to take her hand but hesitated. He still didn't feel on solid ground with Mary Helen yet.

J.T. drove down the highway from the hospital and swung left on Hwy 17 toward Charleston. Before reaching the bridge over the Ashley River into town, he turned right on Hwy 171 leading to James Island and Folly Beach. All of this area up and down the coast he knew well.

He and Mary Helen were both a little quiet on the drive. With the weather a touch cooler, J.T. had the top up on the convertible, and they listened to the radio as they drove past stores, shops, and churches and into the quieter and marshier area leading toward Folly Beach.

Mary Helen gazed out over the marsh as they crossed a bridge. "We're heading into pirate land. I love all the old stories of how this area was once a favorite spot for pirates."

"The word folly means *foliage* in French. This whole place was once densely covered in foliage, very jungle-like and isolated back in the 1700s. It was inevitable, I guess, that it would develop as a tourist spot in time, so close to Charleston."

"I like Folly Beach, but I like Edisto better."

"No argument there." He grinned to hear the words. Turning off onto Bowen's Island Road, he added, "I love the history of Bowen's Island. The Bowen family bought the island in the 1940s for about $3000."

Her eyes widened. "For so little?"

"Land was cheap then and the only route to the island at that time was by boat. When the Bowens first opened their restaurant on the island, you had to boat over to it. Ask Grandad Mikell sometime to tell you stories about boating to the restaurant in the early days."

"I will."

"The bridge makes it easier to get to the island now but you know the restaurant is still sort of a dive."

She laughed. "I like to think of it as a rustic icon, individual and unique."

"Bowen's is that," he agreed with a grin. "If you remember, the building hangs out over the water, has a rough, weather-beaten exterior, graffiti-covered walls, and a lot of old junk inside, but it also has great seafood and fabulous views out over the river and marshes."

"I love sitting near one of the windows or out on the porch upstairs where you can watch the sunset over the water and spot egrets flying in to nest. It's so pretty." She turned to him, a thought coming to mind. "I do hope you keep bug spray in the trunk of your car though."

"A good Lowcountry island boy always keeps bug spray on hand, and we might need it at Bowen's." He smiled at her.

Mary Helen seemed to want to settle back into their old relationship as before, so for now J.T. decided to play it her way.

The paved street soon turned into a gravel and dirt road as it wound its way to a dead end turn where the weathered restaurant sat on stilts out over the creek. J.T. found a place to park under a tree. They spritzed a little bug spray over themselves, and then headed up the wooden ramp leading into the restaurant. Even at nearly five, when Bowen's officially opened, a short line of people waited to get inside to order and get a table.

As they moved inside after a wait, Mary Helen let J.T. place their orders while she went upstairs to snag a good table. He found her a short time later at an outside table on the upper deck, near a corner of the porch. "Do you mind to sit outside?" she asked. "The views are better and it's still nice out."

He sat their drinks on the table. "The temperature reached seventy today; it's still in the upper sixties now." He settled into the chair across from her. "You're wearing a sweater and I've got a couple of old hoodies in the back of the trunk I can get for us if it turns cool."

"Look how beautiful it is." She sighed and gazed out across the seagrass and the sweeping expanse of Ashley Creek. "What time will the sun set?"

"About 6:30, I think. We'll start to see color earlier, though."

"I can hardly wait." She got up for a minute to walk over to stand near the rail. "Come and look at this, J.T."

Eager to please her tonight, he walked over to stand beside her. "There's an egret," he said, pointing to a tall white bird standing in the marshes.

Her voice softened. "Here's what I really wanted you to see." She pointed to the battered wooden post at the end of the porch beside them. "Look on the post about six inches up from the rail. You can't miss it."

He did and then smiled. "J.T. plus M.H." He traced his fingers over the letters, written amid all the other weathered scrawls of initials, words, and names. At Bowen's people wrote everywhere on the rails, porches, and walls. The restaurant was full of graffiti. "I wrote those initials there a long time ago."

"I know. I hoped it would still be here." She leaned against him. "I'm so sorry we have so many quarrels, J.T., that we have so much trouble loving."

He leaned over and kissed her, not caring who saw. "I've never had trouble loving you, Mary Helen. But we have weathered some hindrances and roadblocks in our relationship for sure and experienced far too many times of separation. I don't want any more."

"Me neither," she said, moving away from the rail to sit down again.

"Talk to me now, Mary Helen," he said, dropping into the chair across from her and reaching for his iced tea. "Our food won't be here for a little while."

She sighed, looking out over the water. "I think I want to start by saying I'm sorry. A lot of situations in my early life, and in my later life, built a fear and distrust in me for a certain kind of man."

"Like Miles Lawrence?"

"I think it started there. He was so charming, so handsome, and he had a way with words. He won Suki and me both over—and he was working on Mother. I never saw it coming that he'd be a cheater and a liar. It really hurt."

"You had a girlish crush on him at only nine. I remember you all but swooned every time he came around."

She squeezed some lemon into her tea. "I know. Even today it hurts me to see him."

"You know all men are not like Miles Lawrence."

"I do, deep down inside. But for me it was like being bit by a dog and then feeling leery and afraid of dogs ever since or developing a fear of heights because you fell off something high when small. I was overly sensitive afterward to handsome, charming men— thinking they couldn't be trusted—and I overly noticed every instance when girls showed an avid interest in anyone I cared about who fit that category."

"And I always fit that category in your eyes."

She looked away from him. "Yes, you did. I didn't see it as much when we were little, but I really began to notice it when we grew older. You have an innate charisma women notice, and I had a problem with that I hadn't come to terms with yet."

"You think you have now?"

"Maybe." She nodded and grinned at him. "You are a fine looking man, J.T. Mikell, and sexy, too. I think I've decided to relish that."

He laughed. "Well, that's good, I think. I've always thought the same and more about you as a woman. You turn on every single crank and faucet in me. And no one else has ever done that for me in the same way."

"Thanks." She gave him a shy smile. "I haven't appreciated enough how much you care for me and always have. Gracie Byrd took me to task for that this morning."

J.T. almost dumped his tea over in surprise and he knew his

mouth dropped open. "What?"

"I came back from Waterview, still torn up and indecisive, starting to pack to go back to New Jersey. I popped downstairs to get some things to tuck into my duffle and nearly fainted to see that girl knocking at my door. I mouthed for her to go away but she opened the door and let herself right in, insisting she needed to talk with me."

"Gracie's persistent when she wants something."

"I saw that." Mary Helen nodded. "She got candid with me about why she wanted you, mostly because you weren't interested in her. Gracie said she finally realized she has a problem with wanting things she can't have and not appreciating things she already has." She paused. "It made me realize I'd been somewhat the same, in a way, not appreciating you as I should."

Before he could reply, she added, "She told me that you and Ezra came to see her and her parents last night. Our conversation wasn't entirely edifying, as you can imagine, but I learned a lot about Gracie by listening."

"I felt desperate after seeing you on Saturday." J.T. ran a hand through his hair. "Ezra had been a help to me in the past, and I knew he'd counseled a lot with Gracie. I hoped he might help me think what to do. He said we needed to confront her this time about what she'd done, make her see the consequences of it and that she would not gain from her actions what she wanted—now or ever."

She propped an elbow on the table. "I wish I'd been a fly on the wall for that meeting."

"I'd like to have been a fly on the wall at your meeting with Gracie, too." He sighed and looked out over the water. "I hope we all did her some good."

"See, that's where you're nicer than me. Because she had problems, and made problems for others, I simply disliked and avoided her. You were always kind enough to care about her."

"You mean gullible enough to fall for her theatrics and lies. I need to apologize to you for that. I should, as you said, have learned enough long ago about Gracie to keep from getting taken in by her. Isabel certainly gave me *what for* about being a fool in that way. And she is right. I need to be keener about the motives behind people's words and actions."

"Well, don't toughen up too much." She leaned over to give him a quick kiss. "Your kindness is a part of your charm."

"Not if it loses me the woman I love."

"Well, it hasn't. And I intend to keep a jealous watch over you, J.T. Mikell. Once you have that wedding ring on, all license for women to try to charm you into their clutches will be off. "

"Don't worry, Mary Helen. I'm the faithful type." He reached under the table to take her hand. "We Mikell men are not known to wander or stray after we find the right woman. And I've found mine."

"You sweet thing," she said, leaning across the table to kiss him again. "I'm so glad we've working out our problems."

"We may have other problems in the future, but promise me you'll always come and talk to me about things when you get upset, Mary Helen. Don't shut me out and run away."

"I promise. That's been a fault of mine. I'm going to believe the best of you from now on, always give you the benefit of the doubt, and I hope you'll do the same for me."

"I will."

The waiter came with their food, two heavy Chinet plates piled high with fish, crabcakes, boiled shrimp, fries, and slaw on the side. J.T. had ordered a side of fried oysters for them to share, too, and slices of key lime pie for dessert.

Mary Helen's eyes widened. "As much as I love their key lime pie here, I'm tempted to eat it first." She laughed.

They settled in to eat for a time, enjoying their dinner.

Mary Helen sighed after a while. "You know, I think the meeting you and Ezra had with Gracie might have really done her some good."

"Why do you say that?" he asked, finishing off the last bite of his crabcake.

"Did you know she went back to Tommy?"

He looked up with surprise. "No. Did she tell you that?"

"She did. The conversation you and Ezra had with her, and things her daddy said about Tommy, made Gracie realize she might have taken his love for granted simply because he was readily available. He wasn't something she couldn't get." Mary Helen pushed her bangs out of her eyes. "She went to see him after you and Ezra left."

"No kidding?"

Mary Helen grinned. "She said they made up and she stayed over."

"Well." J.T. wiggled his eyebrows. "That can only be a good thing."

"Evidently, it was." She sampled a bite of pie. "She told me they were getting back together. In fact she was heading home to pack her things to move back in with Tommy at his place today."

"That's great news," he said and meant it. "I've met Tommy Henry. He's a first-rate guy. Stable, good-hearted, kind, and smart. Chuck and I always felt he was too good for Gracie, but he seemed to understand her like no one else did. He always acted so patient and sweet with her." He pulled his pie closer to dig into it. "His business is a prosperous one in Charleston. I heard he had a nice home not far away on Sullivan's Island."

"I'd like a happy ending for Gracie if only to keep her out of our hair." Mary Helen laughed. "Is that awful of me to say?"

"No." He winked at her. "I was doing my own little happy dance inside at your news. I counted myself lucky the day that girl married and left Edisto the first time, and I count myself lucky and blessed she's leaving again. May she live happily ever after at Sullivan's Island and never come back."

They both laughed.

"Oh, look. The sun is setting." Mary Helen pointed out over the horizon to where a big ball of yellow was falling low in the sky, sending out a blaze of orange color and turning the boats on the water into dark silhouettes.

J.T. frowned, a new thought coming to mind. "Did you call and tell your family about us splitting up?" he asked.

"No, for some reason I couldn't do it." She shrugged. "I didn't tell anyone except Isabel. I don't think she said much to anyone around the island, either. Jane didn't seem to know about it, or Elaine and Pete. Usually the Edisto grapevine goes into quick action over gossipy news."

J.T. let his eyes rove out over the glorious sunset. "I know neither Isabel or Ezra said anything to anyone except Gracie and her parents. I doubt her parents will say anything about what happened either. Stanley and Eunice Byrd weren't eager to have Gracie's actions known around the island. Some word may get out eventually that you and I had a spat and broke up, but since we're back together again now, the gossip won't be very interesting to pass on or probe into."

She smiled at him. "I like those words *back together again.*"

"Me, too," he said and meant it with all his heart.

She looked wistful then. "An older lady I talked to at the hospital today said all the things we do and experience in life are just gravy after love and family. I hope you want to have a family, J.T. Seeing those babies really made me start to think in that direction."

He grinned with pleasure. "Fortunately, I know how to make that wish come true and will be happy to soon demonstrate it."

She wrinkled her nose and giggled at his words. "I'm so glad I came back to Edisto."

"Me, too." J.T. said, his heart so full that words seemed hard to find. He looked across at Mary Helen, with the glow of the sunset touching her face, and decided life couldn't get much better than at this moment.

RECIPES from *Return to Edisto*

Frances Mikell's Apple
Butter Cinnamon Tea Cake

2 1/2 cups flour	1 cup buttermilk
3/4 cup white sugar	1 egg
1-cup brown sugar	1 cup chopped pecans
1/2 T. cinnamon	*Apple Cake Icing:*
3/4 cup apple butter	3/4 cup confectioners sugar
1 tsp baking soda	1 T. milk
1 tsp baking powder	1/2 tsp vanilla

Directions:
Preheat oven to 325 degrees. Grease and flour a 10-inch round porcelain quiche pan or 10-inch round aluminum cake pan. With mixer mix together the flour, sugars, cinnamon, and apple butter on low until a sort of coarse pebbly texture is achieved and then measure out 3/4 cup of it and set it aside to use later. Next combine the baking soda, baking powder, egg, and buttermilk. Let this mixture stand about 5 minutes until it doubles in size and gets a little bubbly. Then blend in all the original flour, sugar, cinnamon, and apple butter mixture except for the 3/4 cup set aside. Pour the batter into the quiche or cake pan. Then mix the chopped pecans into the 3/4 cup flour mix set aside and sprinkle this mixture over the top of the mixture in the pan. Bake the cake at 325 degrees for about 45 minutes until toothpick comes out clean. While cake cools slightly, make the icing in a side bowl and then drizzle over the cake. The tea cake can be put on a tiered glass cake plate or kept in the pan. Cut in slices, like pie, and serve, adding extra icing or a dollop of whipped cream if desired.

Jane Edings' Chocolate Chip Cookies

2 3/4 cup all-purpose flour
3 tsp soda
1 tsp salt
2 sticks real butter
3/4 cup white sugar
1 cup finely chopped pecans

3/4 cup lt. brown sugar
1 tsp vanilla
2 large eggs
1 12-oz. pkg. chocolate
  chip morsels

Directions:
Combine flour, baking soda and salt in bowl. In a second bowl beat butter, sugars and vanilla until creamy, then add eggs. Next, beat in flour mixture a little at a time. Stir in chocolate chips and nuts at end. Drop by tablespoonfulls onto greased baking sheets. Bake at 375 degrees for 9-11 minutes. Cool a few minutes and then remove from baking sheet to cool further. Makes 4-5 dozen cookies.
(Note: This was my mother's recipe, which I always loved!)

Chuck Whaley's Edisto Slaw

1/2 head cabbage, chopped
1/2 med. onion, chopped
1 small green pepper, chopped
    1/3 bottle LaMartinique Original Poppy Seed Dressing

1 cucumber, peeled and
  chopped

Directions:
Stir cabbage, onion, cucumber, and green pepper together. Add poppy seed dressing. If desired, add salt and pepper. Chill and serve.

J.T. and Mary Helen's
Shrimp, Crab, and Sausage Gumbo

1/4 cup vegetable or olive oil
1 12-oz pkg andouille sausage, sliced
1/4 cup all-purpose flour
1/2 large onion, chopped
1 red pepper, chopped
1 green pepper, chopped
1 1/2 celery ribs, chopped
5 garlic cloves, sliced thin
3 cups chicken broth
2 14-oz cans diced tomatoes
1/2 lb fresh okra, sliced thin

6 fresh thyme sprigs
2 bay leaves
1 tsp kosher salt
1/4 tsp black pepper
1/8 tsp ground cayenne
2 tsp fresh lime juice
1-cup stone ground or quick-cook grits
1-2 lb lg peeled shrimp
1/2 lb lump crabmeat
1/2 cup chopped fresh parsley leaves
Hot sauce, optional

Directions:

Take out one tablespoon of the cooking oil and put in a large shrimp pot over med-high heat. Add sliced smoked sausages. Cook appx 4 minutes until browned on all sides. Remove to a side plate with a slotted spoon. Add the remaining oil to the sausage drippings in the pot. Whisk in the flour and then cook over low heat, stirring frequently, for about 20 minutes until the mixture is a reddish brown color. Now, stir in the onion, red and green pepper, celery, and the garlic, and then saute over medium heat for about 8 minutes until vegetables are softened and partially cooked. Next stir in the chicken broth (can use fish stock if you have it), the tomatoes un-drained, including the juice, the okra, thyme, bay leaves, salt, pepper, cayenne, and lime juice. Bring all to a boil and then reduce the heat and simmer everything covered for 30 minutes. ...While the gumbo base is simmering, cook the grits, and then cover and keep them warm. ...After the gumbo has simmered for 30 minutes, stir in the cooked sausage and the shrimp. Cook about 4 minutes until the shrimp are done. Then add the crab and simmer until heated. Take out the bay leaves, and stir in the parsley if desired - or use it as a garnish after. You can add a little hot sauce at this time or just put it on the table for guests to add as they desire....Serve the gumbo in a wide, shallow gumbo or soup bowl, spooning the gumbo over hot grits or, if preferred, putting a spoon of grits over the top. This recipe serves about six but can be doubled to serve more.

Yvonne Helton's Lowcountry Bean Salad

1 1/2 cups fresh or frozen green beans
1 lb fresh or frozen lima beans
1 lb fresh or frozen black-eyed peas
1 1/2 cup chopped red or green onions

3/4 cup fresh lemon juice
1 1/2 cups olive oil
3/4 cup fresh lemon juice
Fresh dill, salt, black pepper to season

Directions:
Precook chopped green beans, lima beans, and black-eyed peas separate, each according to directions as to whether fresh or frozen. Best if all beans are fresh but frozen will work, too. Drain and combine all beans in a bowl. Whisk together lemon juice and a little salt and pepper in a side bowl, adding in the olive oil and then the chopped onions—green onions or red onions, according to preference. Pour liquid mixture over beans and toss well. Before serving can add a little fresh dill. Chill the bean salad for about 15-30 minutes before serving or make 4-6 hours ahead and chill until ready to serve....Serves 6 but can be doubled for a larger group.

A Reading Group Guide

RETURN TO EDISTO

Lin Stepp

About This Guide

The questions on the following pages are included
to enhance your group's reading of
Lin Stepp's *Return to Edisto*

DISCUSSION QUESTIONS

1. As the story begins, Mary Helen is returning to Edisto Island. What has happened in her life that caused her to leave her home and job in New Jersey suddenly? Why does she choose to come to Edisto? Do you have a place you go—or yearn to go to— when life becomes painful and difficult? Have you ever gone back home again during a hard season?

2. There is a strong bond between Mary Helen and her younger sister Suki. Where is Suki living as this book begins? Mary Helen says to Suki: "Playing piano is your happy place." Why does she say this and what is Suki doing with her life right now? How are Suki and Mary Helen similar and yet very different? If you have a sister, or sisters, are you close?

3. J.T. (Jenkins Townsend) Mikell is not someone Mary Helen wants to run into on her first night at Edisto—or on any night. Why? Even when J.T. drops by the house on his way home, Mary Helen tries to get rid of him. Why does J.T. stay anyway? How does he help Mary Helen on a difficult night? What was J.T. and Mary Helen's earlier relationship like growing up? What has their relationship been like since she left home to go to college? What is J.T. doing with his life now and how does he feel about seeing Mary Helen again?

4. Mary Helen has been sexually threatened by her boss. What was her experience? What did she do after Wendell Hembree threatened her? Statistics, at the time these questions were written, reveal that every seventy-three seconds an American is sexually assaulted, and one in six American women has been the victim of rape or an attempted rape in her lifetime, with young women the most likely to experience sexual threat. And yet rape and sexual threat is the most unreported crime. Why do you think this is

so? What did Mary Helen do after Wendell Hembree threatened her? Do you think she made the right decision to leave and not confront the company owners about what happened?

5. It is obvious from early in the book that Mary Helen and J.T. have a history together. What did you learn over the book's story about how they met and first fell in love? What caused them to break up? What factors kept them from resolving this old issue when they both obviously still held feelings for each other? The word "trust," listed as the foundation stone of any relationship, is often used linked to their problems. How has trust been lost between them? Why do you think this is so? Why is it hard to rebuild trust after it is lost?

6. Mary Helen has a long-time relationship with her neighbor Isabel Compton, owner of The Little Mermaid. When did Isabel and Mary Helen meet? How did they become bonded over the years? What help does Isabel offer to Mary Helen when she comes back to Edisto? How is she a good friend and wise counselor to Mary Helen throughout this story? One of Isabel's lines of wisdom was: "We don't always know everything about others, even when we think we do." Do you think that's true? How is Ezra Compton also a help to J.T.?

7. If you read *Claire at Edisto*, the first of this trilogy, you met many of the characters in this book before. What changes have happened in Claire's life since the last book? Claire had started to write children's books in the first novel. Has she continued in that work? What books has she written since? Did any changes from the last book to this surprise you?

8. Good friends are always a blessing. J.T. is friends with Leon Johnson, his assistant manager at work, and with two old friends from childhood Chuck Whaley and Andrew Cavanaugh. How are his friendships different with each young man? In addition,

Mary Helen reunites with her old childhood friend, Jane Whaley Edings. How have Mary Helen's and Jane's lives gone in different directions? Yet they rebond quickly. Do you think there is something special about long time friends we've known since our youth?

9. J.T. and Mary Helen have also known Gracie Byrd since childhood, but there are no warm feelings lingering for Gracie. Why has Gracie always been a problem to Mary Helen and J.T.? Although many people outgrow their childhood issues, Gracie has not. What are her emotional issues and how have they negatively impacted her life and the lives of others? What problems does she cause going to the Little Mermaid to see Mary Helen early in the book? What problems does she cause later when J.T. and Mary Helen are engaged? Did you change any of your feelings about Gracie toward the end of the book?

10. If you are a parent, you know that there is a thin, fine line you have to walk in giving advice about the love relationships of young adult children. What did you think of J.T.'s mother—Lula Mikell's—talk with him about Mary Helen? In addition, Mary Helen's mother, Claire, also has two sweet talks with Mary Helen about J.T., one at the Little Mermaid and one later in Beaufort when Mary Helen comes home upset. How did Claire help Mary Helen, and how did Lula help J.T., at these times? Can you recall a time when one of your parents gave you good advice you really needed?

11. Charisma is a social gift that even psychologists have a hard time explaining, but we have all known men and women who have it—and project it. Sexual charisma is an even more enigmatic gift but it often explains the boy all the girls swoon over or the girl all the boys go running after. Social gifts, like charisma, can be both a blessing and a curse. J.T. and his father, John Mikell, along with Miles Lawrence, all possess that special charisma with women.

What problems has it caused for them? Have you ever known anyone with this gift? How can the general gift of charisma be a favorable blessing?

12. While some people have charisma and draw us to them, others have the opposite effect. Winnifred Meggett is one of those people. Even though she is smart and knowledgeable, she has earned the nickname Wacky Winnie. Why? How can people who get too fervent about causes begin to push others away rather than drawing them in? Many, fervent in their beliefs, can become extremists in political, environmental, or other views. It isn't the causes they support that tip them over the edge to extremism but the accompanying rejection of good values that they leave behind. What causes does Winnifred support and what values does she begin to reject to support them?

13. The person or persons causing the poisoning of dogs in this book was a primary mystery in the story. How did you feel about this situation as you began to read about dogs on Edisto being poisoned? Did you have any sense early on in the book as to who was causing this problem? Did you think, like Mary Helen, and most others, that the mystery was solved when the robbers were caught later in the book? Were some of the dogs themselves also problematic in their behavior? What is good etiquette for dogs and owners? How did J.T. help to resolve this situation once and for all?

14. A major life decision we all face is what career path to choose. Often the path demands a sacrifice of time and money for education or training, moves to where a career takes us, and difficult family decisions to make. How did J.T. and Mary Helen differ in knowing the career path they wanted to take? It often helps in life to have someone who believes in you and encourages your choices. Did Mary Helen and J.T. respect each others' choices? How did their differences cause problems in

their relationship early on and as the story progressed? Did you know at an early point in life exactly what you wanted to do, or did it take time and trials to find your way? Who believed in you and encouraged you?

15. Illness and accidents interrupt the planned order of our lives. When Mary Helen falls through the porch floor at the old Mikell plantation and breaks her arm, what plans of hers are interrupted? How was J.T. a good help at the time of this accident and after? How did his kindness in this difficult time begin to change Mary Helen's feelings for him? Have you ever broken an arm, leg, or had an accident that greatly disrupted your life?

16. Faith can always be a help and comfort in our lives, but we too often lean to it after we've first tried to figure everything out for ourselves. Kizzy Helton is a good spiritual help to Mary Helen and J.T. in this story. How did she give good counsel to Mary Helen at the grocery when she first arrived on the island and later to both Mary Helen and J.T. after Mary Helen broke her arm? Another Helton family member, Kizzy's son Farlin Helton, also prays for Mary Helen at his church. J.T. seems to comfortably accept that the Heltons, as he puts it, "live close to God" and that 'Farlin Helton has God's ear.' He respects their counsel and walk with the Lord. Do you believe some people live closer to God than others and that because of this they hear better from God than others?

17. Sometimes unexpected events—and people—can greatly impact our lives. Mad and angry at J.T. toward the end of the book, Mary Helen is packing to leave the island to return to New Jersey. What unexpected call set her on that path? As she's packing, Gracie Byrd shows up invited and insists on talking to her. What does Gracie say to her? While reeling from this unexpected visit, Jane calls, in labor, and Mary Helen heads off to take her friend to the hospital. In culmination to all these

events, a lady Mary Helen has never met before talks to her in the hospital courtyard, saying something that causes Mary Helen to re-examine the course of her life. What did the lady say? What did Mary Helen then do afterward? Have you ever met a stranger that said something to you that helped to change the course of your thoughts and life?

18. This book could have ended in several different ways. Were you happy with its ending? What offer that Isabel presented earlier in the story made it easier for Mary Helen to decide to stay at Edisto? Did you like the final scenes with Mary Helen and J.T. in the restaurant? What did you like best about this book and which character was your favorite? Who do you hope you might meet again in the next book about Suki's life?

About the Author

Lin Stepp

Dr. Lin Stepp is a *New York Times*, *USA Today*, and *Publishers Weekly* Best-Selling international author. A native Tenessean, she has also worked as a businesswoman and educator. A previous faculty member at Tusculum College, Stepp taught research and a variety of psychology and counseling courses for almost twenty years. Her business background includes over twenty-five years in marketing, sales, production art, and regional publishing.

Stepp writes engaging, heart-warming contemporary Southern fiction with a strong sense of place and has sixteen published novels set in different locations around the Smoky Mountains and the South Carolina coast. Her coastal novels in the Edisto Trilogy are *Return to Edisto* (2020) and *Claire at Edisto* (2019). The latest Tennessee and North Carolina mountain novels are *Happy Valley* (2020), *The Interlude* (2019), *Lost Inheritance* (2018) and *Daddy's Girl* (2017), with previous novels including *Welcome Back* (2016), *Saving Laurel Springs* (2015), *Makin' Miracles* (2015), *Down by the River* (2014) and a novella *A Smoky Mountain Gift* in the Christmas anthology *When The Snow Falls* (2014) published by Kensington of New York. Other earlier titles include: *Second Hand Rose* (2013), *Delia's Place* (2012), *For Six Good Reasons* (2011), *Tell Me About Orchard Hollow* (2010), and *The Foster Girls* (2009). In addition Stepp and her husband J.L. Stepp have co-authored a Smoky Mountains hiking guidebook titled *The Afternoon Hiker* (2014) and a Tennessee state parks guidebook *Discovering Tennessee State Parks* (2018).

For more about Stepp's work and to keep up with her monthly blog, newsletter, and ongoing appearances and signing events, see: *www.linstepp.com*.